WHO SHOT THE SHERIFF?

SERIES

An Original Story

By

PROLIFIC, INTERNATIONAL BESTSELLING AUTHOR

JOHN A. ANDREWS

CREATOR OF:

SAUCE

THE PIPS

RUDE BUAY

NY CONNIVERS

BOOK #2

CO-AUTHORS

JONATHAN & JEFFERRI ANDREWS

WHO SHOT THE SHERIFF? SERIES

Copyright © 2012/2016/2019/2024 by John A. Andrews.

All rights reserved.

The publisher must secure written permission to use or reproduce any part of this book except for brief quotations in critical reviews or articles.

Published in the U.S.A. by

Books That Will Enhance Your Life

A L I

Andrews Leadership International www.ALI Pictures.com

www.JohnAAndrews.com

ISBN: **9798301600272**

Cover Design: ALI

Front Cover Design: ALI

Edited by: ALI

Adaptation updates 2014

Optioned by ALI Pictures in January 2014

WHO SHOT THE SHERIFF? SERIES

THE HUSTLE,

THE FLOW, THE VERDICT...

THE MILTON ROGER'S CONSPIRACY...

THE JURY

DEAD MEN TELL NO TALES...

WHO SHOT THE SHERIFF? SERIES

BOOK ONE

The HUSTLE. The FLOW. The VERDICT...

WHO SHOT THE SHERIFF? SERIES

TABLE OF CONTENTS

PROLOGUE...6
CHAPTER ONE..9
CHAPTER TWO...10
CHAPTER THREE...14
CHAPTER FOUR..20
CHAPTER FIVE..24
CHAPTER SIX...28
CHAPTER SEVEN...32
CHAPTER EIGHT...38
CHAPTER NINE..43
CHAPTER TEN...50
CHAPTER ELEVEN..55
CHAPTER TWELVE..59
CHAPTER THIRTEEN..64
CHAPTER FOURTEEN..67
CHAPTER FIFTEEN...70
CHAPTER SIXTEEN...75
CHAPTER SEVENTEEN...81
CHAPTER EIGHTEEN..87
CHAPTER NINETEEN..90
CHAPTER TWENTY..97
CHAPTER TWENTY-ONE...102
CHAPTER TWENTY-TWO...107
CHAPTER TWENTY-THREE...114
CHAPTER TWENTY-FOUR..119
CHAPTER TWENTY-FIVE..121
CHAPTER TWENTY-SIX...124
CHAPTER TWENTY-SEVEN...129
CHAPTER TWENTY-EIGHT...136
CHAPTER TWENTY-NINE..143
CHAPTER THIRTY...147
CHAPTER THIRTY-ONE...152
CHAPTER THIRTY-TWO...160
CHAPTER THIRTY-THREE...167
CHAPTER THIRTY-FOUR..170

PROLOGUE

The luscious green mountainous terrain in the north stretches and recedes towards the low land area golf courses and the elaborate nineteenth-century town square houses south of Mandeville, Jamaica. Mandeville is the capital city and largest town in the parish of Manchester in the county of Middlesex, Jamaica. In 2005, it boasted a total of over 50,000, plus at least another 25, 000 including the suburbs. Today, almost a decade later, that population has more than doubled.

Situated on an inland plateau, Jamaica's only parish capital is not on the coast or a major river. Mandeville is sandwiched in Manchester between the parish of Saint Elizabeth to the West and Clarendon to the East. Additionally, it is located approximately 64 miles from Kingston, Jamaica's capital, and 65 miles from Montego Bay, another capital city otherwise known as MO Bay.

The town square, which is much of an English town setting, has a courthouse, a parish church, a clock tower, and many large, elegant, early nineteenth-century houses that line the winding streets in the town center. The plush green grass adds luster to the

the setting of the old-fashioned town square. The blueprint for this town, nestled in Jamaica, was laid out in 1816 and named after Viscount Mandeville, the eldest son of the Duke of Manchester, who was then governor of Jamaica. Many of those original buildings, such as the courthouse's stature, an impressive cut limestone structure with a horseshoe staircase, and a raised portico supported by Doric columns built in 1820, can still be seen. During the week, this building is usually filled with lawyers and their clients. The oldest dwelling in Mandeville is the rectory beside the courthouse, which was also built in the same year.

IN THE SUBURBS TODAY, many who have struck it rich and returned from North America and the United Kingdom show off their hard work and charisma by building massive houses. So much so that developers keeping up with the trend have complemented these mansions with significant housing developments, most of which are expansive gated communities. It is documented that many of Jamaica's oldest businesses were started in Mandeville, such as the Mandeville Hotel, which began operations in 1875, and the Manchester Golf Club, the first in the Caribbean, was founded in 1868. Some local festivities in Mandeville include the "Manchester Fiesta," held on August 8. The South Manchester sweet potato festival is held every year on October 28. In 1957, in a joint venture with the

Jamaican Government, the Alcan Bauxite Company gave the city a shot when it built houses for its then-mostly expatriate staff. The relatively high wages lured many educated Jamaicans to Mandeville. Subsequently, the town has seen an influx of Jamaicans and foreign intellectuals, including lawyers, doctors, and other high-ranking officials. It is home to the Northern Caribbean University (formerly West Indies College), a Seventh-day Adventist institution of higher learning. It's a great place where the neighbors know each other and frequently eavesdrop on each other's affairs.

Some of the notables from Mandeville include Donovan Bailey, retired Olympic sprinter Charmaine Crooks, Olympic athlete Sheryl Lee Ralph, actress and singer Winston McAnuff, reggae musician Heavy D (born Dwight Arrington Myers), rapper Lovel Palmer, Jamaican and international footballer Garnett Silk, a reggae musician, and Christopher Williams, an athlete. In Peter Tosh's version of "Johnny Be Goode," he sings about a hut on the top of a hill " deep down in Jamaica close to Mandeville." While in Bob Marley's "Mr. Brown," the character is noted as being asked for "from Mandeville to Sligoville." Not to confuse him with "Sheriff John Brown" in I Shot the Sheriff.

CHAPTER 1

WAY BEFORE BOB MARLEY, Peter Tosh, Jimmy Cliff, Dennis Brown, Freddie McGregor, Gregory Isaacs, Johnny Nash, John Holt, and Eric Donaldson entered the musical era, a college professor and Mandeville native, Sebastian Haynes, born way before the Civil Rights Revolution, met and married Megan Williams. Several years later, they gave birth to their first and only son, Wesley Haynes, at Mandeville Hospital. Wesley weighed nine pounds and twenty-two inches. His mom, an obstetrics and gynecology nurse, saw him as the perfect size for a newborn. Mr. and Mrs. Haynes always envisioned themselves as king and queen even before they said "I do" inside Mandeville Park.

Now, in their eyes, their little bundle of joy years later, Wesley was their prince, and he would be privy to the inheritance, that of their imaginary throne.

WHO SHOT THE SHERIFF? SERIES

CHAPTER 2

More than a decade later, Megan and Sebastian Haynes watched with amazement as their son Wesley entered his teenage years. At thirteen, he possessed commanding leadership skills in sports. Wesley Haynes played soccer, cricket, basketball, volleyball, and track at Manchester High School. He became so adept in track and field that his coach, Conrad Fredricks, nominated him for a nationwide competition.

Unfortunately, Wesley could not compete in the tournament. He had worked so hard to qualify. Just one month before the competition, he broke his left leg playing basketball in the neighborhood park. He attended the event but sat there with his leg propped up in a cast. This was tough for the young Haynes, who sat there in limbo, watching others compete while envisioning better days. As his voice deepened, Megan and Sebastian stayed up late at night after a hard day's work and sought out colleges and universities that he could attend and later earn a law degree. The steady influx of lawyers in that fluid community was at an all-time high. You say a *lawyer,* and an imaginary bell goes off in the city of Mandeville, signaling the welcoming of Manchester's baby boomers.

The local Ad Signs posted in multiple locations said we can help you with legal representation for divorce, accidents, personal injury, malpractice, bankruptcy law, criminal defense, child custody, real estate law, immigration law, drug litigation, DUI, and traffic-related tickets.

One astute commuter, who meditated on those billboards every morning and evening while earning his livelihood years later, had this to say:

"It seemed like the legal industry was cashing in while law schools were preparing new students for their gold rush.

Back then, whenever Megan and Sebastian, who were focused on developing potential in Wesley, mentioned their goals for their son to the neighbors, those nationals questioned Megan and Sebastian's intention for wanting their son to become what they called a deep pocket, a traitor. They not only felt that the profession was already saturated there in Mandeville but added:

"Lawyers are a bunch of liars, thieves, and crooks; they will sue their mother if they get a chance." By this time, the few sour grapes in the bunch of legal scholars living in Mandeville were noticeable; some of them smelled so bad that they had become a stench. The number of lawyers not only grew in Mandeville but expanded to other areas of Manchester as well. Even though the city was a breeding ground for higher educational learning, the neighbors saw Haynes' dream as too far-fetched for their son Wesley. On the other hand, Wesley, though he had a knack for legalese and was fascinated by legal issues, saw himself as a musician, and that's all. You say music, and he is ready to spit you a tune. To him, music was life! It had meaning. It was exhilarating! He imagined playing music from sun up to sun down. With his used guitar recently acquired at a garage sale, he roamed the town and villages in and around Mandeville, emulating the likes of Jimmy Cliff, Bob Marley, Peter Tosh, The Beatles, The Temptations, The Isley Brothers, and many others, singing their songs and honing his musical craft. He was euphoric.

On the other hand, his peers saw in him a musically possessed individual engulfed in a world of piped dreams.

As his "Adam's apple" developed, not only did his voice deepen more, but his poignant rhythmic style became the talk of the town. "That Wesley boy can sing, you know," they said in Patios.

Now, suddenly, the switch had flipped. The neighbors, amongst themselves, voiced under their breath, and in Patois:

"That Haynes' boy can sing, you know. He has a very unique style."

Not only were the girls his age crushing hard on him, but also older women. More so, he was like a magnet, beginning to mesmerize them with his musical style and charisma.

Megan and Sebastian finally believed in their son's talent and determination, so much so that they bought him his first electric guitar and an amplifier for his sixteenth birthday. With these new musical toys, Wesley played at neighborhood events, including the sweet potato fest, amped. He wowed the crowd constantly with his music and converted many naysayers into believers.

CHAPTER 3

Success has a price to pay. Not only was Wesley paying it by struggling financially as an artist who bartended while pursuing his dream, but he was simultaneously attracting friends and some enemies alike. Some people loved him, but others, without stipulation, hated his guts.

Although many of those haters had seen and heard the most recent Garnet Silk in Mamma Africa and Place In Your Heart, Heavy D in Mr. Big Stuff and Gyrlz, They Love Me, Sanchez in Missing You and Never Diss De Man, Buju Banton in Murderer and Love Sponge, and Beres Hammond in Tempted To Touch and Pull It Up. They had cut their teeth on the musical vibes of Bob Marley and the Wailers in I Shot The Sheriff and No Woman No Cry, Peter Tosh in Soon Come and Walk and Don't Look Back, Jimmy Cliff in The Harder They Come and Many Rivers to Cross, Dennis Brown in Silhouette and if I Had The World, Toots and The Maytals in Sweet And Dandy, Gregory Isaacs in Night Nurse and My Number One, and Third World in Now That We Found Love and Sense of Purpose.

They had danced to the poignant rhythm of American legends like Otis Redding in Try A Little Tenderness and Hard To Handle, Sam Cooke in Cupid and Bring It On Home To Me, The Temptations in It Was Just My Imagination, Jerry Butler in For Your Precious Love and I Stand Accused, the legendary Barry White in Let the Music Play and You're The First, The Last, My Everything, Al Green in Love and Happiness, and How Can You Mend A Broken Heart, James Brown the Godfather of soul in Sex Machine and Try Me, Smokey Robinson in You Got A Hold On Me with the Miracles, and Cruisin.' Teddy Pendergrass in T.K.O and Turn Off The Lights. Plus, Marvin Gaye in Sexual Healing and Let's Get It On, and Michael Jackson in Billie Jean and You Want to Be Starting Something.

Additionally, not recently forgetting the soothing sounds of Luther Vandross in Never Too Much and A House Is Not A Home, Jaheim in Ghetto Love and Just In Case, Brian McKnight in Back At One and Crazy Love, Lionel Ritchie in Easy and Still, and Babyface in This Is for the Lover in You and Never Keeping Secrets. As well as Usher in Nice and Slow. Plus, the newcomer, Maxi Priest, on the reggae scene in his hit song How Can We Ease The Pain? and Shaggy in It Wasn't Me. Nevertheless, Wesley Haynes is a work in progress. What could he spit that was so exceptional? What can this kid from the block bring to the table?

WHO SHOT THE SHERIFF? SERIES

Many locals still queried despite his plodding emergence into the musical arena.

They couldn't comprehend. Not only that, but the visions in their minds were also too nightmarish. But it was theirs and not Wesley's.

Those who hated Wesley did so mainly because they couldn't envision his dream of making it big and living out his true potential. So, they laughed at him and chipped away at his self-confidence. Even when they applauded, it was mediocre on his behalf - full of envy and bigotry.

On many occasions, those who thought less of Wesley would even attend neighborhood events where he performed to drag down the aspiring singer with their pessimism. Their hypocritical attitude was despicable. It got to Wesley Haynes on many occasions, but he found a way to rebound from their negativity.

Just like you can't hide the sound of thunder, the sight of lightning, or the colors of a rainbow. So also, you cannot put a bushel on true talent mixed with persistence. Put it under a rock, and it will roll that stone away. Even the police at the local station could not escape talking about Haynes as a potential rising music star, and his upsurge was very noticeable. John Brown, the descendant of an enslaver and the lead law enforcement officer in Mandeville wanted to stand out and dub himself the Sheriff. This veteran Sheriff, who had struggled with alcoholism, saw Haynes' success

WHO SHOT THE SHERIFF? SERIES

differently and, filled with hatred, looked for ways to nail Wesley Haynes at every opportunity. He had always nursed a big grudge for people with talent, and now it was Wesley Haynes' turn. Why? Only Sheriff John Brown knew. Sheriff Brown felt that any conviction brought against the young talent would sour the rising star's career, whom he called Singer Man. Brown would secretly but also jokingly ask his deputies:
"Anything yet on the Singer Man?"
When the response was in the vein of: 'Nothing yet Sheriff.'
Brown would remark:
"If he sings, he's got to have some flaws; he can't be that clean."
Brown knew deep in his psyche that one day he would spike Wesley Haynes to the cross, derailing his musical career. In his quest for sabotage, Sheriff Brown roamed Mandeville's streets, looking for any crime to which he could pin Haynes. Although the Law Enforcement Department in Mandeville listed Brown's assignment on the board at the station, indicating he was out looking for Bad Boys - a new term for lawbreakers. Brown would drive by the strip nightly where Haynes resided, pretending he was doing a neighborhood watch to minimize criminal activity.
On multiple occasions, Sheriff John Brown watched Haynes like a P.I. or, some might say, like a hawk by

following him around the neighborhood, oblivious to Haynes, in an unmarked police vehicle. On many weekends, Brown would have his deputy join him in the stakeouts so he could have ample time to follow Haynes around while the deputy concentrated on picking up other criminals. They needed to return to the station with at least a few citations. Brown purposed in his mind: if Haynes' vehicle had a cracked windscreen, a malfunctioned wiper blade, a broken taillight, a burnt-out light bulb, a darker than ordinary tint, a going bald tire, a boisterous exhaust, expired registration, missing tags, or anything he could manufacture or fabricate, be summed up as an infraction tremendous or minor, he was going to cite Haynes and bring him in.

Brown had no problem being the bad cop who would prey on Wesley like a giant hawk for any chance he could get to pounce. Brown was willing to bend the law, twist it, tweak it, or break it to produce the catch inside his net – Wesley Haynes. In his quest, made up of many late-night stakeouts, his searches were futile as Haynes always slipped through his grasp.

Later that evening, the Sheriff huddled with his Deputy and two other high-ranking cops. The topic of discussion was Wesley Haynes' affairs. "Someone has got to cool him before he gets too hot." Says the Sheriff's Deputy.

"I agree. He's such a show-off. I will be keeping a close eye on Singer Man."

The Sheriff responds and immediately leaves the huddle. He goes directly to the chalkboard a few yards down the hall and writes in block letters; I AM OUT LOOKING FOR THE BAD BOYS. The cops in the huddle take notice. The Sheriff departs hurriedly.

Moments later, he pulls up in his sedan on Mandeville Road. A wooden backdrop with multiple posted signs captures his attention. Next to these signs is a POST NO BILLS warning. He focuses on a poster promoting one of Wesley Haynes' events. He exits his car, peels it away from the scenery, and pursues Wesley Haynes.

The singer, oblivious to this pursuit, knew the streets of Mandeville very well and used different routes to get home.

WHO SHOT THE SHERIFF? SERIES

CHAPTER 4

One Friday night, after performing at a club with his newly formed band of four, a bass guitarist Mike, a percussionist Max, a drummer Winston, and a female backup singer Britney, Wesley said one of his frequent long goodbyes. He got inside his compact car and headed home. The drive should take at least 20 minutes using alternate routes. That night, he took the familiar path to get him home in 18 minutes. He realized he was tired but found a way to stay wide-eyed and bushy tailed.

The roads were clear at 2:00 AM except for a few returning home from the clubs, motorists, and taxi cabs looking for the next fare, plus a few buyers and sellers working on their nocturnal high or their graveyard shift making money by peddling drugs.

Like the law of attraction, Wesley stepped on it and was soon accompanied by a trailing vehicle. Familiar with all the streets and intersections in Mandeville, Wesley thought about eluding the tailing vehicle and embarking on a street race. So, he took off through those well-known streets of Mandeville. Now, with sirens and flashing red and blue lights, the tailgater persisted. Sensing more than trouble, Haynes pulled over to the street's side.

Sheriff John Brown emerges from the sheriff's car. He has numerous stripes on his lapel, though most were unjustly earned. He abruptly approaches Wesley's car, posturing his rank-and-file status.

"What happen, youth? Do you think this is a bloody Daytona Race Track? Speeding like a maniac! The speed limit signs are posted for a reason ... too slow for offenders like you, huh?"

Says Sheriff Brown in Patois,

"Sir, it's been a long day, and I was trying to get home soon. I didn't mean to cause any harm. I'm a defensive ..."

Sheriff Brown interrupts in Patois,

"Tell that to the Judge! You no see. I clocked you to do ninety in a forty-mile-an-hour zone. That is fifty over the limit, a whole half a century. Plus, you try to get away..."

"Sir, I am not Brian Lara and wasn't playing cricket ... I was trying to get home."

Says Wesley,

"Oh, you've got cricket jokes. Let me look at your driver's license, proof of registration, and insurance."

He provides the sheriff with the requested documents. The Sheriff goes to his car, and after reviewing Wesley Haynes' documents, instead of issuing him a traffic ticket, Sheriff Brown quickly returns to Wesley's car and remarks,

"Singer Man, step out of the car."

No one had ever addressed Wesley using that name. Anyway, Haynes complies.

Sheriff Brown frisks him down for any possible weaponry. He is clean. The Sheriff roughs Wesley Haynes up and then cuffs him. He escorts him to his Sheriff's car. There, he shoves Haynes inside onto the back seat of his car. Haynes winces during the physical roughness.

"I am The Sheriff!" He reminded Haynes in case he forgot who the brass cop in Mandeville was. Sheriff Brown slams the door shut and returns to the singer's car. He rummages through the car. He finds Haynes' electric guitar, an amplifier, and a notebook filled with written lyrics. He searches for some more but finds nothing else he could use to incriminate the singer. With nothing else to attach Haynes to besides speeding and possibly attempting to elude an officer, he drives him to the barracks, where Haynes spends his first night behind bars after filling up a cup with his urine.

Haynes was permitted one phone call, and that was made to his parents, Megan and Sebastian. They were not at all happy that their son was spending the night in jail. Looking at the time on the clock showed that it was now 4:00 AM on that unforgettable Saturday. Later that morning, they readied themselves, making a trip to the police station to visit their son Wesley. Driving to the station was uncomfortable for Megan and Sebastian Haynes. It was their first visit, and they didn't know what to expect. They discussed the pros and cons of Wesley's musical career choice. Did their son make the right decision to get caught up in the musical industry? Was his dream too farfetched? They reasoned that if he had chosen a law profession, the law enforcers might be a bit more lenient with him regarding a traffic violation.

Upon arriving at the police station, Megan's and Sebastian's facial expressions clearly showed how much they despised the look and feel of the environment. Police officers were coming in and out fully loaded with sophisticated weapons as if they were returning from or going to war. Plus, calls were coming in regarding some of the most hideous crimes. They saw themselves in an extraordinary milieu as neither of his parents had ever visited a police station. Anyway, they posted bail, and Wesley Haynes was released. His urine test came back negative for drug usage. Brown had alleged that he had smelt marijuana odor in the car at the time when Wesley was pulled over. It was all a hoax, an attempt to nail the singer on drug charges. Even so, a charge was brought against Haynes for eluding a police officer in a high-speed chase. That charge, though, was later dismissed.

WHO SHOT THE SHERIFF? SERIES

CHAPTER 5

That one night spent in jail left a bad taste in Wesley's mouth. For the first time in his life, he had been housed with criminals. These undesirables were made up of rapists, drug offenders, pimps, prostitutes, thieves, robbers, arsonists, and murderers, all awaiting arraignment. Most had no qualms about confessing what they had done to wind up where they were.

The stats regarding the amount of black men who ended up going to jail or prison showed they made up. 40.1% of the almost 2.1 million male inmates in the U.S. and Jamaica. At the same time, nearly 75% of them became second offenders. Additionally, about 10.4% of the entire African American male population in the United States aged 25 to 29 was incarcerated, by far the largest racial or ethnic group—by comparison, 2.4% of Hispanic men and 1.2% of white men in that same age group were incarcerated. Compared to the stats in Jamaica, those figures were minuscule because of the densely Black population.

Wesley examined those facts and felt they were despicable. His hometown of Mandeville, in his eyes, bore some resemblance and, therefore, wasn't very conducive to the growth of his potential. He felt like he was now a big fish swimming in a small pond filled with sharks, alligators, and crocodiles, which sought to devour him, namely one tough brass underhanded cop in Sheriff John Brown.

A few months later, Wesley Haynes took his skills to Kingston, the capital city. By now, the rumor was out in Mandeville that Brown would do anything to put Haynes in prison. Haynes saw the handwriting on the wall and sought to change that condition.

Unfortunately for Sheriff Brown, dismissing the charges against Wesley Haynes crushed his ego.

Haynes had researched and found that Kingston accommodated singers with skill and some, down to the core, sweat equity. Haynes was willing to pay that price by any means necessary. To Wesley Haynes, the big city was a busy place where everyone was wrapped up in their hustle and flow, and he understood that genuine success was always up to the individual.

When informed about his decision to move east, his parents, Sebastian and Megan, weren't happy campers. Feeling like their only begotten was not making the right decision, they tried to get Wesley to change his mind. When asked How he was going to survive? Wesley replied,

"I will find a day job and play my music all night. While others are sleeping, I will be hustling. Bob Marley spent a lot of time in Kingston, " he reminded his parents.

"Marley often returned to Ocho Rios where the air and life are cleaner. Don't worry, I will return it when I make it big. I'm going to make it. I believe in the possibilities. This is my time." Wesley reminded his parents.

"We still think that you need to give it some thought. Some real thoughts. Think it over, son."

His mom encouraged him.

Sebastian interjected,

"Son, what you have gone through shouldn't give you a reason to pack up and leave Mandeville. This is your birthplace."

"Dad, it's all about the music. Music is the food of love. I've got to play it. I would rather soar with the eagles than scratch with these chickens." Responds Wesley

"Why don't you sleep on it? Think it over, Wes."

His dad encouraged him,

"Dad, this is all about sticking to my mission. If I had taken up the legal profession and the opportunity arose for me to move to Kingston to work as an intern or paralegal at some unknown law firm. You would have said get them, Wesley. You were born to conquer. But because I've chosen my brand of success – music- you are trying to persuade me to stay in Mandeville, where there are many haters and few lovers. I would instead begin in a place where nobody knows me, where my name has never been dragged through their court system, where no one destroys what I sowed.

I love you both, but I also love success because, as a kid, you always told me I was born to succeed. If I chose to be a janitor, I would want to ensure that I became the best. According to the advice of the late Dr. Martin Luther King Jr."

Megan and Sebastian got the message. They realized their efforts were futile in keeping Wesley in Mandeville when he began to pack.

That night, Wesley packed his clothes in a suitcase, his amplifier in a box, and his guitar in its case. He packed his clothes in another suitcase. Early the following morning, he boarded a bus headed east to Kingston.

CHAPTER 6

Upon arriving in Kingston, the big city, it didn't seem like all it was cut out to be. Most of the streets were filled with potholes. The bus driver did Wesley considerable disfavor by driving first through the slum areas. One of the streets had an abandoned refrigerator in the middle of it. The bus took a detour to the next bus stop and away from the dumped household appliance. Wesley, very early, was presented with a negative picture of his new city. He suddenly woke up to the realization that now he was in a city much different from Mandeville.

Wesley got off the bus close to Main Street. He had not packed a snack for the trip and needed a bite. He saw a restaurant nearby and purchased a beef patty, cocoa bread, and cream soda. After devouring the meal, he continued up Main Street.

Thomas, whom he met on the bus, saw him walking towards Main Street. Driving a little two-seater car, Thomas pulled over, rolled the passenger window down, and asked:

"Wesley, are you staying in this immediate area?" Wesley replied.

"I have not yet decided. I will figure it out."

"You are crazy, mon. This is Kingston. Do you see what's going on all around you?" Wesley looked half a block up Main Street and saw it not only occupied by gridlock vehicular traffic but pimps, prostitutes, Ministers of Parliament, drug dealers, vendors, card and domino players, robbers, and people who, if they could roll it, smoked it. The Weed fumes saturated the mild, dense air. It seemed like suddenly, Ganja smoking was now legal. The partakers didn't smoke a little skinny joint but a big fat newspaper-rolled marijuana spiff.

"Let me give you a lift to a safe place,"

said Thomas, opening the passenger door. Wesley put his luggage in the back seat and jumped in. The car took off through Main Street.

Thomas pulls up outside a small 25-room hotel. He tells Wesley to check out the scene here until he's acclimated.

"You don't have to like it; it's not what you want, but it could be a means to help you get what you want, mon,"

Thomas said.

Thomas also informed Wesley that Clyde Gumbs, the owner, could use some help. He suggested that Wesley introduce himself to Clyde and let him know he is new in town. Thomas told him he might need some help fetching groceries, cutting the grass, and emptying the trash in exchange for lodging, food, and some pocket change.

He also gave Wesley his phone number and suggested Wesley call him to let him know how it worked out with Clyde.

Wesley took him up on it and moments later met Clyde. The hotel owner, Clyde, stuttered and was tall and stocky. He looked like a wrestler and was in his mid-60s. Clyde interviewed Wesley. They bonded quickly. Clyde, also a Mandeville native, reassured Wesley, the out-of-towner. He liked Wesley's ambitiousness and saw him fitting in nicely. Clyde found extra chores for Wesley and paid him extra to do so. Wesley did not forget to call Thomas and thank him.

Soon, Wesley was able to create some savings. So, when Clyde decided to put a for-sale sign on a van that was in the repair shop, Wesley made him an

offer. Clyde sold him the van for $500.00. Wesley continued working for Clyde during the day, and at night, he rehearsed his music and wrote lyrics.

Everyone around Wesley smoked weed, including Clyde, who said his reason was medicine. It wasn't long before Wesley Haynes indulged. Rehearsals were now like a burning bush. As they say, if you spend time together with robbers, at some point, you will end up driving the getaway car, and if you spend time together with pigs, you will find yourself rolling in the mud. Wesley was now rolling them up and getting his regular highs. On the other hand, he stuck true to his objective, though sometimes as high as a kite while playing his music every night. Kingston, like most other Jamaican cities, was full of beautiful women. Even so, he didn't like what he saw in the women he met in Kingston, as most just threw themselves at him. His heart was still set on his Britney in Mandeville. He longed for the day when he could see her again.

CHAPTER 7

Wesley Haynes' wages grew as he continued to save his money. He was earning a living, but his heart was stuck back in Mandeville. One day, he called Britney and asked if she would like to move to Kingston. Britney said yes without hesitation but would have to convince her parents that this move would pay off. Britney had decided to elope, but she mentioned the move to her mom. Her mom, Christine, and her dad, James, were unhappy that their only daughter was moving to Kingston. It was too far away from Mandeville. Plus, she was not about to have her nineteen-year-old daughter shack up with some singer. All he had going for himself in their eyes was raw potential, a guitar, and an amplifier. Britney was raised in the church, where she was immersed in biblical teachings, including that sex came after marriage. Her mom also believed in those related concepts.

Even so, after several days of pleading with her mom to release the reigns, her mom finally consented that she goes under one condition: She was not going to get pregnant before marriage like her mom, Christine, did. Britney gave her mom her word, and the following day, she headed east on a bus bound for the capital city of Kingston.

Wesley rented and moved into an apartment on 'Main Street.' Britney arrived from Mandeville a few days later. She was so excited to see him again. It wasn't long after the reunion when someone stole Wesley's van. Now, they were without transportation. They needed it to get around Kingston, and Wesley also needed the van to continue fetching groceries for his boss, Clyde Gumbs. So, like sliding downhill, Wesley was unemployed, and no groceries came from Clyde due to his no-show-up.

They ate cornmeal porridge and peanut butter and jelly sandwiches for a few weeks, washing the meal with sweet water. While Wesley was without transportation, he got on the bus one day and visited the neighborhood bank to acquire a loan. Mrs. Jacobs, the loan officer, met him and interviewed him. She welcomed him and served him some Jamaican Blue Mountain Coffee.

As they sat down to discuss his banking needs. Wesley requested a loan of $10,000.00. Getting back on his feet was a priority, and that amount could go a long way. Mrs. Jacobs ran his credit report. From the look on her face, it didn't look satisfactory. Then she broke the news, letting Wesley know she had to deny him credit. Wesley returned home for another day of cornmeal porridge, peanut and jelly sandwiches, and sweet water. Later that night, the Kingston Police called and notified

Wesley, they had found his vehicle. He decided to pick it up the following morning. When he recovered the van, it was not only out of alignment but also decorated on one side with graffiti. His dream tank was suddenly convoluted with nightmares, and this domino effect was like a parasite eating away at him.

Throughout this ordeal, Wesley was smart enough to stay connected with Clyde.

To downsize, Clyde decided to sell the hotel and move to a senior citizen home across town. Clyde knew the owners of most of the restaurants and clubs in Kingston, including Milton Rogers, who owned Michael's Bar and Grill. Clyde's entrepreneur buddies had it going on in the big city. So, Clyde made some phone calls on Wesley's behalf. Michael's Bar and Grill invited Haynes in for his debut performance.

Haynes bought Britney a lovely, sexy dress for the event. She liked it and dressed to the nines for the occasion. Britney did backup vocals while Wesley did vocals and played his guitar. They sang some familiar covers. Clyde and Thomas also attended the event. They had a blast and experienced Wesley, the man behind his music, firsthand.

Michael brought Wesley and Britney to perform every week on Thursday and Friday nights. The patrons enjoyed their music. Their weekly calendar was suddenly fully booked as the word spread about their musical style. After most sessions wrapped at 2:00 AM, Wesley and Britney would go to their crib on Main Street and stay awake, counting up twenty, ten, five, and one-dollar bills. They were booking gig after gig, and they liked the flow.

Two weeks later, the other band members joined them. Wesley drove the van to their gigs. He dropped his band members off at their yard after their musical performances each night. In addition to using covers of other singers like Bob Marley, Jimmy Cliff, Steele Pulse, Lionel Richie, Peter Tosh, Dennis Brown, James Brown, and the like, they developed the habit of spitting their tracks. They wrote and practiced extensively for hours. Someone always brought in the weed to their sessions as they took turns. That habit was now evolving in their little clique.

One night, after playing at a club and packing up their equipment, Wesley was approached by a man and his wife. The man, a Jamaican national who later revealed his identity as Bill Parsons and a Mandeville extract, told Haynes he was looking for young, fresh talent to go into the studio and record. Bottom line, he was in the new talent discovery business. Haynes should give him a call to discuss the possibilities further. Parsons had heard about Haynes from his long-time friend Milton Rogers.

Haynes' band members overheard the conversation, and the night trip to their homes took on a different tone. They were laughing and cutting up while reminiscing about their tenure in Mandeville. They felt that coming east was about to pay off big dividends. Max, the percussionist, had to break up with his girlfriend Sofia to move to Kingstown. In a heated quarrel regarding the move, she told him that it was either Kingston or her. He chose Kingston. Mike, the bass guitarist, had no strings attached. He was all in if the band members said they were going to the moon. In his eyes, Wesley and Britney were like the characters Henny Penny and Ducky Lucky, and he was willing to follow.

On the other hand, Winston decided to give up his part-time job as a fitness trainer, which he had for many years. It was tough breaking ties, not knowing when he could pay his bills and continue saving ten percent of his income as he was accustomed to.

But now it seemed like things were getting ready to turn around for the better.

"Most people seek out these kinds of opportunities, but this one sought us out, "

said Haynes, under his smile, with an enthused breath. In their happy mindset, getting home that night felt like one escalated elevated ride. Britney was ecstatic.

WHO SHOT THE SHERIFF? SERIES

She saw herself being able to shop till she dropped and wear the kind of attire actual performers can.

Wesley Haynes called Bill Parsons the following day and set up a time to meet. This good attitude was now so contagious that it transpired in every note they played and every lyric they spat. Their performances now took on true meaning as they sang with passion and purpose and with vision as well.

Those nights and days leading up to the interview seemed to be shortened as the anticipated meeting day drew closer — to being followed by possible studio time.

> WHO SHOT THE SHERIFF? SERIES

CHAPTER 8

The day of the meeting soon arrived, and Wesley Haynes showed up at Bill Parson's office.

Haynes wants the deck stacked on his side, dressed in neat, clean, upscale casuals. He couldn't afford a car wash for the van, which had recently been stolen and graphitized, so he parked it a little distance away from the building so as not to feel embarrassed and, above all, outclassed by the Mercedes Benzes and Cadillac SUVs he expected to find parked outside Bill's office. Haynes was right. As he parked the van around the corner and walked to the office, he discovered a parking lot filled with some of the most desirable automobiles in the world. From Wesley's point of view, Bill Parson's parking spot had his name on it: RESERVED FOR BILL PARSONS.

Wesley Haynes quickly pressed the buzzer to the door and announced himself. A woman answered. As he entered through the revolving glass door of this middle-sized office, he realized that the woman with Bill that night at the club also worked there at the studio. Dressed in a beautiful red dress, the woman addressed:

> WHO SHOT THE SHERIFF? SERIES

"I am Rose Best-Parsons. Bill is expecting you. He is with another client and should be out shortly." Rose assured.

It wasn't long after taking a seat that Rose escorted Wesley to Bill's office with a signed contract and a smile. In the interim, the other client, a woman in her early twenties, exited Bill's office. Bill extended his hand and shook Haynes.' After breaking more ice, the two men talked about vision and potential for a while. Later, Bill Parsons took Wesley on a tour of the back studio lot. Bill talked with Wesley about possibly taking his music to the top. After the tour of the studio, they returned to the office. This was new for Wesley; no one had ever taken him by the hand in his musical career. Haynes felt like he had found his mentor in Bill Parsons.

As a result of that meeting, Haynes and his band booked their first recording session, which was scheduled for three weeks from that date. Wesley left the office elated, seeing his dream materialize. In his mind, coming east was paying off big time.

Haynes couldn't wait to tell the band members the great news, and he did. They, waiting for his return at a local restaurant, were beside themselves upon learning that they were booked for a studio recording session and that Bill Parsons was interested in signing them. Additionally, they realized they had three more weeks to prepare before the recording. Their rehearsals took on major significance, and their gigs were events that made the bodies of their audience tingle.

They were evolving as a superb, talented group with a sense of purpose. After one Friday night gig, Max, the percussionist, said that Wesley sang like a man possessed and heard his guitar speak on separate occasions.

THAT DAY CAME. They entered the studio, ready to lay down their tracks. Upon arriving at the studio, they were met by "Big Bubba," the engineer, an Afro-Asian man in his mid-forties. Big Bubba did his prerecording spiel. Moments later, they were set up to record their first song and gave it all they had. At the end of the session, when the recording studio door opened, they stepped out electrified. Their song This Is My Time was how they felt, and they wanted the rest of the world to know.

Bill Parsons was not present at the studio session but walked in as soon as Big Bubba got ready to play back for Wesley and his band members. Parsons was mesmerized after Bubba, his engineer, pressed playback. So were the members of the entire band. Wesley asked for a rough copy, and Bill Parsons burned him a copy of the recording pending a scheduled mixing session.

Wesley Haynes and his posse left the studio on an all-time high and returned to their dwellings more stoked than when they first came together or even when they

WHO SHOT THE SHERIFF? SERIES

first moved to Kingston. Was it hard for them to sleep that night? You bet! It was. They stayed awake, thinking about the possibilities along the way. However, tragedy struck hard, like those twisted ironies of life that none of us understood that night. Unfortunately, for Bill Parsons, he did not make it home that night. While leaving the studio's parking lot, he was approached by two gunmen who not only robbed him but took his wallet and the keys to his Mercedes Benz. They pumped several bullets into his body, leaving him dead. As if that wasn't enough, they entered the recording studio and walked off with studio equipment, a mixer, and microphones.

The following morning, as the local Television stations reported the news, Wesley held Britney in his arms, in tears. The man opening the door to their career now no longer existed. Big Bubba, it was alleged that it had already made it home when the incident occurred. Bubba stated, as was reported to Wesley by Rose:

"Bill stayed at the studio after Big Bubba left and was listening to that song repeatedly. They both felt they had a great song and couldn't wait to have it mixed and distributed."

The tragedy hit home to the band members in many ways. Was this foul play? Their newly recorded song was left inside the archives of the stolen mixing equipment. But their freshly acquired mentor and primary music connection had lost his life. It was tough for the band members to face the whole situation.

WHO SHOT THE SHERIFF? SERIES

CHAPTER 9

Later that evening, before the band's regular practice session, the five band members Max,
Mike, Winston, Britney, and Wesley stopped at the neighborhood pharmacy to buy a sympathy card. Before rehearsing, they all signed the card and sent it to Rose Best-Parsons with a bouquet. Several weeks later, they mourned the loss of Bill Parsons and the loss of the master recording of their first song.
On the other hand, Wesley Haynes was happy he requested a copy of the song so he could take it home with him. Even though he wasn't optimistic about its superb quality, he felt it had some value and wanted to listen to it that night after the session.
In the meantime, Britney felt like all they had come to Kingston to accomplish was falling apart. She and Wesley argued, and she indicated that she wanted to return to Mandeville. She took it one step further and began packing up her things. One of the things she said was:

WHO SHOT THE SHERIFF? SERIES

"My mom told me not to move to Kingston with a man whose all he had going for him was some potential, a guitar, and an amplifier, but I did."

Those words tore Wesley. He loved Britney madly. Trying his best to convince her to stay seemed not to work out. He told her things would get better. Even so, the road to success was getting more complicated to her, and her patience was growing thin. Looking across at the two suitcases, she left the apartment to clear her head.

Without his knowledge, his girl Britney went to the park to jog and meditate in the afternoon to finalize her move back to Mandeville. While at the park, she ran into a woman who worked as a secretary at a recording studio in Kingston. They talked briefly.

Wesley stayed on the phone while Britney was out of the house and made a series of phone calls to find someone to take on his unfinished project, either re-record a session or mix the tracks he held on to. He got hit with rejection after rejection. It was now mid-afternoon, and after making phone calls to no avail, Wesley heard Britney walk in through the kitchen when he was about to push the project aside.

"Don't give up! I met someone who could help us mix and duplicate that song."

She remarked.

"Really?"

Asks Wesley,

"Yes, I do. I don't know how much they will charge us, but as a secretary, she might be able to do us a favor." Replies Britney,

"How come you did not mention that before now? You are holding out on a brother, aren't you?" Responds Wesley,

"I just met her at the park, Wesley." Britney responds,

Britney grabs the phone, dials it, and strokes Wesley's head while she waits through the dial tone. The phone rings for a while. No one picks up. She redials, and finally, Grace, the secretary, picks up. "Hey, Grace, it's Britney! We met at the park earlier today. I realize you are just back from lunch…"

"Yes, we did. How are you? I like your hairstyle; I'll see if my hairdresser can hook me up with such a hairdo. Girl, I have to come and check out one of your gigs around town. When and where are you playing next?" Asks Grace.

Britney is now animated.

"We'll be at Michael's Bar and Grill this Thursday and Friday evening. Quickly visit so we can hang out a bit. you'll get to meet Wesley and the rest of the band members… I've been telling you about."

Says Britney,

"Sure thing, I can do Friday night. I will get a babysitter. I'll see you there. I got to go; my phone is ringing off the hook. That could be my husband Gregg.

WHO SHOT THE SHERIFF? SERIES

Plus, the big boss is making his presence felt," Grace says to Britney as she abruptly aborts the phone conversation.

"She'll be at Michael's on Friday night, Wesley." Says Britney as she joins Wesley on the couch. They are both staring at the two packed suitcases in the living room and the money for the one-way bus ticket on the center table.

"Can she or can't she help solve the problem?" Asks Wesley.

"I haven't asked her as yet. First, she'll have to meet you and the band. Then we'll talk to the girl a little. Then I will do my BTW. Women believe in the four-play process, but guys want it immediately."
Responds Britney.

"Is that our next song?"
Says Wesley as he kisses her on the lips.

The phone rings. Wesley grabs it on the second ring. Any news at this point is great news, he visualizes, not only to move the project along but also to keep the love of his life, Britney, there in Kingston. It's Big Bubba, the engineer.

Bubba informs Wesley that a reliable source just told him that the Mandeville Sheriff's Department was connected to the robbery and shooting death of Bill Parsons. Big Bubba stated that Parsons had owned several acres of marijuana plantations in the hills of Manchester, north of Mandeville. Also, it wasn't a robbery; it was a cold hit - and organized sting that brought down the entrepreneur and record producer Bill Parsons.

Wesley asks Bubba,

"Is there anything you can do to help us move the project along?

"There is nothing you can do with that song in your hand. If it's mixed, it will be full of scratches, and right now, I have no connections to set you up for a new recording session. So, for now, you may have to can it!"

Britney, still sitting on the couch and staring at Wesley, dumbfounded, and discombobulated about Bill's death, realizes the plot was not the news she wanted to hear. It's not the way to say goodbye to the man who opened the door to their musical career in such a short time. She regains her presence of mind and asks, "What's up, Wes? Is it what I'm hearing? Sheriff John Brown? He struck again, that hatemonger?" "Sheriff again!

Says Wesley,

Britney's jaw drops as it finally begins sinking in that what she is hearing is for real. Wesley continues,

"They were responsible for the death of Mr. Bill Parsons. I don't get it. If they work as cops in the city of Mandeville…. Why are they conducting raids in Kingston? That's outside of their area."

WHO SHOT THE SHERIFF? SERIES

LATER THAT DAY, SEVERAL HELICOPTERS surveyed marijuana plantations in Manchester. In the interim, Jamaican Police, accompanied by U.S. army personnel, moved in. They torched many Ganja plantations, burning down marijuana trees and plantation houses. Ten Jamaican nationals were shot and killed during the confrontation with the police infantry and army personnel.

It was believed that the men killed were responsible for plantation operations and worked for the now-deceased Bill Parsons.

Additionally, it was reported that some areas of the more than half-mile-square (kilometer-square) marijuana plantation resembled a nursery, with small plants in different stages of growth. Other parts were like mature corn fields, with neat rows of forest green plants rising more than six feet to a protective mesh shielding the expanse of plants.

From the aerial view via helicopters, it was said to look like a giant square of asphalt secluded in the Valley areas of Manchester.

Minutes after the plantations went up in smoke, dark black-gray ash clouds hovered over Mandeville, covering it like a thick dark blanket.

Many locals watching the inferno wished they could fetch a few hundred pounds of that weed before it blew up. With its fantastic market value, most would have been set for life.

As a result of the burning weed, the contact from those smoke-laden clouds was distributed and felt in many low-lying areas of the city of Mandeville. Many residents of Mandeville, it was reported, who never partook of the substance, not even medicinally, received their first Ganga high for free - and unchallenged by the law.

WHO SHOT THE SHERIFF? SERIES

CHAPTER 10

It was Friday night at Michael's Bar and Grill in Kingston. The DJ was spinning vinyl while the band members set up their equipment on stage. A few patrons were mingling, enjoying cocktails and appetizers, while others got their groove on dubbing it out on the dance floor. All roads seemed to lead under the strobe lights. Grace showed up as promised. She was dressed to the nines. Britney was on stage, setting up the microphone stands and spotting her as soon as she entered the room. Britney met her moments later and then introduced her to Wesley and the other band members. Grace had a few glasses of Merlot while she chit-chatted with Britney, exhilarated by her make-over hairstyle.

Suddenly, the DJ announced the band's upcoming onstage appearance, scheduled to occur in the next three minutes. As a result of that 3-minute warning, many rushed to the bar to get a drink before the band played. The band took the stage and opened up with Thank you, Lord then segued into THIS IS MY TIME. The audience was now sucked into the musical interlude and were on their feet dancing and cheering.

WHO SHOT THE SHERIFF? SERIES

Amongst them was Grace, partying hearty - applauding while she danced.

During the intermission, Grace talked again with Wesley. She stated how much she liked the song, was happy to have met Britney, and was able to attend the night's event. Wesley thanked her for coming and arranged to drop off a copy of the song the following day.

Grace's boss, Alston Beckles, liked the song and decided to host a recording session. A few days later, Wesley showed up with his band at the studio, and the song was in the can and ready for distribution a few weeks later.

Haynes and his band members were invited to the studio to hear a preview. They liked it. So did the studio. Grace got on the phone and immediately pitched the song. At the end of that same afternoon, she had called several radio stations in Jamaica, the U.S., Holland, and the United Kingdom. Most of them bought into the hype

and decided to preview the song during that same week. Some radio station producers couldn't wait to get a copy.

Leaving the studio on cloud nine, the band members boarded their van, put in the CD, and rocked the song as they partied on their way home.

THAT NIGHT, they thought about taking off but showed up at their night gig instead. Before the first intermission, they sang their new release and handed out a few copies. Even the DJ rocked the song while their band took an intermission. After the break with the crowd yelling, "This Is My Time," the band opened up with This Is My Time. The audience loved the song and wanted more, but their appetite was only wet with a diminutive reprise version.

Haynes' song lit up the airwaves in Jamaica and worldwide the following week. It climbed to Number One on the music charts in less than three weeks. Things began to change with the air of success. The band has now booked improved gigs and even upgraded their musical equipment. Every exclusive nightclub in Kingston wanted them. Their performances were now not only sold-out events but unforgettable performances. Countries overseas, including China, Japan, Holland, Germany, Australia, the United Kingdom, Brazil, the U.S., and hosts of other nations, were jamming the song not only on radio but at clubs and most music-related events. Concert venues throughout the U.S. also joined the list of callers requesting a musical performance. With the well-deserved success, the band members upgraded their lifestyles. Instead of using one van as a means of transportation, they could each afford their own vehicle. Britney went on a much-needed shopping spree.

Grace continued to drive momentum as the record's sales soared, using referral after referral to increase sales.

The song held Number One on the charts for over twelve weeks. It was apparent that Mandeville's rising star had risen in a different town than his hometown. Coming east had brought success to Wesley Haynes.

The singer wisely put some money into savings. He upgraded to a white fully loaded drop top, which was now just one in his fleet of automobiles. Money flowed in like money was going out of style. On a beautiful sunny day, Wesley drove his drop-top to his neighborhood bank, where he still did his banking. He wondered how Mrs. Jacobs was doing. In his mind, a convertible car and a drive-thru went well together. So, he chose the drive-thru versus going inside the bank that day. As he pulled into the driveway, Mrs. Jacobs was at the drive-thru window.

Wesley handed her the deposit slip. She read it, as stated, a $10,000.00 deposit. He opened his bag sitting on the rear seat and handed her stacks of one-dollar bills. The money-counting machine at the bank was inoperative on that sunny Friday afternoon, so Mrs. Jacobs had to count the bills manually. Before proceeding, she told Wesley the machine malfunctioned, so he should bear with her as she counted the bills by hand.

Wesley told her with a smile:

WHO SHOT THE SHERIFF? SERIES

"That's okay. I don't have anywhere to go. I am not in any hurry. I will wait until you are finished." While she counted the bills, Wesley played songs like This Is My Time, The Harder They Come, I Am Gonna Use What I Got, and Black Man Redemption from his MP3 collection.

While Mrs. Jacobs counted the 10,000 one-dollar bills, the motorists in tow of Wesley began tooting their horns in desperation. The counting took a while and aggravated them. Suddenly, there was a mini traffic jam at the bank's parking lot as cars were seen reversing out of the drive thru. Those drivers later opted to go inside the bank and conduct their transactions in a peeved manner.

After Mrs. Jacobs looked stunned, Wesley collected his deposit slip, folded it neatly, put it inside his wallet, and drove off and out of the bank's drive thru.

> WHO SHOT THE SHERIFF? SERIES

CHAPTER 11

During that era, the U.S. placed an embargo on the Caribbean banana trade. They demanded fair trade at The Lomé Convention in September 1997. Caribbean bananas are commonly grown on small, family-run farms and were about to take a hit. A September 1997 World Trade Organization (WTO) decision pressured by the US, backed by companies like Chiquita, had meant that these local producers were forced to compete on a "level playing field" with giant multinationals and Latin-American "dollar" bananas. They entered this pact with South America in many ways that benefited Chiquita, who was near bankruptcy.

It was a tough one for farmers on the islands. Owing to this restriction, most farmers who harvested bananas resorted to growing marijuana as a substitute crop. It became known to the U.S. government, and in collaboration with the local government, they sent in helicopters and members of their armed forces to torch the Ganja crops.

In the interim, Colombia kept growing its marijuana produce in abundance. So much so that they could supply the glut in the marketplace; if you bought some weed in the Caribbean during the burning of the plantations raids, rest assured it was Colombian. It wasn't long before the U.S. backed off from the torching of crops. The hillsides of Manchester and other torched plantations in Jamaica soon became green again.

It was believed that the ash from those fires served as fertilizer to grow the now luscious Ganja trees. Profits soared in the marijuana market.

Not only did Kingstonians now get most of their weed from the hillsides of Mandeville, but it also served as a constant supplier for Canada, the U.S., and the U.K.

Jamaican police, along with American military infantry using helicopters, once again embarked into the hills of Mandeville in an attempt to destroy their Ganja crops. Unfortunately, they met with strong resistance from the locals who not only slowed their entrance into the hills but, in some cases, blocked the streets with used furniture and other significant appliances, trapping and killing the "pigs" – another name for the police. Ganja farmers fired many rounds off at will, injuring and killing some of these anti-drug supporters. Profits have now soared from the Mandeville plantations. The Ganja boom attracted investors, including Wesley Haynes and others who acquired several acres of land in Haynes' hometown. The word leaked to Sheriff John Brown not only that Haynes had struck it big with his music but that he was cashing in on the profits from the booming narcotics industry in Jamaica. So, he sent Deputy Ron Charles to Kingston to capture Haynes and bring him back to Mandeville for interrogation.

By this time, Wesley Haynes had acquired several bodyguards to keep many people at bay. His celebrity status was emerging rapidly whether he wanted to or not. Whenever and wherever he performed, it was known that the singer's heavily guarded entourage was present.

Meanwhile, Wesley Haynes returned to Mandeville for the first time since he moved to Kingston. He spent only the weekend and assisted in moving his parents, Megan and Sebastian, out of Jamaica to a new home in Miami, Florida. This gift was a total surprise to the now-retired couple. Never wanting to leave Mandeville, they weren't sure how they would
fit in. But they adjusted and became acclimated swiftly despite their retirement status.

Sheriff John Brown's deputy, oblivious to the security surrounding Wesley Haynes, went into Kingston on his weekend trip to Mandeville in search of Wesley Haynes. Not only did he not find Haynes, but he also found nothing in the drug trafficking business to which Haynes could be attached. People in Kingston were tightly lipped about Wesley Haynes' affairs. During that unofficial hunt for Haynes, Deputy Ron Charles traveled from nightclub to nightclub and restaurant to restaurant. Yet he did not find Wesley Haynes.

IN THE INTERIM, Wesley and Britney, along with their parents and band members, were now in Miami. After arguing over the time and locale, the two singers finally decided to tie the knot and have a private wedding in Miami before heading to Paris for their honeymoon.

So, the Sheriff's deputy returned to Mandeville empty-handed. This did not sit well with his boss, Sheriff John Brown, who questioned his deputy's failure to deliver Wesley Haynes. Brown later told another deputy that Deputy Charles was not on the same page when bringing in Wesley Haynes and felt that Haynes was paying the deputy off to cool it.

Brown wanted Haynes and would not settle for less than just that. This was now his burning desire. It was his ultimate obsession. The Sheriff vowed to catch Haynes and bring him to justice in his hometown of Mandeville someday.

WHO SHOT THE SHERIFF? SERIES

CHAPTER 12

When Deputy Ron Charles returned to Mandeville without Wesley Haynes in the net, Sheriff John Brown later decided that he would pick up the rod and go after the Singer Man himself. He toyed with the idea of driving to Montego Bay and flying out to Kingston. However, Brown wanted to do things somewhat incognito despite his objective. He was concerned about masking the suspicion that he was after Haynes if it all blew up in his face.

The word had been out that he had a vendetta against Wesley Haynes in Mandeville, though not yet in most other cities. But Haynes seemed to be breaking out of that net with every trap he set. This displeased the Sheriff very much.

So, Brown left for Kingston accompanied by five other Deputy Officers in a large van. Ron Charles was not with them on the trip; Brown wanted him to stay put for allegedly cooling it. They made the van their final transportation choice because it was roomy, brand new, and fully loaded. Plus, news came in that Haynes

WHO SHOT THE SHERIFF? SERIES

had acquired an elite armed entourage, so they had to be prepared against possible retaliation by Haynes's posse.

In that event, they needed to load up as much weaponry as possible onto the van. Several AK45s were amongst their very eclectic handpicked arsenal. Upon arriving in Kingston, Brown found it necessary to use a separate vehicle. So, he rented an unmarked sedan luxury car and went undercover through the streets of Kingston. Before their daily manhunt, carried out mainly at night when the clubs were in operation, they came together to debrief.

One night, Brown and his team looked for Haynes at Michael's. He had received a tip from the Kingston Sheriff's Department that Haynes performed there on Thursday and Friday nights. Sheriff Brown showed up like a hungry lion and exited the club solo. His van and crew staked out a few blocks away, waiting to be dispatched if necessary.

Upon entering the club, he came up against the owner, Milton Rogers. Rogers knew about Sheriff John Brown's vendetta against Haynes. So, he told him Haynes was not there and that he should let the Police in Kingston oversee the business in Kingston. Sheriff John Brown didn't like anyone talking to him in that manner. After all, he was THE SHERIFF. On the other hand, Rogers was a tough cookie and wasn't into bowing down to any Kingston cop, much less an out-of-town law enforcement officer. Also, some of Roger's local law enforcement contacts talked about how much Sheriff Brown's office spent to bring down Wesley Haynes.

Rogers even questioned why that money wasn't being used to build schools and provide a better education system for the residents of Mandeville. Rogers knew that Mandeville had Sheriff John Brown's back for far too long. That's why Brown got away with whatever he chose to do. Both men argued for a while, resulting in Brown displaying his gun during the scorching verbal exchange. Rogers, though, was not at all intimidated. Sheriff Brown later walked out of the club challenged.

Although his objective in visiting Kingston was to bring in Haynes, he had to find a way to get back at Rogers for his trash-talking. So, to prove his authority, he visited The Crow's Nest, a chic nightclub owned by Rogers that overlooked Kingston. Some notables who frequented this joint included the late Bill Parsons. This served as a hole in the wall for most entertainers in the capital city.

Brown pulled outside in his unmarked vehicle, surveyed the premises, and called his team to make arrests. Outside the Crow's Nest, they arrested more than two dozen men and women made up mostly of patrons who had had records as pimps, prostitutes, and drug dealers. Officers jumped out of the van like

S.W.A.T. in action, displaying their sophisticated arsenal of weaponry. Sheriff Brown was about to capture some bad boys on Milton Roger's premises.

In his mind, he didn't get what he wanted, so he took what he could get. Later, not only did the Kingston Police take those individuals to jail, but Brown was able to help orchestrate putting a chain and lock on The Crow's Nest, claiming it was a drug depot. Brown could do that because of his significant connections in law enforcement throughout Jamaica, and that's just how it flowed. Even so, the man he mostly wanted was still large in his eyes and on the hustle.

They continued searching in that city for Haynes, but their search turned futile at places they thought the singer would frequent.

On the streets, the word from pessimistic vagrants and the mentally insane voiced that Haynes was hiding in a bunker back in Mandeville.

Sheriff John Brown did not buy into the epiphany of the bunker philosophy. He was mindful that if one were there in Mandeville, he would have

been the first to know about it. He was the Sheriff, and he had it like that.

Those intellectuals, on the other hand, knew better. They knew Haynes was not a fugitive and was well protected against the vindictive Sheriff John Brown. After all, the word was out and debated amongst them: "The Sheriff was after Wesley Haynes."

WHO SHOT THE SHERIFF? SERIES

As news soon circulated, it was later learned that Wesley Haynes and Britney had gotten married in the U.S. and, after honeymooning, were embarking on an impromptu tour. This tour was centered on the East Coast, from Tampa, Florida, to Boston, Massachusetts. Sheriff Brown was sadly disappointed when he got the news, as he was set on bringing home that big fish to be fried and sautéed — Wesley Haynes.

Overseas, Americans were not only talking about the singer's music in Barber Shops, Hair Salons, Coffee Shops, Eateries, Subway Stations, Airports, and Bus Stations; they were bopping to the beat of his music on office elevators, and during smoke breaks, even prisoners were in the mix at their yard.

Whenever people wanted to be fit, they worked out at the local gyms or jogged down the street. They played his music from Central Park in New York City to Disneyworld in Florida and Disneyland in California. Frustratingly and in disgust, Sheriff John Brown returned empty-handed to Mandeville just like his deputy did. Except that he arrested some bad boys and thought about every possible horrible thing he would do to Haynes when he was captured.

WHO SHOT THE SHERIFF? SERIES

CHAPTER 13

For several weeks, Sheriff John Brown shuffled papers filled with erroneous information presented to him, stating Haynes had finished his U.S. tour and returned to roost in Mandeville. So, once again, he continued his frequent stakeouts. Retrospectively, the American concert venues proved differently for Haynes; he and his band still appeared at scheduled events throughout the U.S., while Brown continued to track him relentlessly and mistakenly down in Jamaica.

One day, while going through his paper shuffling routine, a wire came across his desk, and a ship loaded with marijuana was found adrift off the coast of Port Antonio. According to reporters, it was believed that Haynes had ties to this vessel as it was registered to a U.S. Miami address once used by the singer. However, it was too early to pinpoint Haynes' direct involvement as information remained sketchy. Sheriff John Brown felt optimistic that Haynes was connected in one way or the other. If Haynes had been attached, this would have been Brown's chance to have the singer put away for good in a Jamaican prison, where even the stray dogs would have been treated better, as the word on the street described those prison conditions. So, Sheriff John Brown took a leave of absence from the Mandeville office to visit Port Antonio in an attempt to carry out his private independent investigation on the origin of the narcotics and ship's owner.

It was not an easy task for him to get involved in the investigation as he had planned. The Port Antonio Police Department wanted full access to that boatload of weed. They wanted not out of Towner's next to it, not even some of their policemen. Port Antonio was said to have strong ties to some of the most powerful drug cartels. Plus, the corrupt police department in that city had an affinity with the Colombian Drug Cartels; they brought in revenue unmatched by any other Caribbean city from San Juan in Puerto Rico to Port of Spain in Trinidad and Georgetown, Guyana.

Luckily for Sheriff Brown, one of his colleagues, Lieutenant Samuel Graves, worked at the Port Antonio Police Department and had some seniority, which he exercised in bringing Sheriff Brown on board the investigative team of top brass narcotics agents from Port Antonio. Brown, though, had to get accustomed to less seniority, but he adjusted his status in order to join the investigative team.

Samuel Graves, on the other hand, claimed that Brown was his part-time understudy. So, they went to work unraveling the case about the ship.

> **WHO SHOT THE SHERIFF? SERIES**

Sheriff John Brown was right this time around, as singer Wesley Haynes was alleged to have co-owned the ship that went adrift with over 100 bags of weed — each crocus bag contained at least fifty pounds of chronic weed bound for Miami. The stench coming from that loaded, anchored ship was overwhelming. Before the boat went adrift, Brown had also been aggressively investigating the shipping of marijuana from Jamaica. He was led to believe whoever handled the trade had a great degree of sophistication because no arrests were made on the transportation end of the trade. Haynes was allegedly in the mix, and if this could be validated, Sheriff Brown was coming after him.

BEFORE LEAVING FOR PORT ANTONIO, the Sheriff had a few rounds of liquor to celebrate since his hate parade against the singer began.
During the week-long full-fledged investigation, it was determined the singer was involved.
Based on his findings, Jamaican authorities requested that Haynes be returned to stand trial.
Haynes' Madison Square Garden performance had to be canceled, and he returned to his hometown of Mandeville in handcuffs to be charged before the prominent Judge Christopher Bailey.

> WHO SHOT THE SHERIFF? SERIES

CHAPTER 14

During the trial, which lasted for almost six months, attorneys for Haynes did all they could to remind jurors that Wesley Haynes was an emerging international reggae star whose music was impacting the lives of many. Additionally, during the tenure of the hearing, numerous photos of Wesley Haynes were distributed as flyers outside the Mandeville courthouse. On the other hand, his hit single CD was selling like hotcakes in many places, the U.S., Europe, France,
Holland, Asia, the United Kingdom, Germany, Jamaican cities, and more in Mandeville. After six months of hearings in the Mandeville courthouse, the Mandeville and recently Miami resident, 27-year-old Wesley Haynes, who had faced ten years to life in prison, was sentenced after un-swayed jurors found him guilty of drug trafficking.
Sheriff John Brown testified against Haynes at the hearing. He stated: When he arrested Haynes for speeding late one Friday night, the car in which Haynes committed the offense smelled like Ganja. He claimed that the singer took off on a high-speed chase

through the streets of Mandeville. He further testified that he did not charge the singer for smoking the substance because neither the substance nor any other material portion of its residue was found in the car during the search, which he orchestrated while Haynes was in handcuffs.

Sheriff John Brown made sure he cleverly sounded like he had given those breaks to Haynes during his testimony at the hearing. He did not want to be portrayed as if he had a vendetta against the singer. Jimmy Cliff spat a song called Hypocrites, and this was the Sheriff's MO – being hypocritical. He had to keep that facade down low based on who he was dealing with and the prevailing mitigating circumstances.

Additionally, Brown said that a urine test carried out on the singer proved negative for narcotics. But the singer was speeding like someone high on something. Judge Christopher Bailey, also a high-flying resident of Mandeville, showed no bias and sentenced Wesley Haynes to 10 years in prison for narcotics trafficking. Dozens of letters and emails were sent to Judge Bailey's attention from those supporting Haynes. Bailey ignored them all. He couldn't care less what those outside the courthouse thought. What the jury decided mattered most. He felt that, in this case, justice was served.

Wesley Haynes did not speak at the sentencing.

When asked about the fate of the reggae star?

"With good behavior and time already served, Haynes could be out of prison in five years," one of his attorneys, John Goodman, told reporters in Jamaica and the U.S.

"What happens now to his Madison Square Garden performance?"

Asked one curious Wesley Haynes' picture-on-a large-placard supporter.

"I guess he will find a way to make it up to his fans, said another of his attorneys outside the Mandeville courthouse."

Haynes was quickly whisked away in a police transport vehicle to the General Penitentiary. As the car sped away, one female onlooker in her 50s yelled out:

"They should have tried him in America. The Jamaican Prison System is the worst. The stray dog in the street will probably get better treatment!" Most, on occasion, referred to that prison system as a hell house.

WHO SHOT THE SHERIFF? SERIES

CHAPTER 15

Although imprisoned, Wesley Haynes' reggae music continued to burn in the hearts and souls of many. It wasn't long before his wife Britney could release a remix of his single CD while Wesley Haynes remained incarcerated. This international release hit hard into the musical arena, creating a severe dent. Profits soared; for many of his local fans, it seemed like he was performing for them in the clubs and restaurants in Kingston and concert venues around the country. While others, conscious of the fact that Haynes was still incarcerated, waited in anticipation for those five to ten years to pass.

The band, unable to hang together without its leader, fell apart. Mike, the percussionist, joined another band in Miami. Max, the drummer, performed in local gigs back in Jamaica while peddling and pushing narcotics on the side. Winston, the bass guitarist, became a bartender. Through it all, they were happy that they still received royalties from the hit song "This Is My Time."

WHO SHOT THE SHERIFF? SERIES

THE YEARS WENT BY FAST with Wesley Haynes still inside the Pen. The 911 bombings of the World Trade Center were behind us. People were coming together on different fronts. On the other hand, racism still left its scars and, in some cases, remained a sore. It was well known that the civil rights revolution of the 60s not only diluted racism but left an open wound still in need of healing. Still needing racial healing, America had elected its first black president. On the other hand, Saddam Hussein, the president of Iraq, was captured and killed. Christopher "Dudas" Coke, the drug kingpin of Tivoli Gardens, was extradited from Jamaica to the United States. People were caught up in the epiphany of going green. The age of "i" had emerged, giving birth to i-phones, i-tunes, and most recently, i-pads. Hip-hop music was still taking a hard rap, mainly from the religious sector. Even so, it still had dominance. China and other Asian countries have bought into the hip-hop culture. Reggae music continued to evolve; even R&B singers and pop stars like Rihanna included that vibe in their musical portfolios. Before this, most Reggae artists recorded covers of famous R&B and pop artists. Even songs like What Goes Around Comes Around by Justin Timberlake have a reggae melody submerged within. After almost six years since that ship laden with narcotics was found adrift off the coast of Port Antonio, Wesley Haynes was released from prison on

WHO SHOT THE SHERIFF? SERIES

the grounds of good behavior. He had heard about the changes in the world while inside the Pen. But now, being outside those walls sure put all those evolutions into perspective for the singer. Conversely, Sheriff John Brown was still pompous as that night when he put Haynes in jail and vowed to pull the rug out from under the singer and the day he testified in court deflating the singer's character. Brown remained a hero for bringing down Wesley Haynes in that narcotic trafficking investigation and trial. However, although near the retirement age of 55, he still worked for the Mandeville Police Department.

On the other hand, the way was paved for a strong comeback for Haynes, whose remixed CD single was still doing well worldwide.

With the help of Britney, who always maintained a positive mental attitude throughout the ordeal, Wesley convinced his band members to return. They did, and in addition to their continued performances, they scheduled a studio session and

recorded a second single, CD, A Better Life Must Come, which later laid the foundation for recording a complete album.

Wesley Haynes not only cleaned up his life and disassociated himself from narcotics, but after the tour, he returned to Jamaica and built a mansion in Mandeville when not enjoying his other manor in Miami. Britney, after a few months, gave birth to their first son, Damien Michael Haynes. Wesley was happy to be a dad and create a lineage for his son Damien.

AS FAR AS Sheriff John Brown was concerned, Wesley had laid the issue to rest. He had buried the hatchet. The locals kept growing weed as most people had to keep up with their extravagant lifestyle.

Now, in Mandeville and most other Jamaican cities, most parents struggle to send their kids to school due to the high cost of education. Fewer and fewer men joined the police force because unless their parents had the money to provide them with a quality education, those types of jobs they never got. So, there became a significant glut in the police department. To make matters worse, whenever there was trouble, and the police were called in, most of those police officers never returned alive. It also became habitual for troublemakers to request police assistance regarding numerous fabricated incidents. When the police showed up, the locals would block off the streets, making it impossible for them to return without being slowed. Then, they would capture, beat, and kill the officers and confiscate their weapons.

Most of these criminals are known to have some of the most sophisticated, eclectic forms of weaponry in their collection. Name the gun; if it has not already been confiscated, they have it in their possession. When it comes to arsenal, most of them are on par with the police, while others own weapons more sophisticated than most police departments, not only in Jamaica but around the globe.

Because of a shortage of police officers, most veteran officers maintained their tenure with the Jamaican police force. So did Sheriff John Brown.

CHAPTER 16

Early Friday night in August, Sheriff John Brown and Deputy Charles were in separate parallel parked cars near an intersection in Mandeville. Both drivers' windows were partially closed as the officers conversed from car to car.
In the interim, the light turned yellow, and a speeding black luxury vehicle, unable to stop, ran the yellow light, suddenly changing to red as soon as the vehicle reached the crosswalk on the other side. The two Sheriff's cars, not waiting for the traffic signal to change, took off in pursuit of the motorist.
Sheriff Brown's car, now ahead of the pack with flashing lights and sirens, is chasing the eluding motorist. Deputy Ron Charles' car follows suit with flashing emergency signals. Finally, the luxury vehicle stops and waits on the right shoulder.
The two men dart out of their vehicle with guns pointed toward the idle SUV. As both men got closer to the parked car, two rounds of gunshots in quick succession cut them down to the ground from through the vehicle's rear windscreen. The luxury vehicle takes

WHO SHOT THE SHERIFF? SERIES

off at speed, leaving Sheriff Brown and his deputy Ron Charles bloodied and lifeless on the street. The vehicle races unaccompanied through the streets of Mandeville.

Hours later, the Mandeville police department, with sophisticated weaponry, combed through the streets of Mandeville in search of the killer and runaway driver. They were searching for their number one suspect, Wesley Haynes, who was on Sheriff John Brown's all-time wish list.

Later, detectives, along with police units, arrived at the crime scene. Moments later they surrounded Wesley's house in Mandeville. Like the S.W.A.T. police, they move in. Since no vehicle was parked in the driveway, some occupied that space in take-down style. They demanded Haynes' surrender while displaying their state-of-the-art weaponry. There was

no response. So, they broke down the front and rear doors simultaneously.

They entered the house in that same take-down style. There was no one at home. After perusing through the house, they recovered a gun in Wesley Haynes' bedroom dresser. They were later able to determine Haynes as the registered owner of the firearm that they confiscated.

Still, they continued searching Mandeville for the singer. People, fearing for their lives, got out of their way. If Haynes was hiding under a rock in Mandeville,

WHO SHOT THE SHERIFF? SERIES

they were determined to find him. The officers kept their hands on the trigger, ready to shoot in an instant. Wesley Haynes was nowhere to be seen.

The aggressive news media picked up the story and ran it every way they could. The newspaper headlines read: Who Shot The Sheriff?

Sheriff John Brown and his Deputy were Gunned Down After a Traffic Stop.

Even before Haynes was confronted regarding the shootings, not only were the police at the Mandeville station accusing him of the shooting deaths, but the word on the street was clear: Haynes Shot the Sheriff. At the time of the shootings, no one had heard gunshots go off; a silencer could have been used as detective sources close to the crime later suspected. AFTER THE SHOOTINGS, it later became known that an elderly man and woman, Doris Weeks, and her husband, Claude Weeks, were returning home from church. They had just welcomed in the Sabbath with one of their church members and done some praying on her behalf. On their way home from dropping off the church sister, they passed the two parked police cars on the roadside. Then, the wet, bloody street connected the two bodies lying up ahead.

"Oh my Gosh!"

Said Doris,

Claude saw what she saw and pulled over to the side of the road. They stepped out of their car and noticed the two uniformed officers looking lifeless. They called 119 and waited for the police to arrive. Moments after that call, several police officers converged on the scene. The couple explained what they had seen to the officers as they drove up the street from church. The officers took their statements.

Still, Doris and Claude were taken to the station for additional questioning by Detective Paul Stevens and Detective Mike Jones. Realizing they had no connection to the crime; the couple apologized and were released.

Meanwhile, the police continued to search for Mandeville, looking for Haynes and the vehicle involved in the crime. Because of the enormous amount of glass found at the crime scene, it was evident that the getaway vehicle had a busted windscreen. Mandeville Police visited several automobile glass repair shops, questioning workers about recent glass repairs. Even

So, no information could be linked to the crime.

Like a thumbprint, everyone has an opinion, and most are not afraid to voice it. Most felt that Haynes shot the Sheriff and his deputy because they pursued him. The search also expanded into Kingston, where the singer lived and performed nightly. Tired police officers worked on rotation. Officers from other cities pitched in to help in solving this crime dilemma. The look on the faces and in the eyes of most police officers in

Mandeville said they were in dire need of rest and recovery.

"Mandeville had a few years prior hosted the Haynes drug trafficking trial, which sent Haynes to jail, but it was not prepared to deal with, and endure, the turmoil of this crime."

According to one Jamaican TV reporter,

There was some merit to this as they were working with a tired, understaffed unit. Additionally, many locals were reluctant to give up any information regarding the shootings. Bearing in mind, the same Sheriff participated in seeing Haynes go to prison a few years prior. Recruiting from other police stations on a Friday night in Jamaica wasn't the easiest thing to have happen. With that Friday being a payday period, most were out splurging a portion of their dough. Most police stations needed who they had on staff and some to help keep a lid on weekend crime. With the continued shortage of policemen in Jamaica, it was difficult for most police stations to give up their key players. A few stations nearby obliged anyway. A glass expert, Sam Chang, was brought into the crime lab. After recycling the glass and reassembling it by laying out the tinted windscreen on an adhesive surface, it was determined that the vehicle used in the shoot-out was an Infiniti SUV. Wesley Haynes also owned a car in that SUV league, which fit the description!

WHO SHOT THE SHERIFF? SERIES

Many questions were unanswered as they had not yet caught up to the singer and his whereabouts.

> WHO SHOT THE SHERIFF? SERIES

CHAPTER 17

Wesley Haynes reported that he was last seen at MO Bay airport preparing to board a plane bound for the U.S. His wife Britney and their son Damien were with them, along with two bodyguards.

"Now the evidence seemed to be weighing in against the reggae artist as many, including members of the growing prosecution team, learned that Haynes had possibly killed the Sheriff and his deputy and fled the country.

Says one TV reporter on the station's late-night news "Though many questions remained unanswered: Why did Haynes leave his gun behind in the drawer of his Do you have a bedroom dresser? What happened to the vehicle which engaged in the crime? Where was Haynes at the time of the murders? Did he commit those murders?"

As the Jamaican Police began to put information together, an APB was placed on Haynes. They at least wanted him to help them solve this puzzle with some unanswered questions. Later, after an extensive manhunt for Haynes, they continued searching the

WHO SHOT THE SHERIFF? SERIES

MO Bay airport facility based on a tip from a Mandeville connect. - a parking attendant who recognized Haynes.
A glimpse of the vehicle involved would make it license tags while filling out his nightly report. It is so much easier on manhunt operations and the SUV registered to singer Wesley Haynes was Under investigation. The license tags would be recovered at the airport parking garage.
this whole mystery together or, ultimately, the Police who discovered the black Infiniti SUV sensed The culprit(s) turning themselves in would suffice," Says that it was not the vehicle involved with the lead detective Paul Stevens to his understudy Mike shooting deaths. Still, leaving no room for errors, they had it towed and impounded for the possible evidence in the case.
It wasn't long before corroborated reports poured into the Mandeville Police Department's blood spot samples, hair, and other DNA collection. Haynes, it was evidence.
Did they hit the homerun about Haynes' involvement now that they had recovered his vehicle? They were getting closer and felt strongly he had fled the country. Even so, they had not yet found Haynes, and his truck didn't have a busted windscreen. If he did conduct those double killings, why he didn't turn himself in

and avoid an ambushed manhunt, many police officers queried.

UPON ARRIVING IN MIAMI and watching the late evening news, the singer says he learned for the first time that Sheriff Brown and his Deputy were gunned down, according to one TV reporter who stalked Haynes at the airport before he got inside his limo.

Haynes knew that many fingers would be pointed at him. Still watching the news as it unfolded, he realized that the Mandeville Sheriff's Department and other Jamaican law enforcement agencies were looking all over Jamaica for him. He was most stunned when he saw the tow truck towing his SUV to the pound and the pictures of what looked like S.W.A.T. Police surrounding his Jamaican home.

Later that afternoon, Haynes met with his newly formed legal team in Miami to discuss and be advised. His legal team advised him there was nothing to worry about when they heard his alibi. After all, the burden of proof rested in the hands of Jamaican law enforcement, and as of yet, they had no evidence to arrest the singer.

According to the autopsy performed on Sheriff John Brown and his deputy Ron Charles, results indicated that Brown died at 8:33 PM that evening and Charles at 8:35 PM, two minutes immediately afterward. Both men died from single gunshot wounds.

WHO SHOT THE SHERIFF? SERIES

According to the record, the flight bound for Miami took off at 9:30 PM that same evening. If Haynes were the motorist who committed those murders, based on the timeline, he would not have had enough time to abandon the vehicle and get to the airport to catch his flight. Bearing in mind that the distance between Mandeville and MO Bay, where the murders occurred, is at least 65 miles. Therefore, it seems farfetched to link Haynes to the crime based on the timeline. Could his wife Britney be a coconspirator? Even if his wife drove the SUV to the airport and he took a cab after supposedly killing the two officers, the singer still would not have made it there on time. He would have missed the flight. How about his two bodyguards who accompanied him on the trip to Miami? Could they have carried out the murder and driven to the airport in a Dodge Viper? Would they have made it there on time to catch that flight after going through tight airport security? Would Haynes leave his gun at home and travel with one bodyguard? Even if he did so, the other bodyguard would undoubtedly be able to catch that flight after cleverly getting rid of the still unrecovered getaway vehicle. Detectives at the Mandeville station had too many questions and very few answers.

Additionally, in support of Haynes' alibi, a spokesman for the commercial airline issued a statement claiming that the flight from MO' Bay airport to Miami

International Airport left on time at 9:30 PM, there were no delays, and the Haynes family was on board. Weighing the evidence, the prosecution felt that there wasn't enough evidence against Haynes to carry out an arrest.

Mandeville's Police Department was enraged by the prosecution's decision, but they still felt that Haynes was their man.

Consolatory on the part of Wesley Haynes, after such great news, with enhanced security protecting him and his family, he continued living as he chose. Except he decided to remain tight-lipped when questioned by the media about his involvement in the double murder. Britney, in strong support of her husband, figured that apparently someone tried to frame her husband knowing that the word was out that he had always had a running with Sheriff John Brown. Could someone else be raining on his hit parade? She queried. Haynes' other band members joined him later that day at his Miami home, in support of his presumed innocence. To them, their lead singer and friend said he was innocent of the alleged murder charges, and that mattered most.

It was later learned that the bodies of both fallen officers were cremated, and some ash was stored at the local courthouse in Mandeville. However, two separate funeral ceremonies were held to mourn the loss of the

Jamaican-born Sheriff John Brown and his deputy Ron Charles.

Many mourners were in attendance.

In the interim, Jamaican Law Enforcement pulled the registration profile of every registered Infiniti SUV on the island of Jamaica. A task force was sent out to inspect these vehicles and question the owners. Many drug dealers who owned the same make and model made concerted efforts to ensure their vehicles were free of narcotics. Nothing turned up to support any evidence related to the crime. They later agreed the vehicle used in the shootings could have been unregistered.

WHO SHOT THE SHERIFF? SERIES

CHAPTER 18

Wesley Haynes and his band resumed their tour amidst much controversy that he was responsible for the murder of Sheriff Brown and his deputy Ron Charles. However, Haynes was a suspect, according to sources close to the Mandeville police. The Police had to back off from arresting him as they realized they didn't have sufficient proof to convict the singer of the crimes in question how they wished, though, that they could locate the vehicle which engaged in the murders! The Jamaican Law Enforcement departments launched an island-wide search for that vehicle. They searched Alleys, Trenches, Ravines, Junk Yards, Chop Shops, Auto Repair Shops, Tractor Trailers, Construction Sites, Abandoned Lots, Rivers, Lakes, Beaches, Landfills, Garages, Forests, Parking Lots, Ships, Burial Sites, and anywhere else they thought a vehicle could be hidden. Even so, they failed.
Meanwhile, in New York City, Haynes and his band arrived at Madison Square Garden with an armed entourage. On the outside, many jubilant supporters wore T-shirts reading, "Who Shot the Sheriff?"
Inside, the concert was about to begin shortly. The announcer came on stage, dressed in an all-white outfit. This sold-out crowd was eagerly anticipating

this event, which had been rescheduled after almost six years.

"Ladies and gentlemen!"

Said the announcer, who continued after the huge applause,

"This is not only the evening we've been waiting for but an event that the New York Tri-state area could not do without for much longer. Stand on your feet and give a massive Big Apple welcome to the reggae artist of our time, Mr. Wesley Haynes."

The announcer departed, and the lights went down, fading black. The all-black members of the band took their positions dressed in black. As Wesley walked out dressed in all black, the lights came up. He looked like he was *Coming to America*.

Everyone was now on their feet. Wesley and his band started the event with a mixed reprise version of This Is My Time. The crowd went nuts. Britney joined them on stage, dressed in black as the band segued into a cover song. The audience, from the nose bleeds sections to the floor, engaged in a wave as the performance continued. It was a spectacle to watch. They had waited over six years for this event, and Haynes and his band delivered spectacularly. As the musical vibes continued to reverberate, the entire Madison Garden crowd was rocking and dubbing to the sweet reggae beat. The band played their best, and the singers gave it all they had. The place was in a musical frenzy. After a very entertaining performance, the music faded to the last song of the night. The crowd remained on their feet, waiting for more. They started another wave interlude in anticipation.

Wesley looked across at Britney, and together they looked behind the band. They cranked a 3-minute reggae medley to close the event. New Yorkers had an evening they would never forget. News spread swiftly about the success of the New York City Madison Square Garden concert. Many New Yorkers were still talking about this amazing event days afterward. More so in Mandeville, Wesley Haynes' hometown, even if they had not been physically present to experience the event, they jubilantly commented on it.

CHAPTER 19

It was obvious the prosecution was not done with Wesley Haynes. Pressured by the Sheriff's associates they kept on digging for substantial evidence, enough to make an arrest of the singer. With so much speculation surrounding that crime, but also mainly because of Haynes' alleged involvement in these murders, it seemed as if the powers were secretly planning to go ahead and arrest Haynes anyway, even if he was just a suspect. That was the dialog circulating amongst the police in Mandeville.

On the other hand, they felt as though they were walking on thin ice or eggshells if this whole thing were to backfire. Wesley Haynes could get back at them for making an unlawful arrest. He had enough money to drag their entire department through the mud.

ALMOST A MONTH LATER, the murders are still unsolved, and the authorities are looking for a possible break in the case; the phone at Detective Paul Stevens' office rings. It's Lloyd Matthews from the ballistics department. He is ecstatic.

"Hey Paul, I think we have something we could use to attach Wesley Haynes to those murders."
"Great. Lay it on me!"
Says Paul Stevens,
"According to our ballistic findings, the bullets which claimed the lives of Sheriff Brown and Ron Charles match the handgun retrieved from Wesley Haynes' house on the night of the murders."
"Great! Put that gun in the vault and keep it there."
Says Stevens,
"By the way, fax me your findings ASAP. Thanks."
Paul Stevens walks out of his office stoked. He feels like they have made a dent in the case. He just needed the confirmation.

IT IS NOW ONE MONTH AFTER the murders of Sheriff John Brown and Deputy Ron Charles. The crime lab seemed like they had turned over a double six.

The detectives close to the case were awaiting ballistics confirmation. Detective Paul Stevens teamed up with Mike Jones, and together, they flew to Miami in the meantime and interviewed Wesley Haynes for the first time.

Both detectives met with the singer at his home. Britney, his wife was present and also participated in the meeting.

When asked where he was on the night of August 12 when Sheriff John Brown and his deputy Ron Charles were murdered, Wesley said that he was at the airport heading to Miami. Britney concurred. He was then asked what time the plane departed; he said it left at 9:30 PM sharp. When asked why he was flying to Miami. Haynes mentioned that he and Britney were scheduled for rehearsals prior to performing at the Madison Square Garden Concert.

"Why didn't you take an earlier flight?"

Questioned Stevens,

"It only takes a few hours to fly to Miami from Jamaica. I figured once we arrived we'd get some sleep and wake up the next morning ready for rehearsals the next day."

Haynes was asked if he knew Sheriff John Brown and Deputy Ron Charles. Haynes told the detectives that he was pulled over almost a decade ago and arrested by Brown. Continuing, Haynes added that he saw Brown again during his trial more than 5 years ago. Sheriff Brown had testified at the trial.

What about Deputy Ron Charles? Haynes said that he had no prior knowledge of Deputy Charles and had never met him.

Jones presented Haynes with photographs of the victim Charles. Haynes looked at the photographs and said,

"I never met him, never seen him."

The detectives then asked Haynes if he owned an Infiniti SUV.

Haynes answered,

"Yes."

Detective Jones produced a picture of a black Infiniti SUV and asked Haynes if that looked like his automobile. After carefully looking at the picture Haynes said:

"That looks like my automobile." Stevens then asked Haynes if he had owned a handgun.

"Yes,"

Replied Wesley Haynes. "And where that gun is now?" Asked Stevens.

"Gun's at my home in Mandeville."

Stevens continued,

"Your gun is registered?"

"Yes. It is."

Responded Haynes.

"Why don't you travel with it versus leaving it behind?"

Stevens inquired.

"I don't want to forget it's in my possession while going through airport security. It belongs at the house. Plus, I've made it a habit to let my bodyguards worry about security when on the road. That's what they get paid to do."

Jones asked,

"Mr. Haynes, did you shoot Sheriff John Brown and Deputy Ron Charles?"

At this point, they get poised to squeeze a confession out of him.

"I did not,"

Replied Wesley Haynes,

"What if DNA collected at the scene proved otherwise?"

Stated Paul Stevens,

"I don't think anyone would be crazy enough to plant my DNA at the crime scene."

Said Haynes,

Jones sent a text message to headquarters to find out if there was any new information on the missing vehicle. There was none. Without it they realized they were only standing on one foot regarding arresting Wesley Haynes. With Haynes vehemently denying his involvement with the double murders, the detectives had only one piece of evidence to go on – the handgun. But they still needed confirmation from ballistics that the bullets matched Wesley Haynes' gun. Once again, Stevens produced a picture of the weapon. Although there was no evidence placing Haynes at the scene of the murders, the detectives were willing to throw as many curve balls as they could to get a strikeout.

"I must inform you that the bullets that took the lives of both officers were recovered, and the bullets fired seemed to match your gun."

Stevens added,

"Seemed? I don't see how that is possible. I never shot those guys,"
Says Haynes.
The detectives asked him if he would provide fingerprints and hair samples and accompany them to the station to do so. He agreed. Haynes supplied the officers with fingerprints and hair samples at Miami Police Station.
In the interim, both detectives agreed that Haynes was their prime suspect even though they didn't have sufficient evidence against him. They were persistently and methodically building a case against Haynes, judging his body language and whatever they could glean from him that showed a guilty reaction.
In the interim, the police department in Jamaica had received the faxed confirmation on the ballistics test, and their boss informed Detective Jones via text that they needed to arrest Haynes based on the limited evidence against the singer. They felt that if the timing of death were miscalculated Haynes could have done it. Plus, the bullets matched. With the timeline still in question, they privately articulated that he could have used a car resembling
his Infiniti. Then, he drives his car to the airport and parks it there. Maybe he didn't want any DNA findings from blood drops from the victims, so he chose to switch cars. He knew where the Sheriff placed

his speed trap. So, he sped through that street, encouraged the chase, stopped his car, and when the officers proceeded to investigate, he shot both of them and hid the car.

Additionally, because the bullets matched the gun, they felt firmly up to this point that it was he who had committed the murders and no one else.

Moments later they read Haynes his rights and arrested him based on the ballistics test. Haynes was held in custody with possible extradition to Jamaica in order to stand trial for both murders and face the death penalty if found guilty.

WHO SHOT THE SHERIFF? SERIES

CHAPTER 20

Meanwhile, the legal minds in Mandeville were busy putting their prosecution team together for this high-profile trial. Judge Roger Carmichael was appointed to rule in the case. Carmichael was younger and had recently replaced the senior former judge Christopher Bailey, who had previously sentenced the singer to 10 years in prison and had recently lost his battle with pancreatic cancer. Most locals felt Haynes would get a fair trial with a new judge on the bench. One who was his age group and probably a little bit more understanding of the nature of the murder case.

It was a given that many Jamaicans were still upset about the guilty verdict in the Wesley Haynes narcotics trial almost a decade ago. Many still debated the case at Barber Shops and other establishments, claiming he was wrongfully convicted.

Even so, in this case, Jury selection was set to begin in a few days. The overseas press was gearing up to embark on Jamaica for this high-profile trial of the Jamaican reggae artist. Was the largest city, in the parish of Manchester in the county of Middlesex on the island of Jamaica, ready for all this? In the eyes of most nationals, it was. However, the wavering prosecution team saw it differently and opted out of having the case tried in Mandeville, fearing that the singer would walk scotch-free. There was discussion of a Kingston held trial, but the political ramifications could be devastating for the ruling political party if Haynes won the case. Haynes had developed solid political ties in Kingston and was revered by the entrepreneurs in that town who were strong supporters of the opposition party.

They considered New York, but with most of the Jamaican population abroad living in that city, they imagined seeing almost a quarter of a million demonstrators outside the courthouse in protest. New York turned down their proposal, stating that the singer had no ties to the Big Apple—not even a physical address.

Miami, where the singer lived, owned property, bought a house for his parents, and was held in custody was their next option. After days of negotiations, Miami agreed and jury selection in that city was underway. News soon spread rapidly in Jamaica that the case would be tried on U.S. soil. That decision not only paved the way for several days of rioting from a rambunctious simmering local posse, but several police officers lost their lives during the protests. Mandeville supporters of Haynes demonstrated wearing their Who Shot The Sheriff? T-Shirts in gold, black, and green colors.

One TV reporter asked a black T-shirt-wearing supporter, "Why are you demonstrating against the trial being held overseas?"

The middle-aged woman answered,

"He is like a modern-day Bob Marley, and we believe he is innocent. He was boarding an airplane at the time of the murder. It could not have been him who did it. That Sheriff had always been giving him problems, but I don't believe he did those murders. I really don't think he would get a fair trial in America. They don't understand our complicated legal and political system."

When a member of the prosecution was asked by the same reporter about that woman's viewpoint:

He responded,

"That is for the Judge and Jury to decide whether he is guilty. We believe he is guilty as he had every reason to commit murders. Once again, we will put our faith in the Judge and the Jury."

The demonstrations that erupted in Mandeville started at dawn on Friday and lasted throughout the weekend until sundown. The three-day protests ended when many of Wesley Haynes' supporters had to return to work on Monday. So, by Sunday sunset, the number of people parading the streets of Mandeville began to dwindle.

On Monday morning, the news broke that a different judge, Monica Finley, a native of Kingston and living in Miami, had been appointed to the bench. She was dubbed a no-nonsense judge with a 90% conviction record. According to most prosecutors, her 10-year tenure on the bench in Miami was immaculate. About her, they jokingly articulated:
"There's a method to her madness."
They loved that guilty ratio.
Most of the Jamaican prosecution team stayed in track for the now overseas trial.
The following day, five hours were spent selecting the nine-member jury, which consisted of five men and four women. The Jury consisted of two African American men, one African American woman, two Caucasian men, two Caucasian women, one Hispanic male, and one Asian woman. With the jury selection completed, the trial was set to begin on Wednesday inside the Miami courthouse.
Wesley Haynes elected to go with a new defense team from the one that represented him in his narcotics trafficking trial. He selected Collin Mattes to head up his defense team, a fellow Jamaican from Kingston who lived in and had been practicing in Miami for 7 years.
By this time, many Jamaican reporters and other civilians interested in the case had already arrived in Miami for this all-important trial. To fund the trip,

many hosted Garage sales, and some Tenement Yard sales. Some stayed with relatives, while others stayed at hotels and motels. The U.S. government supported granting visas to those involved with the trial.

WHO SHOT THE SHERIFF? SERIES

CHAPTER 21

It was now Wednesday morning, and the trial was set to begin. The enormous crowd that gathered outside the Miami courthouse was made up of many moonlighting lawyers, fans of Wesley Haynes, non-supporters, divorcees, bored housewives, single women, teachers, firemen, engineers, sculptors, painters, entertainers, writers, entrepreneurs, cab drivers, retirees, farmers dressed in coveralls, newspapers editors, journalists, TV news channels along with their personnel, clergymen, ex-cons,
barbers, politicians, street vendors, off-duty police officers and even people who had never met the singer or heard of him before that day. Many of them tried to crowd into the small courtroom. Only a few handpicked were allowed in. Those who stayed outside seemed as if they had left their problems behind and just wanted to be there to find out firsthand: Who shot Sheriff John Brown and his Deputy? Who pulled the trigger had now, for months, been the gossip worldwide, and the residents of Miami were about to find out whodunit? The crime, in which

the singer and former narcotics dealer, Wesley Haynes, was being charged. If found guilty, the singer could face the death penalty and be killed by way of lethal injection.

OPENING STATEMENTS WERE first delivered by the lead Prosecutor, James Tolliver. In those statements to the jurors, he said the singer and former convicted narcotics dealer had struck the jackpot from his solo CD hit song and he decided to invest it in the booming marijuana industry, which led to his downfall, and not only did he blame the Sheriff for his demise, but he also shot and killed the officer along with his deputy.

According to Tolliver,

"Sheriff John Brown had been a veteran Sheriff in Mandeville for over thirty-five years and did not tolerate bad boys and drug dealers. Sheriff Brown also assisted in the investigation of Wesley Haynes, which later convicted the singer for narcotics trafficking."

Tolliver also told the jurors that Haynes not only dealt drugs but had on one occasion, eluded Sheriff Brown during a traffic stop through the streets of Mandeville. He said that although Brown caught him speeding early that Saturday morning, he did not cite the singer. And even though he suspected him of using narcotics, he only searched his car, arrested him, and took him to the station to provide a urine sample. Haynes was released the next day after bail was posted. Charges were, however, later dismissed.

Sheriff Brown, Tolliver said, was a good man who didn't deserve to die. He kept drug dealers off the streets of Mandeville!

But during the address to the jurors, Collin Mattes for the defense stated that during a cross-examination of Wesley Haynes, it was revealed that the singer was the singer. However, he felt vindicated by Sheriff John Brown, who was like a thorn in his side, Haynes decided to let sleeping dogs lie. He said Haynes had forgiven him. Mattes emphatically told the jurors that according to his alibi, Haynes, the defendant was not in Mandeville during the time of those two brutal murders.

"Wesley Haynes was on a plane with his family bound for Miami during that timeline. A timeline will prove the defendant is not guilty of these murders." Haynes, he said, was scheduled to meet with his band members for rehearsals in Miami before their Madison Square Garden Concert to benefit AIDS victims.

Additionally, he let the jurors know that even though the singer had spent over five years in jail, he was released on good behavior. Haynes, Mattes added, had cleaned up his act and transformed himself into a model citizen working to help victims stricken with HIV aids.

> WHO SHOT THE SHERIFF? SERIES

"It takes a model citizen to forgive his enemies – Haynes did. Wesley Haynes decided not to fret because of evildoers. No wonder many of his supporters dubbed him as a modern-day Bob Marley." Said Mattes,

BEFORE TRIAL BEGAN, however, Haynes, with his wife Britney by his side, told reporters he was happy with the jury selection and felt that they would give the trial their best unbiasedly. The morning, he first opened up with Haynes in very high spirits. He was laughing and cutting up with his lawyers and band members. At one point, he was seen kissing his wife, Britney, on the lips. He came to the trial dressed like a king, in a sharp-looking black double-breasted suit, a striped shirt, and a killer power tie.

In his opening address to the jurors, Collin Mattes also introduced Haynes as "The singer of our times." At this point, the defendant stood up, did a modest profile, and relaxed back in his seat. As the proceedings began, he took out his pen and pad and took notes. He listened intently to the statements made, glancing peripherally at the jurors to see their reactions.

Mattes reiterated to the jurors that Wesley Haynes was innocent and had no connection with dual homicide.

But Tolliver reminded them that Sheriff John Brown and Deputy Ron Charles were shot and killed and that the whole purpose of this trial was to find out who did

WHO SHOT THE SHERIFF? SERIES

it. He told them that he expected them to convict Haynes and nothing short of it. He also reminded them that not only did Haynes have several running with the law, but he also disliked Sheriff John Brown.

Additionally, spending five years in prison could have generated enough venom in the singer to want to take Sheriff John Brown's life and anyone else associated with him.

Tolliver concluded by emphasizing:

"Wesley Haynes deserves to be punished for these crimes of injustice. It is no miracle that the death penalty is in place."

CHAPTER 22

The following day, the court reconvened with Ryan Mundell, who handled the autopsy. After being sworn in, Mundell, in his testimony, explained the cause of death. Mundell states that the gunshot wounds to the throat of Sheriff Brown and to the head of Deputy Charles were the cause of the officer's death. Mundell showed PowerPoint slides detailing the position of the bullet wounds on the bodies of both officers. During his picture-slide presentation, he used a rule to draw attention to the throat area of Sheriff John Brown, where that fatal bullet entered. He further
explained that the bullet lodged in the upper vertebrae of the spine.
Mundell also mentioned that the Sheriff might have had a chance to live at least a bit longer if the bullet's impact had not severed his windpipe, disallowing the flow of oxygen to his lungs. As he continued to show these grotesque pictorial accounts, Wesley Haynes was busily engaged in scribbling notes on his notepad and showed signs of sympathy on behalf of the Sheriff. Mundell then showed slides of the bullet wound evolving from the gunshot to the head of Deputy Charles. With the same ruler, he again pointed to the

middle of Charles' forehead where the bullet entered. He further stated that the bullet went through the brain and lodged in the back of the deputy's skull. Mundell was questioned by both Collin Mattes for the defense and James Tolliver for the prosecution regarding the timeline of these deaths. He informed both men that Sheriff John Brown died at about 8:33 PM that evening and Deputy Ron Charles around 8:35 PM.

Judge Monica Finley ordered a small 15-minute recess and then continued the hearings with Detective Paul Stevens taking the stand.

Stevens testified that he and Detective Jones were called to the crime scene that night, a few hours after the murders possibly occurred. He stated that when he arrived, he interviewed an elderly couple, who apparently called 119, stating that on their way home from church, they saw what looked like an accident. They added that they got out of their car to see if someone needed an ambulance or CPR. At that point, they saw the two officers lying there dead along the roadside.

The couple said that they figured that the officers had been shot as their bodies seemed pierced, one in the neck and the other in the head. They also claimed that they smelled sulfuric fumes like gunpowder. It then was confirmed in their minds the men could have been shot.

We wanted to believe the couple but had to do our duty, so Detective Jones and I had both of them transported to the police station. There, we later questioned the couple more extensively and released them.

We felt that the couple did not commit these murders based on autopsy reports we had just received. The time of death just determined by the autopsy indicated that the deaths could have occurred between 8:30 PM and 8:35 PM.

While at the crime scene, we made it a high priority to glean whatever evidence we could. The fresh, broken glass at the scene indicated that the shooter could have fired the bullets through the back windscreen because a mini antenna was found amongst the broken glass. We collected the fragments of glass along with the two guns still held tightly in both officers' hands and delivered them to the crime lab. The coroner was called onto the scene by Detective Jones, and the bodies were later transported to the hospital.

That same night, we visited Wesley Haynes' home. Haynes was listed as a prime, possible suspect because of his previous running with Sheriff John Brown. We were also informed he could be dangerous because of his prior narcotics associations and his entourage of bodyguards who worked for him, so we went in with not only backup but with a strong police presence. At his home, we recovered a gun which, after ballistics tests, linked his gun to the bullets that have been determined to have claimed the lives of the Sheriff and his deputy on that fatal night.

More than two weeks ago, after interviewing Wesley Haynes at his Miami home, we fingerprinted him and acquired a hair sample. We didn't have enough proof to arrest him then. We later received confirmation on the ballistics and then arrested Wesley Haynes and charged him with the murder of both officers.

Judge Monica Finley asks the lawyer of the defendant if he has any questions for detective Paul Stevens.

"Yes your honor," says Mattes.

Mattes confers with Haynes, then stands up.

"I apologize, your honor."

"Next time counselor, ask my permission before conferring." Says Finley, "I will your honor." Mattes responds.

Mattes approach and address,

"Detective, your name is Paul Stevens is that correct?"

"Yes."

Responds Stevens,

"And you are an officer at the Mandeville station?"

"I am."

"And you just swore to tell nothing but the truth?"

"I did."

"How long have you been with the Mandeville Police Department?"

"I've been with the department for twelve years."

Stevens responds,

"How long have you known Sheriff John Brown?"

"For as long as I've been working at the Mandeville station."

Responds Detective Stevens.

"How would you describe the man you have known in a working environment for twelve years?"

"Objection!"
Says Tolliver,
"Sustained,"
Says Judge Finley,
"Do you know Mr. Haynes?"
"No, I don't."
"When was the first time you met Wesley Haynes prior to this trial?"
"I first met Haynes at his Miami home when Detective Jones and I interviewed him before arresting him." States Detective Paul Stevens.
"Were you aware that the singer Mr. Haynes and Sheriff John Brown was at war with each other?"
"Objection your honor!"
Says James Tolliver, on behalf of the prosecution, "Objection sustained, says the judge.
"Have you ever heard Sheriff Brown say that he is going after Haynes, and he will bring him in to be sautéed like Escovitch fish?"
Detective Stevens fumbles,
Objection, your honor, this is tampering…
"Objection overruled. Answer the question detective Stevens," Says the judge.
"I did hear mention that Haynes was on his wish list, but it could have been from a fellow officer. I don't recall hearing that statement directly from Sheriff Brown. I also did not hear the Escovitch fish marinating analogy."
"So, you did hear something to that effect from one of your fellow officers?"

Asks Mattes,
"Yes. But I am not sure who said it."
"So, Wesley Haynes' name was a station word in the green room, the smoke oasis, the early morning breakfasts, on the beat, the firing range, the stakeouts, and in meetings at the Mandeville Police Station?"
"Objection your honor!" Says Tolliver.
"Sustained," Says the judge.
"When did you consider Haynes a suspect, at the time of the murder or during the interview?"
"Haynes has always been a suspect we just didn't have enough evidence to make an arrest. Not until we ran the ballistics on his gun and later interviewed him regarding his alibi, was that confirmation received regarding the ballistics test."
Says Stevens,
"At what time did you visit the Haynes' home after the murder?"
Asks Mattes,
"It was around 10:35 PM on the night of the murders."
"Was it before 10:35 PM or closer to 10:45 PM?"
It was closer to 10:35 PM." "No further questions your honor," States Mattes as he takes his seat.
The Judge looks over at the prosecution team. "Mr. Tolliver?" She says.
Tolliver responds,
"I have no questions, your honor." "Detective Stevens you may step down," Says Judge Finley.
Finley hits the gavel and continues, "This court is now in recess. We'll reconvene in thirty minutes."

Haynes closes his notepad and moseys outside with his wife and the rest of the defense team.

It was beginning to seem that whenever things heated up in the courtroom, Jude Finley would take a break so everything could simmer down before she continued with the next witness. Her mindset was to keep an orderly courtroom and not allow tempers to flare as things got out of hand.

CHAPTER 23

When the trial was reconvened that afternoon, Jude Finley invited Sam Chang, a crime lab expert with glass and metal suaveness, to the witness stand. Chang began by stating his credentials as being actively involved with that area of criminology for over 15 years. He also said collecting evidence from the rear windscreen was very unusual. Mostly, it's the front glass or front windows that get damaged in a vehicle gunshot-related incident. Usually, in an incident like this, the front windscreen gets shattered because a gunshot is fired in a face-to-face manner unless it's a drive-by shooting, then the glass on the front door doors tends to get blown out. He further said that the tiny antennae found amongst the shattered glass was a huge indicator that the glass was from the broken rear window of the vehicle.

Chang also said the glass on the ground contained no tire marks, so it could not have been the front windscreen unless the vehicle moved in a parallel direction, which is highly impractical. Also meshed into the glass fragments he was able to discover

WHO SHOT THE SHERIFF? SERIES

sulfuric fumes and smoke residue. Chang explained the tedious process of recycling the glass and making the pieces fit like a jigsaw puzzle. Then he explained how he glued the fragments of glass again using Crazy Glue.

Chang walks over and removes the windscreen from its paper wrapping.

Mattes, the defense lawyer, approaches the table and takes a good look at the windscreen. On the windscreen, there are two holes. Chang indicates that the two bullets fired from inside the car went through those holes. Wesley Haynes takes written notes while he soaks up the information. In his imagination, Haynes sees the windscreen as one that looks identical to his automobile.

Jude Finley says,

Mr. Mattes, you may cross-examine the witness. Mattes approaches.

"Great job, Mr. Chang. I can only imagine how much effort it took to put those pieces of glass back together again; every splinter has to be in place. "Thank you!" says Chang.

Mattes continue,

"Is it possible to determine when the shots were fired through that piece of glass?" "I am afraid there is no way to determine the time of bullet impact through the glass."

Says Chang,

"So, Mr. Chang, what is the purpose of reconstructing a piece of glass if one cannot tell the time of impact through it?" Asks Mattes.
Objection," Says Tolliver. "Objection overruled," Says Judge Finley.
"Sir, the main reason for reconstructing the glass fragments into a whole piece of glass is to be able to determine the make and model of the vehicle used in committing a crime when that vehicle involved in the crime is missing and not part of the crime exhibit."
Answers Sam Chang,
"No further questions."
Says Mattes, "Mr. Tolliver?" Says Judge Finley.
Tolliver approaches,
"Mr. Chang, your work is commendable." Chang acknowledges.
Tolliver continues,
"In your analysis of the windscreen, were you able to determine the tenure of the tint job?"
"Yes, sir! The tint was done recently. The way the glass loosely attached itself to the tint is a clear indication that the tint job was still new. The tint job had to be done within three weeks to a month before the incident as the glue was still mending with the glass. It was a high-grade tint that was durable. The type they use in limousines."
Mr. Chang, in your findings, were you able to determine who got shot first in this brutal incident?"

WHO SHOT THE SHERIFF? SERIES

"That was one of the first things we looked at while putting the pieces of glass back together. The first bullet pierced the windscreen on the left. Ironically, that bullet did not remove the windscreen. But the second did."

Chang points to the hole inside the windscreen on his PowerPoint illustration.

Chang continues,

"According to our analysis, that bullet struck Sheriff John Brown, who was approaching on the left side of the vehicle and towards the gutter. The second shot, which came through the right of the windscreen, completely detached it from its holding. Once again, because of the way the windscreen was dislodged, we could find other samples like pieces of hair and car fragrances."

"What scent were those fragrances?"

"A pina colada scent."

"What other evidence was found on the dislodged windscreen, Mr. Chang?" Ask James Tolliver.

Mr. Chang continues,

"We were able to retrieve fingerprints as well." Wesley Haynes and Mattes exchanged a glance that Haynes had initiated.

"Thank you, Mr. Chang. At this time, I have no further questions."

James Tolliver returns to his seat.

"Mr. Chang, you may step down, "

WHO SHOT THE SHERIFF? SERIES

Says the Judge.

CHAPTER 24

The Judge next calls Phyllis McPherson, another crime lab expert, to the witness stand.
McPherson is a tall and beautiful African American woman. She is an expert in hair samples and works in the crime lab with the Mandeville Police Department. McPherson was sworn in.
"Counselor, you may proceed with your cross-examination of the witness."
Says Judge Finley to Collin Mattes,
Mattes approaches,
He sizes up McPherson, a scientific expert employed by the city and called by the prosecution. He visualizes this as an uphill climb, knowing from experience that these types of witnesses are almost like the Good Book. Plus, when Mattes looks around at his table, there are no experts present except for the church couple. How he wishes he had some full-fledged experts on his side. He moves closer to the stand, almost in the witness' space. Meanwhile, James Tolliver is looking at him, thinking, what is this moron doing?
"Hello, Miss McPherson, how are you today?"

WHO SHOT THE SHERIFF? SERIES

"I am doing great,"
Responds Phyllis McPherson, "I've noticed you've been involved in a few trials before this one. Is this trial of any major?

WHO SHOT THE SHERIFF? SERIES

CHAPTER 25

Mattes asks:
Significance to you?"
"Objection!"
Says Tolliver,
"Objection sustained!" Says the judge.
"How long have you been working for the crime lab, Miss McPherson?"
Asks Mattes.
"I have been doing this work for the last fifteen years. I have now worked seven years with this particular crime lab in Jamaica."
Says McPherson,
"Miss McPherson, you know that millions of hair samples are similar, don't you? Plus, in most cases, hair samples can only determine an individual's race." Phyllis McPherson, feeling the pressure, responds promptly,
"While that is possible, a carefully studied DNA could, in most cases, link that offender to the crime." Responds McPherson.

"Did you pick up these samples yourself from the crime scene, or were they delivered`?" Tolliver looks across at Mattes and shakes his head, thinking: where is he going with this one now? Should I object again? I'd rather not. This might seem like the prosecution is losing a grip on the case.
"The crime lab maintains high integrity and trust with the detectives on how evidence is collected and delivered to the lab."
Collin Mattes probes,
"Based on your findings, would you conclude that the hair sample collected by the detectives on that night when the two Sheriff officers were gunned down in Mandeville matches that of the defendant Wesley Haynes?"
"It is not a 100% match, but at least 75%, which, in my experience, I would say is probable,"
states Phyllis McPherson.
"How probable?"
Asks Mattes.
"Quite probable.
"And you feel that a 75% quite probable is enough to convict someone?" "Sir, those are our findings," Says McPherson.
"No further questions,"
Says Mattes as he returns to his seat.
"Mr. Tolliver!"
Says Judge Finley,

Tolliver approaches,

"Miss McPherson, thanks for all your hard work at the crime lab. May I ask how many pieces of hair you examined based on evidence provided by the Mandeville Police?"

"We looked at two pieces of hair."

"Were they all the same in texture and color?"

Asks Tolliver,

"No sir, they were all different,"

Responds McPherson,

"How different?"

"They were both from the black race but different colors. One was jet black, and the other was brownish."

"Were any of these dyed or artificially colored?"

"No, sir. They were original."

"No further questions."

Responds Tolliver, who, before he takes his seat, glances across the way at Mattes as if to say: "Wesley Haynes is going down. You can bank on it. Heck, yes, I'm like his new Sheriff; nothing he plants will grow. We are going to make that soil toxic. I'll watch as he gets electrocuted."

Wesley Haynes senses Tolliver's angle, trying to attach him to the crime.

Judge Finley strikes the gavel with authority, claiming: "This court is in … recess! We will resume in 15 minutes."

CHAPTER 26

Narcotics arrests controlled most of the marijuana traffic up and down the Caribbean Coast. He said "Haynes supplied him weekly with at least 100 pounds of chronic marijuana back then. He also said that the ship that went adrift was loaded with a shipment, part of which was heading his way in Miami. Davis claimed that he paid Haynes for the narcotics in advance, also the shipping charges, which were very expensive.

According to Davis, that shipment never arrived. He never got the weed and did not receive a refund from the dealer, Haynes. Davis said that when he asked Haynes about the goods, Haynes told him to go to hell and that the Sheriff had captured the ship John Brown and dry-docked it at Port Antonio.

Davis further said that Haynes told him a conversation about how Sheriff Brown was always raining on his parade and that one day, he was going to dry up those angry clouds.

Davis said he also asked Haynes how he planned on getting rid of the Sheriff, knowing he was the most powerful Sheriff to ever wear a badge in Jamaica. A drug dealer named Marcus Davis and Davis said Haynes responded: "According to Jimmy, currently

serving time for drug trafficking, Cliff, Time Will Tell, Time alone will tell.
Charged with drug possession and having an unregistered Collin Mattes approach the witness stand intending gun in his possession was brought in by the on questioning Davis' credibility.
The prosecution began cross-examining Wesley Haynes.
"Mr. Davis, are you here today at your own volition?" The prosecution thought that by getting him to gather "I'm not. I was requested to be here. Because I had some dirt on Haynes, they might have a chance to do business with Haynes."
The prosecution endeavored to squeeze a conviction out of this case. After being sworn they went for his jugular:
"Mr. Davis, I understand that you are currently Marcus Davis testified that Haynes, prior to his serving time. Is that correct?
"Yes, I am,"
Says Davis,
"Is your testimony against my client part of a deal to reduce your sentence?"
"Objection!"
Yells Tolliver.
"Your honor, may I proceed?"
Requests Mattes,

Some conversation residue ensues amongst court attendees, including Tolliver and Mattes.

"Order in court!"

Yells Judge Finley.

"Counselors, if this type of behavior continues in my courtroom, I will have to reprimand both of you. The objection is overruled!" Continue the judge.

"Mr. Mattes, please continue."

"How many years is this grand appearance taking off your 15 years prison sentence for drug trafficking and the possession of an unregistered firearm?" "None. I volunteered after being asked to do this because I felt that justice should be served in the shooting death of Sheriff John Brown and Deputy Ron Charles."

Says Davis,

"You swore to tell the truth a few minutes ago, right? States Mattes,

"I'm all for the truth. I have nothing to hide."

Says Davis,

"How much are you getting paid to do this?"

Asks Mattes,

"I am not here for the money."

"What are you here for then?"

"Justice." "Justice…?"

Asks Mattes.

"I have no further questions about your honor," says Mattes.

> WHO SHOT THE SHERIFF? SERIES

IN THE INTERIM, news broke globally that Wesley Haynes's song "A Better Life Must Come" had just been nominated for the Grammys. Radio stations played his song over and over again.

Finally, his name was back in the news in a positive light. Commuters in New York, Boston, Chicago, Washington DC, Seattle, Utah, France, London, China, and other cities and countries were now not only talking about the Haynes' trial but also bopping again to his music.

In the minds of his fans, this timely nomination would possibly sway the jury to a no-conviction. On the other hand, Haynes' non-supporters were still opposed and questioned why other songs instead of Haynes' weren't nominated for the Grammys. They claimed that Wesley Haynes had been charged with the murder of two law enforcement officers and should not have been given such public celebratory accolades. Plus, he faced the death penalty in these charges if convicted.

Before the reconvening of the trial, the following day after the Grammy nomination news hit, Judge Finley informed the jurors in a closed meeting that people were attempting to try the case in the media. She also told them that they were, however, the only ones entrusted with the outcome of this case.

The Hispanic woman juror and one Caucasian member were absent from the meeting. It was earlier brought to the judge's attention that the two jurors weren't feeling well and would not be continuing the trial. Judge Finley informed the other jurors that the two jury members would not continue because of ill health. Also, the court will be adjourned for one day until those jury replacements are made. The other seven jurors were happy to be away from the courtroom for an extra day. Although some of them would instead continue with the same core of jurors selected before the trial.

On the other hand, some felt it would be good to bring in some new blood, facilitating a fresh aura in the jury box.

This was a much-needed break for the prosecution and defense to cool tempers and get a fresh start before the trial continued in two days.

WHO SHOT THE SHERIFF? SERIES

CHAPTER 27

Wesley Haynes, while in prison entertained frequent visitors. His wife Britney was the most popular. She would visit several times a week and be present next to him inside the courtroom. His visitors were always well-screened. The palladium surrounding the singer was always very tight. Now that the news about his Grammy nomination surfaced, security around him was beefed up instantly by prison officials. Haynes was not sure what his fate was going to be. He couldn't see how he got entangled in this website. Even so, he depended on his defense team to make the right decision regarding his fate in the trial.

While in prison, he kept very much to himself except when he had visitors. He didn't trust anyone on the inside, but he knew that those who visited him were well-screened.

Now, with enhanced security, he felt protected within those walls. His cell, #11, adjacent to #12 and #13, colored shiny light gray on the inside with a window that served only as a skylight. His two neighbors, Reggie occupied # 12 and Nigel in # 13. Reggie, in his mid-30s, was on death row for killing five police officers in South Beach. While Nigel, now in his 50s was serving a 25 to life sentence for a series of rapes. Nigel had already served 12 years of that life sentence and seemed not to give a darn about being paroled.

Every morning Nigel, before the breakfast alarm sounded, would call out the names of his rape victims: Cynthia, Thelma, Mavis, Maria, and Isabella as loud as he could. Though he had been sent to the hole on several occasions for that type of behavior he didn't care. Apparently calling out their names was his therapy. He had done it so often at this point the wardens sensed that he was immune to the hole, so they ignored his boisterous, insane attitude. Although, at times, they did put him in mainly to set precedence. Many inmates said that Nigel was still possessed by these women after being incarcerated for almost two decades. Some saw him as an outright lunatic. Other inmates at Westview were also constantly sent to the hole. It seemed like to them a dark revolving door. Most of the prison incidents that warranted this punishment stemmed from fights, loud noises, threats, and stealing. The men who smoked were only allowed to do so under supervision in a room known as the smoke oasis.

While at the smoke oasis, most inmates kept their cigarettes back in their cells under lock and key. No one trusted anyone. That's how the relationship was at Westview.

Breakfast was served at 7:00 AM daily. If you missed it you didn't get any. The ration made up of scrambled eggs, grits, and watered-down coffee was served 7 days a week.

Lunch and dinner were the same meal except that it was served at different times. Sometimes, it was pork, and at other times, chicken. It is comprised of a scoop of steamed rice, a piece of broccoli or carrot, a small portion of mashed potatoes, and a piece of meat. If you didn't eat pork you would enjoy a meatless meal on the days it was served. Most people ate chicken. The ones who claimed they were Vegan or Rastafarians received no substitute. To wash the meal down watered limeade or water were the only two choices. Some viewed the limeade drink as urine. Most inmates preferred water which they called H20. So, at mealtimes, H20 was highly favored over limeade.

Most inmates at Westview prison shared a bunk bed that was cemented to the wall except for Wesley, Nigel, and Reggie.

The exercise grounds, securely gated and the size of almost three basketball courts, were their community sanctuary. The gossip, the sports news, the presidential elections, the gas prices although none of them were currently driving a vehicle, how the stocks traded was one of the favorite topics, even though no one invested or had money to do so. If something happened or was going to happen it was aired here. Women are known to gossip a lot but most of the men at Westview had them beat.

Some inmates played Frisbee while others played dominoes, monopoly, and basketball. Some of the biggest cheats in Monopoly were housed at Westview. Regarding basketball, the Piston Bad Boys of Detroit could not step in the shoes of the ten players usually allowed to grace the court. After every basketball game, it was like a bloodbath. You had to come ready to play and be prepared for fights either during the game or afterward. There were no officiating referees, so no one fouled out. Those not prepared for basketball played another game or watched from the sidelines.

Yes. On the inside, it was very much a dog-eat-dog world as those in had no problems confronting another prisoner looking for a fight. So, when that inmate retaliated, a fight ensued. As a result, they would be reprimanded and were sent to live a more constrained prison life. Like it's said: misery loves company. Inside those prison walls, it was a fact! Wesley Haynes, though he loved basketball, feared to thread. He had enough dirt thrown at him on the outside, so he avoided any confrontation within those walls. To him, there was enough rivalry in the courtroom. So, he would resort to his cell and do pushups to keep fit. The inmates referred to him as Mr. Goody Two Shoes. To Haynes, it didn't matter. He wanted to be out of there.

Lockdowns were held twice daily, from 4:00 PM to 5:00 PM and then at 10:00 PM. The inmates at Westview did not celebrate this event much. You could tell by their body language that something was getting ready to happen, which annoyed the heck out of them even before the command was given.

Inmates such as Nigel found it despicable and overly structured, but that was life within those walls. During the first event, they counted the heads and filed reports. Afterward, they had dinner.

Some people, including Wesley Haynes, went to their cells or to the library, while others just hung out playing ball, shooting Frisbees, or enjoying an intense game of dominoes or monopoly.

At 10:00 PM the day was a wrap, followed by lights being switched off. When the Warden made that announcement, it was official. It was understood. Even if Henny Penny or Ducky Lucky showed up and said that the sky was falling, it was a wrap! Those two characters would be looking up to the skies all by themselves.

Wesley did not enjoy this lifestyle. Although it was a lot better than the conditions he had endured while in a Jamaican prison. It was understood that even the stray dogs on the street were treated better than the prisoners in Jamaican jail. He couldn't see himself living like that for much longer. "Something had to change," he told himself. As was stated earlier, his quiet time was spent reading and writing, including doing pushups to keep himself fit. His small library included a Bible along with motivational literature. He read a lot from the "Proverbs," "Ecclesiastes," and "Revelation." In the Book of James, he completely soaked up.

At nights before the "lights out" command. He wrote lyrics to songs and meditated before hitting the sack. Haynes knew that his fate was in someone bigger and more significant than himself. He held on tightly to the idea that, late in the midnight hour, God was going to turn things around.

Haynes watched the news and read the papers, not only about the status of his trial, although he tried avoiding the repetitious drama in which he was involved. He was there, seeing it unfold LIVE before his eyes. Even so, his name had surfaced all day in the news on two fronts, so he indulged in keeping aware.

Plus, not only were people talking much about his Grammy nomination, but most were reveling in it. He couldn't avoid soaking up all the press, although behind those walls at Westview, he kept a very low profile.

On this particular night, he was not only excited about his Grammy nomination but also happy about the adjournment, which gave him a break from the courtroom the following day.

WHO SHOT THE SHERIFF? SERIES

On the other hand, he wondered how the new jury replacements would affect his trial. He tried not to worry about it too much, but the whole thing consumed him.

Haynes questioned his own fate, wondering if the new jurors, who were on the outside, would be looking in for days. He hoped they would not bring the mindset of his non-supporters to the trial. Haynes wished they would have continued with the same jury even if he didn't know what verdict they would have assisted in presenting to the court.

Newly replaced jurors tend to want to try the case based on what the public is saying, even if they are told not to, as he envisioned.

"How could they, after discussing a case with others, not bring their opinions into the Jury Box?" he asked.

Overall, he had to go to sleep to be fresh and ready for what, in his mind, would be a new day in the chapter of his trial. He didn't know what to expect except that there would be a different aura from inside the jury box. The warden passed by his cell and announced: "Lights out!"

Haynes realized that the day was a wrap. Yet he struggled with the idea and finally forced himself to sleep.

CHAPTER 28

The trial resumed the following day on schedule. Defense lawyer Collin Mattes wanted a win for his client and nothing less than that. He sensed that evidence was lacking. So, what do you do when evidence is lacking? You apply pressure on the opponent and get into the heads of the witnesses. Like in basketball, when you smell a victory, you put the other team under defensive pressure, causing them to turn the ball over. That morning, he showed up with his game face on.

Wesley Haynes showed up looking his best in a nicely tailored gray suit that looked like it was made for him. His dotted shirt appropriately complimented his new tie. Looking across at the jury box, nine jurors were present.

He didn't want to treat this day as the day of the verdict, knowing that many more witnesses were still in the lineup; his lawyer had hinted to him that it could be a lengthy trial. Judge Finley had a history of dragging things out, maintaining order, and taking long breaks. She wanted it all delivered in her courtroom.

WHO SHOT THE SHERIFF? SERIES

The jurors were poised. The view of the jury box was inescapable.
Wesley Haynes scanned it thoroughly for the demographic makeup. He was not sure if that would have anything to do with changing the outcome, but the thought was there, and he was subconsciously holding on to it. He noticed, however, that an East Indian female juror and a Philippine woman replaced the two sick jurors.
"Let the show begin!"
He said in his mind. He pulled out his pad and readied himself. How he wished today was the finale. Sitting next to her man was Britney Haynes, dressed to the nines.
At nine o'clock on the dot, the court was called into session. Judge Monica Finley took the stand and announced the jury replacements. Judge Finley looked like she had tanned deeper with what could have been a possible spa treatment during her one day off the bench. She was upbeat.
Finley then addressed the jurors:
"Ladies and gentlemen of the court, I must let you know that the two new jurors have already been briefed and are very much up to speed on the unfolding events in this trial. With that said I would like to call our next witnesses to the stand." In no time, the following witnesses were introduced, the first for the defense: A couple, Claude and Doris Weeks, who

were the first to arrive at the crime scene after both the Sheriff officers were gunned down. The couple looked like they were dressed in their best church outfits. The oath was read and taken. Mattes, invited by Judge Finley to cross-examine the following two witnesses, approaches. "Mr. and Mrs. Weeks, good morning! I know this is not your conventional environment, but an innocent man's fate is at stake in this trial, and as a witness, that fate is also in your hands. You were the first people on the scene on that night when two Officers, John Brown and his deputy Ron Charles were gunned down on that Friday evening of August 12th. Take the jurors back to what you witnessed on that late evening."

Claude, speaking for the couple, addresses:

"Thank you, Mr. Mattes. You are correct. This is not where we choose to be. My wife Doris and I are pastors of a Seventh-Day Adventist church in Mandeville. We would rather be out caring for the sick and afflicted, but this is where we are called to be.

We live a few blocks from the church and also from where the shootings occurred. Normally, we don't take that route home, but on that evening, we gave a sister in Christ who was going through some tough times a ride home after praying with her at the church. After dropping her off, we took what you might call the "back roads" to our house. On the eve of the Sabbath, our desire to get home was a priority so we could be fresh and ready for church the next day.

We saw two Sheriff cars parallel parked along the roadside. The vehicles looked suspicious because none of their parking lights were on.

"Why would two police cars be parked in that manner?"

Doris asked.

I told her something must be wrong, and I wondered if someone had stolen their car.

As we continued up the street, we saw two bodies on the ground over the side of the street. I was going to drive past them. But my caring wife asked me: What if they needed an ambulance or CPR? In the same breath, she reminded me of the story of the Good Samaritan. So, I pulled over. There was broken glass and blood on the street. When we looked closely at the two men it sank in that they were two Sheriff Officers, by their uniforms and badges. Their guns were still in their hands.

The smell of gunpowder was thick in the air, which added to the bullet wound in the neck of one officer to the left and the other wound in the head of the other officer on the right. They were lifeless. We realized that there must have been a shooting that left them dead. Doris reminded me that, that was a crime scene, so try not to touch anything. She also questioned why the police had not been here on the scene.

"They haven't taken care of their sheep."
She said,
"There are two missing sheep. Where is their shepherd?"
I wanted to leave; it had been a long day. Plus, we had to get home and get enough rest to officiate in church the next day. Doris reached into her purse, grabbed her cell phone, and called 119 to report the incident. We both felt obligated to stay until the police arrived, so we waited a little bit longer.
When the two detectives, Stevens and Jones, arrived, we told them what we had seen. They questioned us about who we were and where we were going. We told them the gospel truth. They put us in the back of their car. As we waited, other police officers and coroners showed up. The two detectives continued collecting evidence, taking pictures, and sweeping up pieces of glass.
We felt it was time to leave but wanted to be obedient citizens. We were later driven to the station in Mandeville by Detective Stevens and Jones. At the station, we were questioned some more before we were released."
Inside Judge Finley's courtroom, it is so quiet that you can hear a pin drop!
"What additional questions were you asked?"
Questions Mattes of the defense,
"Questions like: Do you know Sheriff John Brown and

Deputy Ron Charles?"

"Do you own a gun?"

"Have you fired a gun before, even at a shooting range?"

"Do you own a second car?"

We told them no and that we do not own a second car. They asked what make and model it would be if we did.

I told them that we weren't materialistic. At this point, Doris was more tired than I was and said, "The Word says: "Lay up for yourself, treasures in heaven … "'We don't need a second car.' Then, they released us and drove us back to our car.

"No further questions, your honor." Mattes takes his seat.

"Counselor Tolliver?"

Says Judge Monica Finley,

"Mr. Weeks, in your recollection: When did you first arrive at the crime scene?" Asks Tolliver,

"We were there at 9:30 PM."

Says Mr. Weeks.

"How soon did the police arrive?"

Asks Tolliver,

"They were there 15 minutes later at 9:45 PM."

Says Mr. Weeks,

"No questions for the witnesses your honor." Finley strikes her gavel.

"This court is in recess, let us reconvene in 15 minutes." Britney looks at Wesley, he looks at Mattes. They then look across at the jurors.

CHAPTER 29

The trial hearings resumed for yet another day, and Britney Haynes, the wife of defendant Wesley Haynes, was called to the witness stand. Judge Monica Finley invited Mr. Tolliver, a lead member of the prosecution team, to cross-examine Britney Haynes, another defense witness. Britney was sworn in.

Mr. Tolliver approaches,

"Mrs. Haynes, good morning."

"Good morning."

Say Britney Haynes,

"This must be a horrendous task being here every day with your husband, who is on trial for murdering Sheriff John Brown and Deputy Ron Charles. You understand the due process, I am sure." Britney gives a partial smile.

Mr. Tolliver continues,

"You understand the oath that you have just taken, right?" "I do."

Says Britney,

"And you do swear to tell the truth?"

"I do."

Says Britney,

"Tell us about your husband." Wesley pays attention as if he doesn't want to miss a word.

"Wesley and I have been married for almost 8 years, having been together for two years prior. Wesley has been a leader in everything he has done, including track and field. My parents were skeptical when they realized we were serious about each other. I must tell you he shocked them.

Wesley is a good family man, a great husband, a great dad. He did not commit those murders of which he is accused. He was with me and our son Damien at the airport in preparation for boarding a plane to Miami when those murders were committed. This is a complete waste of our time dealing with a crime we have no connection to. This is not due process. This is processing dues, and we are paying with our time."

Britney breaks down in tears.

She draws everyone in.

Britney finally composes herself.

"What time did you arrive at the airport Mrs. Haynes?"

Asks Tolliver,

"Wesley, our son Damien, and I arrived at the MO' Bay airport at about 8:30 PM," States Britney.

"Were you wearing a watch at the time Mrs. Haynes?"

"Yes, I did."

Says Britney,

"Did you check your watch arrival at MO' Bay?"

Asks Tolliver,
"I didn't."
"Why not?"
Asks Tolliver.
'We take this trip to the airport regularly. It takes us about an hour to get to the airport from our house. We left our house at 7:30 PM."
Says Britney,
"At what time did you and your family board the aircraft?"
Asks Tolliver,
"We boarded at 9:10 PM when everyone else did."
"What time did that flight depart?"
Tolliver questions,
"The flight departed at 9:30 PM," States Britney.
"What was the purpose of that Miami trip?"
Questions Tolliver,
"We were visiting Miami for rehearsals before a Madison Square Garden Concert," Responds Britney.
"What was the tenure of your rehearsals?"
Tolliver asks,
"We rehearsed for three days," Responds Britney.
"Your event was scheduled for May 27th, Memorial Day, according to the New York Times. You still had a two-day window."
Asks Tolliver,
"We took our son on a tour of New York City."
Responds Britney Haynes,

"Thank you. No further questions."
James Tolliver says as he returns to his seat,
"Mr. Mattes, do you have any questions for Mrs. Haynes?"
States Judge Finley,
"Yes, your honor."
Mattes addresses Finley as he approaches the witness, "Mrs. Haynes, you have been through a lot during the last eight years. You have raised your son while your husband was imprisoned. Here, you are going through yet another trial. How do you manage all this?" Asks Mattes,
"I believe in God, and I believe in my husband Wesley. He's got many rivers to cross, but this is his time," States Britney Haynes.
That statement emotionally affected Mr. Mattes. "Thank you, Mrs. Haynes. I have no further questions." Mattes ambles back to his seat.

CHAPTER 30

Three weeks, including weekends, had elapsed since the trial began. However, many witnesses had already testified and been cross-examined. That Monday morning, Wesley Haynes, and his wife Britney, along with the courtroom regulars, were back in Judge Finley's courtroom. After saying good morning, Finley had Max Richards, the band's percussionist, called to the witness stand. The Judge then invited James Tolliver to cross-examine Richards, a witness for the defense.

Richards was questioned about his tenure with the band. He was further asked if he knew Sheriff John Brown or ever met the Sheriff. Max Richards never met him or Deputy Ron Charles, so he told the court he didn't. When asked if he ever heard about Brown? Max said it was hard for people who lived in Mandeville not to hear about such a prominent individual unless they lived under a rock.

"You seem to have a great relationship with Wesley Haynes, the defendant. Have you ever heard him make any threats on Sheriff John Brown's …?"

"Objection, your honor!" Yells Collin Mattes for the defense.
"Objection sustained,"
Says Finley, who continues,
"Mr. Tolliver, I am warning you …,
Tolliver continues,
"Have you ever heard any threats made by anyone in the band regarding Sheriff John Brown's life and that of Deputy Charles? Did you make any of your own?"
"No sir, I heard none and made none."
"Tell me about your Madison Square Garden Concert."
"Objection, your honor, that question is irrelevant," Says Mattes.
"Counselor Tolliver, what does that question have to do with the trial?"
Asks Judge Finley. Collin Mattes is now on his feet.
"Your honor, may I approach the bench?" says Mattes.
"You may,"
Says the judge.
The two counselors approach the judge's bench.
"Your honor, all I am doing is trying to determine the motive behind the defendant's trip out of the country, right at the time when the two murders were committed, with his gun linked to the crime." "You may want to address your question differently, counselor. We are taking an unscheduled recess for fifteen minutes. Please meet me in my chambers," Says Judge Finley.

"This court is now in recess for fifteen minutes." The judge strikes her gavel.

Inside the chambers, Judge Finley warned the two counselors about the importance of sticking to questions on the trial.

"We don't need to deal with all the irrelevant stuff. Not in my courtroom. Let's keep it professional and respect the juror's time." Says Finley.

THE TRIAL RESUMED. That afternoon, Detective Mike Jones was asked to take the stand as a witness for the prosecution. Jones was the accompanying detective dispatched to the scene of the murders with his senior partner, Detective Paul Stevens, on the night Sheriff John Brown and Deputy Ron Charles were gunned down. He also accompanied Stevens to Wesley Haynes' Miami home, where they cross-examined the singer before making the arrest. The jurors had heard from his partner Paul Stevens before, and so did Wesley Haynes, who readied himself by taking copious notes.

Judge Finley invites defense lawyer Collin Mattes to cross-examine. Mattes asked Jones to describe what happened on the night of the murders.

Detective Jones talked about being called to the scene and not knowing what to expect. He stated that with the 119 calls coming in relayed by a civilian who was at the scene where two Sheriff officers were gunned

WHO SHOT THE SHERIFF? SERIES

down, there was a degree of skepticism. Mainly because it was common for civilians to make those kinds of calls, and when officers were dispatched to the scene, they realized it was a hoax. By then, it's too late as these officers are ambushed, robbed of their weapons, and in most cases, killed. He reiterated how frequent those crimes were. He said in his mind, the callers could have been connected in some way to those murders also. So, he expected the worst. Arriving at the scene of the murders, he and his partner questioned Claude and Doris Weeks, an elderly couple who claimed they saw the bodies in the street on their way home from church and called 911. Jones later showed pictures of the evidence retrieved from the crime scene on PowerPoint slides. Those graphics included the corpse of Sheriff John Brown and his Deputy Ron Charles, the shattered rear windscreen of the getaway car, glass fragments on the street, the tire imprints of the vehicle, and the two parked Sheriff cars. Next, Jones shows slides of Wesley Haynes's vehicle parked at the airport parking lot along with it being towed, Wesley Haynes' recovered handgun, and a wide shot of the crime scene showing the intersection, Sheriff's cars, and the gunned down officers. Mattes asked Detective Jones:

"Detective Jones, at what point in your investigation did you feel you had enough evidence to arrest defendant Wesley James," Jones said.

"Upon receiving confirmation on the ballistics test."
"And when was that?" "At the police station."
We asked Mr. Haynes if he would accompany us to the station for fingerprinting and a hair sample. He agreed, though we sensed he was uncomfortable. He was very nervous about the process. Plus, we felt he was our man by his nervous reaction when we told him that the ballistic test connected his gun with the shots which claimed both officers' lives."
"No further questions." Says Mattes as he returns.
Wesley Haynes' two Bodyguards were next to the stand. The defense asked them about the timeline of traveling from Montego Bay International Airport to Miami on the night of the shootings. Both men confirmed a 9:30 PM departure from MO Bay to Miami.
The prosecution then quizzed the bodyguards concerning Wesley Haynes' alibi. The guards confirmed they departed MO Bay airport at 9:30 PM on that Friday night. Tolliver also asked if he had anything to do with the shootings of Sheriff John Brown and Ron Charles. Both men denied any involvement in the shooting and death of Sheriff Brown and his Deputy.
The court then heard testimony from Denzel Fraiser, one of Haynes' bodyguards. Another day in the trial was concluded. Meanwhile, outside the courtroom, Detective Stevens and Jones left hurriedly in a car.

CHAPTER 31

It was now Friday and almost two months into the trial would have elapsed. Without the getaway car, James Tolliver, the lead prosecutor, knew from the outset he had a legal challenge to face in this case. The lack of hard evidence against the defendant was factual. The only thing he had to go on really was the recovered handgun and share speculation mixed with he says, she says. But he was willing to fight to the very end. Death by lethal injection faced Wesley Haynes if Tolliver was able to pull out this win for the prosecution. This high-profile case would show him off as an elite prosecutor. Additionally, Tolliver was eager to see Wesley Haynes fry.

Tolliver had supplementary evidence like the hair sample which could have belonged to anyone else than Wesley Haynes. He had character witnesses who didn't care about dragging the defendant through the mud. He had some expert testimony which so far didn't hold much ground in the case. Although he had the possible murder weapon, the non-corroborating timeline didn't put the defendant at the crime scene in the opinion of most.

How he wished the getaway car would surface during the trial. Thanksgiving and Christmas had passed, as did the New Year. Still, when it came down to hard evidence, Tolliver did not deliver any treats. The late-breaking evening news stating the SUV believed to have been involved in the murders was spotted in a ravine was nothing but a hoax. Anyway, after being investigated thoroughly by the new arrivals in Jamaica, Detective Stevens and Jones, this unregistered vehicle was rechecked, and keys found at Wesley Haynes' Jamaica house matched the ignition. Even so, the car had a busted rear windscreen, but that original back windscreen, mainly around the corners, was still intact.

THE COURTROOM FELT AS if things were winding down. It's just like the last two minutes of a basketball game. Except no one had yelled - two minutes!
Sitting as usual next to his wife Britney and defense lawyer Collin Mattes, Wesley Haynes showed signs of impatience although still ready to write.
The ballistics expert Lloyd Matthews was called to the witness stand and sworn in. Matthews had been recently appointed by the Mandeville Police Department and assigned to the case after the shooting deaths of Sheriff John Brown and Deputy Ron Charles.

He had previously worked for the Kingston police for 10 years. Matthews, by far, was the prosecution's star witness. He held the keys to unlock the only major piece of evidence thus far that could connect Wesley Haynes to the murders – the handgun.

After taking the oath, Judge Finley invited defense lawyer Collin Mattes to cross-examine the witness. Mattes steps up in front of the witness stand. "Good morning, Mr. Matthews. It seems like you have been handed a very delicate assignment. One which could most likely determine if my client Wesley Haynes, who is facing the possible death penalty, be convicted of the crimes of shooting Sheriff John Brown and deputy Ron Charles on the evening of August 12th. Mr. Matthews, what process was used by your lab to determine if the bullets that killed both officers on that night were fired from the gun belonging to the defendant, Wesley Haynes?"

"A basic procedure was followed where a bullet from the defendant's gun was shot into a tank filled with water. After that bullet was recovered, it was viewed under a comparison microscope and determined it was a match."

Matthews responds,

"Did you perform the same test on the guns of Sheriff John Brown and that of Deputy Ron Charles?"

Asks Mattes,

"No. I did not." Says Matthews,

"You did not? I can't believe this. Really? May I ask you why not? The two officers, Brown and Charles, allegedly died from gunshot wounds; two guns were recovered at the crime scene belonging to both men. Another gun was recovered from the defendant's home belonging to the defendant. You conducted ballistics tests on the defendant's gun but not on the guns of Sheriff John Brown and Deputy Ron Charles. Why not Mr. Matthews?"

Asks Mattes, demanding answers,

"There was no reason to. I didn't think it was necessary. I had already discovered that the bullet matched the gun of the defendant." "What type of gun was found on Sheriff Brown when he was shot and killed?"

"A Glock 38,"

What type of gun was found on Deputy Charles when he was shot and killed?

"A Glock 38."

What type of gun was found and retrieved from the home of Wesley Haynes on that same night? Matthews responds,

"A 38 45 GAP"

"Same guns, Mr. Matthews,"

"That is correct," Says Matthews.

"My common sense would tell me if three guns are identical, there is more than an 80% chance they could discharge the same bullet unless that gun had been reconstructed."

"Probably,"

Says Matthews,

"Probably or most likely?"

Asks Mattes,

"I would say probably,"

"Were any of these guns reconstructed?"

"Not to my knowledge,"

"Mr. Matthews. Are you mindful of a crime known as friendly fire?"

"Objection!"

States James Tolliver,

"Objection overruled!"

Says the judge,

"Your honor, I would like to propose that the court takes a recess so Mr. Mathews can complete ballistics evidence on the guns of Sheriff John Brown and Deputy Ron Charles."

Asks Collin Mattes for the defense, "Objection to such a decision! This is an attempt by the defense to prolong this trial,"

States James Tolliver,

"Objection overruled."

Says Judge Finley,

"You honor, may I approach the bench?"

"Yes, counselor, you may."

Tolliver does.

> WHO SHOT THE SHERIFF? SERIES

"Your honor, the defense is trying to sway the jurors' minds."
"Your honor, how could I sway the jury? They have not yet deliberated the case. They have no hard evidence against my client except for those manufactured and hearsay. How could he not have done ballistics on the other two guns? Is this a ploy to convict my client?" "Gentlemen, you need a timeout." Judge Finley says to the two lawyers.
Judge Finley asks James Tolliver:
"Mr. Tolliver how long would your witness take to return to the court his ballistics findings on both guns:"
"I have no idea. I could find out for you during a recess."
"Thank you, and let's get to work."
To the court, the judge orders,
"This court is in recess for 15 minutes!" During the break, Tolliver met with Lloyd Matthews. After making a few phone calls, Matthews determined it would take at least 5 hours to return the necessary ballistics findings to the court.
The court was called back to order. Judge Finley informed the court that the trial would be adjourned until 3:00 PM. When it did, they continued with the cross-examination of ballistics expert Lloyd Matthews.

LATER THAT EVENING the trial resumed with ballistics expert Lloyd Matthews on the witness stand.

Defense lawyer Collin Mattes continues his cross-examination of the witness.

Mattes continues and goes straight for the jugular. "Mr. Matthews, based on your recent findings, is there any discovery you would like to share with the Jurors?"

"After putting the guns of Sheriff John Brown and Deputy Ron Charles through the same ballistics test as was done for Wesley Haynes' gun. It was determined that those fatal .45 bullets were in close resemblance to those also fired from the officer's guns during the test. The mystery remains: How did all three men wind up with the same type of weapons?"

Mattes asks:

"Which of the bullets examined in your tests was the closest to the ones that killed both officers?"

"After comparing all five bullets under a comparison microscope, they all look similar." States Matthews,

"No further questions, your honor,"

Says Mattes as he saunters to his seat. Haynes is taking copious notes.

Judge Monica Finley looks at Tolliver.

"Mr. Tolliver!" Says the judge,

Tolliver approaches,

"Thanks for all of your hard work, Mr. Matthews. In conclusion, based on your findings, would you say that the defendant's gun is exempt as the possible weapon used in the murder of Sheriff John Brown and Deputy Ron Charles?"

"No. It doesn't."

Says Matthews,

"No further questions, your honor."

James Tolliver, returning to his seat,

WHO SHOT THE SHERIFF? SERIES

CHAPTER 32

It was almost the end of the day. Several witnesses had been heard from. Defense lawyer Collin Mattes had just finished drilling the ballistics expert. After that episode, the courtroom should have been due for a recess.

Judge Finley looked across at the clock on the wall at the rear of the courtroom and then at the tired jury. "It has been a long trial thus far," Says Finley with empathy,

"We could leave our final witness for tomorrow, but my gut instinct says we should get to the end ASAP. With that said, I would like to invite Mr. Milton Rogers to the witness stand." The court announcer echoes,

"The court calls Mr. Milton Rogers!"

Milton Rogers ambles his way from the rear of the courtroom to the front. He takes the oath and settles down in the witness chair. The judge calls Collin Mattes to cross-examine.

"Good evening, Mr. Rogers! Sir, tell us about your relationship with the defendant, Mr. Wesley Haynes." Rogers composes himself and proceeds.

"I first met Mr. Haynes over 8 years ago in Kingston. He was introduced to me by a dear friend, Clyde Gumbs. Clyde was a patron at my restaurant for many years. He called me one afternoon and said he met a very ambitious gentleman, a singer with style- Wesley Haynes. He told Haynes that he had recently moved from Mandeville to Kingston. Clyde noted that Haynes had worked for him, and besides being a talented singer, he was trustworthy. Clyde Gumbs asked me if I would hire Wesley Haynes to perform at Michael's Bar and Grill, a restaurant I owned. I then looked at my schedule and told Clyde I could use the singer on Thursdays and Fridays and have the young man call me to talk further.

The next day, after lunch hour, I received a phone call from Wesley Haynes. I told him I was busy for the next two days, but I would love to have him come in so we could talk. He showed up on Monday afternoon, and after the interview, we booked him for Thursday and Friday of that same week. He was excited and told me his girlfriend Britney was his backup singer, and she would be accompanying him.

Haynes's music wowed the guests on both nights, so I rebooked him for those nights every week. A few weeks later, Max, Mike, and Winston, three band members, joined them. It wasn't long before they blew up as their music caught on—so much that I had no choice but to turn many guests away on those nights due to a lack of space.

The rumor was out that Sheriff John Brown from Mandeville was looking for Haynes to pull the rug out from under him. While entertaining some guests at Michael's one night, I saw a car pull up. The driver refused to valet the park and blocked the driveway. The parking attendant called me over to intercede. Out walked a man in street clothes. I could tell by the bulge in his waist that he had to be armed. No sooner did he flash his Sheriff's badge.

He asked me if I was the owner. I said yes. How may I help you? He said he was looking for Wesley Haynes. Wesley and Britney had been gone for over a week, so I told him they were not there. I then asked him who I should tell them to stop by. He said Sheriff John Brown. He asked me several times, "Are you sure you are not hiding them? Because if you are, I will arrest you for obstruction of justice?"

"I have no reason to hide anyone,"
I said.

"He asked me the same question again. I then told him I didn't think it was any of my business to relay the man's whereabouts. He searched through the crowded restaurant, displayed his gun, and then left upset. One of my managers later informed me that Sheriff Brown visited one of my other restaurants and arrested some innocent patrons."

Concluded Rogers,
"Have you been in contact with the defendant since that incident?"
"This is the first time I have seen Haynes since his performance at Michael's. However, we've talked a few times during the last 8 years."
Mattes asks,
"What was the nature of those few sporadic conversations?"
"We talked about the hit parade - the progress of his music,"
Says Rogers.
"Was the Sheriff accompanied by other officers when he visited your restaurant looking for the defendant Wesley Haynes?"
"No, he was by himself and, as I mentioned, carried a gun which he displayed," Replies Milton Rogers.
"What type of gun was it, Mr. Rogers."
Asks Mattes, "A Glock 38."
Says Rogers,
"Did he tell you why he was looking for Haynes or did he say that a warrant was out for his arrest?"
Probes Mattes,
"No, he didn't."
"Did he leave you any of his contact information?"
"No, he didn't,"
"Have you ever driven any of Wesley Haynes' vehicles?" "Never did." Responds Rogers.

"No further questions, your honor."
Mattes says as he returns to his seat.
James Tolliver, for the prosecution, approaches the witness, Milton Rogers.
"Mr. Rogers, you claimed you spoke with the defendant over the years. Were those conversations constant or sporadic? And who initiated those conversations?"
"We spoke sporadically. Sometimes, I called, and at other times, he did. He's a busy man, and so am I. All we did was touch bases." Answers Rogers.
"Would you say once a month, twice a month, or every day?" Ask James Tolliver.
"More like twice a year."
"During those sporadic conversations, did he say anything to you, or did you ever overhear him say he was going to shoot Sheriff John Brown and his deputy or that he had killed both men?" Questions Tolliver.
"Wesley Haynes never did." Says Rogers.
"Mr. Rogers, did you or anyone you know shoot and kill Sheriff John Brown and his deputy Ron Charles?"
"No. I didn't and don't know anyone who did."
Says Rogers,
"Mr. Rogers, do you drive or own an Infiniti SUV?" Asks Tolliver.
"No. I don't," Says Rogers.
"Did you know the late Bill Parsons?"
Questions Tolliver,

"Yes."
"What was your relationship with the late Bill Parsons, his posse, and how did you fit in with the music industry in Kingston?" Questions Tolliver.
"Objection!" Yells Mattes,
"Objection overruled, answer the question, Mr. Rogers."
Says Judge Finley,
"Bill Parsons was a patron of mine. He brought a lot of high-profile clients, most of whom were in entertainment, to eat at my restaurants throughout Kingston. He liked our food and bragged about it to his peeps."
Responds Rogers,
"Was Bill Rogers a drug dealer?"
Asks Tolliver,
"Objection!"
Says Mattes,
"Objection overruled."
"That I don't know. He never told me." "What did he tell you he did for a living? I am sure he divulged."
"Parsons said he was a music producer. He was very well respected. That is the most I know." Says Rogers.
Tolliver presents an envelope. From it, he removes a bunch of keys.
"Have you ever seen these keys before? These keys match a black, unregistered Infiniti SUV listing you as the owner. I will ask you again: Are these keys yours?"

WHO SHOT THE SHERIFF? SERIES

A bullet hits Rogers in the chest. At the rear of the courtroom, there is a struggle between Gregg Nichols, the husband of Grace, and the Court Officer for a pistol. Wesley and Britney rush to Roger's aid. He falls to the floor to his death.

The Judge yells as police intervene and arrest Gregg. "This court is in recess!"

CHAPTER 33

The courtroom was eerie as the trial entered the closing arguments phase with a post-tragedy. However, some felt there should have been more evidence for this drawn-out, almost two months of trial. Collin Mattes went first and went through a list of some of the high points of the testimonies presented by witnesses and said: "The prosecution has presented nothing to find my client Wesley Haynes guilty of the murders of Sheriff John Brown and Deputy Ron Charles. This has been nothing more than a case lacking crucial hard evidence. There has been more tragedy attached than substantiating evidence. Again, I ask: Where is the vehicle from which these bullets were fired? Which of the three guns recovered was the one from which those two bullets were fired that claimed the lives of Sheriff John Brown and his deputy Ron Charles? Those essential questions are still left unanswered. Men and women of this hard-working jury, I know the matter rests in your hands to decide if the defendant, Wesley

Haynes, is guilty or not guilty. You will do a calculated job to return with a not-guilty verdict."

James Tolliver was the finale. He spent almost thirty minutes arguing, reviewing what the witnesses said in support of a guilty verdict and the recent courtroom tragedy.

After this, he gave his intelligent interpretation of justice and why the jurors should return with a guilty verdict. About justice, Tolliver said: "What is justice? Justice is a fair, just, or impartial legal process. What is justice when wealthy people can buy their way out of a crime? What is justice when the wealthy can get away with murder? Innocent people lose their lives every day, and those who are responsible for those deaths, if they are rich, are often allowed to walk. This has to stop. We cannot progress when the guilty are allowed to go free. Our system is ruined from the ground up when it comes to justice.

We've heard many testimonies during this trial. Two men of the law were gunned down in cold blood on that fatal Friday night in August. It is your duty..."

James Tolliver stares at the jury and continues, "To deliver justice in this case. Justice will only be delivered by a guilty verdict. As a jury, that climax rests solely in your hands."

The prosecution and defense both rested. Judge Finley gave the jurors until the following morning at 9:00 AM.

to return with a verdict. The jury retired that afternoon to begin their deliberation.

EVERYONE IS SITTING on edge in the courthouse except for the Jurors and the Judge.
Judge Finley:
"Good morning, ladies and gentlemen of the Jury. Have you reached a verdict?"
"Yes, we have your honor!"
"Would the defendant please rise?" Wesley Haynes stands.
"Will the foreperson please read the verdict?"
"Yes, your honor.
On count one of the shooting and death of Deputy Ron Charles, we, the jury, find the defendant, Wesley Haynes, not guilty.
On count two in the shooting death of Sheriff John Brown, we, the jury, find the defendant, Wesley Haynes, not guilty."
Judge Finley says,
"The court is dismissed."
Britney grabs, hugs, and kisses Wesley. Collin Mattes waits for his turn to congratulate Wesley Haynes and does so to Haynes and his wife. Other Haynes supporters are jubilant not only in the courtroom but around the globe.
The crowd outside the courthouse yells:
"Hip, Hip, Hooray, Hip, Hip, Hooray!"

CHAPTER 34

Much effort had been put into the well-anticipated Grammys. Ever since Wesley
Haynes received a Grammy nomination for his hit song "A Better Life Must Come." The Grammys were peppered with controversy as to why the song of a prisoner and an alleged murderer had been nominated for such a prestigious award. Even though the song had a positive message, many church organizations planned to boycott the event.

The committee, on the other hand, felt that no matter what, they were going to host the event. They realized history was filled with events in the past threatened by a boycott. They were not going to bend; they were not going to fold.

Wesley Haynes' song was still rocking the charts at number one.

WHO SHOT THE SHERIFF? SERIES

It was Grammys night. Haynes had been found not guilty in the murder of Sheriff John Brown and Deputy Ron Charles just a few days prior by a jury of twelve.

Many still doubted him, thinking he was the only one who could have done it. The verdict spoke differently.

The event was packed. Haynes supporters lined the streets wearing their A Better Life Must Come T-shirts. The winner was finally announced.

Many at home were glued to their TV sets, supporters and non-supporters alike.

The host returned after the featured band did a number. In a very emotional state of mind, the host addressed:

"What is to happen will, and there are no coincidences. This year's Grammys goes to Wesley Haynes for his song A Better Life Must Come. The entire room went into applause.

Everyone was now on their feet, applauding. The room was transformed from frenzy to unrest, and lights from the many cameras flashed everywhere. Wesley and Britney Haynes graced the stage, and the applause grew louder. Wesley accepted the award, gave it to Britney, and took the microphone. Wesley's parents, Megan and Sebastian, Britney's parents, James and Christine, Rose Best-Parsons, and Grace were all in attendance. They cheered…, "Thanks to an awesome God, they meant it for evil, but He meant it for good!" Thanks to my wife Britney and our parents! Thanks to band members Max, Mike, and Winston, mentors, the naysayers... Thanks to the Grammys! This is indeed a better life!" The singers, holding hands, returned to their seats. The audience continued to cheer. Crowds on the streets cheered, including those in foreign countries and different time zones. People at home watching the Grammys on TV were cheering. The radio station's phone lines were jammed with people calling in and requesting the song. The radio stations did let his music play!

WHO SHOT THE SHERIFF? SERIES

WHO SHOT THE SHERIFF? II

An Original Story

By

INTERNATIONAL BESTSELLING AUTHOR

JOHN A. ANDREWS

BOOK TWO

CO-AUTHORED BY:

JONATHAN & JEFFERRI ANDREWS

WHO SHOT THE SHERIFF? SERIES

THE MILTON ROGERS' CONSPIRACY

WHO SHOT THE SHERIFF? SERIES

TABLE OF CONTENTS

BOOK #2..173
CHAPTER ONE...176
CHAPTER TWO...178
CHAPTER THREE...184
CHAPTER FOUR...190
CHAPTER FIVE..196
CHAPTER SIX..201
CHAPTER SEVEN..204
CHAPTER EIGHT...207
CHAPTER NINE...210
CHAPTER TEN...214
CHAPTER ELEVEN..219
CHAPTER TWELVE..224
CHAPTER THIRTEEN...229
CHAPTER FOURTEEN...232
CHAPTER FIFTEEN...236
CHAPTER SIXTEEN...240
CHAPTER SEVENTEEN...248
CHAPTER EIGHTEEN..252
CHAPTER NINETEEN..255
CHAPTER TWENTY..259
CHAPTER TWENTY-ONE...262
CHAPTER TWENTY-TWO..265
CHAPTER TWENTY-THREE.....................................270
CHAPTER TWENTY-FOUR.......................................274
CHAPTER TWENTY-FIVE..277
CHAPTER TWENTY-SIX..281
CHAPTER TWENTY-SEVEN....................................284
CHAPTER TWENTY-EIGHT.....................................287
CHAPTER TWENTY-NINE.......................................291
CHAPTER THIRTY...294
CHAPTER THIRTY-ONE..297
CHAPTER THIRTY-TWO..302
CHAPTER THIRTY-THREE.......................................306
CHAPTER THIRTY-FOUR..310
CHAPTER THIRTY-FIVE..313
CHAPTER THIRTY-SIX..317
CHAPTER THIRTY-SEVEN......................................321
CHAPTER THIRTY-EIGHT.......................................324

WHO SHOT THE SHERIFF? SERIES

CHAPTER 1

A gray gated cell door slams shut and reverberates with a loud echo. The silhouette of two human beings lingers. Burnt-out fluorescent light bulbs flicker continually. Meanwhile, Bats come and go in droves, crowding the upper deck of the North Terrace cell block. Their call and echolocation peak while the after-sunset-rays dwindle, welcoming the beginning of dusk.
A horrid stench from this banal and dilapidated North Terrace cellblock rises amidst a gentle breeze.
Simultaneously, the simmering chatter of multiple eaves-dropping inmates perched diagonally across the way and upstairs on both sides erupts like a bee hive in distress.
Adding to all this, these insane, boisterous prisoners pounce, cheer, chant, chat, and revel as if their favorite football team had just scored the winning touchdown. Not a lame dash into the endzone but one with a zero point nine-nine seconds left in the game. In reality, there is no end-zone, no pompom girls, no quarterbacks, no refs calling flags on the play, and of course, no pig skin, just crazed inmates and cell blocks

with units stacked up on top of each other. Conversely, an incarcerated newbie, not yet revealed to inmates, seemed to be the leading cause of prisoners going hog-nasty-wild.

Some cop multiple look-see through their tightly locked-down iron bars, while others push up against cell doors like sharks sensing some fresh human blood. Even so, revelation is still sequestered. Their bark doesn't generate a bite.

In the interim, rectangular silver and brass padlocks hanging on their gated cells rock back and forth due to these inmates' investigative and relentless charged pursuit.

Yes, sizing up this newly arrived conviction has become their priority and their utmost, white-heated obsession. In their eyes, the blanketed arrival of this newbie frustrates them. Disclosure is long overdue. Never before have inmates prowled and chanted to become hitched at North Terrace. They drool like a dog desiring a bone. Their hostility and bewilderment are overbearing. Across the way, in front of that cell, the governing backsides of two Wardens preside. Their clothing, midnight blue garb, decorated with green, yellow, and black shoulder patches depicting Broward County Prison, is like the aroma of raw onions in the eyes of these restricted inmates, who continually press for revelation.

WHO SHOT THE SHERIFF? SERIES

CHAPTER 2

These two unorthodox Wardens, still focused on securing a big rectangular brass padlock on that cell door, wouldn't let up…privacy is locked down tightly even with those flickering lightbulbs still illuminated. For some time, though, the brass lock didn't conjoin. "Snap-Click-Snap," it finally does. The lock dangles after being securely fastened. What a relief…
The two Wardens high-five each other; they buoy up; it's a glory hallelujah moment. They leave in high praise. Carrying the prisoner's abandoned shackles, the shorter of two guards, FREDDIE KNOWLES, is a stocky, dwarfed Caucasian less than five feet tall. His cohort is a slim fair-skinned African American woman with her backside still in obstructive view. He proceeds. She follows in tow. With his swagger, he exhibits a little Napoleonic stature. Street chants accompany this swag-man attitude:
"Punk, it served you right!"
Knowles echoes and continues in a braggadocios humdrum. "There's no glory on the outside, but inside here can be like a living hell, Gregg Nichols." Observing these overwrought and animated jailbirds,

WHO SHOT THE SHERIFF? SERIES

Knowles skillfully creates two balls with both hands using those abandoned shackles. He mimics, he steps, he elevates, he bolts, and his swag intensifies and sizzles like a new musical fusion "bap, per dap-dap, bid-de per-dap." He sticks up his right index finger high above his midget frame as an indicator that he's numeric uno and sole prison guard since Cain killed Abel. Knowles draws some applause. However, some return that index finger notion to their sender. He feels challenged.

"Chirp, chirp, chirp..." his hand-held radio interrupts the flow with clarity segued behind some intermittent disappearing static.

"Freddie... report to East Wing pronto ... check on inmates smoking contraband... I mean, it smells like weed smoke going on in the East Wing. How the heck did they get contra... up in that place? They brought in hacksaw blades in hamburger meat inside upstate New York, Methamphetamine in Colorado, and old saw blades in Alcatraz... don't turn this into no dummy making your own "Oink" and "Oscar" show. Are they trying to brand us with some... Bad Press? Can't stand the bad press. Let's not repeat the Escape from Alcatraz. Not under my ... watch." Knowles immediately collapses the chains inside one hand. It weighs...on him. He reaches for his radio now dominant on his belt with the other hand, and responds:

"Copy that...Copy that, Chief Myers! That new guy is uncanny; he's got voodoo written all over him. ...driving those other inmates wild...as soon as he landed in number 9."

The delayed-in-action KEISHA THOMAS has a cute face along with her bulged thighs. She has already secured a key ring laden with keys to her baggy below-the-butt pants' loop. She bounces in to try to catch up with Knowles amidst the laughter of inmates. She hustles towards the mission. The keys jingle, bouncing back and forth against her swift moving-in-stride bow-legged and abnormally bulged thighs. Knowles propels and regains his swagger as well as her flow. He feels he's back in his stride again and elevated above the prison universe. "Darn, that is some good shit!"

"Yeah!"

Says his singular unit, still lagging in the distance.

Catching up with Knowles is now a challenge for Keisha. She immediately unhinges her baton, swings it high above her head like a propellant dividing the dense air saturated with clouds of smoke, and whistles loudly, "I did it my... way."

As these two Wardens complete what looked like a time-consuming we-got-you-sucker formality, they move out of view from the cell inside the abbreviated cul-de-sac. The number 9 on the cell door becomes visible. For some time now, the hidden attraction –

WHO SHOT THE SHERIFF? SERIES

GREGG NICHOLS- has not only been revealed to his unrelenting neighbors, but he comes face to face with this bunch of crazed inmates for the first time. This mid-30s African American handsome male figure like a manikin has not only emerged center stage for them to see but finds himself morphed into their continued laughing stock.
"Turn off the lights and light up a candle! Also, bring us, Juice Simpson."
Yells one promiscuous inmate with no shirt on. Inside cell number 9, Gregg, standing erect, rubs his nose continually to lock out the mixed pong emanating from his surroundings. The strong BO and chronic weed fumes saturate the air and escalate like gray scattered clouds traveling upwards to heaven in the distance.
Meanwhile, mean-spirited, penetrative looks from those inmates housed in double-decker cells across the way still taunt Gregg to no avail. To ease the tension, he looks to his left and right. Even so, he finds no relief from their oppressive tweets.
Those prolonged looks, some provocative and a few welcoming, while others are downright complicated and counter-friendly. The latter, as if to say: inside here, in this man's world of incarceration, criminality, and flames... On this North Terrace, ya block, you are our next victim, Greg-o-ry.

WHO SHOT THE SHERIFF? SERIES

In Gregg's mind, he could not only see them racing through the corridor to join that weed-smoking party but also sawing off that rectangular padlock on his cell door with hacksaw blades and in hot pursuit. In their eyes they see themselves taking turns - victimizing the heck out of Gregg.

His nervous thoughts rattle and submerge underneath his breath: "I can't trust none of these pricks...such scumbags, sex-deprived creatures and happy-handed faggots. I can't trust the system either. Who can be trusted? They've put me in here to terrorize the heck out of me."

As if Gregg has been smoking marijuana too, paranoia sets in from his imaginary high... he sees himself floating in mid-air like a runaway kite across the galaxy's Milky Way.

Trying to maintain his level-headed composure, Gregg stares at his neighbor's soiled and wrinkled prison garb. He zones in.

Gaining focus and clarity, he reflectively admires his clean and neatly pressed blue prison attire. Superiority sets in on his behalf, and he gently unbuttons his collar, sticks out his chest, and profiles for them with the confidence of a Stallion.

A few smiles are in order from his fellow convicts. Even so, Gregg Nichols does not buy into their sentimentalism. In his mind, and rightfully so, they are not to be trusted. He remains non-verbal, like a brick, and still not trusting, even in the air they exhale or the contentment inside their heart. He chooses not to become one bit unraveled- externally. Some spew out their saliva at Gregg. Some call him a pussy; others call him a pleasure. Suddenly, someone yells in patois: "Me, Mumma Gattar, and Puppa Raymond! Where are you when ma need you? Blood seed!"

WHO SHOT THE SHERIFF? SERIES

CHAPTER 3

Gregg Nichols inspects his six-by-ten, four dark gray walls and the sparsely furnished abode. Graffiti lingers, no doubt etched by its last great-fisted occupant. A half-made-up bunk bed stares back at him. BO mixed with Lysol and mildew also presents an unusual funky odor combination. Before Gregg Nichols could bask in disparity, he hears dripping sounds - bipp bab, bipp bap. Looking up, he sees drippy liquid running down his cell wall and on top of his cotton-plaid bed linen.

While he investigates the moisture's origin, the babble of innumerable voices blitzes his cellblock's outer limits. Through all that confusion, he recognizes some declarations: some more flagrant, others in a Southern twang, and some in unorthodox uninterrupted patois. The huge wave of opinions subsides, and then someone coughs cynically as if bringing more wet gravel to the beach from their adulterated throat holes. Gregg looks up agitatedly as this trickling downpour escalates and meanders into a - drip, drip, drip. There is still a blanket of evidence regarding the source of the liquid, the chemical composites, and the culprit. Even

WHO SHOT THE SHERIFF? SERIES

so, he isn't amused as the constant drip and flow of experiment number one prevails.

"What did you do, Mr. GQ, shoot Sheriff John Brown and his Deputy? Then you blame it on Wesley Haynes and Milton Rogers just because you can't get up off your bum boo cloth grudge and grass cloth prejudice? You are nothing but a play-hater and rass bigot." A voice in a thick Jamaican dialect vents.

One can see nothing but hate and jealousy in the eyes of this callous inmate who calls himself The SON OF JUDAH. He's a dreadlocks-attired, coarse-looking six-feet-plus figure. The Dread – as his peers sometimes refer to him, seems to be now standing on an apple box, which makes him pull off his new height of almost seven feet six tall. His head nearly kissed the roof.

Nevertheless, Gregg ignores the rhetoric and facade of hydraulics in action across the way. He focuses on his dilemma: that stream that smells like fresh adult human piss tapering off on his yet-to-be-slept-on multicolored plaid cotton bed covering.

"Relax, GQ, you are too ... uptight." Another disparaging voice mutters and continues after a brief pause...

"Don't believe all that hype they fed you on the outside about us in this North Terrace. We might sound rowdy right now, but we uphold standards of a mellow mood. We have never seen anyone like you up here. So, what

do you expect?" He scans the cellblock and continues: "We'll be easy on you. We have earned our stripes. It's all about community in here: What's yours is ours after your initiation." Son of Judah slurs.
He waits for a much-anticipated response from Gregg. None emanates.
"Bigotry! Did Gregg Nichols shoot Milton Rogers to kill him? So, hear me, God? No, I solemnly swear…it was an accident, your honor." Says KYLE CHANG, an Asian Jamaican from the upper deck above Son of Judah and perpendicular across the way from cell number nine.
Still, Gregg is stone-faced, sautéed inside what has become a game of verbal roulette. He grabs his cell door, shaking it with a vengeance. Across the way in cell number 10 and noticed by Gregg for the first time, is a shiny-haired Gerry-curled African American Male.
"They call me CAT DADDY."
He says.
Gregg lets up to hear him.
"I am a puss, and I can be your daddy. I am as lame as a Goldfish but bite like a Shark!"
Cat Daddy continues in a deep Southern twang.
"Another weirdo to deal with… They couldn't house him in Alabama, the Carolinas, Mississippi, Georgia, or Tennessee?"
States Gregg underneath his breath.

Suddenly, he hears movements like footsteps overhead. Upstairs and directly above his compartment resides a dwarfed Caucasian named RAYMOND HYBELS, wearing washed-out and dirty dreadlocks that are obscure to Gregg's vision. He would rather be called Ray or Hybels...never Raymond. That name evokes the demons in him and pisses him off. Hybels yell rhythmically and in patois as what seems like the battle of words continues:
"That neophyte shot both men and then shot Milton Rogers, who paid him to shoot the Sheriff and his Deputy. That is what I call conspiracy 101... mobster style, to rarted. You alloyed bigot."
The reek of urine now silences the other odors and burns like ammonia inside Gregg's nasal cavity, combined with the dwarfed-sized Hybels pinned inside his imagination. The Newbie on the cellblock, Gregg Nichols, with his cup running over, and piss all over his cell, lashes out:
"Let the Games begin! I say Let the...Games begin! Will the real man stand up and show his stinking face...you puss... You pissed on my bed. A puss is a puss and will always be a pussy... When dis yah dog step... the puss better go into hiding. Cause I am worse than a Rock-wilder and a pit bull in unison. You had better go into solitary confinement before mey catch you bum boo-rass cloth. When I leap, I am coming for your jugular."

"Me throw me corn, meh nah call no fowl. Who the cap fits let them wear it. So says Bob Marley... dead and gone and will rise up again. I believe in the Duppy... but I am no co-conspirator or rass cloth Glock gunman." Says Hybels.

Jumping up and chanting to support Hybels, the six-footer Son of Judah, now off the apple box but still maintaining seven feet with every jump, yells: "Time will tell, Mr. Gunman, time will tell. You'll do no see? I reside by the rivers of Babylon. Jah Jah... covered I, and nothing shall encompass about I." Son of Judah pauses and then continues:
"No voodoo, hex, or necromancy can touch the I."
"You've got a problem too, Big Man?"
Asks Gregg, looking out and into the face of Judah's son. The son of Judah becomes confrontational, holding on to his gated door with both hands. He becomes overly animated and imitates Gregg's previous act — settling the scores.
"If you drop those words again, we will have some real PROBLEMS up inside North Terrace... Real Problems, big man." Gregg ignores him.
He continues,
"Don't talk to me about problems...I and I was raised inside West Kingston ... I was born in massive problema! Ask anybody where this ya dread come from..."

"Lunch! Lunch!" yells the same two prison officers who threw Gregg inside the lockup. Keisha Thomas parades the cell block with her male underling, Knowles, in tow. Once again, waving her baton high above her head, she gaits.

Inmates retreat as she does. She hoists her ring laden with keys and unlocks the cell doors sequentially. Inmates file out hastily towards the prison's lunchroom.

CHAPTER 4

Lunch is served. The long line of crooks diminishes. These Jailbirds congregate and sit around immovable chairs and tables. On each plate, a ration of steamed rice, a piece of pork, broccoli, carrots, and some watered-down lime juice. Before the starved and downtrodden Gregg Nichols could partake after fetching his seat, he sees an inmate waving at him with the grin of a Cheshire Cat in the distance.

Gregg Nichols avoids initial eye contact. The male subject is persistent and now more animated than before, with signaling and beckoning hands thrown in the air.

Gregg Nichols remembers him from the Wesley Haynes trial.

"That blabbermouth who testified against Wesley Haynes. Another puss! Darn pussy! Whey dem find yo?"

Gregg says once more underneath his breath this time immersed with patois, while he stays put.

Gregg looks in his direction, but the puss has disappeared. Finally, as Gregg partakes of more grub,

he sees the stalker probing towards him from inside the corners of his eyes. He lands and sits down directly at Gregg's table and partakes of the food ration. "Gregg Nichols, how are you? I heard you made North Terrace stand on edge... upon your arrival,"
Gregg pleads the fifth.
"Remember me? MARCUS DAVIS, I heard about your incident. What a travesty! Only in America. We have a black man in the White House, but things are not getting better for us as black a black race. I don't understand why bad things happen to good people like us, and it isn't ISIL, Syria, or some radicalized terrorist. It's our system."
Says Marcus Davis.
Gregg Nichols once again pleads the fifth.
Marcus eats some more broccoli from his meatless plate and drinks a mouthful of watered-down lemonade like it's a thirst quencher.
"Hey, I'm on the East Terrace; you should come over and hang out sometimes. Smoke a little weed, play some dominoes... We have no problems with getting in our contra... whatever you want in narcotics we have it over there. Just bring some money with you." Before Gregg could thaw out. Marcus Davis continues... "You don't trust anyone, huh? Not even Ray Hybels... I know the feeling... 'In God we trust. In man, we burst.' They should engrave the latter on our almighty dollar in Jamaica. Michael Manley and

Edward Seager blew that opportunity, and Portia Simpson Miller also had a chance. Now, it's all about what they call women's lib. Liberate what? Now, it's just like it was in the seventies when women took over and dominated the workforce. These days, the have care nothing about their have-nots. People like Wesley Haynes and Milton Rogers should pay for their debts. That will bring about true liberation as far as I am concerned."
Says Marcus.
Gregg does not see most of his logic in that statement and responds:
"Sorry, wrong man; I am not into the gossip. I see sad stories. Hear sad stories. However, I speak no evil of my fellowman."
"If you want to know anything, just ask me. I am better than CNN, ABC, CBS, NBC, the Huffington Post and FOX combined. I get all the gossip up here. I hear about every Pre-Madonna who goes whoring or pushing drugs while their man is inside the Pen. I heard someone pissed on your bed, and it wasn't even you. Matter of fact you had not even slept in it yet." Says Marcus.
Gregg is furious on the inside but hums a tune to "Someone pissed on my bed, but it wasn't me." He turns the piece of pork over and examines it with the plastic fork. He sticks it. It bleeds.

WHO SHOT THE SHERIFF? SERIES

"I am worse than a crossed-bred dog; my bark is as vicious as my bite. I latch on and don't let go." Gregg says as he pushes the half-cooked piece of meat and the rest of the meal to one side. The blood swims around on the plate and merges with the fatty liquids from the same piece of meat.
"You want out of here, huh?"
Ask Marcus Davis.
Gregg Nichols nods his head.
"Like I want to puke right now. This place not only sucks, but it also stinks worse than a gory cesspool." Marcus leans in.
"Your friend Wesley Haynes still owes me that money for the undelivered shipment of chronic seized on that ship in Port Antonio. Could you get him to pay up? I need my money, bald head." "Don't get me involved." Says Gregg.
"One hand washes the other. You wash mine, and I'll wash yours."
Gregg is not buying into Marcus' hand-washing shallowness.
"When I get out of here, I will make sure the bum-boo cloth pays up. That wretch! A thief and a scamp."
"When are you getting out of here?" Asks Gregg.
"I am hoping to get into that witness protection program or parole, whichever comes first as soon as I am cleared. Create a new identity for myself. Move

into a plush apartment suite with round-the-clock security and some bad, bad dogs." Says Marcus.

"My name is Gregg Nichols. I don't have an AKA, and I have never needed one. I don't even have an "A" in my name. I only use "K" as a short form of okay whenever I text. I just wanted to be a good husband to my wife and a great dad to our two daughters, Raina and Rayan. I don't need to be drawn into all this drama." Marcus looks away, scanning the perimeter.

"How does that thing work for an innocent man?"

"No. Only the guilty. It could have worked for Wesley Haynes, Milton Rogers, and Bill Parsons, those bastards."

Says Marcus.

"What did you do to end up in here, Marcus?"

"Never let your right hand know what your left hand did. Just in case it turns into a rat. You know those boneless ones that crawl underneath doors?" States Marcus Davis.

"You've got it wrong. Matthew 6:3-4 KJV: But when thou doest alms, let not thy left hand know what thy right-hand doeth: That thine alms may be in secret: and thy Father which seeth in secret himself shall reward thee openly. And yes, I know a rat when I see one." Gregg replies.

"Lunch is over!"

Yells Keisha Thomas pacing in circular motions.

"Why did you say that?" Gregg says in Ebonics. "Those guys were outstanding citizens. They meant well." Continues Gregg Nichols as both men get up from the table.
"To be continued."
Responds Marcus Davis.

WHO SHOT THE SHERIFF? SERIES

CHAPTER 5

The next afternoon Deja visits Gregg at North Terrace for the very first time. Sad but elated she is seated inside the visitor's center on a wooden bench, while Gregg is brought from his cell block by Knowles. As she waits and looks around the perimeter, that pale look she exhibited since Gregg's incarceration – becomes magnified. Her mindset of coping with the entire judicial bureaucratic process while playing the role of a single mother for their two daughters, Rayan and Raina, and much more, haunts her. She envisions: Something has got to change soon.

Inside this sitting room, which accommodates a few inmates as well as visitors, the Nichols couple seeks privacy but finds none. Gregg's mindful: Everyone eavesdrops on each other's conversation and then lies like maggots inside nuts when they congregate. Additionally, visible, and invisible cameras capture every move made by inmates. Starved sexually, the two kiss passionately like the aftershock of a first kiss. As if by magic cameras come in tight on their upper body just in case Gregg swallows saliva and anything else with it. Bottled water? Non-existent. Generally, in

WHO SHOT THE SHERIFF? SERIES

this type of meeting between lovers at the North Terrace visiting room, if the inmate is suspected of swallowing anything in the act of kissing, that inmate immediately undergoes an internal body scan for any consumed contraband, whether his windpipe responds to swallowing narcotics or not. In the past, visitors have been known to circulate drugs during a sensual kiss. Which they later pass out in their monitored feces.

Gregg asked about the kids. In a subdued tone, Deja told him how much they missed him at home. "It's been a decade since you've been away, Gregg. I bought Rayan her first training bra yesterday." At this point, Gregg scans the room, sizing up all the deviant inmates. He puts his finger on his lip, suggesting that Deja keep those comments low. Finally, after a dull look on Deja's face, Gregg catches himself.

"You what? Do you check her Facebook and Instagram for those perverts?" Gregg asks.

"You can't put the brakes on one's development... I've told her she is banned from social media until you come home."

"Sorry. That is something my Dad would have said. What did she say?"

"Something about she can't leave her BFF's hanging. One day this boy sent her a shirtless picture. She sent him back a post telling him how cute he was." "Tell her

WHO SHOT THE SHERIFF? SERIES

to tell those FFs I am a double black belt, plus... Remind them that when I bite, I don't let go. How is my little princess, Raina?" Gregg states.

Deja responds: "Raina sobs constantly, wondering when you are coming home. This place is turning you mad, Gregg. You look so pale. You were never so violent. Now you want to bite out everyone's jugular and spit it out."

"Deja, I would never have said that. It seems like you bring more violence in from the outside. It's not helping me much. After all, I might bite it out and swallow it." "Gregg, please stop your cannibalistic gestures." Says Deja.

"Anyway, tell Raina soon. Her daddy will be home soon. And keep those perverts away from my girls, " says Gregg.

"Really?"

Asks Deja.

"She won't even eat breakfast. She has gotten very skinny. The child misses your singing in and around the house. There is no daddy to serenade her, " says Deja.

Their grip on each other's hands tightens.

They embrace. "How are they treating you here babe?" Asks Deja.

"This is no place for a real man to be...

The ration they feed us here is what you would feed your dog with when you run out of dog food. At least

> WHO SHOT THE SHERIFF? SERIES

I get a shower frequently. That might increase their water bill."
Says Gregg.
"I've heard this jail is full of Happy Hands. It must be hard on them. The only opposite sex they see are the female guards, right."
Says Deja.
"You are so right. That's what's up in this facility. They are very possessive…"
Says Gregg.
Deja tunes him out.
Gregg continues…
"I'll break their arm if they get too close to me or, better yet, bite it off. Last night, Hybels from the cell above me pissed on my bed."
"He was inside your room, Gregg? Can't you curb your enthusiasm?"
She asks double questioningly. "I don't play that. He pissed inside his cell and the urine trickled down onto my bed."
Says Gregg.
"Oh. Okay. This is so overrated. This is Yuki!"
Says Deja.
Gregg doesn't get it.
"I know. That's what our princess would say – yuk."
Says Gregg.
"Visiting hours are over!"

Says the eavesdropping, pouncing pompous prison guard, Keisha Thomas, waving her baton with much jealousy in her eyes.

Gregg and Deja Nichols embrace, and then she departs, blowing a kiss at him in the wind. "See you at the trial. They can't stop us, Gregg! They can't stop us!" She yells.

He tries in vain to hold back his tears. But like a river flowing downstream, they are unstoppable. So, he curbs them with his shirt sleeves.

Keisha spins quickly in his direction after Deja is out of sight and briskly escorts Gregg back to North Terrace.

WHO SHOT THE SHERIFF? SERIES

CHAPTER 6

A boisterous crowd gathers outside the Miami courthouse. Chants of "Free Gregg Nichols, he's innocent. Lock up the real gunman," reverberates. "It's nothing but a conspiracy," compliments those chants. Waving multi-colored and multi-designed placards accompany those multiple-escalated chants, echoed by Gregg Nichols' peeved and disgruntled supporters. Police with riot gear move in but cautiously. Stoked TV reporters, legal analysts, and Radio personnel are busily warming up their equipment.

News editors stationed in mini-trucks record footage captured from the preliminary coverage.

Several protesters engage in discussions, thus igniting the tense first day of the trial. Even local Clerics converge, dressed in power ties. Their female counterparts are adorned in pantsuits.

This accusation has been well documented plus recently attained viral status: Gregg Nichols not only shot his associate Milton Rogers, but he could have shot Sheriff John Brown along with his Deputy.

WHO SHOT THE SHERIFF? SERIES

Even so, Gregg has always maintained his innocence. Even though he had stated he did not pull the trigger, the blanket evidence still advocated he touched the gun that did.

On the other hand, Gregg's supporters still point their fingers at the court officers, ERROL CLARKE, and QUENTIN DALEY.

With that said, the conjecture remains that Daley, who struggled with Nichols over Glock 38, could have pulled the trigger of the gun and snuffed out Rogers, as he testified on behalf of his good friend Wesley Haynes. Also, there could have been some collaboration on Clarke's part.

In any event, Gregg is the one charged with the shooting death, incarcerated, heading to trial, and, if convicted, could rot inside the Pen, or fried in Florida's electric chair.

Instantly, a black SUV pulled up, followed by a flashing blue light sedan. Gregg's defense lawyer SEBASTIAN

DAVIS leaps out of his utility vehicle. Gregg and two white-collar officers follow him. Armed officers step out of a sedan. They probe the area while trailing behind Gregg, his lawyer, and his escorts.

The radio and TV media are now hot as an oven, and microphones are poked in the direction of Gregg Nichols and his entourage to cook up some hot news. "Mr. Nichols, you have been charged with the death of your friend Milton Rogers. Others believe you could be responsible for the deaths of Sheriff John Brown and his deputy. Are you ready for what might turn out to be a three-dimensional trial?" Asks one overzealous TV reporter to get ready for the end-zone reply from the defendant. "No comment!" Says Gregg.

"We have nothing to say. My client upholds his innocence."

Says Sebastian Davis eloquently. The entourage proceeds up the courtroom steps.

More reporters press, trying to boil him softer or, in other words, squeeze a confession of guilt out of the defense team even before the Judge and the Jury are announced inside Judge Melendez's courtroom.

CHAPTER 7

With looks of apprehension inside the courtroom, Gregg Nichols enters through the side door, hustled by the two escorts. They seat him in the front row next to his already-settled attorney, Mr. Sebastian Davis. Those two accompanying officers disperse through the same side door from whence they came and lounge inside the waiting area after closing that door behind themselves.

Gregg Nichols looks to his right, glancing at the prosecution's cast of characters. They loom large like Mt. Everest in his eyes.

MARK CONNOLLY, the District Attorney, is standing engaged in conversation. He interrupts Gregg's stare with a penetrative return look.

Gregg probes. On the front row sits three other prosecution attorneys poised like vultures as they compare notes from their yellow pads.

Gregg scans further and recognizes new faces as well as some familiar ones, mainly from the trial in which Wesley Haynes was acquitted of shooting the Sheriff along with his Deputy.

Additionally, inside that same courtroom in which Gregg Nichols was charged for shooting Milton Rogers, weighty images emerge. They haunt him—especially those portraying Milton Rogers falling backward on the witness stand.

Trying hard to keep his mind now, as if to make matters worse, the Jury Box presents itself with 12 hard-nosed individuals.

The seven men and five women are eager to decide their fate inside the box. The thought of a split rattles Nichols' mind like an overexcited snake. He amuses the thoughts of them hanging themselves during deliberation.

Friends and family are limited in attendance in the courtroom. There is no Wesley or Britney Haynes. However, his eyes are linked with Collin Mattes, the lawyer who appeared in Wesley's defense. What a brilliant job by Mattes, as thoughts of the previous trial ran like cobwebs through his frazzled mind.

Simultaneously, various officials file into this already-packed-to-capacity courtroom. Nichols' eyes zone in on Quentin Daley, taking a seat. The infamous court officer with whom he struggled over Glock 38, which claimed the life of Milton Rogers. A murder for which he has been charged and imprisoned. He reflects Gregg Nichols shot and killed Rogers... Those press clippings still saturate his mind, followed by indents. He mops cold sweat from his brow... Many believed he did shoot the Jamaican Mogul. However, the media has some lingering doubts, especially among Gregg's peers. Most artists cherished the notion that Quentin Daley shot Rogers to attain much-needed heroic status. Some even claimed that Daley believed strongly that Rogers was the gunman who shot the Sheriff and his Deputy, Ron Charles. Some even claimed Daley wanted to be dubbed the next Lee Harvey Oswald, a mystery killer. So, he portrayed the character in order to identify. Gregg replayed the shooting tragedy in his mind over and over like a worn-out tape and saw himself coming out of the struggle with the gun in his hands. Only to be arrested moments later, escorted outside to the police car, forced inside, and driven away to the prison and later housed at the despicable North Terrace with these lovers of men.

Suddenly, as if by design to obliviously relieve him from his Déjà Vu, his lawyer nudges him to make room for his wife, Deja, who had just walked in dressed to the nines. She sits beside Gregg and kisses his lips, leaving her full red lip imprints.

That act of sentimentalism drew massive attention from attendees inside the almost maxed-out courtroom.

WHO SHOT THE SHERIFF? SERIES

CHAPTER 8

The name REUBEN MELENDEZ stands out, etched in gold inside a wooden fixture on the
Judge's bench. It peaks like a bull's horn. The Judge enters in a statesmanlike fashion. In his late 50s, elegant, sporting a fresh haircut and of Latino heritage, he enters - announced. All rise, he takes his seat, and the rest of the room except for multiple court officers in white shirts, black ties, and visibly shaped bulletproof vests underneath. They gait, not taking any chances.

Melendez, recognized among his peers for his strong convictional reputation, glances at the twelve jurors with a shallow smile and a slight nod.

The Jurors reciprocate respectfully and modestly. Meanwhile, Melendez settles comfortably into his chair, leaning forward with poise and forthrightness. This time, he takes in Gregg Nichols as he begins to address the audience.

"Men and women of the jury. A few months ago, inside this very same courtroom, Milton Rogers was shot while testifying in the Who Shot the Sheriff? trial. The fact remains that whoever shot Sheriff John Brown and his Deputy Ron Charles is still a mystery. Even so, as members of the jury, you are commissioned by the state of Florida to determine who pulled the trigger that claimed the life of Milton Rogers." His eyes connect with the Bailiff's interaction with the court reporter. "I guess we are ready?" The Judge continues. He shuffles some papers, looks them over, and then calls DA Mark Connolly to deliver his opening statements. The Broward County DA, with pomp and finesse, approaches the podium.

Ladies and Gentlemen of the jury ... ONE man is on trial in this courtroom. I want that to be understood. Not several as claimed by the populous. Milton Rogers was shot and killed on Valentine's Day while testifying in a case having to do with the murder of two Jamaican law enforcement personnel: Sheriff John Brown and Deputy Ron Charles.

This court and the world at large believe you have been selected to find the defendant, Gregg Nichols, guilty of murder. The weapon recovered from the crime scene was a Glock 38, owned by an officer of the court, Quentin Daley.

However, according to eyewitnesses, who we will hear from during the trial, Nichols and Daley were caught up in a struggle for that gun immediately after Milton Rogers was gunned down. There is much validity to this question: Why would a civilian struggle with an officer of the court over the officer's gun? Except to take the officer's life or the lives of other courtroom attendees.

If Milton Rogers were alive today, the state of Florida would have had two fewer crimes to solve — one inherited from another country.

Justice was obstructed by shooting Rogers inside that courtroom. The defendant, Gregg Nichols, having known Rogers for a long time along with his associates, had plausible cause to commit this horrific crime. Along with a probable motive to blanket evidence.

The state of Florida supports the death penalty. It is your responsibility to produce a conviction: Sending Gregg Nichols to the electric chair is for the magnitude of the crime.

Mark Connolly returns to his seat.

Melendez doodles with pen and paper. He scans the courtroom.

Court officers assist while new arrivals money inside the courtroom are seated.

The stenographer is still typing away no doubt capturing and sub-texting. Gregg Nichols converses with his defense team. He patted his defense lawyer, Sebastian Davis, on the back. Melendez scans the courtroom once more.

CHAPTER 9

The defense lawyer, Sebastian Davis, puts pen to paper, and like a sponge, he soaks up Connolly's opening statement. Gregg Nichols steals a look at Davis's copious notes, neatly etched on a yellow notepad. Peripherally he can see his focused defense at work.

Davis had been note taking since before Mark Connolly began his opening arguments and remains diligent.

Davis wards off a pestering creepy-crawly.

"You okay?"

The concerned Nichols asks his attorney. "I'm okay as can be. Connolly is working hard to influence the jury. I've got this, plus the bug, too." Davis responds.

"What did the bug bring, good news?" Asks Nichols.

"It says they don't have enough evidence to convict." Replies Davis.

"Really?" Asks Nichols.

Deja Nichols, freshening up her bright red lip gloss, interjects:

"We've got your back, Gregory!" That name, seldom heard since his Adam's apple evolved, tugs at Gregg's heartstring. He nods, "Yes." Eventually, Attorney Sebastian Davis is called upon for his opening remarks. After addressing the judge, jury, and court, Davis connects with his client Gregg Nichols as if to recalibrate before refocusing on the twelve fate-deciding jurors. They are yellow pads and paper-mate pens ready. He adds some imaginary inches to his stature and delivers…

"Good afternoon your honor, jurors, court officials, and attendees. In this trial, we find two defendants at its very core. Although both men are currently inside this courtroom, only one has been accused, charged, and incarcerated. The other is free to roam and enjoy a life of sanity. He doesn't have to eat ration aided down his esophagus with watered-down lime juice. At this moment, he's still classified as a witness, that's all.

I still don't believe anyone has all the facts relating to the shooting death of Milton Rogers. Gregg Nichols and Quentin Daley are the only ones who do. Both of their hands handled that gun. The gun which fired the fatal shot. The bullet that snuffed out one of the most critical witnesses in that trial…leaving us with this fiasco.

It is nothing new for innocent black men to be locked away in jail while the guilty ones go free. This is an awakening reflection of our dissident judicial system. Imagine two men caught struggling for a gun after Rogers was gunned down. Yet, guilty fingers are still pointing at my client, an associate of Mr. Milton Rogers. My client has no motive for committing such a crime."

Gregg leans forward, trying not to miss a word.

"My question is WHY?

Because the defendant is black?

Because he is talented?

Because he attended that trial in support of his friend, Wesley Haynes?

Because his prints were found on the gun from which that fatal bullet was discharged? Others also touched the item now classified as exhibit one, as you will learn later in these proceedings.

Members of the jury you are faced with a problematic task... disseminating this story. The fingerprints of several people recovered from the gun snuffed Milton Rogers out, and no authentic witness statements were recorded. What we are left with is a shared motive. Who really had a motive to kill Milton Rogers? That is the big question.

In this trial, we are going to need some strong hard evidence. Not evidence manufactured, fabricated, or imagined, evidence not bought and sold but original.

It is going to be tough for you, the jury, to point fingers at my client unless someone produces the real truth regarding this tragedy — the truth and nothing but the truth.

There's no doubt that evidence will prove that my client Gregg Nichols did not pull the trigger, which snuffed out the life of Milton Rogers.

Attorney Sebastian Davis connects visually with the entire courtroom and the jurors and then retires with poise.

He strolls to his seat next to Gregg Nichols. Deja looks at Attorney Davis and approves with a smile. The defendant's look shows that he is happy with Davis heading up his case.

Judge Melendez calls for a 15-minute recess and returns to his chambers. Attendees mingle. The prosecution team huddles. The defense chit-chat and powwow with Gregg and Deja Nichols.

Other courtroom attendees file out of the room.

WHO SHOT THE SHERIFF? SERIES

CHAPTER 10

Amidst the hustle and bustle of tight security, anxious North Terrace inmates entertain their visitors. Richard Hybels meets with a beauty named Yuki Barnes inside the visitor's lounge. Meanwhile, Gregg Nichols, expecting no guests, takes it easy to scan the newspaper inside cell # 9. Yuki is African American in her thirties, attired in a decoded gray sweatsuit, Gray and white Nike sneakers, and a white Kangol hat to match. Both sit on a bench in semi-privacy. In the distance sits Cat Daddy, drinking soda from a plastic cup. He eavesdrops. Some jailbirds mingle, soaking up what's left of visiting hours. Some with no one to greet them and mind their own business, while others try to read the lips of the visitors, no doubt looking for gossip.

"Are we wired?" Asks Yuki, scanning the vicinity.
Wired?
Asks Hybels. "Tapped! Are you clean?" Asks Yuki.
"No. Only being watched like a hawk by these electronic Peeping Toms. Every black bulb you see in the ceiling is a freaking Peeping Tom with Ray Ban sunglasses on."

WHO SHOT THE SHERIFF? SERIES

Says Hybels, also casting an eye over the locale. Yuki clues in by staring at multiple surveillance cameras, especially those designed as dome-shaped tinted bulbs.

"They are very tight on us... Is this the making of a prison movie? Are they audio enabled or just faking us out?" Asks Yuki.

"That would constitute a breach of one's privacy." Responds Hybels.

"Back to this matter. Are you a candidate for the Witness Protection Program, or do you have any affinity with the feds?" Asks Yuki.

"No desire to. I would rather make my money...my way. Frank Sinatra said: I did it my way. Someone else said; it's my way or the Highway. They locked me up. That is the only relationship I have with their system. Everything else is my own business." Responds Hybels.

"Cut the crap Richard; time is money. Okay... how much do you want and how soon do you need the stuff?
Asks Yuki.

"Fifty grams to start. If it moves well, which I think it will... you can profit big time. Contra does well inside here as soon as the word gets out...Chi Ching! After that, you will most definitely have a repeat client. BTW, I have a few depots in South Beach... if you need some high heels to tread down Babylon Avenue instead of those name-brand sneaks." States Hybels.

"I detest this place for more reasons than one. BTW, who pays on time for those drop-offs in South Beach, and especially Babylon Ave? ... I don't deal with IOU's." States Yuki.

"I will text you coded locations. Just say this is Yuki, and you are all set; nothing else exists. They will be expecting you."
Says Hybels.

"Leave my name out of it in case they tap into that busted screen Metro PC gadget. BTW it would help if you had an upgrade on that signal because I don't play to lose... And am I your only supplier?" States Yuki candidly.

"Not really. If you need an advance, see me..." Before Hybels can finish his thought, Yuki surveys the perimeter again and responds with concern: "I need five thousand USD to begin. Will have to stock this shit, you know."

"You accept Jamaican dollars?"
Asks Hybels.

"In God, we trust, no Jamaican, Guyanese, or Chinese bills. They assume too much space. No 'in man we burst' ... USD only."

Cat Daddy walks over and makes a timely introduction.

"Hey baby, I am Cat Daddy. Those lips of yours shine as the noon-day sun. And like butter against sun, they are poised to…run."

Yuki studies the slick Gerry-curled-up character, Hybels. She sees in him: nothing but a smooth-talking pimp and reasons,
"No wonder he's known as Cat Daddy."
He continues,…
"That's what they call me. I'm like a cat and your daddy."
Yuki concurs. "They call me Yuki." She responds.
"Pretty name for a sister." Responds Cat Daddy with glistening eyes.
Hybels hands Yuki a copy of the perspiration-laden Miami Herald newspaper, which he has held for the entire duration of their conversation.
Yuki smiles and departs in a flash.
Cat Daddy gleans two-eyes-full of her curvaceous backside with a smile, followed by an exclamation, "Darn! I wonder who's tapping that." Returning to her car, Yuki runs into a man dressed in a suit. He's the replica of Cat Daddy accentuated with a pimp's attitude.
In her mind, could these two cats be identical twins…or is this Déjà vu?" Yuki races to her car, avoiding the carbon copy. She gets in and takes off. About one mile up the road, Yuki pulls over and parks

WHO SHOT THE SHERIFF? SERIES

along the roadside. She peruses the newspaper. Inside is an envelope with fifty-one hundred dollar bills in U.S. Currency. She sticks all that cash deep inside her bra, tosses the sweaty Herald out the window, and drives away from the curb. She tunes into her favorite radio station and covers the upbeat song already in progress.

CHAPTER 11

Inside the courtroom, the ambiance is tense as the world is set to hear testimonies in the trial.

Cameras and their operators are poised, ready to televise. Deja Nichols graces the witness stand. She looks more made up than ever and probably just entertained a spending spree. Every strand of her hair and clothing is in place. Her stylishness spells – impeccable.

Unprecedentedly the wife of the defendant debuts.

Could this be the testimony to convict Gregg Nichols or the one to set him free? A widespread two-sided epiphany embellished by most in the media.

Inside the courtroom, Deja takes the oath.

DA Mark Connolly approaches the podium. "Good morning, Mrs. Nichols," he says. "Good morning, Mr. Connolly," Deja responds respectfully.

"Deja Nichols, you are married to the defendant Gregg Nichols. How long?" "I am. Over 8 years." Responds Deja.

"It is my understanding that you were sitting in this same courtroom on the evening Milton Rogers was gunned down."

WHO SHOT THE SHERIFF? SERIES

"Unfortunately, I was. What a horrific occurrence on Valentine's Day." Responds Deja.
"Did you expect this to happen?" "Objection...counsel is leading the witness!" Yells Sebastian Davis.
A wave of grumbles rises from the cluster of Gregg Nichols' supporters in the courtroom. "Silence in court! The objection is overruled, " says Judge Melendez.
"Why were you in the courtroom on that evening Mrs. Nichols?"
"I was watching the trial."
"Did that visit your only visit during the entire trial? If so, why?"
"No. I have been in attendance more than a dozen times prior."
"All of those times with your husband, the defendant?" "Objection!" Says Attorney Davis. "Objection sustained." Says the Judge.
"Did you always accompany your husband to the hearings?"
"I did."
"Mrs. Nichols, would you say your husband was an associate or a friend of the late Milton Rogers?" The Judge is listening intently. So do the Jurors, the prosecution's clique, the defense's cluster, and most of all, the one with the most to lose – Gregg Nichols. "I would say both."

Says Deja.

"Would you also say he was a celebrity chaser? A stalker or a con artist?"

"Objection!"

Davis shouts, now on his feet. "Counsel, no obstruction inside my courtroom. Please take your seat."

Says the Judge. Davis lounges.

"Gregg was not that kind of person. He was none of the above. He was a business professional. Not a criminal in any way." Replies, Deja.

"Tell me about this business association between himself and the late Milton Rogers."

"My husband is a quality businessman. Always has been. His ties to Milton Rogers came through his love for music. Gregg loves what he does."

Gregg nods.

Deja continues.

"We owned a CD packaging and distribution company. Wesley Haynes became one of our clients after his business became too big for my boss, Mr. Beckles, to manage.

We met Milton Rogers through our friends Wesley and Britney Haynes. My husband has always maintained tremendous respect for both men. He revered them... so to speak. "Revered enough to take his life?" Interrupts Connolly.

"He didn't."

Says Deja.

"How do you know that Mrs. Nichols?"
"Whenever they had an event, we were always invited. I felt bad when I couldn't always attend some of their events."
"Did Gregg attend solo?"
"He did. When he returned home to me and the girls, he always shared his experience about the wonderful times spent together." "What did he tell you about Milton Rogers' character?"
"Rogers was very comedic but outspoken. He didn't hold back his tongue. A class act."
"How did your husband feel about Wesley Haynes?"
"Objection! Mr. Haynes is not on trial. My client is." Says Davis.
"Overruled!" Says the Judge.
"Did Wesley Haynes and Milton Rogers always get along?"
Asks Connolly.
"As far as I know, they were like buddies. Most of the time, joking and cutting up."
"Did your husband have a good relationship with both Haynes and
Rogers?"
"He did. He was like their water carrier…always willing to serve." Says Deja.
"Did you see your husband shoot and kill Milton Rogers, or did he tell you he did?"

"No. I did not see him shoot Milton Rogers, and he did not tell me he did so. This is all a conspiracy to keep my husband behind bars. Our system continues to set a bad precedent for black men—one which is destroying our kids. Gregg needs to see our two daughters grow up. This system is like a sponge sucking out the virus out of too many black families. This has got to stop. I want my husband home with me! Not in prison, humiliated by a bunch of homos."
"Thank you, Mrs. Nichols. No further questions." Gregg smiles and then, with tears running down his cheeks, gives a thumbs-up to Deja. The jurors read into that emotional exchange between the couple.
Deja glances at the Jury Box and tears up.
Connolly is back in his seat. Judge Melendez looks at his watch. Attempting to take a recess, finally…
"This case is adjourned until tomorrow at 10:00 AM." Deja steps down from the witness stand. She embraces her husband Gregg while shedding additional tears.
Gregg consoles her as his tears fall, moistening her fancy hairdo.
Two escorts rush through the side door into the courtroom. They accompany Gregg and rush him through that particular courtroom exit.

> WHO SHOT THE SHERIFF? SERIES

CHAPTER 12

Back at North Terrace Longue, the contended mingle and the stressed – stress. Gregg Nichols and Marcus Davis face off in a domino game usually designed for four players. Even so, the duo squared up for what could be a friendly game. There's no money on the table and no contraband underneath. Marcus shuffles the deck methodically. Then, he shoves the deck in Gregg's space and removes the double blank from the stack as if it were marked or X-rayed by him. He pushes it next to Gregg's right hand.
Gregg's eyes move by Marcus disputably. Marcus draws seven cards. Gregg does the same. Marcus pushes the remainder of the cards to the other side of the table. The remaining thirteen cards nest up close to double-blank.
"How did you know which card was the double blank? Did you mark the cards?" Gregg asks.
"Funny you should ask that. These are not my dominoes; you saw me borrow them from the recreational center. Didn't you? Just play the hand you

have. Do you have double six? Only amateurs study the game for so long. It's easy, Math…just aim and shoot. So, play Mon."
States Marcus.
Gregg still stares at the double blank while scanning the dominoes in his hand.
"As far as you I know. If I were you, I would study what double blank means. It might come in handy. A blank is a blank. It will always be a blank. A blank from blank leaves nothing. Double six, play." "How do you know I have Double six? Do you know something I don't?"
Gregg says while posing double-six.
"Double six at you. Go to the pack!"
Marcus has no choice. He searches through residual domino cards. He accumulates. Finally, he produces a six-ace, which he slams down on the table as if it were a hot piece of coal briskly discharged from his right hand. He even blows on his hand after the card lands on the granite tabletop.
Gregg takes a sip from the bottled water next to him. Marcus follows suits from a giant bottle.
"Let me drink my gallon. Before Simon Peter walks on it." Marcus downs most of it, still staring at six-ace nestled against Double six. "You got me on that one, Gregg. I hope you can be that good when you testify in court."
Says Marcus.

"If I testify."
Responds Gregg.
"Deja did a great job on the witness stand. I am sure the world is waiting to hear from you."
"Yep...Deja was brilliant. She has more to go."
"You are not going to? You've got to cover your A... She can't do it for you. You depend on a woman to save you? Understand that you are not a Wesley Haynes. If you had the money and the fame he has, you would have a chance at a non-guilty verdict without testifying...but?"
Gregg plays Double-ace.
"I'll cross that bridge when I get to it. Six-ace is still your play...You pass?"
Responds Gregg.
"Me pass? Never!" Says Marcus.
"Well, play, mon ...you are holding up the game. What happens? Six-ace! Did you cool off? Is that why you drank the gallon of water?"
Marcus starts singing 'Like a Bridge over Troubled Waters' as they continue. Now, he has no choice but to study the game.
"You know Milton Rogers built those restaurants with drug money?" Asks Marcus.
"Really?'
Asks Gregg.
"You never saw his investment portfolio? The man was loaded like a freight train."

WHO SHOT THE SHERIFF? SERIES

"No." Says Gregg.

"That's why he derailed. Rogers always presented himself like Donald Trump. Never knew his closet was full of extortion and excess baggage."

"Did you waste him, Gregg? Tell the truth, it's just between me and you."

States Marcus Davis.

Gregg Nichols is deep in thought. He stares at the double-six card he posed and the six-ace that Marcus played later. He drops the ace deuce on the table and slides it against the Double ace. "My play before yours. You must wait your turn." Marcus goes to the deck in search of a matching domino card. He produces Six-deuce.

"Deuce to you. Play now." Marcus stands up, excited. "Clap your hands if you pass."

Gregg slams down a double Deuce and blows the imaginary steam off his playing hand. "Eight bullets! Seven missing. I just wished there were more bullets inside that Glock."

Responds Gregg Nichols.

"Rogers was a big deal. They said the Feds also wanted him dead." Says Marcus.

"Why are you staring inside my hand, Rasta? You can't play a friendly game with cheating?

Asks Gregg.

"Once a man, twice a child."

Says Marcus.

"Enough of your parables,"
Gregg says as he throws in his hand and merges all the cards on the table close to Marcus' hands.
"I see one man who can't stand the truth." Gregg gets up and sticks a hand in Marcus' face.
"Lockdown!!"
Yells prison guard Keisha Thomas, waving her baton high as usual and strutting her stuff. She subsequently gathers up all the dominoes. Gregg Nichols heads to the North Terrace while Marcus Davis saunters to the East.
Gregg Nichols spits his second song since incarceration: If those walls could talk on his way to his cell block. Inmates listen pressed up against their cell doors. Some are mesmerized, some mimic, others are muted. Subsequently, the lights go out.

> WHO SHOT THE SHERIFF? SERIES

CHAPTER 13

Inside Judge Melendez's courtroom, Deja Nichols continues her testament with poise and diplomacy.
The defense attorney asks: "Mrs. Nichols, what is your current profession?"
"I am a singer first, entrepreneur second, and mother third."
"What kind of entrepreneur are you?"
"CD packaging and distribution."
"What genre of music?"
"I sing mostly R&B, some reggae. Now and then, I'll drop some funk."
"I've heard your R&B and Reggae, never your funk."
"You've heard 'Mind your own business, Mr. Babylon. It's a fusion."
"Not yet."
Says Davis.
"It is epic, branded, my IP… don't worry."
Says Deja.
"Tell this court about your second vocation."
Says attorney Davis.

"Gregg and I own a CD packaging and distribution company. We both have worked in that field for over five years."
"Profitable?"
"Yes. Our business exploded in the last year of operation."
Says Deja.
"You have a few major clients? I am sure." States Davis.
"Yes."
"Wesley Haynes being one of them?"
"Objection!"
Says Connolly.
"Objection sustained."
"Yes. We took on Wesley Haynes as a client last year just before he won the Grammys."
Says Deja.
"Did Haynes bring his business to you, or did you solicit his business?"
"I had introduced Wesley Haynes and his wife Britney to my ex-boss, Mr. Beckles when they were trying to produce their first song. That song turned out to be a mega-hit. They wanted to give back, so they approached us with their CD packaging and distribution needs."
"Are they still in your Rolodex?"
"They are."
Responds Deja.

"Milton Rogers?"
Asks Davis.
"He is still in our Rolodex. He will always be."
Says Deja.
Gregg gives multiple supportive nods.
"How did you meet Milton Rogers?"
"When Wesley and Britney Haynes' first song went platinum, we were invited to the celebration, which was held at his restaurant in Kingston. We had a blast. There, we met Milton Rogers for the first time. He introduced himself and asked if we were enjoying ourselves. He treated us with much respect and kind hospitality. He's very businesslike but such a gentleman."
"What was your husband's relationship with the Milton Rogers after that meeting?"
"Gregg always had the utmost respect for Mr. Rogers."
"He did?"
"Yes."
"Would you consider Gregg a gunman or a waterboy?"
Deja laughs.
"Gregg couldn't shoot a fly!" She yells sarcastically.
"Does your husband own a gun?"
"Gregg does not. He's not a violent person. I don't think he knows how to pop one off. He only does karate on rare occasions. Like a sponge, one has to

squeeze that craft out of him. He can indeed hurt you like that with his eagle and snake."

Says Deja.

"Did he discuss with or conspire with you in any way to end Milton Roger's life."

"No, he did not."

"You were sitting next to him in that courtroom. Did you see him shoot and kill Milton Rogers? What did you see, Mrs. Nichols?"

"Gregg jumped up from his seat and wrestled with the court officer. Rogers went down. Gregg persevered in trying to take that gun away from the court officer."

"Did he tell you why he wrestled with the court officer?"

"Gregg didn't know if he was going to shoot us next. Or, on the other hand, shoot everyone else in the courtroom. The man was acting like a psycho...I've seen moves like those on TV."

Says Deja.

Judge Melendez leans forward in his chair, relaxing his torso.

"Mrs. Nichols, I have no further questions."

Says Davis before returning to his seat.

"Thank you, Mrs. Nichols."

Says the Judge.

Deja retreats to her seat next to Gregg, accepting his approval.

CHAPTER 14

The Court Announcer calls Detective Mike Jones to the stand. He swears to tell the truth and sits down. DA Mark Connolly connects viscerally with the jury before approaching the podium. Jones is in a lovely black suit with gray pinstripes, a white shirt, and a dapper paisley tie.
He sports a new faded haircut.
The jurors buoy up.
"Good afternoon, Detective Jones."
Says Connolly.
"Good afternoon."
Responds Detective Jones.
"A case of Deja Vu, I must say."
Connolly continues.
"It certainly is...twice in six months. Same courtroom, almost the same crowd except for a few new faces."
Says Jones.
"What were you doing in this courtroom on the evening when Milton Rogers was shot and killed?" "I

was assigned with my partner Detective Paul Stevens to the Who Shot the Sheriff? case."

"And what happened then?' "During Milton Rogers' testimony, a gunshot went off. Milton Rogers reacted to being hit; blood flowed from his chest. He fell over backward, holding his chest. His hand was saturated with blood. My partner sitting in the row before me yelled: 'Unbelievable!" Unbelievable! This is ... Unbelievable.' We raced to the two men still struggling over the gun at the rear of the courtroom. We discovered later the two men were Gregg Nichols and court officer Quentin Daley. Nichols had the gun pointed at Daley when we arrived. We commanded him to drop the weapon on the floor. He hesitated, then tossed it to the side." "What type of firearm was it?"

Asks Connolly.

"A Glock 38."

"Who owned the Glock 38, detective?" Asks Connolly.
"The gun was assigned to Quentin Daley, one of the court officers on duty during the trial." "Do you know who fired the fatal shot from that gun that killed Rogers?"

"I am not sure. However, Nichols' body language indicated he was the aggressor in the gun struggle."
"Objection...speculative!" Says Davis.
"Overruled." Says Melendez.
"What happened after that?"

"Moments later, we handcuffed the nervous Gregg Nichols to our cruiser. After driving him to the station, we booked him."

"Nervous?" Asks Connolly.

"Yes!"

Responds Detective Jones. "In your career, you have encountered several nervous offenders like Nichols. Haven't you?"

Asks Connolly.

"Yes. Wesley Haynes was a prime example." Wesley Haynes, sitting at the rear of the courtroom, shows disapproval.

"Thank you, Detective Jones; I have no further questions,"

Says Connolly.

The Judge announces a brief court recess.

CHAPTER 15

The trial reconvenes with Defense attorney Davis, who is pressing Detective Mike Jones. The veteran cop is up to the test, sitting comfortably in his seat.

Deja Nichols once again freshens up her bright red lip gloss. Her lips glitter under the courtroom light. From her purse, she removes her mirror to validate her beauty.

"Detective Jones, earlier you testified: you saw nervousness on the part of the defendant Gregg Nichols moments before Milton Rogers was shot. Are you an expert on body language?"

Asks Sebastian Davis.

"I would not say I'm an expert, but I understand this reflective trait in criminals. Thus, leading to multiple arrests and multiple convictions."

Says Jones.

"Really?"

Asks Davis.

Detective Jones hesitates.

Attorney Davis goes to his notes. He postures, he ponders.

"Detective Jones, in the recent case Who Shot the Sheriff? You arrested Wesley Haynes... Isn't that so?"
Asks Attorney Davis.
"I did."
"However, you claimed that you observed, and I quote, 'his guilty body language,' which gave you a reason to believe he committed that crime."
"Yes, I did."
Says Jones.
"But he did not." "He didn't?" Asks Jones.
"You attended the trial, didn't you? Citing that case, the defendant, Wesley Haynes, was found not guilty. How come?"
Asks Davis.
"That's what they said. I still don't buy it."
Says Jones.
"So, detective, you have reasons to believe otherwise?"
"I do... Justice was not served, in my opinion." Says Jones.
"Opinions are like noses; everybody has one. Different size, different shape, different color."
Things seem to be getting out of hand, as both are engaged sarcastically, but the Judge refuses to let them ramble on.
"What grades did you receive in your Criminology-Body-Language-Class, Detective Jones?"
"Objection!"
Says Connolly.

"Objection overruled."
Says Melendez.
"Are you aware, Detective Jones, body language could be a facade and isn't transparent enough to be used as evidence in a court of law?"
"Objection!"
Once again, Judge Melendez overruled the objection.
"Detective Jones, you stated earlier you were assigned to the Who Shot the Sheriff? case."
"Yes, I did."
"Which one?"
"I didn't."
"According to your recollection, what was the result of that trial?"
"Objection!"
Yells Connolly.
"Objection overruled. Answer the question." Says the Judge.
"Wesley Haynes was found not guilty. He should have been retried," Says Jones.
"That is a pretty passionate statement, I must say, from a law enforcement officer. Thank you, detective. I have no further questions, your honor."
Says Sebastian Davis, who strolls back to his seat with a swagger in his strut.
The afternoon in Judge Melendez's courtroom, she was finished with Jones feeling the venomous sting of those

brutal jabs from defense Attorney Sebastian Davis and vice versa.

DETECTIVE PAUL STEVENS WAS next to testify. He supported most of Det. Jones' testimony. However, Attorney Davis asked him if they were hungry to attempt convicting another artist, seeing their efforts failed in the previous Wesley Haynes trial. To which Stevens replied with a straight face:

"No. We were doing our jobs."

After a series of objections by Connolly. Attorney Sebastian Davis encapsulates his cross-examination by saying:

"I love police business when they serve and protect. However, I distaste for bad, rancid, and rotten police business."

Connolly questions Detective Stevens later in the trial to corroborate Detective Jones' sparring testimony with the defense.

> WHO SHOT THE SHERIFF? SERIES

CHAPTER 16

Quinten Daley was the next witness called on to testify. Grumblings from various courtroom attendees emitted before court officer Quentin Daley arrived in front of the witness stand, sending a message of justice wrongfully administered by the system. However, those clatters ceased as the evictor readies himself to intercede. It was obvious most of the court awaited this moment. If Nichols was not going to testify, at least they were privileged to hear from the next accused…however, they were not charged.
"Do you solemnly swear to tell the truth, the whole truth and nothing but the truth, so hear me God." the bailiff eloquently articulated.
"I do."
Says Daley.
Once again, anti-murmuring erupts from the defense's section of the courtroom.
DA Mark Connolly approaches and begins the cross-examining of Quentin Daley, the prized eyewitness.
"Mr. Daley, you were the court officer on duty when Milton Rogers was murdered inside this courtroom on

Valentine's Day of this year, wasn't you?"
"I was."
Mr. Daley, Jamaican immigration stamped your passport, indicating you visited that country between August 1st and 16th last year. The Bailiff brings the passport over to Daley. "Is this your passport?" Asks Connolly.
Daley examines it.
"Yes, this is my passport.
"Were you in any way involved in the previous incident: the shooting death of Sheriff John Brown and his Deputy Ron Charles on August 12th?"
"I was not. It wasn't me."
"Do you know anyone who might have been involved?"
"Objection!" Says Sebastian Davis.
"Objection sustained."
Says Melendez. "No. I do not." Says Daley.
"What was the purpose of your visit to Jamaica in August last year?"
"I was on vacation with my wife and our teenage son. Jamaica had been on our vacation wish list since we honeymooned there over a decade ago." Responds Daley.
"You had a great time?"
"Yes, we did."
"Did you collaborate with Milton Rogers regarding any criminal activity on this trip? And as far as you

know, was he involved in that double shooting of the Sheriff and his Deputy?"

"I don't know if he was. I had never met Mr. Rogers... Never heard of him until the trial."
Says Daley.
"Do you know if Gregg Nichols was involved in the shooting of the Sheriff and his Deputy?"
"I do not know if he was. He resided in Jamaica at the time, burning CDs and other business... who knows what else."
"Did you know Gregg Nichols before Milton Rogers was shot and killed? Did you maybe spend time together with him and smoke a joint or two? I drank a beer and played dominoes. Any involvement you can recall?"
"No. I did not know Gregg Nichols before that shooting. As I've stated, That was the first time I met. Gregg Nichols when he removed my gun from its holster by surprise and shot Milton Rogers."
"So, when he grabbed your gun from you, that was the first time you met the defendant?"
"Objection."
Says attorney Davis.
"Objection overruled."
Says the Judge.
"Did you give the gun to Gregg Nichols to shoot Rogers, or did he grab it from you, Officer Daley?"

WHO SHOT THE SHERIFF? SERIES

"He took it from me… grabbed it!"
"Liar…I tried to stop you from shooting him."
Says Nichols, rising out of his seat and pointing in Daley's direction.
"Order in court,"
says Melendez.
Nichols returns to his seat.
"How many rounds did he discharge?"
"One round."
"How come?"
"That's all I saw."
"Mr. Daley, was your gun fully loaded before Milton Rogers was shot with that same gun?"
"No, it was not. Partially…"
"How many bullets did you recall loading inside that gun?"
"Seven."
"And you say seven out of eight inside that magazine was partial?"
"Yes!"
"Was that partially loaded gun a planned activity, or did some of those bullets just happen to be missing at that time? Did they fall out of the gun when you opened it, and you forgot to put them back inside?"
"I am unaware of any bullets falling out of that gun."
"And Mr. Daley… you didn't plan it that way to be accosted by the defendant ? Did you?"
"I did not."

"Did you shoot Milton Rogers?"
"No. I did not."
"Well, if you didn't, Mr. Daley, Who did? Who positioned themselves and pulled the trigger?"
"The defendant Gregg Nichols. He shot Rogers."
"Whose gun did Gregg Nichols use to commit that brutal murder?"
"Mine."
"How? I mean, how did he do it?"
"He grabbed my gun away from me, opened the magazine, inserted his bullet, and shot Milton Rogers."
"So, he used his bullet. He didn't trust yours to do the job… taking out Rogers?"
Gregg is agitated.
"Liar! Liar! That is highly impossible."
Says Gregg Nichols.
"Silence in court."
Says the Judge, striking his gavel. The murmuring residue fades to the emittance of a pin drop sound, which emerges swiftly and resides.
Heads turn to see what caused the dead silence.
"Counselor, you may continue."
Says Melendez.
"So, your gun could have been tampered with prior and left empty?"
"Possibly."
"By whom?"
"I have no idea." Responds Daley.

"Did you share information regarding the status of your gun with the defendant or anyone else?"

"No. I had no communication with anyone regarding my gun."

Says Daley.

"Mr. Daley, did the defendant push or shove you to wrestle your gun away from you?"

"No. He did not. He grabbed me by the seat of the pants. Lifted me off the ground and took my gun away."

"What did you say to him?"

Asks Connolly.

"You need to back off and return to your seat. Don't try anything funny, or you'll be dead meat."

"Did you reach for the handcuffs you carried as an officer of the court?"

"No. There was not time enough to do so."

Connolly signals the court bailiff to the square next to the Stenographer. On the table, the bailiff retrieves a large envelope. Connolly opens the package. The bailiff takes out a Glock 38, unholsters it, and checks it to make sure it isn't loaded. It's not. Safety is administered. The bailiff hands it to Connolly holstered.

Connolly un-holsters.

"This is a Glock 38, the same ammo recovered at the scene after the fatal shooting. Does this look like the

gun you carried and was taken away from you when Milton Rogers was shot inside that courtroom?"
Says Connolly.
"Objection. May I approach your honor?"
Says Davis.
"Yes. You may."

says the Judge."
Sebastian Davis approaches, removes his smartphone, and takes multiple pictures. Other lawyers representing both the prosecution and the defense also do this.
All picture-takers return to their seats.
"Counsel, may we proceed with your cross-examination?"
Asks the Judge.
Connolly hands the gun to Quentin Daley.
"Looks familiar? Are you sure this is the gun?"
Asks Connolly.
"It does."
Responds Daley.
"Please show this court and the jurors where your gun was when it was taken away from you by Gregg Nichols."
Instructs Connolly as he now passes the gun's holster to Quentin Daley.
Daley puts on the holster and positions the gun inside it. The gun and holster are attached to the right side of his pants waist.

"This is where my gun was positioned when the defendant snatched it away from me."
Says Daley, pointing confidently to the right portion of his waist.
"Did the defendant point it toward you before he shot Milton Rogers?"
Asks Connolly.
"No. He grabbed the gun away from me, loaded it, and immediately shot Milton Rogers after loading."
"No further questions."
Says Connolly, strolling back to his seat.
"Mr. Davis, your witness."
Says Judge Melendez.

CHAPTER 17

Sebastian Davis approaches. First, he studies Quentin Daley like a textbook. Second, he connects visually with the jurors and the rest of the courtroom. Third, he cross-examines…

"Mr. Daley, what was the purpose of your trip to Jamaica in August last year?" "As mentioned, I was on vacation with my family."

"Which hotel did you use for that trip?"

Asks Davis.

"Sandals." Replies Daley.

"Sandals? Must have been one heck of an expensive vacation."

"It was!"

Responds Daley.

"Who picked up the tab, your contractor? Very coincidental, so you showed up in Jamaica right about the time Sheriff Brown and his Deputy were shot and slain. You postponed the vacation you stated earlier for at least five years. Months after you returned, a prominent Jamaican was gunned down inside a courtroom under your watch. Do you expect us to believe you had nothing to do with these crimes?" States Davis.

"I have already taken an oath. Didn't I?" Responds Daley.

"Mr. Daley, how many bullets were inside the chamber of your gun when Milton Rogers was shot?"

"That is a hypothetical question. Are you asking me about before he was shot?"

"Did you fully load your gun before attending the trial that day?"

Asks Davis.

"I did not."

"Why not, Mr. Daley? You were an officer of the court, functioning in a high-profile case. Why would you not fully load your gun to protect the courtroom if necessary?"

"When I picked up the gun, I thought it was loaded as I left it the day before."

"You assumed? Do you not brush your teeth in the morning instead of claiming it was already brushed the night before?"

"My gun has always remained in whatever condition I left it."

"Mr. Daley, you mean to tell me, as an officer of the court, you show up at a trial, not knowing if your gun was loaded and, secondly, if there were multiple rounds inside your gun chamber? What if you had to discharge multiple rounds to protect the entire courtroom? This is America... what if you had to deal with a lone wolf? Or did you deliberately put one bullet inside the gun so you could shoot Milton Rogers, and as you were confronted... click – empty gun? So, you saved yourself from getting shot? Just like in the movies, huh?"

"I don't know what you are talking about. My gun is normally fully loaded."

Says Daley.

"But it wasn't on this occasion. You stated earlier it was partially…" "It was. I believe…"

Responds Daley.

"You believed but it was not a fact. Do you believe you have your car keys on you, or do you know that for a fact?"

"I know that for a fact."

Responds Daley.

"Mr. Daley, you earlier testified: my gun is normally fully loaded. Those are your words. However, it wasn't. Plus, you either failed to check it, or it was already your knowledge that the gun was fixed with one bullet inside its chamber, or you deliberately put one bullet in the gun with Milton Rogers' name on it. You wanted to kill him execution style. Didn't you, Mr. Daley? So, you planned it, executed it, and boom!"

"Objection."

"Objection overruled."

Says Melendez.

"How many bullets were inside your gun chamber before Milton Rogers was shot?"

"I don't know. I don't recall. I know that Gregg Nichols tampered with its chamber before shooting Rogers."
"According to the ballistics report, your gun was empty after discharging the bullet that claimed the life of Mr. Rogers. That would imply, mathematically, that it contained one bullet before discharge. You could not miss it. You must have shot many bullseyes at the shooting range. Yes?"
"I don't know how many shots were fired at Mr. Rogers because I did not shoot him." "Who did Quentin Daley? Who did? Tell the court they are waiting for your answer."
"Gregg Nichols did."
"Did he eat the rest of the bullets which he found inside your gun chamber?"
"I don't know that?"
Says Daley.
"Whose responsibility was it to ensure the gun you carried during the trial was fully loaded?"
"It was mine."
"What you are telling the court is negligence on your part. Do you expect us to buy into that? Like your unscheduled trip to Jamaica back in
August."
"I have told you the truth."
 Says Daley.
"Thank you, Mr. Daley. No further questions."
Judge Melendez strikes the gavel.

"This trial will reconvene tomorrow at 10:00 AM!

CHAPTER 18

Legal Analysts and other news media descend on courthouse grounds like starved flies onto molasses. They buzz over each other to report the news. Attendees exiting from the full-to-capacity courtroom are mesmerized by such historic media commotion. The growing noise of confusion covers the entire courthouse sidewalk. Finally, a legal analyst burrows through the crowd and forays on Quentin Daley, who is encircled by an entourage of lawyers.

"Mr. Daley, you finally got your chance to testify in court in an uncanny case which many have dubbed - a Milton Rogers' conspiracy. How do you feel now that you've shared your story?"

"I feel great. Finally got the monkey off my back."

"Sure, must feel good."

Says the reporter, taking back the microphone. "If you had to do it all over, you would be sure to check your gun to ensure it was fully loaded. Wouldn't you?" The reporter hands the microphone back for Quentin Daley's POV.

WHO SHOT THE SHERIFF? SERIES

Multiple microphones are now perched in Daley's face, waiting to receive the answer to this crucial question.

"I would. You know things happen. If it was fully loaded, I might not have been here today. On the other hand, Nichols might have shot and killed me, too. By far, that was his intention, an imminent clean sweep...the outcome could have been worse; many more lives taken."

Another analyst interrupts...

"Why didn't you say that to the judge? You claimed you were innocent. What were you afraid of, Mr. Daley? Do you still see fingers pointing at you?" The microphone is shoved back at Daley. The other analyst regains his stride and interrupts. "Were you hurt as Nichols grabbed you by the seat of your pants during that ordeal?"

Ask that Analyst.

"Daley, you are a wicked man. You lied on the witness stand. You shot Rogers and pinned it on Gregg Nichols. Just like you shot the Sheriff and his deputy, then they tried to pin it on Wesley Haynes!" Yells a Nichols' non-microphone bearing supporter and legal scholar.

"That's enough, guys. We've got to go, "
says one of Daley's attorneys as he directs the multiple legal entourage off the sidewalk.

WHO SHOT THE SHERIFF? SERIES

The lawyers rush Quentin Daley inside the waiting car. The car departs speedily. They follow in tow.

CHAPTER 19

Gregg Nichols returns to "North Terrace," wishing the trial were over and that all those guilty fingers were pointed at Quentin Daley instead.

After entering his cell block, the Son of Judah emerged like a snail out of its shell.

"Long time! You are back, Gregory Nichols. When do we party...I mean, get it on?"

Gregg Nichols pleads the fifth.

The son of Judah feels ignored.

"They said you did shoot Rogers. So, you deliberately shot Milton Rogers? If there were more bullets inside that gun, you would have shot the court officer, too. Make it a bang, bang instead of a bang. That bauy Quentin Daley: Blow him rass cloth head off. Wouldn't you?"

Gregg Nichols is still mute.

Hybels, invisible to Nichols. However, he resides above his cell but is only visible to the Son of Judah and other inmates from their vantage point; he says in patois: "There is a grass cloth trend. A sequence... You hypothetically shot the Sheriff and his Deputy. Then you shot Milton Rogers. One man standing was

Quentin Daley next to the gunman. If bullets were still inside the gun, that court officer would be dead too. As Judah just explained. We have to start calling you the rass Glock man instead of the gunman. That name fits your MO."

"He's got to have a deputy. Maybe Errol Clarke is in on it, too."

Son of Judah replies.

"You are right. I've got to have two victims at once. Two caskets instead of one. Any two will do. Who will be next? I wonder who my next deuce would be…come on, deuce, deuce. The eagle for one and the snake for the other. Who wanna test me, old schools? Piss against the wall, punks."

Says Nichols as he practices his karate moves, mirroring himself on the dark gray cell wall.

The two prison officers yell, changing their tense mood. The entire cell block is evacuated.

NICHOLS MULLS OVER HIS FOOD as he sits solo at the 4-seat round table inside the prison cafeteria. Son of Judah, Hybels, and Kyle Chang walk in with their ration servings and plop down at his table. There is dead silence.

Gregg Nichols takes a bite of the cold broccoli from his plate. He again pushes the meat aside as if the cooks didn't get the memo.

"Calm down, Nichols, we've got your back. Whatever happened to your domino-playing mentor, the Buay

Marcus?"

Asks Hybels.

"I heard he went to "East Wing," fixing to join the witness protection program and get out of here. Is he taking you with him?"

Asks the Son of Judah.

"My mother used to say: What your right hand knows, never make your left hand know."

Says Kyle Chang.

"That's pearls of wisdom. Never cast your pearls before swine; they will turn around and rend you. The key word is rending. Now, he is fixing to tell on your rass... Don't you understand Mr. Artiste? You are confiding in a snitch. We thought you knew better. You didn't learn much in that department from the blind old man, Mr. Beckles.

Says the Son of Judah.

Gregg Nichols reflects.

They seem to have placed Gregg Nichols into a tight vice and gradually tightened it with their fists full of physiological witticism. Gregg examines the plastic fork methodically. The cutlery breaks during its probing investigation.

"Gentlemen, it should have been apparent that I needed solitude. However, seeing you joined me uninvited, and I welcomed you into my space. That says Gregg Nichols deserves some respect. That said, I'd prefer you keep your comments to yourself."

All three of his neighboring inmates immediately stand up, initiating a physical confrontation—daring Gregg to retaliate. Gregg is about to get even.

In the interim, Keisha Thomas and Freddie Knowles rush in their direction. Keisha, waving her baton high, says:

"Gentlemen, don't start a fire up here. Put out that spark, or all four of you will go to the hole. We are the only voice up here. You listen to us or pay the consequence for real."

The quartet disperses back to North Terrace, mostly swearing and in patois under their breaths.

CHAPTER 20

Outside the South Beach Bar and Grill, high-end automobiles double park instead of receiving attention by Valet parking attendees. Inside the crowded facility, patrons groove on while the DJ drops some of the latest tracks. Overlooking the bar, the sizeable gold-framed clock displays 9:55 PM. Frequenters, mindful that the main attraction for the night will take the stage in five, rush to the bar to fill up or get refills. Those seated at tables signal waiters and waitresses to serve their tables quickly.
The high fashioned Emcee takes the stage.
"Ladies and gentlemen, let's give a warm South Beach, Miami welcome to the undiscovered artist, but not for long - Yuki Ba-r-nes!"
Loud hand clapping and cheers follow in applause. Yuki Barnes takes the stage dressed to the nines. She drops one number. A loud applause follows. While the four-piece band extends the beat Yuki steps closer to the edge of the stage.
"Good evening, Miami... How are you all doing at South Beach? You are all looking great tonight. Are

you ready to party? Ha, hah hah… The man in the red shirt looks very patriotic. I can tell you are ready. Before I lay the next couple of tracks on you, I just want to give a big up to Gregg Nichols in the Pen. Also, to his lovely wife Deja, who is probably going through some tough times since he's been locked up?" Most of the crowd raises a glass in support of Deja. "It must be tough on that woman making a living now with her man inside the pen—no daddy for her kids. No money… No money, no honey, especially when you are locked away with such bastards."

Yuki tears up and gains the sympathy of patrons, both women and men. One woman rushes on stage with a box of paper tissues for the artist. Yuki thanks her and wipes the tears away.

"She has been a great inspiration to many. Women are made of extra stuff, aren't we?"

The audience, mostly women this time, applauds heartily as the next song plays. However, a few men chime in hesitantly.

"These are some of my favorite Boss Woman Deja's tracks. Are you ready? Turn it up, Mr. DJ! You ready South Beach?"

Says Yuki.

Yuki Barnes sings three covers Deja style. The crowd wants more. The eager DJ pulls up the last cover dropped as Yuki exits stage right.

WHO SHOT THE SHERIFF? SERIES

Outside South Beach Bar and Grill, Yuki readies to board the taxi. Fans rush towards the taxi cab. Pushing pen and paper at her. She autographs a few.
"You were great tonight. You did an awesome job with Deja's songs."
Says one skimpy-dressed woman after collecting the Yuki's inscription on a napkin.
Yuki blows a kiss in the wind as customarily.
The cab takes off.

> WHO SHOT THE SHERIFF? SERIES

CHAPTER 21

The media has been inundated for over a week with news regarding the infamous witness, Marcus Davis. Rumor has it: Davis recently joined the witness protection program to turn in mega Drug Lords from Jamaica, Colombia, and Mexico who trafficked in the U.S. While some refer to him as the Snitch who tried to bring down artist Wesley Haynes during an unconventional testimony in the Who Shot the Sheriff? trial. Still, some believed Marcus Davis, known by his peers as "The Parrot," was a paid witness in that case. Some advocated that the witness protection program was nothing but a hoax or publicity stunt concocted by Davis to strike a deal with his parole officer. It was believed that a man who liked that much publicity would do anything to get his name out there. Thus, drawing sympathy to his cause was an easy decision.

On the other hand, to thwart the press, Marcus Davis claimed Wesley Haynes owed him money on a shipment of weed bound for his drug depot in Miami that never arrived. The ship "On Time," which never

WHO SHOT THE SHERIFF? SERIES

arrived and was identified as carrying his shipment, was seized in Port Antonio by Jamaican police.

After that, the ship's origin was investigated by top cop Sheriff John Brown and Port Antonio's top brass DEA Lieutenant Graves. Wesley Haynes' whose name surfaced as co-owner of that ship, was sent to prison for ten. Haynes was later released early, after five years of good behavior. Marcus Davis still maintained a venomous grudge for Wesley, not only because he claimed the money had been owed him from the aborted shipment of weed but because of Wesley's stellar success as an international reggae artist.

With many bystanders yet to be called in this trial, it was uncertain if Marcus Davis was among them or the BFF of Deja Nichols, Britney Haynes – the wife of Wesley.

Some even claimed that Wesley Haynes would be among those witnesses. However, many still suspected his involvement. Haynes was already found not guilty of shooting the Sheriff and his Deputy. So, in some minds, that hatchet should be buried. Yet some just couldn't let go of even top intellects inside the legal arena.

Legal Analyst Bradshaw, a Haynes advocate, echoed: "Even though the victim Milton Rogers was a friend and mentor of Haynes, staying out of that environment would do Haynes much justice.

Additionally, it was evident Haynes did not pull the trigger, which snuffed out Sheriff John Brown and his

Deputy, as he was acquitted of those charges on Valentine's day."

Yet, many non-Haynes supporters debated his return to that courthouse and his placement on the witness stand. Legally, it's not practical to try a person twice for the same crime.

"If Haynes testified on Nichols' behalf and made a single blunder or told a white lie, it could be like the opening of an old wound. The masses wouldn't be tolerant to all that inflammation from a wound that should have already been healed. Instead, any new cut would suffice — at least anyone who owned a similar Glock 38 and detonated a single round.

So those anxious debaters tucked their tails between their legs, at least for now. In other words, they cooled it.

In the meantime, one radio station broke the news that Wesley and Britney Haynes were on their way to Paris to drop their new song.

WHO SHOT THE SHERIFF? SERIES

CHAPTER 22

It is another day inside Judge Melendez's courtroom. The atmosphere grows tense as excessive movements recede to almost zero.

The court requests Marcus Davis. He steps up to the witness stand and takes the oath. DA Mark Connolly steps into position and begins his cross-examination of Davis.

"Marcus Davis, good morning."

"Good Morning." The witness responds.

"Second time around?"

"It is."

Marcus Davis responds.

"Are you getting paid to testify in this case?" "No. I am not getting paid one red cent. Only here for justice to be served."

Responds Marcus Davis.

"Marcus Davis, is this courtroom familiar to you?"

"Objection!"

Says his namesake, Sebastian Davis, for the defense.

"Objection sustained. Answer the question." Says

Judge Melendez. "It is. I was here on Valentine's Day." Says Marcus Davis.

"What happened on Valentine's Day?" "Objection. Leading the witness. Your honor, we are privy to what took place."
Says Sebastian Davis, who is now standing.
"Objection overruled."
The defense lawyer retreats.
"We all know what happened on Valentine's Day. How much did you know Milton Rogers?" Asks Connolly.
"Counselor?"
The Judge cautions. "How much? A little? A whole lot?" Asks Connolly.
"Milton Rogers came from Mandeville. He grew up across the park from where Wesley Haynes lived. He was a smooth talker. Drove expensive automobiles. Rogers later moved with his drug-pushing attitude to Kingston because of multiple threats made to his life.
"Unsubstantiated!"
Yells Nichols.
"Mr. Nichols! You may continue, Mr. Davis."
Says Melendez.
"When he arrived in the big city, he immediately bought two restaurants and additional fancy rides with hydraulic suspensions and rag tops. He upgraded and expanded these eateries just before Wesley

Haynes moved to Kingston. People in Manchester and Port Antonio were after Rogers like a hawk after young chickens. They said he owed them money. However, no one in Kingston allowed anyone to turn him in, not even the cops. They revered him. When Haynes told me he was purchasing a ship with Rogers to transport weed, I laughed but wasn't surprised; I knew there would be repercussions. I saw them as two buck rats in one nest with short tails.

However, I told Haynes to be careful. He turned out like Rogers and spread all over Jamaica like a stage-four cancer.

Haynes went back and told Rogers what I said that dirty dog. Milton Rogers later called and told me I would starve. They will dry up my turf and watch Me as I morph into a leftover pretzel, gnawed at by rodents."

"The man is lying! That snake."

Gregg Nichols is taking a page from Wesley Haynes' playbook.

"On a subsequent shipment, Haynes told me to pay before delivery. I did but never received the shipment."

Marcus Davis continues.

"What happened?"

"The ship was seized in Port Antonio."

"What did you do when you found out the ship was seized?"

"I asked Haynes what's up. He gave me a sorry story. So, I called Rogers and told him I knew he co-owned the ship and needed my goods or my money back. He said there is no money-back guarantee in the files. The loss is a part of business, and I am not the only one suffering. When I asked him to name other sufferers, he said it was confidential, but Babylon was suffering, too. And those who bring you news will also sosoo pan you."

"The ship seizure? When did all this happen?" Asks Connolly.

"Five to six years before Sheriff John Brown and Ron Charles got shot." Responds Marcus Davis.

"How much do you know the defendant, Gregg Nichols?"

"I know him well. We play dominoes at North Terrace. He's amateurish; he wastes too much time reading the game. Nichols joined the Rogers and Haynes posse right after Haynes moved to Kingston. I also frequented nightclubs in Mandeville during the first half of August last year. When both Sheriffs got shot. I recently spoke with him a few times in the Pen... He looked very discombobulated. He showed signs like he had lost his marbles."

"Marcus Davis, do you know who shot Milton Rogers on Valentine's Day?"

"No."

"Did you shoot Milton Rogers?"

"I did not."
"Did Gregg Nichols tell you he shot Rogers or conspired to do so?"
Asks Connolly.
"Objection! This is not a circus. This is a trial!"
Yells Sebastian Davis.
"Objection sustained."
Says Melendez.
"You may answer the question."
Says Connolly.
"He didn't tell me outright. However, I wouldn't put it past him. He did tell me how he wished there were more bullets inside that gun. And all he was thinking about was a courtroom clean sweep."
"Objection, speculation, hearsay!"
Yells Davis for the defense.
"Objection overruled. Counselor, you'll have your chance."
Says Melendez.
"Did Nichols confide in you in prison?"
Asks Connolly.
"He did. Maybe he also had weed on that ship, which never left Port Antonio. He never said it, but Birds of a feather flock together. "
"Your honor, I have no further questions."
"Attorney Davis, your witness."
Judge Melendez says, glimpsing at the clock on the courtroom wall and the Jury box.

CHAPTER 23

Sebastian Davis began drilling by asking Marcus Davis if anyone could trust him.

"Ouch!" Marcus Davis says in his mind, "no one has ever asked me that." Marcus Davis replied after considering that many people trust him as far as he knew.

The frown on Gregg and Deja's faces told one that their answer didn't sit well with them.

"Really?"

Asks Sebastian Davis.

"The ones who don't trust me cannot trust themselves either." Marcus Davis continued in a rather sarcastic overtone.

The defense lawyer then asked him if he aspired all along to join the witness protection program. With a broad smile on his face, he told the court:

"When you do good, great things get thrust upon you. However, all that program analysis stuff is still purely speculative."

Sebastian Davis then asked Marcus Davis how long he had cherished his desire to join the program. Connolly objected to this question. Nevertheless, the Judge

insisted that Marcus Davis provide an answer, to which Marcus replied, "over ten years, sir."
Sebastian Davis continued pressing his namesake about his statements made prior in testimony regarding Milton Rogers. "Did you have a vendetta against Rogers?"
Asked the defense lawyer.
"I did not. However, I've always seen him as a small fry. Although he functioned like he was some big potato."
Says the witness.
"Watch your words!"
Says Nichols under his breath but loud enough to draw a response from Judge Melendez.
"Silence in court!"
Barks the Judge.
"The man's a liar! A blatant liar, a conspirator."
Continues Gregg Nichols.
"Gentlemen I am warning you."
Says the Judge.
One could now hear a pin drop inside the court room after that warning...with the stenographer now on hiatus and court officers ambled back into position, the Judge says:
"Please continue Counselor."
"You seemed to be at odds with Wesley Haynes, the man who you referred to as Rogers' partner. It is hard for me to believe you didn't have it up for Milton Rogers and wanted to see him get rubbed out."

WHO SHOT THE SHERIFF? SERIES

"Wesley ran his mouth too much and so did Rogers, Parsons and his Water-boy Gregg Nichols."

"Were you involved in a conspiracy to kill Milton Rogers?

"No, I was not. No reason to." Says Marcus Davis.

"Do you know of anyone who was?" "No. Rogers and Wesley Haynes shot the Sheriff. That's what's still on the street nowadays. Most likely, someone was now after Rogers. That's how the mop flops."

"What grounds do you have for that statement?" Asks Sebastian Davis.

"Come on, it was common knowledge. Whatever you do to others will be done unto you... that's Biblically correct? Rogers was a crook. He owned an Infiniti SUV and a Glock 38 just like Wesley Haynes did. Maybe the same dealer reassembled both guns? They found his Infiniti. Where is his Glock? Ok! It shouldn't take a rocket scientist to figure that one out. Two infinities could have been included instead of one. You guys are the lawyers, not me. Go figure...I don't get paid to do that stuff."

"Mr Davis were you not on parole at the time when Sheriff John Brown and his Deputy Ron Charles were gunned down? Did you visit Jamaica back in August of last year?"

"Jamaica?" Ask Marcus Davis.

"Yes, Jamaica. A stamp in your passport indicates you did."

Says Sebastian Davis.

"I was. That is my birthplace. I go whenever I choose to go to the moon. I wasn't born ah foreign...scene?" Says Marcus Davis. "Who did you rub out on your trip?"

Ask Davis for the defense.

"No one."

"No further questions."

Says Sebastian Davis and briskly ambles to his seat. Gregg Nichols gives his lawyer a thumbs up in approval. Deja shares smiles with both men seated to her left. The Judge takes a 15-minute recess, which later evolves into an adjournment of the trial's proceedings for the day.

… WHO SHOT THE SHERIFF? SERIES

CHAPTER 24

In Paris, after being interviewed and dropping a sample of their new hit song "Someone Has Got to Pay" at a studio session, Britney and Wesley returned to their hotel.

Upon entering they find themselves immersed in the Late Breaking News flashing across their TV screen: Woman shot in Drive-by is identified as artist Deja Nichols.

The news broke early this morning: Last night Deja Nichols, the wife of Gregg Nichols was rushed to Mercy Miami Hospital. It is reported the artist/entrepreneur was gunned down while walking toward her car in South Beach. According to the reports: At 10:30 PM last evening. Deja Nichols was traveling to her car and carrying an empty duffel bag. Several bullets rang out. According to one eyewitness' account. The artist fell backward onto the sidewalk a few feet away from her parked BMW. A speeding black automobile departed from the scene. That lone eyewitness, an elderly man riding his bicycle after dark in the park, states that he spotted a grayish black or what looked like a black car speeding away from the scene. The car displayed temporary license tags. Deja apparently took a bullet to her right arm and was minutes later rushed to ER, where she appears to be in stable condition. Meanwhile, the drive-by assailant(s) is still on the loose. It was just a few days ago since Deja testified on her husband Gregg Nichols' behalf inside a Miami courtroom. He has been charged in the shooting death of Jamaican Mogul, Milton Rogers. According to sources, singer Britney Haynes was distraught upon hearing about Deja Nichols' incident. The two female artists were very instrumental in Wesley Haynes' rise to fame and fortune.

MEANWHILE IN MIAMI news of the shooting incident saturates the printed media as well as Radio and TV. The Miami Herald front page headline reads: Woman shot in Drive-by is identified as Deja Nichols. Many in the media theorize, why was Deja in that area of South Beach after midnight? An area dominated by pimps, prostitutes, and Drug Lords. The artist recently testified in her husband's trial.

In the meantime, her very close friends Wesley and Britney according to sources inside Haynes' camp, are on the way back from an abbreviated trip to Paris. Where they just signed a mega deal for their next album: Someone has got to Pay.

WHO SHOT THE SHERIFF? SERIES

Britney Haynes is a potential witness for the defense in the case surrounding Milton Rogers' death. Deja was instrumental in helping Wesley and Britney Haynes land the contract for their first song, which became a mega-hit.

Gregg Nichols picks the news up at breakfast inside the North Terrace lunchroom, headlined in the Miami Herald. He is pissed and almost drowning in tears. Several make-believe supporters huddle around him, including Hybels, Chang, and Son of Judah. Instead of talking to Gregg, they converse with each other in an unknown tongue, gesturing and using sarcasm. The news repeated itself across many major Radio and TV networks:

"Meanwhile, Miami police are looking for the vehicle in question along with its suspect(s) who are still at large. If you have any information regarding the shooting incident you are asked to contact Crime Stoppers immediately."

> WHO SHOT THE SHERIFF? SERIES

CHAPTER 25

Late breaking news concerning the shooting of Deja Nichols continues to predominate the media. Upon hearing the summary from other inmates, Gregg Nichols becomes more rattled and unnerved. He mentally aches from his venom and immediately goes into solitude. He envisions that not only is there no Deja by his side inside the courtroom, but his two daughters, ages seven and nine, have to be without the company of their mom and their dad for a while. He is granted permission to make one telephone call per day. Even so, when he calls home, no one picks up. "Whatever could go wrong just did," he mutters under his breath after hanging up the jail phone. "They did it to Wesley Haynes, now they are doing it to me." He continues.

North Terrace's inmates continually make a mockery of him and have no qualms for expressing their views openly.

"Somebody else is eating your chocolate ice cream while you incarcerate Mr. Lover, Lover..." Says the Son of Judah.

"Your wife owes me money... lots! I need to get paid in full."

Says Hybels.

All this is not only news, real or fabricated but salt in the wound as far as Gregg is concerned. Ever since Hybels pissed on his bed, in Gregg's eyes most of what he says comes through one ear and goes out through the other.

Additionally, it has been rumored among his fellow inmates that his wife was dealing drugs in South Beach at the time of the accident. Even so, there was no evidence to link her to any substance transfer.

Gregg, on the other hand, tries as much as he can to ignore them but can't. He subsequently resorts to a solitary lifestyle. Daily, he washes his face, anoints his head, and survives on liquids in search of redemption. So painful...there's not even a song he can spit.

IN JAMAICA, as well as other islands in the Caribbean, news circulated that the Jamaican police may have played a key role in Milton Rogers' death. Rogers was known as a shaker and mover, who aligned himself with the late musical tycoon Bill Parsons. With Parsons in the picture, more wounds were now opened up. The media claimed Rogers, at one point, not only questioned the transparency of Jamaican Law Enforcement but accused that entity of wasting the country's money on the tracking down of Wesley Haynes instead of putting it into the education of young people – keeping them off the streets of Kingston.

Rogers never cared much for Sheriff John Brown nor Deputy Ron Charles. The late, outspoken, uninhibited entrepreneur Milton Rogers had no problems expressing these concerns and more. "He certainly did not hold his tongue back as far as those matters were concerned."

One Radio talk show host echoed:

"After the Infiniti, which was registered to Milton Rogers, was discovered in a Jamaican ravine. Peers of Sheriff John Brown and his Deputy Ron Charles pinned the rub out of their two top brass officers Milton Rogers. Therefore, they sought revenge and rubbed out Rogers in an assassination that will never be forgotten by anyone who ever stepped inside a courtroom or even watched a LIVE trial on TV."

A version of the theory also suggests that the people who assassinated Bill Parsons the late Jamaican music producer and also a close ally of Milton Rogers, paid off Miami Law enforcement to do their dirty work in this tragedy.

Meanwhile, conspiracy theorist continues pointing fingers at Gregg Nichols in the shooting death of Milton Rogers. They theorize as far as Gregg Nichols' involvement: Wesley Haynes set him up. Haynes knowing with Milton Rogers out of the picture, the Haynes' Empire would turn into an instant monopoly. Haynes would automatically become the next Jamaican Mogul controlling the entire music world. Every beat and genre would have Wesley Haynes' branding, even country music. According to media leaks, it was reported that even the Jamaican government, in collaboration with the U.S., England, Holland, and Germany, wanted to stop this monopoly before it got out of control.

CHAPTER 26

The trial was reconvened inside Judge Reuben Melendez's courtroom. Two court officers, Daniel Edwards and Errol Clarke, testified.

Daniel Edwards claimed he was situated at the rear of the courtroom and to the right of Quentin Daley. According to Edwards: Gregg Nichols emerged out of the struggle with Daley and allegedly held on to court officer Quentin Daley's gun.

After the bullet was discharged, Edwards was the first court officer to arrive at the scene. He landed immediately behind detectives Paul Stevens and Mike Jones.

Edwards basically stated to the defense that he saw both men fighting over the gun after Milton Rogers was gunned down. According to Edwards, his main concern was who was going to get shot. So, he rushed to the scene with his gun pointed and demanded: "Drop the gun! By then the two detectives were already forerunners making the same demands of Nichols.

Edwards claimed by the time he was three feet away from the apparent shooter, the detectives were putting handcuffs on Nichols. The gun was thrown to the ground and kicked aside after failed attempts by Nichols to discharge any additional rounds at this point.

Errol Clarke, on the other hand, when cross-examined by Davis, testified that he was on the right side of the room during the shooting of Rogers. By the time he arrived where Daley and Nichols were struggling for the gun, Nichols was already being handcuffed by the two detectives. So, Edwards arrived on the scene moments before Clarke did.

Sebastian Davis asked: Why did it take Clarke so long to arrive at the rear of the court room seeing he had a clear path from the front of the room and only two corners to navigate on the path he chose? Clarke, looking at the location in the courtroom from where the bullet emerged stated:

"I hesitated because I was coming in the direction from whence the bullet which killed Rogers was discharged. If I moved straight ahead, other bullets could have cut me down from straight ahead as I approached the zone of conflict. It was a calculated gut decision I had to make."

The defense then asked Clarke if he was fearful of being shot when he, too, was armed with a Glock 38. To which he responded:

"It all happened so fast. My thought was, what if I removed my gun from its holster and someone grabbed it from me? They could have embarked on a shooting spree."

THERE WAS A CHUCKLE from inside the defense's camp earlier during Connolly's cross-examination of Clarke. The DA asked the witness if he had ever seen this before inside a courtroom. To which Clarke jokingly responded: "Never before in my life. Not even in the movies!"

CHAPTER 27

The court next hears testimony from Claude Jefferson, the coroner right after lunch. DA Mark Connolly is profiled at the lectern eager to get on with the trial.
"Mr. Jefferson, from where did you attain your coroner's degree?"
Asks Connolly.
"UCLA School of Medicine."
He responds.
"I see. How long have you been performing duties as a coroner?" Ask the DA.
"I moved to Miami right after school. It has been a few months shy of twelve years."
Says Jefferson.
"Thank you. I've noticed you've been involved in several high-profile cases prior and that your findings seem to be very accurate." Sebastian Davis objects and yells:
"Leading!"

Judge Melendez sustains the objection. "I am looking at the more than two dozen cases you've testified in. The record indicates that you have always been able to support your findings."

"I believe in professionalism. Thank you." Says Jefferson.

"Who performed the autopsy on Milton Rogers?" Asks Connolly.

"I did."

"Mr. Jefferson, please educate the court regarding your findings."

"Mr. Rogers died from a single gunshot wound to his right side just below his ribcage. The bullet penetrated and lodged in his spine." "How soon after being shot did the victim die?" Asks Connolly.

"Rogers died on the spot in less than five minutes."

"Was there an inscription on the bullet, and if so whose name was etched on it?"

"Yes. There was, the name Milton Rogers." Says Jefferson.

"Do you think the victim could have survived?"

"That's possible, but with that much damage to this spine, he could have been crippled for life." Says Jefferson.

"Thank you, Mr. Jefferson. No further questions." Sebastian Davis steps up and begins questioning the coroner. Among several leading questions without

WHO SHOT THE SHERIFF? SERIES

objection from the prosecution, he asked Mr. Jefferson if it was possible to determine the distance from which the bullet was discharged. Mr. Jefferson stated about 50 feet, the distance of at least one New York MTA train is approximately the length of the courtroom. The defense had no further questions. As a result, Judge Melendez set the continuation of the trial for the next afternoon.

Ramblings continued as attendees made their exits.

CHAPTER 28

Not only did Wesley Haynes and Britney Haynes return to Miami from their trip to
Paris, but Deja's status was upgraded to satisfactory and released from the hospital. The media, upon announcing Deja's release, also claimed the bullet that struck her was a .45 and fired from a .38 45 GAP, the same make and model registered to the Miami courthouse and assigned to Officer Quentin Daley.
This bullet went through the upper biceps in her left arm.
One stalker claimed Deja was seen walking in the park on Sunday morning with her two daughters. That prowler also claimed a well-wisher noticing them in the park, yelled out: "Deja, we love you!" It was said: the artist smiled in recognition of the intentional get well sentiment. Her daughters also shared in.

HEARINGS IN THE CASE continued on that Monday afternoon. The first afternoon commencement session since the trial began almost two weeks ago. Even so, the courtroom staff was seen shuffling back and forth, signs of unpreparedness for the afternoon's court proceedings. Even the Judge arrived a few minutes late behind his bench. Other signs of unrest were also visible, not only inside the jury box but among courtroom attendees as well. The Bailiff hands a one-page document to Melendez. The Judge puts on his horned-rimmed glasses after cleaning the lens carefully to rid of any residue. He then peruses through the page carefully.

"This could be an extended evening if necessary. I just wanted to make everyone aware, " he says as he sits back in his chair. The court announcer picks up his cue of readiness. She calls Britney Haynes to the witness stand. Some applause accompanies the artist. It seems like many had forgotten the rules of the courtroom and indulged in extended applause. Britney accepts their sentiment with a modest smile.

However, Melendez quickly called the court to order after glancing at the clock on the rear wall of the courtroom, accompanied by yet another strike of the gavel and a candid look on his face.

Gregg Nichols, in recognition, turns around and gives thumbs up to his biggest client and great friend Wesley Haynes, who is encircled by his lawyer Collin Mattes and manager Mr. Singh. The trio, freshly attired as if they went shopping with stylists in Paris, acknowledges Gregg Nichols. Wesley returns kindly. They are present at a time when Gregg really needed a boost.

WHO SHOT THE SHERIFF? SERIES

Britney Haynes takes the oath after which DA Mark Connolly begins cross-examination.

"Mrs. Haynes, good afternoon."
Says Connolly with a slight amount of apology in his voice.
To which Britney responds with glee. "Mrs. Haynes these series of events must be very troubling. I assume."
"They are. For yet another time we are dragged into this debacle."
"The judicature has to do what it must do Mrs. Haynes."
Deja is present in the courtroom and with her arm in a sling shakes her head in disagreement regarding the DA's statement.
"No. It's the system!" Deja says.
"Mrs. Nichols, I am warning you."
Says the Judge.
"Please tell the court about your relationship with the defendant Gregg Nichols."
"I first met Deja Nichols over a year ago when my husband and I were at a low point of our lives and our musical career. More accurately we were about to break up. She introduced me to her ex-boss, Mr. Beckles. At the time, I was a basement music producer. Deja was very influential in moving our single hit song to a Grammy contender, and eventually a win.

When we met in the park that day, I had no idea all of this would materialize. She later introduced us to her husband Gregg. How I wished Wesley could adopt some of Gregg's humble qualities." Wesley, sitting multiple rows from the front, smilingly, leans forward in a zinging posture. Britney perks.

Meanwhile, Deja tears up. Large segments of tears run down her blushed cheeks. After that pause, Britney continues.

"Gregg took over the business from his boss who was blind and experiencing deteriorating illness. Our second song became a big hit mainly because of their efforts. They are not only associates, but we consider them close friends."

Deja dries her tears, clutching onto Gregg's left arm. Inside the jury box, Jurors take copious notes.

The Judge loosens his tie and demands a recess after witnessing Deja's tears trickle down and fall onto the courtroom floor.

CHAPTER 29

District Attorney Mark Connolly visually connects with jurors before proceeding.

"Mrs. Haynes, you were inside the courtroom when Milton Rogers was gunned down. Were you not?"

"I was. My husband and I were the first to arrive as he fell backward off that witness stand."

"Did you see Gregg Nichols shoot Milton Rogers? Asks Connolly

"No. I did not."
Says Britney

"Did he tell you he shot Milton Rogers for fame or an inheritance of his estate?" Asks Connolly.

"He did not. Gregg is not that kind of person." Says Britney.

"Mrs. Haynes, are you also one of the beneficiaries to Milton Rogers' estate?" Attorney Sebastian Davis objects.

Judge Melendez sustains the objection.

"You may answer the question."
Says Connolly.

"I am not a beneficiary."
Replies Britney Haynes.

"Mrs. Haynes, in regard to your friend Deja Nichols: Do you know her by an alias or what some may call an aka?"
"I do." "And what's that?" Asks Connolly.
"Grace!"
"Do you know her by any other aliases?"
"No. I don't." Responds Britney.
"And the defendant Gregg Nichols?"
Asks Connolly.
"I only know him as Gregg."
Says Britney. "No further questions, your honor." Says Connolly.
The Judge eyes the clock.
After a pause in the trial's proceedings: "Your witness counselor."
Says Melendez.
Sebastian Davis, after greeting Britney, compliments her for a unique display of courage in a back-to-back trial and in the same courtroom. Britney sobs continuously like a running stream. The Judge suggested Britney take a minute or two before continuing her testimony as she remained engulfed in tears.
"I am fine."
Says Britney.
Gregg Nichols focuses on Deja, now engulfed in the secondary courtroom drama – a tear-jerking episode accompanied by sobs of suffering.

"Oppression Never Done!"
Yells Gregg Nichols.
Court officers amble towards the section of the room where those three words echoed.
"Silence in court!"
Says Melendez.
Residual murmuring continues.
"Let's clear out the courtroom."
Summons Melendez.
Court officers pounce, and subsequently, the courtroom empties out.

> WHO SHOT THE SHERIFF? SERIES

CHAPTER 30

The trial reconvenes after yet another prolonged unscheduled intermission—a coordination and calm-down interruption, to say the least, or better yet: a long time out. This intermission was much needed to get everyone back on cue. Defense attorney Sebastian Davis continues,

"Mrs. Haynes, please tell this court about your relationship with the victim Milton Rogers."

"Milton Rogers gave Wesley and me our first job when we moved from Mandeville to Kingston. He took us under his wings, so to speak. Rogers was a great friend and mentor to Wesley. He would always say to Wesley: 'The heights by great men reached and kept were not attained by sudden flight, but they, while their companions slept, were toiling upward in the night.' Wesley took that statement to heart. It seemed to have entered every fiber of his being. It became his mantra. We will always be grateful to Mr. Milton Rogers."

"I see. Did you or your husband conspire to murder Milton Rogers?"

Asks Sebastian Davis.

"We did not. We loved Mr. Rogers; he had done so much for us. We would never entertain an ungrateful thought towards him. Milton Rogers paved the way for Wesley and Me."
Responds Britney.
"Do you know of anyone who did?"
Asks Davis.
"No. I do not."
"Mrs. Haynes, if you were asked to etch the epitaph on Milton Rogers' tombstone what would you write?"
Britney thinks for a moment. She breathes before answering.
"Here lies a man who gave and gave until there was nothing else to give to the advancement of international music."
Says the multiple Grammy winner, Britney Haynes.
"Thank you, Mrs. Haynes. No further questions."
"Mrs. Haynes you may step down."
Says Melendez.
At this point, Britney Haynes is once again engulfed in tears.
Two aids accompanied by Wesley Haynes emerge and escorts Britney outside the courtroom. Wesley's lawyer and manager follow in tow.
Deja reflects and once again tears up. Gregg puts his arm around her and consoles her. Melendez call for yet another post-tear-jerking-recess. Many believed that

the unusual amounts of tears in the courtroom had a traumatic effect on the Judge.

CHAPTER 31

After the break, DA Mark Connolly approaches the lectern. Ballistics expert
Lloyd Matthews is on the witness stand.
Connolly begins cross-examination. "Mr. Matthews, the record states you are from the island of Jamaica and were recently transferred to the Ballistics department here in Miami. Is that correct?"
"That's correct." Says Matthews.
"What's the tenure of your career?"
"Ten years and counting…"
"Mr. Matthews, you were inside this courtroom on Valentine's Day when Milton Rogers was shot. Were you not?"
"I was."
"Would you say that was coincidental on your part?"
"Yes. It was."
Responds Matthews.
"Tell the court what you saw." "I saw Rogers react to being shot after a single round of gunfire. I then turned around, looking to see where that shot originated. My eyes saw and locked in on two men struggling over a

gun. I found out later the wrestlers were Gregg Nichols and Quentin Daley."
"Did you ask to be assigned to this case?"
"I did not. They sought me out." "Based on your findings, what type of gun was used in the shooting death of Milton Rogers?"
"It was a Glock 38."
"Have you worked on other cases where the type of gun in question was used?"
"Objection!" Shouts Sebastian Davis.
"Objection overruled." Says Melendez adjusting his glasses. Mr. Matthews, I cite in the Who Shot the Sheriff? Case vs Wesley Haynes, you testified: three replicas of Glock 38s were used. Isn't that so?"
"I did."
"You testified earlier that one bullet was fired in that incident on Valentine's Day, inside this courtroom.
"I did."
"Based on your findings, how many bullets remained inside the gun's magazine after that fatal shot was fired?"
"The gun was empty."
"What's the capacity of a Glock 38 magazine?"
"Eight rounds."
"How many bullets were recovered from the victim's body?"
"One bullet."

Based on your findings, how many bullets were discharged from the gun?" "One single bullet." Replied Matthews.

"What test did your lab perform to determine the bullet matched the gun recovered at the crime scene?" Asks Connolly.
"Our regular procedure was once again followed. A bullet from that gun was fired into a tank filled with water. After that bullet was recovered, it was viewed under a microscope and determined a match." "Mr. Matthews, to your knowledge were there any additional guns used in that shooting incident?" "It is clear there was one gun. One bullet with its shell residue which displayed the name Milton Rogers on it."
Responds Matthews.
"Was the name etched in caps or lowercase?"
"It was etched in sentence case and italicized." The Bailiff presents a package. Matthews opens it, removes a slide, and places it into the projector. The fragment shell casing is visible. He zooms in and shows a close-up of the etched shell.
"This is exhibiting number two."
Says Mathews and returns to the witness stand. "Were there fingerprints on the gun and whose?"
Asks Connolly.
"There were prints lifted for Quentin Daley and

Gregg Nichols and Errol Clarke."
"Were any of these prints widely distributed on the Glock 38?"
"Yes, in and around the trigger area. I must say Gregg Nichols prints dominated the entire gun, as well as inside the gun's magazine." "Objection. Your honor, I move to strike the last sentence."
Says Sebastian Davis. "Objection overruled." Says Melendez.
"So basically, the defendant had maximum control of the weapon as indicated by a dominance of his fingerprints inside and out?"
Says Connolly.
"That is a given."
Responds Matthews.
"What percentage of Errol Clarke's fingerprints was found on the gun?" "A small percentage."
"How small?" Asks Connolly.
"At least 20%."
Responds Matthews.
"What percentage for Quentin Daley?"
"At least 30%." Says Matthews.
"So, that means the defendant, Gregg Nichols' fingerprints dominated with a whopping 50%?"

"Yes. I would say that..." "Objection! Move to strike." Says Davis.
"Overruled." Says Melendez.

"Based upon your findings, Mr. Matthews: did the defendant load or reload the gun?" "That is possible. The location of his prints on that gun would suggest he did."

Says Matthews.

"Thank you, Mr. Matthews. No further questions." Says Connolly.

The DA walks back to his seat. On the witness stand, Ballistics expert Lloyd Matthews stays put.

CHAPTER 32

Sebastian Davis approaches with strides of determination and focus. He must be going for the jugular that of Lloyd Matthews' – Gregg reasons.

Restlessness exudes from within the Jury Box. Poise resounds on the face of Gregg Nichols. Deja's face shows genuine support.

"Mr. Matthews, you testified earlier, you were inside the courtroom when Milton Rogers was gunned down. Is that correct?"

"It is correct."

Says Matthews.

"Why were you there at that time?"

"I had just finished testifying in the case vs Wesley Haynes, and seeing Rogers was going to be the last witness in the case, I wanted to witness his testimony. Thoughts of leaving entered my mind, but I decided to stay."

"So, did you witness the shooting of Milton Rogers?"

"No. As I explained, I heard a round of gunshots and saw Milton Rogers fall backward on the witness stand, holding his chest." "You did not? Didn't you see the defendant Gregg Nichols shoot and kill Milton Rogers?" Asks Davis.

"You are putting words in my mouth. I am here to testify about my ballistics findings as an expert. From my vantage point, I did not see who fired the fatal round. However, when I turned around, I saw Quentin and Nichols fighting for control of the gun. I must say: based on any findings, Nichols' fingerprints dominated the weapon." Says Matthews.
"I thought you saw everything." Says Sebastian Davis. Connolly is standing at this point but gracefully sits back down.
Attorney Davis continues.
"Expert! Didn't your findings err in the case Wesley Haynes vs Sheriff John Brown and Deputy Ron Charles?"
"Err?"
Asks Lloyd Matthews.
"Yes... Err. For the use of a better word slips up, or in error?"
"The court granted permission to my department to further investigate the bullets which shot the Sheriff and his Deputy. I provided them with those results per their request."
"So, as an expert, is your work sometimes in error or not definitive or conclusive?" "I do my job the way I was trained."

Says Matthews.

"So, you are trained to err or slip up now and then to manufacture a misleading conviction?" "That's not how I do my job."

Says Matthews.

"You also testified earlier that it is possible the defendant loaded or reloaded the gun."

"I did."

"Where did he put the bullet or bullets he removed from the gun's magazine? They were not found on his person."

"Hypothetically, he could have swallowed them."

Says Matthews.

"All eight bullets were swallowed without a glass of water?"

Asks Sebastian Davis.

"I don't know how many rounds were present inside the gun before Rogers was shot."

Says Matthews.

"Did he pass any bullets out in his stool?"

Asks Davis.

"We don't know that."

Says Matthews.

"Did anyone check?"

Asks Attorney Davis.

The courtroom erupts with laughter. The striking of the gavel restores some sense of order. "No one did. Several days had passed before the remains of that

fatal bullet were transported to me by the coroner's office. Nichols had already been locked up for several days. We had no way of knowing. Or else someone could have monitored his feces."
Says Matthews.

"In addition to the fingerprints of the defendant Gregg Nichols and court officer Quentin Daley, were there other prints lifted from that gun?"
"Yes."
Says Matthews.
"Whose?"
Asks Davis.
"Court Officer Errol Clarke."
Says Matthews.
"Interesting ... so he too was in contact with that gun. Yet, he didn't pull the trigger. Your honor, no further questions."
Says Sebastian Davis, staring into the vicinity of the Jury box before returning to his seat.

> WHO SHOT THE SHERIFF? SERIES

CHAPTER 33

Heaviness emerges from lawful psychoanalysts as to why court officer Errol Clarke's fingerprints were found on the gun that shot Milton Rogers. Now, the nucleus of media-related debates began filtering into the trial. Many feared the jury would become polluted with outside influence.

It is a given Clarke didn't say too much in his testimony. However, many legal experts felt there was more to be told from the co-worker of Quentin Daley, the officiating partner, to the possible gunman, even though he might have been accused yet not officially charged.

Clarke's prints on the gun were unsettling as many legal experts tried to unravel the case outside the courtroom. Meanwhile, inside Judge Melendez's courtroom, as if it were an act of fate, Errol Clarke was recalled to the witness stand. After what seemed like a swift reading of the oath, cross-examination began. DA Mark Connolly proceeded to the lectern.

"Mr. Clarke, did you load or reload your co-worker's gun before the trial on Valentine's Day?"

"No. I did not. I saw him load that gun himself."
Says Errol Clarke.
"How many bullets did he load into that gun's magazine?"
"One bullet."
"Didn't it concern you that your co-worker was carrying a gun with only one bullet inside its magazine?"
"I don't check my co-workers' weapons to determine how many rounds they have loaded inside."
Says Clarke.
"Were there other bullets inside that gun?"
Asks Connolly.
"I don't know." Says Clarke. "No further questions."
Says Connolly.

ATTORNEY SEBASTIAN DAVIS steps into the witness' paint, attempting to score a few points. "Mr. Clarke, in your testimony earlier, you stated you had never seen any incident in the courtroom like Roger's shooting. Were you implying an incident of such magnitude had to be properly executed?" "It had to be well planned." Says Clarke.
"So, you concur it had to have been well planned?"
"Yes. Proper planning is the foundation of any well-executed venture."
Says Clarke.
"Did you share the same dressing room with Officer Daley on the day Milton Rogers was shot?"

Clarke hesitates.

"Did you, Mr. Clarke?"

"I did."

"Your fingerprints were found on his gun. That same gun that took the life of Milton Rogers. What was your intent?"

"We carry the same guns of the same make and model. A Glock 38 gray is a Glock 38 gray. It is quite possible I accepted his gun by mistake while getting ready for the trial."

Clarke states.

"By mistake?"

Asks Sebastian Davis.

"So, did you touch his gun or tamper with it while it was inside the shared dressing room?"

"I don't recall touching his gun. If I did, it was by accident."

"Did you open his gun and reload it?"

"I did not. If it was a mistake."

"A mistake to reload?"

"I did not. As I said, I don't recall overseeing his gun. If
I did it was an unconscious mistake."

"Unconscious? Mr. Clarke, did your unconscious decision also limit you from rushing through the center aisle in the courtroom to the aid of your fellow officer while he tried to recapture his gun?"

"I don't understand."

Says Clarke.

"You said in previous testimony: Instead of going through the center aisle, you went left, turned the corner, and headed towards the rear of the courtroom."

"Yes. That is what happened."

"Why did you choose the longer route instead of the shorter and more direct one? Were you trained to wait or to respond?"

"I made an instinctual decision."

Says Clarke.

"Just like the one you did when you tampered with your co-worker's weapon. Your honor, I have no further questions."

CHAPTER 34

There were no more eyewitnesses called in the case. It seemed that was it for all the testifying in this case. The court took an extended recess.

It was widely distributed: Gregg Nichols shot Milton Rogers. Even if many flaunted the epiphany or the conspiracy theory: Rogers shot John Brown and his Deputy Ron Charles, now Rogers was also snuffed out. As far as it seemed, Gregg Nichols was their man; in their eyes, he was guilty until proven innocent. If he is not acquitted, he could die in Florida's electric chair or, on a lesser charge, be locked away for life if eventually convicted.

However, it was also heavily debated among legal experts: others could have been responsible for that double homicide in which Wesley Haynes was found not guilty. That same entity could have also orchestrated the Milton Rogers' ambush. Even if no one claimed responsibility for the Mogul's death.

When the trial resumed, Melendez asked Connolly to present his closing statements.

DA Mark Connolly rose to the occasion. He straightened his tie, unbuttoned his jacket, and greeted the judge and then 12 jurors with a broad smile. They responded in kind but modestly. His decorum was like a fresh beginning in the trial, which has now lasted more than a month since jury selection.

"Your honor, jurors, other court attendees. It has been a long and tiring six weeks of hearing testimonies and weighing through this preponderance of evidence. I am sure you're like me wanting to put this whole matter to rest. On Valentine's Day last year, Jamaican Mogul Milton Rogers was gunned down while testifying inside this courtroom. Some saw Milton Rogers shoot Rogers after which he engaged in a struggle for the court officer's gun. Although some may argue it wasn't the defendant Gregg Nichols who fired that fatal shot that killed Milton Rogers. There's a preponderance of evidence stacked up against Gregg Nichols. It is clear, based on the testimonies given, that he had multiple motives for killing Rogers, even though the defense may beg to differ. Gregg Nichols could have been in search of fame. By shooting the Jamaican Mogul, he would join the club of Whodunit Murderers like the Lee Harvey Oswald' of the world.

Nichols could have shot Rogers in order to cover up information in the death of Sheriff John Brown and his Deputy Ron Charles.

Wesley Haynes was Nichols' close friend. Chances are Nichols was afraid Rogers would disclose relevant information to support Haynes' guilty verdict. So, he snuffed out Rogers.

Knowingly that Rogers and Haynes had strong financial ties.

Wanting to replace Rogers in the musical chain could have been paramount, so he snuffed out Milton Rogers.

Those are strong and possible motives for shooting Rogers inside that courtroom. To think anyone else could have been responsible: is nothing but ludicrous. Gregg Nichols is guilty of shooting Milton Rogers, as the evidence has shown.

Members of the jury it's your responsibility to deliver justice in this case. Allowing a guilty man to walk free would be forever on your conscience if you do not convict him.

"We, the prosecution, rests."

Multiple eyes are fixated on the defendant while DA Mark Connolly strolls across the front of the courtroom and takes his pew.

CHAPTER 35

Melendez wasted no time calling on defense lawyer Sebastian Davis. With his chest stuck out, Davis approached the jury box and engaged them.

"Ladies and gentlemen of the jury. In a trial that has lasted almost two months. It is apparent the gunman who shot and killed Milton Rogers isn't a first-time offender. I don't believe my client Gregg Nichols shot and killed Rogers. I think this assassination-style killing was not only well orchestrated but a collaborated effort.

Case in point: Court officer Errol Clarke's fingerprints were lifted from the gun belonging to his co-worker, Officer Quentin Daley. My question to you is: Why? Why would someone else fingerprints appear on a weapon which he is not permitted to have in his possession? Quentin Daley, the court officer, was allowed to carry that gun to protect the judge, jury, law enforcement personnel, and other courtroom attendees. Why was there only one bullet inside that gun's magazine? Why wasn't that gun fully loaded by this court officer? Who supplied that one bullet? It is still a mystery. Did it come through osmosis, divine providence, or some heartless killer who wants to see my client convicted for a crime he did not commit?

If Gregg Nichols detached the other seven ammunitions, what did he do with them? No bullets were recovered inside the courtroom nor on his person. Some might argue that Nichols could have swallowed the bullets. It takes time to gulp one horse pill with water, much less without water. The bullets used in that Glock are much grander than horse pills. Suppose it takes at least five seconds to swallow a bullet with water. We can assume it would take three times that time to swallow one without water. It would, therefore, take 105 seconds to swallow all seven bullets without breathing after each ingestion.

Detectives Jones and Stevens were present inside the courtroom and seated a few rows away. They would have gotten to Nichols before he had an opportunity to discharge that fatal bullet. The bullet that Rogers had had Rogers' name etched on it, according to the ballistics report. Let's say the gun was fully loaded with eight bullets. Let's say Nichols removed the other seven bullets, how did he know which bullet had Milton Rogers' name etched on it?

Additionally, if Nichols had to reload Quentin Daley's gun with a bullet that he brought with him through tight security, and there were 8 bullets inside that gun prior, that's an extra 15 second elapse to swallow another bullet. Thus, making it 120 seconds, which, the last time I checked, equals two full minutes. So, did Nichols swallow all those bullets in 2 minutes and then pull the trigger? In essence, four thirty-second commercials would have been aired before he pulled that trigger.

Let's say it took him 1 minute to tackle court officer Daley, and 15 seconds to open the gun's magazine and remove eight bullets, 2 minutes to swallow them. Then let's say it took him 15 seconds to load the etched–fatal bullet, close the gun's magazine, get the perfect aim, and then shoot Rogers. That is 3 and 1/2 minutes. A total of seven 30-second commercials aired since he confronted Quentin, the court officer, to the time the fatal bullet was discharged. I don't buy that, and neither do you. It doesn't add up.

If Nichols loaded that gun with one bullet, then it is evident the gun was empty. This means that court officer Daley was unarmed during a high-profile case. That crime should be punishable by law. We must ask ourselves: Was the Rogers' shooting collaborative between Errol Clarke, Marcus Davis, and Quentin Daley?

Marcus Davis testified he had a long-lasting beef with Wesley Haynes and Milton Rogers over a shipment of undelivered marijuana.

Additionally, Marcus Davis planned to join the witness protection program to shield himself from any

crime. The fact remains: Did Marcus Davis collaborate with court officers Clarke and Daley to eliminate the Jamaican Mogul Milton Rogers inside the courtroom? All these questions we must ask ourselves. I do not believe the defendant, Gregg Nichols, shot Milton Rogers. Time and Time again, I've seen men go to prison for a crime they did not commit. This has to stop. This trial is our opportunity to stop this trend. My client is a decent citizen who wishes to continue living a fulfilled life. Let him go so he can do just that." Sebastian Davis moved in a full circle and wound up directly in front of the jury box, tapping on their heart doors.
"I look forward to your nonguilty verdict concerning my client."
Sebastian Davis walks back to his seat to get a thumbs-up from Gregg Nichols.
Judge Melendez announced the jury would deliberate and return with a verdict in three days. The agitated courtroom attendees file out.

CHAPTER 36

Returning to North Terrace, it was Gregg Nichols' objective to get some much-needed R and R. With deliberation already underway, he couldn't wait to lay his head down and rid his mind of the hearing of testimonies ordeal. His desire was to be free once again, living the life he always envisioned as an artist and entrepreneur. Even so, one more uncertainty beckoned – the verdict. That night at North Terrace oblivious to Gregg Nichols, his neighbors concocted a plot to avenge him.

They had watched that day's proceedings in the trial via the prison's flat-screen TV hitched high above their heads inside the recreation room. Evidently, they had been well informed regarding the current status of the proceedings.

While Nichols walked towards his cell, he felt someone stroking his neck and shoulders. As he turned around, he came face to face with Hybels, his upstairs neighbor, who had maliciously poured urine onto his bed on his first night at North Terrace.

"What is your problem?"
He asks Hybels.
Smilingly, Hybels states:
"I want to get you off my calendar. One big check mark."
Coming at Hybels with a clenched fist, Nichols asks: "You do? Really?"
"You have been sitting far too long on my - to-do list. It's time to check you." Responds Hybels.
Nichols punches him hard in the face. Hybels retaliates, favoring his non-functioning left arm. It has been recent news: Hybels' left arm was paralyzed after his prolonged use of contaminated methamphetamine. Both inmates exchange vicious punches. The fight escalates, with Gregg Nichols gaining the upper hand. Hybels wished there was a bell. None chimed, and no referee interceded.
The duel continues for several minutes until Hybels is sent to the ground, twirling with a straight kick from Gregg Nichols.
"I am sorry man."
Says Hybels.
Son of Judah, witnessing those final moments of the bout between Hybels and Nichols, grabs the mop stick from the janitor, who is trying to access his handheld radio to usher in backup. Moving towards Nichols, he swats the janitor across his neck with the mop. The fabric portion of the mop severs from the stick. Before

closing in on Gregg Nichols, the Son of Judah breaks the stick into two halves and comes swinging at Nichols. It doesn't take long. Nichols disarms him. Hybels gets back up and charges at Gregg Nichols. Gregg administers two quick kicks into Hybels' stomach. Hybels gets back up and charges at Nichols. Another kick plants him to the ground. Now he is badly hurt and favors that other arm.

Son of Judah, now back on his feet, comes charging and swinging at Gregg. They pursue each other aggressively. Son of Judah finally puts Gregg to the pavement locked into a clinch with the arm behind his back. Hybels emerges to even the score. Gregg pries himself out of the clinch and seizes the opportunity to administer blows to the Son of Judah's body, sending him reeling to the ground. Spectating inmates yell from their cells:

"Fight! Martyrdom!

Dead meat! As well as other catchwords for a grotesque bloodbath.

Kyle Chang, as high as a kite, emerges from out of nowhere and immediately confronts Nichols. He displays multiple eagle-like karate moves: first, some eagle moves, and then the snake. Nichols's ineptness does not match Chang's adeptness. Inmates chant louder in favor of Chang.

"Give him the Chinese move. Bruce Lee and all. Flying tiger and hide that dragon. Bite him like a snake and claw him like an eagle."

Nichols is on the ground as a result, coughing up blood accompanied by droplets of the same, which are emitting from his face and upper body as a result of some viscous clawing administered by Chang and directly towards his throat.

The two officers, Knowles and Thomas, spring onto the scene. Nichols is still down. No one counts to ten. Chang tries to get away. They trap Chang before he does. Officers retrieve a water hose from the now-standing janitor and hose down both Chang and Nichols. The sons of Judah and Hybels are subsequently carried away from the scene on gurneys. Chang and Nichols spend that night in the holes.

CHAPTER 37

Back inside the courtroom the following day. It seems as if everyone is waiting for the ball to drop. Gregg Nichols enters the courtroom through that side door just like he did at the beginning of the trial. Except for this time, his left arm is in a sling, and multiple concussions saturate his face and head.

The aura inside the courtroom has transformed since his entry. No late-breaking news announced the cause of the defendant's injury.

Consequently, many believed it was all a hoax, an attempt to sway some sympathy toward Nichols. Even so, Gregg Nichols appeared to be in severe pain and discomfort.

Defense lawyer Sebastian Davis walks in, leaving ample space between himself and Nichols. On the other side, Deja Nichols carefully mops her husband's brow with a rag now soaked with his blood, sweat, and tears.

Judge Melendez strikes the gavel in readiness. "Let me remind this court that our duty here today is to obtain a verdict from the jury and nothing else." Judge Melendez had been briefed earlier by prison officials at

WHO SHOT THE SHERIFF? SERIES

North Terrace regarding the altercation between Gregg Nichols and three other inmates. However, the judge was hesitant to call off the trial for fear that the jury, with too much time off, might toss some pollution into the verdict.

"Is the foreperson ready?" Melendez asks.

"Yes, your honor."

The six-foot-plus Caucasian man replies.

"Wait one moment."

Melendez says he checks to make sure the courtroom has been adequately staffed with court officers. Noticing one of the officers engaged in conversation with a Miami Police officer, he addresses:

"Gentlemen, this court is already called to order. Are you ready to proceed?"

The two officers quickly part company.

"Go ahead, Mr. Foreman."

Instructs Melendez.

"Your honor, during our deliberation, we produced a multiplicity of charges. This might be somewhat unorthodox in a trial, but these are the verdicts." Many heads turned as the last word dropped in its plural state.

The foreman continues: In the shooting death of Milton Rogers, we find the defendant Gregg Nichols not guilty."

Page 322 | 491

The defense section goes ballistic. Deja plants a big kiss on Gregg. He aches from her act of affection but exhibits jubilance. Many attendees begin to file out.
However, the foreman is still standing. Melendez strikes his gavel once again.
"Silence in court!"
He yells and continues.
"The foreperson is still standing, which means we are not yet finished with the court's business."
Those who exited return as if more time has been added to the clock. The score is tied as we go into overtime. You can now hear a pin drop after court attendees take their seats.
"Your honor, on the count of perjury, we find court officer Errol Clarke guilty." A state of wonderment engulfs the courtroom. Melendez once again strikes his gavel. "On the count of murder of Milton Rogers, we find court officer Quentin Daley guilty."
The foreperson takes his seat.
Hugs follow on one side of the courtroom.
Gregg Nichols re-injures his left arm as Deja squeezes on him with her injured right arm.
"Ouch"
Says Gregg as he flinches once in pain.
"The truth has been told. Justice has spoken. Free at last!" Those were the only times he glued many sentences together during the trial.

WHO SHOT THE SHERIFF? SERIES

CHAPTER 38

Three days after the sentencing of Errol Clarke and Quentin Daley, news broke, stating that Hybels was removed from the hole now with his other hand in a sling as a result of the beating from Nichols. In other related news, sources claimed the Methamphetamine, which was responsible for paralyzing Hybels's other arm, was supplied by Deja Nichols, aka Yuki Barnes.
Deja Nichols was subsequently arrested and detained by Miami Police.
Meanwhile, according to sources, an elderly man from South Beach followed Deja as she made a drop off of Methamphetamine to a prison officer at the same building across the street where she was shot a month ago. The elderly man had also witnessed the drive-by shooting incident in which Deja was shot in the arm while he was riding in the park.
Following the tip, police were led to the 'North Terrace' cell block at the Broward County Prison in Miami. Freddie Knowles, the prison officer, delivered that to

Raymond Hybels every time he was brought to the hole.

Police also said Deja Nichols used the aka Yuki Barnes to make her drop-offs at the drug depot in South Beach. Over half a million dollars in contraband money was later discovered in a multiple-layered trash bag in an underground manhole at North Terrace leading to Son of Judah's cell.

Medical experts are claiming the Meth supplied by Yuki was contaminated and mixed with a foreign substance. Many inmates, including Richard Hybels, used the substance provided by Yuki and later wound up with non-functional body parts.

MARCUS DAVIS WAS ALSO ARRESTED hours later in the drive-by shooting incident of Deja Nichols, aka Yuki Barnes, several weeks ago. According to sources, multiple shells shot from the same gun that injured the artist were recovered from the crime scene in South Beach.

Additionally, one eyewitness who preferred to be unidentified provided information that led to Davis's arrest. Police followed that lead to an abandoned BMW. A collection of reconstructed Glock 38s was also recovered from the automobile's trunk.

Ballistics findings indicate seven bullets were fired from the gun found on the front passenger seat. The one bullet that remained inside that gun's magazine had Wesley Haynes' name etched on it.

WHO SHOT THE SHERIFF? SERIES

FLASHBACK ALMOST ONE YEAR AGO:

NIGHT CLUB IN JAMAICA...AUGUST 12th. The surveillance camera shows Marcus Davis driving away from the parking lot inside a black Infiniti, bearing temporary license tags on that same night and hours before Sheriff John Brown and Ron Charles were gunned down.

WHO SHOT THE SHERIFF? SERIES

BOOK # 3

WHO SHOT THE SHERIFF? SERIES

WHO SHOT THE SHERIFF?

III

DEAD MEN TELL NO TALES/THE JURY

WHO SHOT THE SHERIFF? SERIES

An Original Story By INTERNATIONAL BESTSELLING AUTHOR

JOHN A. ANDREWS

Copyright © 2018 by John A. Andrews.

All rights reserved. Written permission must be secured from the publisher to use or reproduce any part of this book, except for brief quotations in critical reviews or articles.

Published in the U.S.A. by

Books That Will Enhance Your Life

A L I

Andrews Leadership International www.ALI Pictures.com
www.JohnAAndrews.com

WHO SHOT THE SHERIFF? SERIES

TABLE OF CONTENTS

```
BOOK #3..................................................................327
CHAPTER ONE..........................................................331
CHAPTER TWO..........................................................334
CHAPTER THREE.......................................................338
CHAPTER FOUR.........................................................341
CHAPTER FIVE..........................................................344
CHAPTER SIX............................................................347
CHAPTER SEVEN.......................................................351
CHAPTER EIGHT.......................................................353
CHAPTER NINE.........................................................356
CHAPTER TEN...........................................................360
CHAPTER ELEVEN.....................................................362
CHAPTER TWELVE....................................................366
CHAPTER THIRTEEN.................................................370
CHAPTER FOURTEEN................................................374
CHAPTER FIFTEEN....................................................376
CHAPTER SIXTEEN...................................................379
CHAPTER SEVENTEEN..............................................381
CHAPTER EIGHTEEN................................................384
CHAPTER NINETEEN................................................387
CHAPTER TWENTY...................................................392
CHAPTER TWENTY-ONE...........................................394
CHAPTER TWENTY-TWO..........................................400
CHAPTER TWENTY-THREE.......................................403
CHAPTER TWENTY-FOUR.........................................405
CHAPTER TWENTY-FIVE..........................................408
CHAPTER TWENTY-SIX............................................411
CHAPTER TWENTY-SEVEN.......................................416
CHAPTER TWENTY-EIGHT.......................................420
CHAPTER TWENTY-NINE.........................................423
CHAPTER THIRTY....................................................426
```

WHO SHOT THE SHERIFF? SERIES

CHAPTER 1

Debris from thunderous explosions skyrockets float toward the night sky, followed by a residual of dense smoke and acidic fumes. Fire flames heighten from multiple cell blocks, aligned as a horseshoe. Meanwhile, in the distance, sounds of sirens and vehicular horns crescendo. Westview Penitentiary's yellow and red fire engines race toward the South Wing. There, primarily female inmates lodge. Their estrogenic pow-wows intensify. It sounds like Anguish 101 – the East and West blocks scorch.

Firefighters barge out and unlock cell doors aided by crowbars. Mega water-laden fire hoses, hoisted from the engine, assume their aerial position. They forcibly dowse the compound. Few inmates make it out alive. In the intervening time, at the Eastern cellblock, marked units one through fifteen, agile firemen evacuate multiple inmates.

Unfortunately, Cell's sixteen through twenty, nestled on the cul-de-sac, hosts the roasted remains of its dwellers. The rancid scent, like barbecue meat, permeates. Among the roasted dead is Deja Nichols aka Yuki, originally from cell number sixteen. Her body gets pulled from the rubble. Deja was arrested on narc charges and co-chairing a Glock reconstruction entity. Her vicious death occurred just one week before boisterous, notorious Marcus Davis was set to be tried for shooting and injuring her. That failed-to-kill accident occurred months ago during a narc deposit that Davis orchestrated from behind bars. It was widely circulated that Davis had people outside doing his dirty work. As a result of those prison fires, the next morning, her third-degree burnt corpse, along with five other inmates, traveled in body bags to the prison morgue on a flatbed truck aided by some rough-looking prison personnel.

Ironically, Deja's husband, Gregg Nichols, was recently released from cell # 11 in the East Wing, at least a city block from those fires. That's where the male prisoners were housed. A block known for housing newbies, life-sentenced recipients, along with some hardcore veterans like Nigel, locked away for life on multiple rape convictions.

It wasn't long ago that Gregg Nichols, accused of the shooting death of Milton Rogers, bid farewell to those holdings after his acquittal. How could someone kill his close friend and mentor? Some questioned. Plus, the colleague to Rogers' friend, Grammy winner Wesley Haynes? How could he? The double questions lingered.

WHO SHOT THE SHERIFF? SERIES

For Rogers' death, 12 jurors found Gregg Nichols not guilty. Instead, Quentin Daley, the courtroom officer was sent to prison for that rubout. Many inside that courtroom saw Milton Rogers mysteriously gunned down while testifying on behalf of the singer Wesley Haynes. Yes, Gregg Nichols did serve time, until he was able to beat the wrap. As a result, he was now a free man. Destined to put his life back together again. However, it seemed like bad karma was in pursuit of Gregg. Yes. That story would have had a successful conclusion, but salt was abruptly added to that wound as Gregg prepped for his wife's funeral.

Gregg Nichols was cut down in cold blood by a gunman outside The Rose Garden flower shop on Front Street in downtown Miami. His carnage for hours decorated the sidewalk with a wreath in each hand. That perpetrator is still at large.

One eyewitness claimed that the gunman disappeared in a no-license-tag-bearing Land Rover. A vehicle, similar to the make and model frequently used by the Jamaican Police Department or JPD.

> WHO SHOT THE SHERIFF? SERIES

CHAPTER 2

These incidents saturated the Newscasts in the Caribbean and the US. Late Fresh Breaking News interrupted with this coincidental complex story: "Hair particles cited as experiments in the Wesley Haynes trial reportedly matched the head hairs of Claude Weeks…"

The deal with the Sheriff and his Deputy should have been buried. However, the boogie man mentality was paramount in the mindset of Jamaican law enforcement. As a result, Quentin Daley was imprisoned and like vultures, law enforcement wanted more blood out of this episodic trial. Claude Weeks was the pastor along with his wife, who, according to police, were first responders on the scene, immediately after the Sheriff and his Deputy were slain over a year ago.

In the meantime, while Claude was arrested, police raided his house. There, they came up empty. The raid

WHO SHOT THE SHERIFF? SERIES

soon extended to the church where he presided as pastor. Inside his office drawer, they retrieved a Glock 38. A handgun that was restored and housed similar bullets was used in the shooting of Sheriff John Brown and his Deputy Ron Charles. Claude, arrested without bail and awaiting to stand trial in the multiple murders, was found dead inside his cell. According to an autopsy result hours later, Claude reportedly died of a related heart ailment.

Rose Best-Parsons' fingerprints were lifted from the Pina Colada fragrance canister found in the SUV pulled from the ravine, believed to be owned by the late Milton Rogers. Her DNA was found on a tube of red Lip Gloss, plus a hair sample on the mat under the driver's seat. Meanwhile, Claude Weeks' hair sample was found on the passenger seat. Rose, recently arrested outside a Mandeville Salon, seemed appalled regarding the charges brought against her. Convinced this case was already dead and buried, she was aghast when confronted with this ghost and placed into handcuffs.

"It wasn't me!"

She shouted. Meanwhile, many clients at the salon that she owned and managed felt she shot the Sheriff and his deputy to even the score with her husband's killers. It's still indelible in her mind while she was handcuffed. Bill Parsons, her late husband, was taken out execution-style while in Rose's company over a year ago at their music studio.

So, now, in this elongated saga, two individuals were still tied to the case as complicit. In the meantime, according to an independent investigation, the late ally of the Sheriff, Deputy Ron Charles' home, was searched, and the computer server that stored beats and songs belonging to Bill Parsons Studio was recovered. Was Deputy Ron Charles in on his boss' killing? Both officers were slain at the exact location. That cover-up? Will we ever know? It was no mystery; multiple individuals were implicit in the Sheriff's assassination.

Were multiple individuals complicit in the murder of the Sheriff and his Deputy? If all it is alleged, those acquitted and those who were already dead participated in those two brutal murders, law enforcement had their hands complete with multiple pencil erasers.

This whole thing should have been laid to rest despite tainted investigations, such as the glove not fitting. Instead, it resurged like a cat with nine lives. All these late but new findings permeate the news media and fester like stage four cancer masticating moment by moment. Law enforcement in Jamaica was caught with its hands tied or, as some would say, like a dog with its tails between its legs. Did they drop the ball? They

WHO SHOT THE SHERIFF? SERIES

were forced to reopen the Who Shot The Sheriff? Along with his Deputy's case.

CHAPTER 3

This resurrected uncanny set of inexplicable entangled circumstances was poised to begin and tugged back inside the courtroom precisely six weeks from now. With Jury selection now in progress, work is in progress.

On the other hand, the Jamaican Labor Party wanted the trial conducted in Jamaica, juxtaposed to the opposition party, the People's National Party, which contested that move and preferred a Miami trial.

They fought back and forth like the Democrats and Republicans during the 2018-2019 government shutdown. Fearing that if the case were Jamaican tried, there would be grave repercussions like causing pandemonium and heated uprisings, street riots, and shootouts. They feared these consequences would affect their chances of toppling the Jamaican Labor Party during the upcoming general election. In reverse, the Labor Party questioned the validity of rerouting this trial, which is now on its third go back to Jamaica. "If they are going to try Jamaicans, it's time to do it on the home turf."

WHO SHOT THE SHERIFF? SERIES

Articulated by numerous legal experts. To them, it was like a homecoming party filled with media, courthouse spectacle, and tourists.

"Anything for the bottom line," voiced the Jamaican Minister of Tourism, bent on raking in the almighty dollar.

Through it all, most locals wanted to put the Who Shot the Sheriff? trial to bed and never shift the covers. Even so, Jamaican Law Enforcement wanted answers badly. They sensed there was a needle somewhere in that haystack and were determined to find it, even if they got pricked deeply. In their opinion, justice had to be served, go high or low. Their elasticity was steroids.

In the meantime, some locals dreaded it all with a ten-foot pole. Distancing themselves in their minds provided solace. They weren't putting food on their table or paying their costly JEP light bills. So, they couldn't care any less.

Supporters of the Jamaica Labor Party felt that the first trial, which was supposed to be held in Jamaica – did. The Jamaican Mogul Milton Rogers would not have been shot.

They debated: Quentin Daley, born and raised in Miami, and the Court Officer, perpetrated gunman accused of pulling the trigger that snuffed out the mogul Milton Rogers.

Some also queried: "If that case was tried on Jamaican soil like it was supposed to, there's no way a court officer would have pulled that trigger." His shooting tactics would have been easily detected before he found the right trajectory through that crowded courtroom.

Others deliberated: "He would have taken into consideration before pulling off such a feat that it would carry major consequences. The Don would target his family and friends to implement community justice and the country's political agenda."

Some cynics still believe it's a myth. However, most intellectuals beg to differ; Don runs things in Jamaica. Inside out, next to the prime minister, He looms large. In the case of "Sponji Edwards," a Don who hails from Tel Aviv, Jamaica, and sub-planted in Mandeville. He was notorious and rambunctious in nature and recently changed his name to "Glock Edwards."

Many now know Sponji as the Don who orchestrated the reconstruction of Glock 38s along with his co-conspirator, Deja Nichols.

Additionally, Sponji controls the politicians, the guns, the shots, the bleach, and the money redistributed in communities such as Mandeville and Tel Aviv. In some cases, he is known to have access to more rounds of ammunition than the police and even a more eclectic collection of weaponry and cohorts.

Pre-trial proceedings rolled on with Rose Best Parsons' name making headlines moment by moment.

WHO SHOT THE SHERIFF? SERIES

CHAPTER 4

Wesley and Britney Haynes, currently on a European tour, were saddened when they learned that their ally Rose Best-Parsons was arrested and charged in connection with the murder of Sheriff John Brown and his Deputy Ron Charles. Knowingly, the circumstances they endured before their acquittal. They arguably showed their frustrations: 'It could never be Rose Best Parsons."

They debated without having all the facts to support their perceptiveness.

Even so, the Haynes couple chose to detach themselves from the entire debacle as fingers remained pointed at them by some locals, especially in Law Enforcement circles. Although they were acquitted of those crimes more than a year ago, the scars of two trials involving the Sheriff still showed when it came down to Wesley Haynes' state of mind. Nevertheless, according to News sources, Wesley stated:

"We still feel an existent bond with Rose Best-Parsons. It was Rose who opened the door for me in preparation for my musical career's first interview. I'll always be grateful to Rose Best-Parsons and her late husband Bill Parsons."

The News Media immediately launched into overdrive, covering multiple related stories. A female Miami judge, Linda Lopez, was picked, not based on Jamaican politics but by the US-based prosecution team.

The 12 Jurors, seven men and five women, were now in place. The trial was inching closer. Rose Best – Parsons is the only known defendant alive and about to be tried for the double homicide. If convicted she would face the death penalty. The discussion marinated and festered throughout the media. On the other hand, multiple questions surrounded Sponji Glock's relationship with Yuki Nichols. Was he her mentor who flipped and orchestrated her sudden death? Also, it was widely speculated that the two were having an affair while her husband, Gregg Nichols, was incarcerated. Gregg, no doubt, died with those two wreaths in his hands as an exhibit of his love for Deja. He held on to her in life despite her rumored triangular affair. In death, he was digging in, visibly with those two farewell treats.

Reportedly, Sponji Glock Edwards affiliated himself with Yuki Nichols after Gregg Nichols, her husband, was imprisoned on charges for the shooting of Milton Rogers.

It was claimed that Sponji also supplied Yuki with narcotics, bankrolled her operation, and endowed her with the rights to the reconstruction of Glock 38s. When it was leaked, Yuki had inside information on who shot the Sheriff and his Deputy. She was roasted in her cell at Westview Penn. Police for years have been trying to bring down Sponji Edwards. He proved slippery as an eel, surviving multiple assassination attempts by law enforcement. However, they were never allowed to do their jobs properly because The Don dominated several communities. Known as a community protector, he kept his peace.

According to one insider:

"When it comes to the politicians, too many questions could be asked about drugs in Jamaica, with few answers to suffice. Those answers could be incriminating. So, many cooled their lips."

CHAPTER 5

While many questions remained unanswered politically and legally, most concerned the rise and fall of Bill and Rose Best-Parsons' empire, which remained inside a vacuum. This troubled those whose bread basket was musical entertainment and some legal scholars.

They were known to have provided a huge payday musical. As alleged: Why were Rose Best-Parsons' fingerprints and lip gloss found inside the vehicle believed to have been implicated in the rub out of Sheriff Brown and his Deputy? Was Rose Best-Parson having a steamy affair with Milton Rogers after her husband's death? Why was her lip gloss found inside the SUV owned by Rogers? Reportedly, Rose could have used that vehicle to commit the murders. Was Milton Rogers the driver and Rose Best-Parsons the trigger-pulling heroine?

According to sources, Rose came from a family of massive wealth. Her parents were plantation owners

WHO SHOT THE SHERIFF? SERIES

in Portland, St. Mary, and the hills of Manchester. She was their only child and the heir to their kingdom, so she inherited a large slice of their pie.

The Aston Martin, which Bill drove was shot up ferociously when Bill was gunned down. One source claimed that Rose gave those wheels to Bill for their 25thanniversary gift. For years, this gift has caused a sore eye for many underachievers. Additionally, sources claimed the recording studio was also purchased by her, not Bill, as he seemed to make Wesley Haynes assume. It appears Bill Parsons ran things, but Rose Best-Parsons was the real Boss Woman. She held the keys to the empire. After her arrest, law authorities drilled down deep to find out if Rose and Bill had invested heavily in the narcotics trade, which originated in Mandeville, as some were insinuating. Still, no paper trail indicated that this entrepreneur couple had made such investments. Plus, the real estate which her parents owned in Manchester was sold off before their death. Rose was delighted in cash, and she inherited much of it. Even so, Bill told Wesley Haynes that he diversifies and does not believe in putting his eggs in one basket. The fact remains: Was he fabricating to Wesley, or all along, putting up a front to indicate what Rose had been his also, as both of them were one, blanketed like two peas in a pod?

During her arrest, Big Bubba, who had collaborated with the moguls as an engineer and chauffeur for many years, was present when Rose was arrested. He recently pulled up a late-model red Lamborghini. A car he drove to shuffle the boss woman. Bubba had tanned somewhat, grew a beard, and wore ponytailed hair. A complete makeover from the look displayed on the day Bill Parsons was gunned down. Bubba, at the time, was also questioned by police, but there was nothing he could be tied to concerning the Sheriff and his deputy's murder.

WHO SHOT THE SHERIFF? SERIES

CHAPTER 6

Inevitably, the media could not get their hands out of the what-ifs. The deeper they drilled down, the richer this mysterious Alfred Hitchcock-type real-life mystery loomed. This case had more probability than anyone could shake a stick at. Not forgetting the number of dead witnesses as well as their co-conspirators. During this new installment of the saga, Court Officer Daley, who is now locked away for life in the shooting death of Milton Rogers inside that Miami courtroom on Valentine's Day, stated:
"I had nothing to do with the deaths of Sheriff John Brown and his Deputy Ron Charles. I am as innocent as a newborn baby. Other perpetrators are still being tried. So, there is no reason to keep me behind bars." Not much attention was paid to his plea. As far as they were concerned, Quentin Daley was not charged and convicted in the assassination of Sheriff John Brown and his Deputy Ron Charles, but he was, for the mogul Milton Rogers.
Meanwhile, new information surfaced: Quentin Daley, while on vacation in Jamaica before the rub out of both officers, met privately with Glock Edwards at the

Sandals resort in Montego Bay before returning to the US. Airline tickets and other travel receipts showed he met with Edwards at some of Don's hideouts.

Text messages retrieved from his iPhone exposed that Edwards provided limousine transportation for Quentin to and from Michael Manley.

International Airport.

Daley could have picked up a Glock 38 from the Jamaican Don during his stay. The gun, which some ballistics experts believe could have been reconstructed, and the gun used to snuff out Sheriff John Brown, his Deputy Ron Charles, Milton Rogers, and possibly Bill Parsons? All four key figures are dead without corroboration in this extensive real-life epic.

Multiple Legal Experts claim, "If Quentin Daley had ties to any of these four murders, Glock Edwards most likely supplied the Amu...as well as the intelligence."

As we recount these tragedies, mysterious findings surround the death of all four victims. The following Op-Ed, which appeared in a Jamaican newspaper, cited: "An individual filled with mystique, intrigue, and a reconstructed Glock could have been responsible for four deaths," authored by yet another prominent legal expert.

"If this is the case, and Daley is the gunman responsible, then there would be no need to hold Claude Weeks in prison," said a Church Elder caught up in the semantics of the Op-Ed. The Elder attended the same Wednesday night prayer meeting at the church where Claude Weeks was the resident pastor. Conversely, with Quentin Daley demanding a release, many felt he did put his foot inside of his mouth. They sensed Daley knew too much about the narrative and seemed to be involved at a much deeper level.

On the other hand, Rose Best-Parsons should also be released if that Daley theory receptacle holds any legal water.

Still, some people probed: the police and prosecutor made too many blunders; people were imprisoned, and the real assassin, based on continued hearings, was still out there. The name: Rose Best-Parsons emerged like sweet plasma, and like a sponge, they were prepared to suck her dry. If found guilty, her holdings would no doubt be transferred to the Jamaican government.

Nothing changed in the judicial process surrounding this case, except the government kept drilling down. They were moving ahead full steam despite the existent suppositions. They were dug in on the what-ifs.

Law enforcement in Jamaica was gearing up for the gossip, but they were not receiving their marching orders for a local trial.

As many locals prolonged their demonstrations, hoping the winds of fate would change the judicial process and bring the savoring scent of the trial directly under their noses, trial proceedings in Miami were salivating anyway.

CHAPTER 7

At home in Jamaica, demonstrators march around one of the most ancient landmarks in Mandeville, the Old Courthouse. A memorial was erected back in the 1820s. The black, gold, and green flag draped around the two pillars flutters and ropes the upstairs veranda. It accentuates the Jamaican team spirit and patriotism. The protest quickly upsurges. If noise could help bring that trial home, they would be happy.

Who Shot the Sheriff? flyers and decorate the wall adjacent to the chain-linked fence—the conundrum spikes keep out the riffraff.

Some signs feature ex-Mandeville native and platinum recording artist Wesley Haynes. The platinum recording artist was previously acquitted of shooting the Sheriff and his Deputy. Another depicts Glock Edwards, the Don of Mandeville. Others pose a twin-pack featuring Rose Best-Parsons and Pastor Claude Weeks, the two remaining alleged cop killers. In the meantime, a large group of Protestants, mainly students from the local church where Weeks served as a Youth Counselor, assembled in a one-mile march heading toward the courthouse.

WHO SHOT THE SHERIFF? SERIES

Meanwhile, on the courthouse grounds, an exterior air conditioning unit buzzed full blast. A large white sign hanging head-high reads: Ministry of Justice Mandeville Magistrate Court Office hours are 10:00 A.M. to 3:00 PM.

Closer to the building, a yellow sign with blue lettering reads: Urinating is Strictly Prohibited. Weed whackers and a clean-up crew speedily enhance the grounds. An elderly man, part of Pastor Claude Weeks' congregation, saunters on a walker. Looking anxiously, he prayerfully expresses his desire for a home trial. To him, his deceased pastor should have some post-life intervention and procure a miracle to bring the trial to the homeland supernaturally.

Meanwhile, tourists inside idle taxicabs grab a few photos using their smartphones. Drive-by taxis honk their horns in a protest against the legal system. Locals in a huddle mumble in patois displayed pictures of the alleged charged victims who were already dead.

WHO SHOT THE SHERIFF? SERIES

CHAPTER 8

One week later, a massive crowd from just about every social class assembles outside.
Boomed microphones pry over the heads of some placard-bearing demonstrators. Media vehicles and journalists are poised to go live. Not long after the arrests of Claude Weeks and Rose Best-Parsons, the renowned journalist Bob Casey, out of New York, flew to Jamaica to see what juice he could squeeze out of the story.
Bob Casey, an American Journalist dressed in casuals, a Canon Sports camera strapped around his neck, and a clipboard in his hand. He waits - poised.
A vendor chops away at a colossal coconut using a dagger. The client pays and partakes. While police dressed in white shirts and black pants with red stripes to the side and bearing M16 rifles ambulate. Uniformed court workers file in and enter the upstairs of the courthouse. In the meantime, a remixed version of I Shot the Sheriff blasts from a spectating Millennia's

iPhone. The teen continually puts the gadget to his ears and then removes it, matching the sound of the beat. All this goes into preparation for a possible Jamaican-held trial. Moments later, it became breaking news that the pending Jamaica trial was shifted to the Sunshine State and the city of Miami. When the news broke, it was a tremendous disappointment to Jamaican locals. They protested some more.

IN MIAMI, outside the courthouse, a car pulls up.
Attorney Stephanie Reid, representing Rose Best-Parsons steps out. Another car pulls up, from which two escorts accompanying Rose Best-Parsons step out. Instantly, boom microphones drop to accommodate.
"Attorney Reid, how do you feel about your chances in this case?" asks one TV reporter.
"I feel great about our chances. Rose Best-Parsons is innocent as far as we are concerned."
Says Reid with multiple folders underneath her arm.
"Mrs. Parsons, you claim you're not guilty. Who do you think did it?"
asks the Reporter.
"I guess that's what this case is all about. Finding out who did it."
Says Mrs. Parsons.
"Do you think they'll be finally able to put this case to rest?"
At this point, Attorney Reid ushers her client past the courthouse entrance. An eclectic entourage follows in

tow as she enters the courthouse stairs. Multiple guards inside escort the jurors.

WHO SHOT THE SHERIFF? SERIES

CHAPTER 9

Still in Jamaica, after multiple weeks of stalling on the part of Glock Edwards, the Mandeville.
Don finally took the bait for an exclusive interview with New York's Journalist Bob Casey. Bob enters the downstairs apartment after being searched for and scrutinized by Sponji Glock's entourage. Customarily, he has a clipboard in one hand and his Canon camera around his neck. Oblivious to Glock's security team, the unit carried by Casey was already in record mode and flash disabled. Glock, adorned with dark sunglasses and most of his face obscured, welcomes the New York Journalist inside a remote Kingston hideaway.
"How do you feel about all the tensions in Mandeville over the third go around in the same case?"
Asks Casey.
"It is what it is, Bob; life goes on."
Responds Glock Edwards.
"How long since you've been an activist for this Mandeville community? Your people seem to adore you?"

WHO SHOT THE SHERIFF? SERIES

Casey asks.
"It's been 15 years since I moved here from Tel Aviv to run things up here."
States Glock Edwards.
"Have you ever seen it like this?"
Casey asks.
"No, man! Like Bob said: 'Man to man is so unjust. You don't know who to trust. Some will eat and drink with you. Then behind them so-so pan you.'
States Glock Edwards.
"Do you believe in the late Bob Marley?"
Asks Casey.
"Of course, the man saw things happening, happening, and those things are about to happen. And he knew the effects of them all."
Says Edwards.
"What's happening in this, right yah, right now? Who shot the Sheriff's case? They should close this whole ordeal."
Says Glock Edwards.
'Is that so?"
Asks Bob Casey.
"Yes! The man even sang about such things to come. The only difference was that Bob couldn't even shoot a fly. I guess he was referring to the anonymous. They say it was Wesley Haynes, Milton Rogers, Deja Nichols, Gregg Nichols, Claude Weeks, Quentin Daley, Rose Best-Parsons, and a whole heap of us.

They even said it was Eric Clapton because he sang I Shot the Sheriff. Even if he didn't write it."
Says Edwards.
"Do you know who might have shot the Sheriff and his Deputy?"
Asks Bob Casey.
"Things happen, people cool their lips, nobody will come forward…fess up? Dead Men? Dead Men tell no tales as far as I am concerned."
Says Edwards.
"Why not? Why wouldn't anyone fess up to these two murders?"
Asks Casey.
"What happens in Mandeville stays in Mandeville. Like what happens in Vegas stays in Vegas. You understand?"
States Glock, looking away as he attends to his ringing cell phone.
"Dread, me kinda busy right now. Let me call you back later. I have company. You no see?"
Glock says into the phone and hangs up. Casey interjects:
"So, you will not say who did it even if you knew?"
"I think Gregg Nichols was involved. He had access to the reconstructed guns. They were inside his attic. Why would anyone arm people with a pistol if they know you are going to use it to kill? Go figure. It wasn't Yuki. Ah, him whey arm Rosie with it."

WHO SHOT THE SHERIFF? SERIES

Says Edwards.

"Thanks for talking with you about who shot the Sheriff. And his Deputy."
Bob Casey wraps up the interview.

CHAPTER 10

The trial was now in its closing arguments phase. Bob Casey apparently had no intention of leaking the Glock Edwards interview to the media. He probably intended for it to air after the judgment in the case or on MSNBC Highliners, thus causing a wrench to be thrust into the end result and creating chaos in the media. Unfortunately, on his way back to MO Bay airport, his car was rear-ended and shoved off the road, collapsing into a deep ravine.

Several locals heard the crashing tumbling sound. Some saw the vehicle descend. Many responded to the rescue. Although they failed in an attempt to save Bob's life, they walked off with his camera equipment along with the interview footage. The automobile was later sawed open to extract Bob Casey's body. Later that same night, the Glock Edwards interview footage ran on a local Jamaican TV station. Hours later, a Miami Cable Station followed suit. Law Enforcement in Miami swarms over the Late Breaking news like flies over molasses. Yet, no one claimed responsibility for leaking the news.

Many wished the news had been released before the closing arguments to impact the trial. Most came to grips that the stable was already closed. Even so, the defense went to war with the prosecution, although the new evidence was inadmissible. However, many claimed it had merit and could have changed the trial's outcome.

CHAPTER 11

Meanwhile, outside of the Miami Courthouse: multiple protesters demonstrate. The hip hop. they swagger, they wave hand-made signs that read: ROSE BEST-PARSONS IS INNOCENT, ROSE COULDN'T SHOOT A FLY, SET HER FREE FROM THIS TRAGEDY. They chant. "Free Rosie! Free Rosie!" A Vendor presses into the crowd, handing out white T-shirts. They read FREE ROSIE. SHE'S NOT GUILTY. News Reporters converge attempting to engage demonstrators. Protesters remain preoccupied.

An agile News Reporter lands and latches onto a DEMONSTRATOR, who's holding up a sign, reading: ROSE COULDN'T SHOOT A FLY.

"Hello. Are you anticipating a non-guilty verdict?" Asks the Reporter.

"That's right. She didn't do it." Replies the passionate Demonstrator.

Law Enforcement, including Court Officials, remains on high alert in case the protest gets out of hand.

"What gives you that assurance?" Ask the Demonstrator.

WHO SHOT THE SHERIFF? SERIES

"Rosie wouldn't hurt nobody. We were classmates. She does not believe in violence. Plus, she's a total giver. She gave me a loan when I was struggling with buying my first car... Without Rosie, I'll still be on the bus." Says the demonstrator as the protest crescendos. Inside the Courtroom: Some court attendees file out perplexed. The Defense team, seated on the front row with closed folders, waits in wonderment. The Prosecution sits parallel on the other side, huddling. They feel the odds are very much in their favor. The defendant, Rose Best-Parsons, looks shattered, still perched on the witness stand. Inside the hot Jury Box, twelve seemingly tired Jurors reside. Some fans aggressively use their notepads. Some look confused and sweating.

JUROR 7, a Jamaican man in his 50s, looks vindictively savvy and antsy. He chicken-scratches additional notes on a disheveled notepad. JUROR 2, a short Napoleonic Latino in his late 30s, seems overanxious as he constantly drones the courtroom clock while eying the clock on the wall. JUROR 8, a woman of Jamaican descent, powders her nose, primps her hair, and applies bright red lip gloss.

JUROR 12, an Asian woman in her 30s seems distracted with matters of her own.

JUROR 6, a flaming French man steals notes from JUROR 5's notepad. He's an Australian man-40s. JUROR 4, a man of Indian descent in his 30s seems unsure of himself and the court proceedings. JUROR 3, a very opinionated Italian man in his 40s, peruses through his body of notes.

JUROR 9, an African American woman in her 30s powwows with JUROR 10, a Hispanic woman of her age. Meanwhile, JUROR 11, a Caucasian woman in her 40s is focused on the Judge.

The HEAD JUROR, a man of Caucasian descent, scans through multiple notepads and then mops his brow with a large multi-colored hanky.

JUDGE LINDA LOPEZ, a Latino Woman in her 40s, finds herself doodling with her pen on a pad. She scans the courtroom. Locked in on the Jury Box, she gavels. There's complete silence for a moment, and then Judge Lopez speaks authoritatively. "Ladies and Gentlemen of the Jury... "

The Head Juror gives his undivided attention. Judge Lopez continues:

"You've seen the evidence and heard the testimony in this extensive and complex trial."

Rose Best-Parsons is poised, unsure of her fate. "You've heard the closing arguments articulately presented by both the defense and the prosecution. A case in which two outstanding Law enforcement giants in Jamaica, The Sheriff, and his Deputy, were gunned down in cold blood. If there's probable cause, you should present a unanimous guilty verdict without any reservation."

She pauses as the Prosecution team chatters, getting their attention. They finally zeroed in on her reverently.

"If there's no probable cause, you should deliver a unanimous not guilty verdict similarly. I expect you to perform your duty and provide justice in this case. Premeditation murder is a serious charge and this trial certainly bears its DNA. It warrants the death penalty in our system. The jury will now retire and begin to deliberate with ambition, justice, and integrity."

The Judge gavels again. The twelve Jurors Exit are concerned.

WHO SHOT THE SHERIFF? SERIES

CHAPTER 12

Additional court attendees file out. The number of Demonstrators increases. They press close to the revolving door as some court attendees clear away. They are louder than ever, bearing extra signs: I SHOT THE SHERIFF, I AM THE GUNMAN, WHO IS THE REAL GLOCKMAN? Once again, News Reporters engage with demonstrators pressing for excerpts.
Signs billboard: DON MAN AIN'T NO KING KONG.

LOCK UP THE DON MAN, HE'S THE GLOCKMAN.

SET ROSIE FREE! NO JUDGE, NO JURY!

At the same time, inside and above the held open door by a neatly dressed female GUARD. It reads JURY ROOM. The Jurors enter. The Guard displays her southern hospitality with colossal style and pizzazz. A large conference room with a huge conference table and twelve chairs waits. The walls seem like they have

recently been freshly painted. Some Jurors, irritated, blow their noses in disgust. One wall features a dry-erase whiteboard with markers and an eraser. Another wall is mostly bare except for a detailed map of Miami on one side. On the next wall, a circular clock displays Roman numerals points at 5:00.

There are multiple windows, some half-opened from the top, except for the one with the NO SMOKING sign, which kisses its ledge. The windows backdrop downtown Miami in an afternoon setting. A kitchen sink houses a coffee maker for sake decoration. At the same time, a water fountain with paper cups inside a cup holder memorializes. Two adjacent doors read Restroom/Banos. One reads Men and the other Women.

The Jurors are all in and buzzing in pre-deliberation mode. Some are still sweating—the Head Juror surveys.

"Can you cool it down for us a bit?" He says to the Guard.

"Will do!"

The Guard responds enthusiastically.

The Head Juror, courtly:

"Thanks. We'll call you if we need anything."

The Guard surveys. She gets a head count and closes the door.

The male Jurors remove their jackets. Most Jurors take their seats. Some wander while others huddle in pow-wow mode.

Juror # 5 hastily heads to the Men's room. Multiple eyes are focused on the huddle. Which, Juror 2 is preoccupied with. He's grouped with Juror 7 at that no-smoking sign window. Outside? Pouring down rain dominates.

Juror 7 turns to Juror 2 as he mops his brow. "At least it's not so hot in here. It was hot inside that juror's box. I couldn't wait to get out of there." Immediately, Juror 6 lands in the huddle. He's flaming.

"I've never been to hell. The closest I came was watching that movie To Hell and Back, but the theatre was air-conditioned."

Juror 7 eyes Juror 6 after that remark.

"Thanks to Jah. His rain is here to cool us down. Come on and cool me down! Cool me down!" Juror 2 weaves into the window for a closer look at the pouring rain. Juror 6 follows suit.

Back at the conference table, other jurors pounce. Some add to their already collected notes.

The raindrops decrescendo. The element draws another onlooker - Juror 3 eavesdrops.

"The Heat plays tonight in all of this?" Asks Juror 2 somewhat tellingly.

"Why, do you have tickets?" Asks Juror 3.

"I wish we could hurry up and get out of here." Says Juror 2.

Juror 7 says Juror 2:

"These things, you never know how long they go. This one can be a marathon."

Juror 6 responds.

"Why? She's guilty as hell. Unless Milton Rogers stole her lip-gloss and planted it inside that abandoned SUV."
The Head Juror attempts to bring Jurors to order with a wave. That doesn't work.
"Excuse me, let's get down to business. "
The cluster of Jurors dissolves.

CHAPTER 13

The twelve Jurors are back in their seats at the table. The Head Juror presides:
"As you know, in this trial, we have a defendant who faces the death penalty. Guilty or not guilty, our verdict has to be unanimous. We can get this over quickly and return the verdict to Judge Lopez." Juror 12 seems disengaged and unmoved by the proceedings thus far.
"What's the rush? Aren't you going to give us time to recollect our thoughts and think about this case through?"
She asks.
"What's there to think about? She's as guilty as thunder follows lightning." Says Juror 2. Suddenly, Thunder blasts followed by lightning bolts. "See? Even the elements are in sync. That's what I'm talking about. Team spirit!" Continues Juror 2. JUROR 9 shares her notes with JUROR 10. While JUROR 11 eavesdrops on their collaboration.
"Well, I guess we are ready."
Says Juror 9.

"I guess we are. Let's talk it through."

Agrees Juror 11.

The Head Juror zeros in on all twelve jurors, commands order and continues.

"If we are ready to let's do it or if we need to discuss it, so be it. Okay? Two, Three, Four, Five, Six, Seven, Eight, Nine, Ten? Who is missing?"

"What's his name? He went to Banos. I hope he finds it."

Says Juror 6.   He draws unanimous attention.

"So, he got lost?"

Asks Juror 10.

"Poor guy. He must be suffering from TB. I mean Tiny Bladder."

Juror 2 insinuates.

Meanwhile, Juror 5 returns. He completes drying his hands with a white rag and takes his seat at the table, looking somewhat edgy. The Head Juror is taken aback.

"Next time, let us know. Will Ya? Not that we need to know. But we do. Do you know what I mean? We need to know where everyone is all the time. Including their votes."

He continues.

"So why are we here? That woman sure pleaded her heart out, for all I know…"

Juror 12 eyes him intently.

"So, you've already made up your mind?"

"I did not say that. I was reflecting. Tossing things out loud in my mind."

The Head Juror retorts.
Juror 12 remains with intent.
"You must be a writer. It is said that writers think 95% of the time and use the other 5% of their time to ink their ideas."
"How did you know? I am."
Responds to the Head Juror. Most of the Jurors wish he left self-promotion out of the deliberation process. He feels their penetrative stare.
"So, as I was saying. The Sheriff and his Deputy are at a speed trap preceding the semi-lit intersection. Weather condition? Almost dark…"
"Dusk. We call that dusk!"
Interrupts Juror 8.
The Juror is persistent.
"Dusk or almost dark? Same thing according to a thesaurus. A dark SUV whisks on by. They follow ardently, sirens, flashing lights, and all. The SUV tries to elude them. They wouldn't let up. Finally, the SUV pulls over. The sheriff's and his Deputy's car lights are still flashing. They park, leave, and cautiously proceed towards the now idle SUV. Bang! Bang! Two shots rang out through the rear windscreen of the parked SUV. The Sheriff and Deputy are cut down. The SUV takes off through unlit Manchester streets."

Juror 4 raises his hands contentiously.

"Who witnessed those killings?"
He asks.

Juror 7 takes Juror 4.
"No one."
To Head Juror, Juror 7 continues adamantly:
"It's all circumstantial evidence."

CHAPTER 14

The Head Juror continues on a roll. The Pastor and his wife showed up, pronto.
Blood splattered along the roadside. Broken glass everywhere." Juror 7 counteracts. "We can't include the Pastor's statement. He's already dead. Deceased. Gone. Lifeless. They said it was a heart attack. Whatever the cause? Dead men cannot testify in a court of law. That's why he wasn't brought in..." To that statement, the Head Juror replies: "I don't trust people who say they are Christians and don't live as Christ did."
Jurors 7 and 8 are caught whispering with each other. The Head Juror is focused on Juror 7. "So that's why you voted not guilty?" To which Juror 7 replies: "I am just exercising my right as a member of the twelve."
Juror 11 interjects:
"I can't believe we are still caught up in this red wave-blue wave conundrum. Are you sure both of you think she's not guilty?"
Jurors 7 and 8 nod yes.
Juror 11 shows her disgust with the Head Juror.

"If this continues, we could be here all night."
Juror 2 chimes in.
"I concur! All night long. All night long. I hope we end up Easy or Dancing from the ceiling." "Ok. Let's try this again. This time we'll do it by ballot. I'll pass out a slip of paper to each of you. Please write your vote down, return it to me and we'll go from there."
Says the Head Juror.
"Before you do Mr. Head Juror. You are the Leader of us all. It's you who is designated to speak for all of us when we return to that hot jury box. I feel like we are wasting our time. Majoring in the minors."
States Juror 5.
He pauses, scans the room, and continues. "If they claim they are not guilty, we need an explanation. Find out why they feel the way they do. Don't you think? Judge Lopez expects us to deliver unanimously."
Juror # 2 looks first at the clock and then out that sign-bearing window. He attempts to light a cigarette but changes his mind.
Juror 7 asks Juror 2.
"You need a Nicorette gum?"
Juror 7 accommodates. Juror 2 takes two sticks of gum.
Juror 7 surveys the room.
"Any other takers?"
Juror 2 attempts to grab another. Yet, he changes his mind.

CHAPTER 15

The rain intensifies. Lightning flashes. Thunder rolls.
The Head Juror focuses on Juror # 8.
"Please explain why you voted not guilty. Will you?"
Juror # 8 stands erect. She takes in everyone.
"I didn't see her do it!"
Multiple Jurors chuckle.
Juror 6 is staring her down.
"Oh. Come on, lady. None of us did. That's the reason we are here."
"I was asked to speak on the matter. Now, do you mind if I continue?" Says Juror 8.
The Head Juror focuses on her.
"Please continue."
"Do you know who Sponji Edwards is?"
Asks Juror 8.
Juror 5 is all over it.
"He's the Don. That Jamaican Mafia who gave that last-minute interview to Bob Casey from the Cable News Channel… and later Casey was found dead." "Bob Casey? Another dead man. They seem to have popped up everywhere."
Laments Juror 9.

WHO SHOT THE SHERIFF? SERIES

The Head Juror gestures for Juror 8 to continue.
She does.
"Do you know what a Jamaican Don does? And no. He's not a Mafioso, as you just described. A Mafioso is small fries compared to that Jamaican sweet potato."
Juror 2 raises his hand high.
Juror 8 ignores. All eyes are now focused on her.
Juror 8 continues.
"They are capable of installing a Prime Minister during a general election. They own more bullets than the Jamaican Police Department, more guns, more ammo, and have more children than Abraham... and the twelve tribes of Israel. They populate..."
Juror 5 interrupts.
"Were those the same guys who killed Malcolm X,
Peter Tosh, Tupac, and Big E?" Juror 9 standing competitively:
"What does all this have to do with this case? Malcolm X?"
"Cockroach don't attend cock fowl party. I'm very happy with my vote: Not guilty." Juror 8 states and takes her seat.
You can hear a pin drop in the room after that remark. Eyes engage those of other jurors. in slow motion.
Head Juror turns to Juror 8.
"Are you saying, if you voted guilty? The Don will come after you and your family and burn your house down?"

"I guess you can read between the lines. Ah, how do the songs go? There are more questions than answers. I shot the Sheriff, but I didn't shoot no Deputy."

Juror 8 responds. She gets up from the table, goes to the window, and looks out. She again sucks them into her vacuum of thoughts.

WHO SHOT THE SHERIFF? SERIES

CHAPTER 16

The rain subsides. The Miami Harbor has a clear view. Juror 8 is still at that window and on the flow.
I can see Miami Harbor now from here. Invaders, Immigrants, a whole boatload. There's no southern border here. There is no wall. There are no steel slats. They must have come through Cuba or Haiti. Juror 2 tries to interrupt her. She ignores his tactics and persists.
"How did the defendant's DNA get on that tube of lip gloss? How did her prints get inside that vehicle? Why was only one strand of the defendant's hair recovered from that SUV, abandoned in the ravine? You don't mess with Don. He's more lethal than Putin,
Kin Jun Um, MBS, and King Kong." The Head Juror scratches his head as he cools his lips.
Juror 5 jumps in.
"She has a point. If this guy, Sponji Edwards, the Don, was sitting at the table when the first reconstructed Glock rolled out. He has preeminence. No wonder he out-arms the police. He says jump, and the villagers ask How High? He installs Prime Ministers. He oversees drug cartels; plus, he bankrolled the entire

Milton Rogers Empire, which included nightclubs, hotels, casinos... I would dread him." To which Juror 9 responds.

Another dead man. Milton Rogers, the conspirator. Who else is dead inside this cagy complex whodunit? Juror 7 informs Juror 9.

"Bill Parsons, Milton Rogers, Deja Nichols, Sheriff John Brown, Deputy Ron Charles, Gregg Nichols, and Bob
Casey. So far."

"Will you let her continue, please?" The Head Juror asks. Juror 9 interrupts. "Why wasn't Sponji Edwards called to testify?" Juror 4 responds:

"Because we only learned about his last-minute interview with Bob Casey during closing arguments. How convenient? Plus, the US cooled its heels regarding Edwards' extradition."

CHAPTER 17

Juror 3 is all wound up. He addresses Juror 7. "Milton Rogers? What a closure to nothing! A man was shot during his testimony. What a debacle! A comedy of errors? Such juxtaposition?"
Head Juror's eyes are fixed on Juror 7. "Let's focus on the defendant Rose Best-Parsons. Why is the defendant not guilty?"
We sense Juror # 7's uneasiness.
Juror 7 zeroes in on the Head Juror.
"Where were you born?"
"Hollywood."
Responds the Head Juror.
Juror 7asks:
"Hollywood? So, you were in the movies? Did you taste the Good, the Bad, and the Ugly? Tinsel Town?" "No. Hollywood, Florida."
Replies the Head Juror.
Juror 2 eyes the clock.
"Look at the time. Where are we going with all of this, to the full length of the court? I hope we are going to dunk. No missing that basket." Using his hands, he immolates an arching free-throw shot.
Juror 7 continues:

"Mr. Head Juror, where I'm from, I didn't grow up flushing. I went to the out-house." Juror 6 asks:
"Out-House? You mean the S - Hole?"
Juror 7 responds,
"POTUS 45 referred to it as an S - Hole country. If, for some reason, I accidentally fell in when I visited. Not only will I have been submerged or trying to swim out of eight feet deep of... No plunger can bring me back." Juror 11 squirms.
"By then not even the flush from a water hydrant can save me. Not even snaking could. So, why should I go down that S - hole with you? Why are you trying to take me down that slimy rabbit hole? Come on, I said she's not guilty." Juror 6 whisks
"How insensitive are you? A Rabbit hole can never be that treacherous, deep, and slimy. That rabbit will forever lose its furry coat. She's guilty like that S-Hole is." "She smells!"
Shouts Juror 2.
"Now, where are we on the voting?"
Asks the Head Juror.
Juror 9, the African American female juror, and Miami native, raises her hands.
"Mr. Head Juror. I've changed my mind. Not guilty."
Juror 3 is ticked off. "Who's adding to the pile?" Juror 7 counters.
"Watch your mouth. That was relevant to my childhood not to my stance in this trial. I have the right

to decide. I vote not guilty." The Head Juror remains focused on Juror 9.

Juror 3 is animated.

"So, now you've joined both of them. Siding with them. We should have known you would. I saw it in your eyes when you walked through that door. Even the guard looked at you funny. Birds of a feather…" Juror 9 reemerges.

"I don't have feathers. Neither do I flock. I just flipped. That's my prerogative. What's wrong with flipping? It might soon become our constitutional duty to walk things back. Well, I misspoke earlier... Finally, realigning what I said." Juror 2 is calculative.

"Now we are 9-3. Nine for guilt. Three for not guilty. This is what I gave up on the Heat vs Knicks for? Whatever happened to unity? Togetherness? United, we stand. Divided, we hang ourselves."

Juror 12 chimes in.

"We keep missing the bucket, the cup, the hole, the basket, whatever? It's becoming more evident: We do not understand how much this trial costs. Neither were the sacrifices being made to come to a verdict. We can recoup the money. Time is something we can never get back."

The Head Juror writes on the dry-erase board: 9-3.

"I think it's time for a stretch break. Let's reconvene in two minutes."

They recess.

CHAPTER 18

The jurors mingle in multiple groups. Near the signposted window. Juror 6 groups with Juror 7. Juror 6 asks Juror 7: "Where in Jamaica are you from?"
"Mandeville, Manchester." He answers. "You are in the thick of it all, aren't you?" Juror 6 asks.
"Yep."
"Are they still rioting over the changed venue for this trial?"
Asks Juror 6.
"No. That's water under the bridge now. They are more focused on the verdict." Juror 6 presses: "I overheard you are a lawyer in the making. The bench on your mind?"
"Yes. Indeed." Replies Juror 7.
"So, you think your home girl is not guilty?" Asks Juror 6.
"How could she be? The evidence against her is insufficient and corroborated. Relatively, it doesn't matter what I think. It has much to do with what all 12 of us decide unanimously."
Juror 7 defends.

WHO SHOT THE SHERIFF? SERIES

"I've been to Jamaica. It's a beautiful country. I had such a wonderful time..."

Says Juror 6.

Juror 5 emerges and interrupts. "I've watched cricket at Sabina Park. Played a few holes of golf. Love the food as well as the culture. I heard you are a banker; I heard." Juror 6 continues:

"Yep. I hated banking with passion. "Really. Why?" Asks Juror 5.

Juror 6 responds:

"I've grown tired of counting another person's money."

Juror 5 responds

"Been there. Done that, Mate."

Juror 7 interjects,

"So, what keeps you busy besides playing golf?"

Juror 5 replies,

"Investments, portfolios, stocks, bonds, mutual funds. The whole shebang." "So, you graduated from counting another person's money to now counting your own? That's a major step up." States Juror 7.

"Adda Boy."

Says Juror 6.

Juror 5 responds,

"Yep. Total freedom..."

Juror 12 joins the huddle and interrupts. "Yep. Money and freedom sure go together. Extreme Money Makeover. That's what I teach my clients. Some get it. Some don't. Just like this whole deliberation process."

Juror 7 responds,

"I like freedom. Believe in freedom. I would die for freedom."
"You sound like MLK. I am happy to join you today in what will go down in history as the greatest demonstration for freedom in our nation's history. Close quote. The great deliberation. We're getting ready to reconvene."
Says Juror 12. The other jurors are reassembling at the table. Jurors 7 and 12 press 5. Juror 7 continues,
"So, how do you get sucked into this jury business? Locked away in a room with a large conference table, 12 chairs, eleven individuals you have very little in common with?"
Juror 5 states:
"Justice. Mate. Justice."

CHAPTER 19

Jurors 5, 6, 7, and 12 head to the table and take up their positions.

Most jurors at the table seem more relaxed. However, Juror 2 seems preoccupied with what is happening outside the deliberation room. The Head Juror gets his attention and presides.

"We've said much but not much to do with this case. Maybe that's why our vote is 9-3. A sheriff and his deputy are dead. We are here to determine if the woman accused of the crime is guilty or not guilty. Her fate has been placed in our hands. We are required to vote unanimously. Are we on the same page? Let's take another vote before we proceed."

Juror 2 contends,

"Yeah. Let's vote so I can catch up on the score. They've got to be deep in the last quarter by now."

Juror 5 shoots back:

"Don't worry. They'll get blown out by the Knicks in the final 2 minutes. Swish! Swish! Swish! Three-three-pointers in the last minute. Game over!"

Juror 2 retorts,

"Not in Miami. Maybe at Madison Square Garden. Our home crowd is so ruckus, you can hardly hear the whistle."

Head Juror interjects:

"Please write your verdict on the piece of paper before you. Fold it in two halves and pass it back this way."

They vote.

The Head Juror tallies up the votes. He articulates.

"It's still nine guilty and three not guilty."

Juror 6 is unraveled.

"Unreal! I don't like disharmony. I don't handle them well. It seems we are further away from the plain truth..."

Juror 2 follows suit.

"It looks like we are going to be here all night long. I can't stand the waiting game."

Juror 2 leaves the table abruptly and goes to the window. He continues:

"When it rains, it pours? I thought at least I could catch the last minutes of the game. Anybody has access to ESPN or NBA TV?"

"Knock it off. Let's pull it together."

Says the Head Juror.

Juror 6 states:

"Yes. What do we know about defendant Rose Best-Parsons?"

He proceeds to count his fingers.

WHO SHOT THE SHERIFF? SERIES

1. Rose was born to wealthy parents - slave plantation owners.
2. She grew up with a gold spoon in her mouth.
3. She married the famous music producer and mogul Bill Parsons at age 17... Juror 5 interrupts. "What does all this have to do with this trial?" The Head Juror intercedes.

"Let him finish. I hope this is all leading up to unanimity."
Juror 7 interjects:
"Come on! Have some faith in the process. This woman's life is at stake. Pz, puff and her life is fried out of her like a drop of water in a hot frying pan?" Juror 6 is agitated.
"If I may continue, that would be great." Juror 2 focuses his attention on Jurors 7 & 6.
"Are you the new Head Juror? Give em an "EL." They take a Line. Come on, hurry up."
Juror 6 proceeds.
Number...? Where was I?

4. Whoever killed her husband, Bill Parsons, is possibly still at large.
5. Her wealth has more than doubled since her husband's death.
6. The Glock 38, which was recovered in her SUV, was reconstructed. Her fingerprints all over it. The gun is a replica of the one found

at Wesley Haynes' house after the Sheriff and his Deputy were killed. She stated the weapon wasn't hers. Yet, her secretary testified that she always carried it inside that black, tinted glass beast of a car, Lamborghini. How did her secretary know it was always there, and the defendant didn't?

7. Her DNA was found on the tube of red lip gloss recovered from Milton Rogers' abandoned SUV.
8. The defendant testified that Sheriff John Brown was an obnoxious cop who insulted her after a traffic stop. After this, he issued her a ticket for driving above the speed limit. 'I was not even speeding.' She testified. Really? Come on!
9. Additionally, she said she assumed that the Sheriff knew who assassinated her husband, Bill Parsons. She stated it was her opinion. The Sheriff knew every rub-out-bandit in Mandeville.
10. She's guilty as the rain follows the rainbow.

Juror 9 yarns and then responds:
"You have given us much to unpack. I hear what you are saying. Yet, none of us can prove beyond a reasonable doubt. It would be on my conscience to put

this woman to death by a guilty vote. With that said, my vote is still not guilty."

Those jurors supporting a guilty verdict become unraveled. Those supporters of a nonguilty verdict maintain poise.

Juror 2 is eyeing the clock.

"This is unreal. When are we going to agree unanimously?"

Juror 5 asks:

"Why don't they rerun the trial so some of us can get up to speed? When are we going to look at the real facts?"

"We are for crying out loud!"

States Juror 6.

CHAPTER 20

Juror 5 is relentless.
"If she went on 5th Avenue and 42nd Street in New York. Video security cameras were surveilling the entire intersection. She pulled out her reconstructed Glock and shot up multiple pedestrians. Put the gun back inside her Gucci purse. She gets back inside her Lamborghini.
Most of you would still say she's not guilty. Why? Because she's got money. Lots of it. Remember OJ? He was so loaded... so the glove didn't fit."
Juror 9 responds:
"Yeah. That glove sure didn't fit. No matter how much they forced it on. I wonder why?" Juror 3 presses.
"Even if she paid me off. That woman is still guilty. Her motives are strong enough to personalize a vendetta and shoot the Sheriff. Realizing the Deputy was alleged, although not charged, for illegally acquiring Bill Parson's beats..." Juror 7 interrupts. "I guess he was planning on becoming a rhythmless reggae artist." Juror 3 continues.

"Maybe. the defendant immediately cut him down, feeling he had something to do with her husband's assassination. In my eyes, Rose Best-Parsons is guilty, guilty, guilty!"

"So, based on our recent decision, we now stand at 4 claiming not guilty and 8 for guilty. It seems we are now further away from being in unison..." Says the Head Juror.

Juror 2 responds.

"This thing should have been over by now. We seem to be going one step forward and two steps backward. We can't find the basket. It seems like the hoop has moved to Orlando or New Orleans." Juror 5 is animated and on his feet.

"I agree. Rose Best-Parsons had multiple motives. She was present when her husband was gunned down.

She testified she wasn't able to identify his killers. It has been well-circulated that law enforcement was involved. At the time, Sheriff John Brown headed up the department. She, no doubt, held on to the thought of the Sheriff's involvement. So, she stalked him. Located his speed traps. Then, when the time was right that night in August, Rose Best-Parsons was sped by his hideout. Knowing that would provoke a chase. The Sheriff and his deputy took off in pursuit."

Juror 8 converses with Juror 7.

WHO SHOT THE SHERIFF? SERIES

CHAPTER 21

Juror 8 is reddened.
"When did she find time to do that and run multiple businesses?"
Juror 5 states:
"She never said...
So, she pulled over to the curb and waited. The Officers got out of their cars and carefully walked towards her SUV. She saw them coming. As they got closer, she perfected her aim. Bang! Bang! Rose Best Parsons shot both of them. Colored her lips red and drove away from the scene through a Manchester unlit street." "I concur! Now, we all can re-vote and get out of here. We've been breathing each other's air for too long."
Says Juror 4, who has been silent for most of the deliberation. Juror 2 gives him a thumbs up.
Juror 9 is adamant.
"Not so fast. Why would a woman color her lips after committing a double homicide?" Juror 12 exclaims.

WHO SHOT THE SHERIFF? SERIES

"The lip gloss was red. The color of blood is always red, instead of having their blood on her hands. She placed it on her lips. So, she can brag about it—the price for the alleged killing of her husband. Additionally, she vows not to tell the truth if she gets caught. How sweet a vendetta. I can see that on a billboard in downtown Miami. How Sweet A Vendetta! The Cop Killer!"

"There's nothing factual about what you've just said. Come on?"

States Juror 10.

The Head Juror tries to maintain leadership. "Okay. Let's not get carried away. Remember, we are in search of a verdict that mirrors the evidence and the testimonies in this case. Anything else shows bias."

Juror 8 gets up from her seat.

"We seem to have overlooked some facts on this case. Wesley Haynes was incarcerated. He was later put on trial and acquitted of these same murders. He's still alive, living large while bragging about his innocence."

Juror 7 zings her.

"Bill Parsons, the defendant's husband, according to evidence, was assassinated weeks before both of these officers were slaughtered. Some have stated the sheriff could have had a hand in his slaying, even if they have no proof."

Juror 7 supports.

WHO SHOT THE SHERIFF? SERIES

"Milton Rogers, the high-flying music producer, was gunned down inside the courtroom next door. He was an amigo and an ally of Bill Parsons—the man who gave Wesley Haynes his break to stardom.
Claude Weeks, the pastor?"
Juror 10 is intent.
"Was he a pastor, a cover-up, or a murderer?" "That's what the evidence claimed. Weeks and his wife Doris were the first people on the scene while the blood of both officers was still pumping. Ironically, Claude Weeks' hair sample was found inside that abandoned SUV owned by Milton Rogers. After spending a few weeks in jail, Claude Weeks suffered a heart attack, and he's now a dead man. Departed! Deceased! Gone! Below Ground!"
Juror 5 tries to get in on the debate. Juror 8 is resilient.
"Quentin Daley was incarcerated for shooting Milton Rogers inside that courtroom. He also visited Jamaica during the time both officers were gunned down..."
"Where is all this taking us?"
Asks Juror 5.
Juror 2 is fixated on that clock on the wall.
Head Juror addresses:
"Let her address the matter, will you? There's some life in what she's saying."
Juror 8 continues:
"Deja Nichols, aka Yuki Nichols, accused of aiding in the reconstruction of the Glock 38. The murder weapon

WHO SHOT THE SHERIFF? SERIES

of choice. Subsequently, she was roasted inside her cell. Gregg Nichols, the choir boy, and her husband died on the streets of Miami. He was gunned down outside a flower shop with a wreath in each hand."
Juror 12 is fluid.
"Eighty percent of those accused are already dead. Who's alive to tell the tales? Plus, this trial is costing the US a fortune. It would have bankrupted their government if this were held in Jamaica."
Juror 8 stands in confrontation. She eyes Juror 12 despicably.
Juror 8 continues.
"So, what are you trying to say?" Juror 12 chimes in.
"There's no reason to be offended. I'm trying to say that Jamaica has sold almost everything it owned: Air Jamaica, the Bauxite company, and the Sugar factory. What else? They even sold Red Stripe to Heineken for how much...? Maybe pennies."
Juror 8 is furious.
"You better watch your mouth!"
Juror 8 takes her seat.
The Head Juror restores calm.
"Okay, Juror 12. As you stated concerning Gregg Nichols, he was gunned down outside the flower shop... Let's stay on that track."
"That's right."
Says Juror 12.
Juror 8 responds.

"The only person alive to defend herself is Rose Best Parsons. The truth she did tell. According to her, She does not know how to operate a handgun. With that said, I'm standing by my vote - not guilty."

The room is in an uproar. Jurors pow-wow.

Juror 2 wipes his sweaty brow.

"Why didn't you say you were of that same opinion five minutes ago? Because one of our fellow jurors alluded to selling some of the greatest Jamaican enterprises? You are biting in like a Pit-bull."

Juror 8 rebounds.

"Jamaica is not on trial. A Jamaican woman who's not guilty of a crime she's accused of is. That electric chair will stay idle. She will not sit thereon." The jurors are listening carefully. More so, the head juror. The debate slips into high gear.

Juror 12 is furious.

"Despite your patriotism, sentimentalism, and optimism about your country. The evidence in this case shows that Rose Best-Parsons committed those heinous murders and should face the electric chair." Jurors voting guilty express affirmative mannerisms. The rain is still pouring down buckets. Thunder has taken its boisterousness to a new level.

Juror No. 5 has a floor. He's vibrant and thunderous, competing with the element. "This is inconceivable. Women hunt. They fish. They visit the shooting range. Most gravitate to trigger happiness during an intense argument with a significant other. One of my classmates related a situation to me. According to him. He was involved in a heated argument with his ex-wife. She jumped up on top of the bed. Stood there. Raised the tempo to another level. He persuaded her to calm down. She didn't. He later jumped up on the bed. She lashed out at him. He tried blocking the blow. She later called the cop and said he struck her. I don't mean to sound sexist. Some women don't have an issue striking out when submerged with a vendetta. It's a given: Any woman who wants to shoot, she shoots - Bang! Bang! She feels she's the big winner if it's a man." The female gender shows disdain over his domestic violence remarks. Anyway, he continues. "The mere fact her fingerprints were lifted from the weapon in her possession indicates:

1. She practiced using it.

2. She used it to defend herself or

3. She used it to shoot Sheriff John Brown and his Deputy Ron Charles…

Juror 6 is inching to say something since Juror 5 touched on that delicate story. Interrupts.
"Me? I've never used a gun, loaded a gun, been to a shooting range, or owned a gun. I don't know how those things work. The closest I've come to one of those weapons was during this trial."

WHO SHOT THE SHERIFF? SERIES

CHAPTER 22

The Head Juror recalibrates.
"Okay. Well, now that the gun thing has become an issue. Let's revisit the testimony of
the ballistics expert. Shall we?"
Juror 7 jumps up. Other eyes penetrate him. He composes himself.
"According to the testimony of that ballistics expert: After putting the guns of Sheriff John Brown and Deputy Ron Charles through the same ballistics test, as was done for that of the defendant. It was determined, according to the expert, that those fatal bullets were similar to the ones found inside the magazine of that gun in the possession of the defendant. The expert later claimed all of the guns were reconstructed." Juror 5 exhibits his discontent. "The expert did testify: After shooting a bullet from the defendant's gun into that tank filled with water and then inspecting it under a microscope. The bullets which killed the Sheriff, and his Deputy were analogous."
Juror 7 is back in stride.

WHO SHOT THE SHERIFF? SERIES

"How did all of these reconfigured apparatus wind up in the hands of civilian and law enforcement alike? Was it possible those two officers didn't want any evidence to leak or surface? Any evidence which could link them to other crimes using their guns? Was all this an attempt to suppress evidence? Make it untraceable. Make both the gun and the bullets untraceable?"
Juror 8 supports.
"That ballistics expert's testimony was the identical scenario he delivered when Wesley Haynes was tried for the murder of both officers. I feel like this is heading to another mistrial."
Juror 5 is combative.
"The reconstruction of the Glock, according to the second witness for the defense is nothing but a hoax, a witch hunt, a charade." Juror 12 follows suit.
"I totally disagree. Everything about the reconstruction of a Glock 38 was posted there on Google for the whole world to surf. Suddenly, after that same ballistics expert testified for the prosecution and against Wesley Haynes for those two murders, the link was instantly removed. Who did it is still unknown. I'm sure it wasn't China. Was it Russia that removed it, Saudi Arabia, Iran, or Venezuela?" Juror 6 states:
"I guess we'll never know.
The prosecution really had a good case until they began talking about the rebuilding of the Glock. Too much complexity. If they took all of that mumbo jumbo

out of the case, they would have a chance of convicting Rose Best-Parsons. Focus on her motives..."

Head Juror turns to Juror 6.

"So, what are you saying?"

Juror 6 responds:

"What I'm saying, based on that cluster of evidence? I have to change my vote to a not guilty..."

"You are kidding me! We had this whole thing locked up. I thought a verdict of guilty was close until that restoration business was introduced into these deliberations. We'll never get out of here tonight." Says Juror 2.

Juror 5 responds.

"Don't worry about that basketball game. The Heat is going to lose in the final two minutes. They'll choke."

Juror 2 senses a Heat loss.

"Don't count us out. We're resilient. A little momentum down the stretch? You know we can shoot three balls like none other. Not even Golden State Warriors can compete when we get going."

The Head Juror gets up from the table. He goes to the board. Erases the 8-4 vote status with 7-5. The Head Juror is steadfast. There's a conclusion in his eyes.

Bringing it home becomes paramount.

He remarks.

"Let's get a head count on the votes. I wished we all could be yea or nay unanimously, instead of stretching this thing elastically."

CHAPTER 23

Juror 10 turns to the Head Juror in disgust.
"I hate the voting process. It's irregular.
Remember, the infamous Hanging Chards and Dimples across town in Broward County? Gore vs Bush 2000.
Resulting in a Bush 271 electoral votes to Gore's 266."
Juror 7 responds:
"Chards and Dimples? ... sounds like a musical group to me. Broward County? It's still the same. Rick Scott vs Bill Nelson 2018. You can't get a good vote out of that place anymore." The Head Juror responds.
"Okay. Let's leave politics out of our deliberations and get on with the vote. The clock is ticking. Juror 2?"
Juror 2 turns to Head Juror.
"I still say guilty. Guilty as a Pimp in a double-breasted suit!" The Head Juror is intent.
"Okay. # 2 guilty. Juror # 3?"
Juror 3 says,
"Guilty!"
"Okay. # 3 guilty. Juror #4?"
Juror 4 says, Guilty!
"Okay, # 4. Guilty. # 5?"

Juror 5 says, "Guilty. She's guilty!" Head Juror zeroes in on Juror 6.

"Okay. Juror # 6, how do you vote?"

Juror 6 says,

"I say guilty. And would not change my mind."

Juror 5 asks:

"So, you voted with most of the women. I wonder why?"

Juror 6 responds,

"Yes. Me Too, rules. I was selected out of a jury pool just like you."

"Calm down."

Says the Head Juror.

Juror 6 is irate.

"Tell your Australian mate to calm down. He should mind his own business. This is not counting another person's money."

CHAPTER 24

The Head Juror goes to the fountain and fetches a drink.
"You all are not making this easy."
"Whoever said this was supposed to be easy? The Judge said it was a complex case. This thing is filled with way too many probabilities. I guess she knew we would never reach a unanimous verdict."
States Juror # 6.
Head Juror responds:
"She must have a Crystal Ball or believe in the serendipitous."
Juror 2 says:
"The Judge should have done this herself." "Blame the ancient Greeks. They called it *dikastai*. You are lucky there are not 500 of us in this room."
Head Juror responds:
Really? Dik-as-tai? Juror # 7, what's your vote?
Juror 7 answers,
"Not guilty. She didn't do it. Couldn't do it. She wouldn't do such a thing."
"Juror # 8, where are you on this?"
Asks the Head Juror.
Juror 8 responds.

"Not guilty. She didn't do it."

"Juror # 9, what's your vote?"

Juror 9 says:

"My vote is still not guilty."

"Juror # 10?"

Juror 10 says:

"Right now, I'm deadlocked. Please get back to me later. Sorry."

"Come on! That's not how it's done. You signed up for this didn't you?" Says the Head Juror. Juror 10 responds:

"Tough decision…"

Twenty-two jurors' eyes are focused on Juror 10. "You don't want me to guess, do you?"

Juror 6 responds:

"At least someone else has the guts to stand up. Although it's a bad roll of the dice."

Juror 12 is focused.

"Will you PLEASE stop trying to contaminate the Jury? Thank you."

Head Juror points at Juror 11.

"Juror # 11?"

Juror 11 answers.

"She's not guilty. I'm holding onto all my cards."

The Head Juror asks Juror 12 for her decision.

Juror 12 responds.

"Head Juror. You know where I stand in all of this. The wealthy always think they can pay their way out of a crime. Not on my watch. She's guilty."

CHAPTER 25

Juror 7, energized with sarcasm, states: "The Heat just lost the game. It was a blowout."
Juror 2 scans the room.
"There is no Television in here. How did you find out?"
Juror 7 responds:
"It suddenly got frigid inside this room."
Juror 2 asks,
"It wasn't a complete blowout, was it?"
Juror 7 responds:
"No. The cold air keeps blowing from the outside. When it rains here in Miami, it's worse than Downs River Falls."
"That's an overstatement. Okay. Let's regroup and get back to this discussion."
Says the Head Juror as he writes on the board 6-5-1.
He zones in on Juror 10.
"Juror 10 we need your vote. Are you ready with your decision?"
Juror 10 responds:
"I guess I would say she's NOT guilty. She couldn't have done it sleepwalking." Juror 2 responds: "Now

we are tied. What a cumbersome series of missed layups! Now we're split right down the middle."

The Head Juror erases the stats from the board and writes 6-6. The 6 Jurors who voted guilty vacate the table and huddle at the water fountain.

The jurors regroup. Juror # 2 looks more frustrated than ever. He's so agitated he paces. He's eyeing the clock.

"We've been making a go at this for hours. We are no closer than when we began. It seems we have drifted further away from the basket. We missed the lay-up, the dunk, the stuff. Now we can't even drain a free throw, much less shoot from the top of the key. It's clear. The ball goes in. The ball bounces out. We fail to score points. We'll be here all night trying to score. This has gone over time. It could be heading toward double OT..."

Juror 5 interrupts.

"Yeah. It seems like some of us take this for a Cricketing Test Match. They don't play those anymore. It's now all in one-day games. Now, the momentum has shifted toward a not-guilty verdict. It is said that momentum is hard to get and easy to lose. That's a truism. It doesn't matter if we keep voting indefinitely. I'm still convinced. The defendant is guilty. She did it."

Juror 7 gets up, goes to the fountain, and gets a cup of water. He stays next to the fountain, drinking all of it.

Throw the empty cup in the trash. Juror 5 continues during Juror 7's absence.

"She shot the Sheriff and the Deputy. All evidence points to her. Her motives were clear. The Jamaican system had been very insensitive to her by orchestrating her husband's death. So, to even the playing field, she shot and killed both officers in cold blood."

Juror 7 returns to his seat at the table.

Juror 2 responds to Juror 5 comments.

"I'm with you. I like that kind of talk. She's guilty as hell. Why was she carrying a Glock if she didn't know how to use it and had never even shot a fly? Knowingly, it was the weapon of choice because it was reconstructed. On the other hand, being unable to trace the seller or the buyer is no excuse for her defense. According to the witnesses' testimony, two individuals in Jamaica initially had full access to the reconstructed handgun: Sponji Edwards and Deja Nichols, aka Yuki Nichols."

WHO SHOT THE SHERIFF? SERIES

CHAPTER 26

Juror 4 has a floor. He seems resurrected. "That Yuki Nichols was some character, wasn't she? She lived a double life. How cool. What a masquerade?"
Juror 2 interjects.
"She was. Yuki was introduced to the music industry by Bill Parsons. The defendant's husband. As the witness further testified, Yuki Nichols went gangster after the rub out of the Sheriff and his Deputy. It was disclosed that on the day before those brutal murders, Yuki and Rose were seen at a club owned by the late Milton Rogers in a lengthy conversation. Could Yuki Nichols be telling Rose Best-Parsons how to use Glock 38? We don't know. The Sheriff reportedly visited the same club and threatened to shut it down. All we know is one day later, circumstantially, both men were killed with a Glock."
The Head Juror goes into note-taking mode.
"If one day after the meeting between Putin and Trump in Helsinki, the US suffered a major tragedy. Of

course, Trump would be blamed. We cannot find out what was discussed between the two women. We cannot find out what was discussed between those two world leaders. In the case of the sheriff incident. Yuki Nichols is dead."

"So, how did the Deputy get shot?" Asks the Head Juror.

"Like it was said earlier. The deputy got in the way. He wound up at the wrong place at the wrong time." States Juror 2.

Juror 10 is robust.

"When asked why all the evidence found inside that abandoned SUV was not handed over to the crime lab? Detective Paul Stevens, while producing a picture of that abandoned SUV, stated: The crime lab had full access to the vehicle for months. They should have swept it clean."

Juror 7 asks:

"Why not?"

He gets everyone's attention.

"It was evident they wanted to nail Wesley Haynes for those crimes. It seems Detective Jones and Stevens had it in for Wesley Haynes. It was all a botch job. For months, that abandoned SUV was not recovered. When its locale surfaced, it was discovered nestled in a cobweb. This recovery occurred almost at the end of Wesley Haynes' trial. So, you see why I'm sticking to a not-guilty decision."

WHO SHOT THE SHERIFF? SERIES

Head Juror asks: "Juror # 9, why are you holding onto the decision of a not guilty vote?"
Juror 9 replies,
"When asked if she ever met Sheriff John Brown? The defendant, Rose Best-Parsons, said She first encountered Sheriff John Brown one Saturday night in Kingston. He rolled up at a restaurant co-owned by her and Milton Rogers. He arrested several of her patrons, claiming they were prostitutes, pimps, and drug dealers."
Juror # 7 urges her on.
Juror 9 continues.
"She further testified: upon hearing the commotion outside on the patio. She stepped out to investigate. The Sheriff was getting inside his car while the van with the arrested drove away. The Sheriff yelled: I'll shut this joint down. He later did." Jurors listen intently.
"When asked her opinion of the Sheriff? Rose Best Parsons said he seemed to be very shady.
When asked why she thought so, she answered that Brown couldn't even keep a straight face. He couldn't look her in the eye during his boastful remark. She also stated: Moments before he showed up at the restaurant, Milton Rogers phoned her, complaining that Sheriff John Brown acted similarly. Many had a vendetta against him. He wasn't to be trusted. He was as crooked as a tree root.

They want to put her in a chair and flip the switch. Execute her? Have you ever in your existence witnessed a man being executed? I have seen at least six."
"Never have." Says the Head Juror.
Juror 9 continues. While Juror 11 visits the water fountain.
"You need to. Everyone who said she's guilty needs to."
Juror 11 fills a cup with water.
"He begs. He spits. He kicks. His eyes roll. He pisses and shits in his pants before he goes to the other side. Could you imagine what a woman does? Picture it! Picture a woman with her farewell white dress on. Well, if you haven't. Why are you asking me to change my vote?"
Juror 11 dumps the whole cup of water. "That's grotesque. I'm changing my vote."
Says Juror 11 as she returns to her seat.
"Oh. Come on! Another one just died!
Says Juror 3.
The jurors become bedraggled.
The Head Juror writes on the board 5-7. He then commands order. Several Jurors remain disgruntled. Mainly Juror 2.
"We've made it out of 200 potential jurors. We are required to submit a unanimous verdict. Even if this

thing lasts for a week or a month, however long it lasts. It's our obligation."
Says the Head Juror.

CHAPTER 27

Juror 2 paces the room.
"I didn't sign up for all this. Who manufactured those rules? What if the jury gets choked? I mean hung."
Head Juror responds:
"That's not the result we are looking for. It says we aren't together in our voting." Juror 3 is enraged:
"How many other police officers did Rose Best Parsons rub out with that reconstructed Glock? We don't know. According to the evidence, the prints lifted from that gun matched the gun of Rose Best-Parsons - the defendant." Juror 10 states: "Do our hearts seek the truth or our minds? A good person produces good things from the treasury of a good heart, and an evil person produces evil things from the treasury of an evil heart. What you say flows from what is in your heart. Luke 6:45 NLT. The defendant said vehemently, 'I believe that the Pastor committed those twin murders. He claimed that he and his wife were first responders. Claiming they were fresh from attending a prayer meeting at their church. What hypocrisy? No coincidence he died of a heart attack."

"Another dead man. The dead does not substantiate our deliberations."
Says the Head Juror.
Juror 10 remarks:
"Based on the facts. The defendant claimed the pastor and his wife stated they were there first. What if they shot him? According to a detailed statement, They arrived while both officers' blood was still warm and pumping. She reiterated that's the statement the pastor gave to the police while detained with his wife shaking like a leaf on a tree at the Police Station. What about that Glock found at his church?" Juror 12 is on her feet. "Mr. Head Juror, you stated a while ago that this thing could go for weeks or even months. Please understand that this trial is not paid for in Jamaican dollars. Jamaicans are proud people.
Judge Lopez should have known this could cost a fortune, even if Jamaicans are more sympathetic with their kind.
This trial should never pan out in the United States of America. In God, we trust. US taxpayers shouldn't have to foot this bill. Let Sandals of Jamaica pick up the tab."
Juror # 3 is adamant. He gets up from the table and paces back and forth.
Juror 3 states:

WHO SHOT THE SHERIFF? SERIES

"I like that Marcus Davis' testimony. The man who was incarcerated lived on the same cell block as Gregg Nichols, the husband of Yuki Nichols.

Marcus Davis testified: One day, he and Gregg Nichols played dominoes. Nichols boasted about his new hit album. Yet, in the can. As he stated, His wife wouldn't let go of the Sponji Edwards affair. The Glock reconstruction expert. He also bragged about the relationship between Yuki and Rose Best-Parsons.

Davis asked Gregg Nichols how long Rose Best-Parsons had been associated with his wife Deja, aka Yuki. Gregg Nichols responded: Their relationship began after Wesley and Britney Haynes failed to reproduce a scratched-up CD containing their hit song. Deja introduced Rose to her producer, a musician who was blind from birth."

Juror 7 shows impartiality.

"According to Marcus Davis, I'm reading from my notes."

Says Juror 3.

The pad from which he reads is moist from sweaty palms.

He continues.

"Gregg Nichols said: It is no fate; Rose Best Parsons acquired a reconstructed Glock handgun. Deja not only spearheaded the operation, but I had a friend who needed to be armed. I would have readily armed her.

When was Marcus Davis asked if he believed the late Gregg Nichols? He said he didn't have a reason to lie.

There was much on Gregg's chest as he tried hard to get acquitted. Even if he had to throw his wife Deja under the bus."

Juror 7 remains independent.

"I don't believe in any of Marcus Davis' testimony. I don't see why you took those notes. Marcus Davis is a traitor, a Con Man, a known liar. In the trial Gregg Nichols vs Who Shot The Sheriff? I cite Marcus Davis's testimony: Nichols, while in prison, told him how he methodically orchestrated the assassination of Milton Rogers. He made it a clean sweep. Subsequently, Gregg Nichols was acquitted, and Court Officer Quentin Daley was implicated in that assassination."

CHAPTER 28

Juror 2 seems wearied. He gets a drink of water from the fountain.
"There are way too many entanglements in this case.
It becomes visible the Head Juror is pressed and looking everywhere for answers." Head Juror asks:
"Have we examined the defendant's state of mind?"
Juror 2 responds:
"I don't know if that will prove anything. Her mind was to be a cop killer."
Head Juror states:
"At the time of her arrest, she claimed The gun could have belonged to her husband, Bill Parsons. He was accustomed to arming himself. Her statement revealed. When asked why it was inside her car, The defendant said: I was cleaning out my car. I saw the pistol. I moved it over to get enough space to fit my large bottle of hand lotion…"
Juror 3 interjects.
"So, she came upon a gun in her car. She didn't put it there as she claimed. Why didn't she call the police to

WHO SHOT THE SHERIFF? SERIES

remove it? If she didn't want to have anything to do with guns?"
Juror 12 states:
"I'm afraid of snakes. Suppose I find a snake inside my car. The first thing I do is scream bloody murder. Secondly, after regaining my presence of mind, I'll call for help to remove it. Touching it is a no, no." Juror 7 counteracts.
"A gun is not a snake. It's a serpent. A snake moves of its own accord. A gun moves when it's aided by movement. The defendant could have ignored it. Sensing, it was a treasured means of protection."
Head Juror asks:
"Did the defendant "know" or "appreciate" that her conduct at the time of storing an illegal weapon was proper? Additionally, do you desire to use it? Was she "compelled" to use the weapon to commit the criminal act? Did the defendant "premeditate" the crime? She allegedly spoke at length with others regarding her distaste for the Sheriff. Was she aware of the risks her conduct posed? Did the defendant, Rose Best-Parsons, feel that harm was imminent, and that violence was the only way to take action against Sheriff John Brown?"
Juror 8 goes to her notes.
"Her chauffeur, Big Bubba, testified the defendant did on numerous occasions share her dislike for the Sheriff. Even though he said he didn't see her commit the murders or believed it was something she was capable

of pulling off. Even if you gave her a belt, I don't think she could have killed a fly. Much less two. In my view, that best fits this narrative."

Juror 12 is furious.

"You are kidding me! So, are you prepared to allow this multi-cop killer to go free? So, can she remove any law enforcement individual she's not too happy with? What are we proposing? If a cop cites a motorist for running the red light. Instead of going to court, fight the ticket. We build up a hated nexus. Stalk him and eventually gun him down? I did not sign up for this. Locked in a stuffy room for hours and hours. I hate being sequestered. Challenged by a judge to produce a unanimous verdict. When this deliberation all began, we were closer to the truth. Now, everything seems to be diluted like ink saturated with water. Look at where we've gotten. Our decision has swayed. Our taxpayers are being mugged. If flipping was an easy thing… I don't mean that. Please allow me to walk it back. All those of you who flipped on the government's case. You should be ashamed of yourselves. At this point, my vote is still guilty."

CHAPTER 29

Juror 8 looks at Juror 12 intently.
Why don't you just go over the edge and flip?
Don't you see you're the only woman still holding out?
This is the age of ME TOO!
Juror 2 states:
"I had no idea the results of this deliberation were based on gender." Eyes are now focused on Juror 6.
Juror 6 states:
"Why am I being targeted? Because I'm the minority inside the room?"
Juror 8 says to Juror 6.
"You are neither a witness, a subject, nor a target." Then to Juror 2.
"I had no idea it was based on if the Heat beat up on the Knicks during the last two minutes of the game."
The Head Juror tries to maintain a calm deliberation.
"Okay. Our duty here is to find a story that assimilates the known facts more completely, more consistently,

and with fewer inferences. Although there might be competing stories. We need to find one we all can agree on." Juror 12 picks up from where she was cut off. "The defendant was found with a Glock in her possession. It wasn't in her hands but in the glove compartment of her automobile. She claimed she didn't know how it got there. It could have been placed there before she became a widow. Two cops were shot months before this gun possession incident. She didn't have a prior criminal record. Squeaky clean. Except for a possibly manufactured moving violation."

Juror 2 eyes the clock.

Juror 12 continues.

"Probably she never used a handgun. Maybe someone who interacted with her did shed her hair sample in their vehicle, or she rode in that SUV at some point, refreshed her lips, and forgot her lip gloss upon exiting. That hypothetical is unique, economic, coherent, and consistent with the defendant's character. Therefore, I'll have to change my vote to not guilty."

Juror 2 responds:

"I saw that coming. Now we are getting higher and higher toward hanging ourselves."

Several jurors voting guilty toss their notepads and pens on the table and walk away. The head juror tries to bring calm to the deliberations. The court officer peaks inside, wondering what has transpired.

Head Juror prompts.

"Don't worry about it. A slight disagreement just seemed to have gotten some members rattled. I've got this. Thanks for all you do." The Head Juror closes the door. He goes to the board and writes 4-8.

Juror 2 is still high-wired.

"Moments ago, those numbers were reversed." Juror 2 walks away from the table. He goes to the same window. Pops another Nicorette gum. The Head Juror is entirely focused. He discusses. Rose Best-Gordon had the right to see what evidence the prosecution had against her before the trial. Which means she had the right to discover in the case. Have we focused on her alibi? Where was the defendant? If she said, she's not guilty. Where was she?

Juror 7 defends.

"She wasn't there. There's no evidence placing her at the scene of the crime. It's all circumstantial. What ifs. It's like the pretense in a good crime novel.

Juror 2 asks,

"Really?"

CHAPTER 30

The Head Juror peruses through his multiple notepads.

"Okay. Let's revisit the circumstances. Sheriff John Brown and his Deputy Ron Charles are conducting a traffic watch. The light changes from yellow to red. A black SUV speeds through the intersection. The two Sheriff's cars are not waiting for the traffic signal to change. They take off in pursuit of the vehicle...

Sheriff Brown's car, ahead of the pack, now with flashing lights and sirens, is chasing the eluding motorist. Deputy Ron Charles's car follows suit with flashing emergency signals. Finally, the luxury vehicle stops and waits on the right shoulder..."

Juror 8 interrupts.

That motorist wasn't the defendant, Rose Best Parsons. It had to be someone else." Head Juror counters.

"The two officers dart out of their vehicle with guns pointed toward the idle SUV. As both men got closer to the parked car, two rounds of gunshots in quick succession cut them down to the ground from through the vehicle's rear windscreen. The luxury vehicle takes off at speed, leaving Sheriff Brown and his deputy Ron Charles bloodied and lifeless on the street. The vehicle races unaccompanied through the streets of

WHO SHOT THE SHERIFF? SERIES

Mandeville..." Juror 12 interrupts.
"That sounds like something a known, skilled criminal would do. The defendant was unskilled...remember?"
The Head Juror continues with his summation.
"Detective Paul Stevens testified that he and Detective Jones were called to the crime scene that night of the murders. He stated that when he arrived, he interviewed an elderly couple, who called 119, stating that they saw what looked like an accident on their way home from church. The couple, Claude, and Doris Weeks, further stated that they got out of their car to see if someone needed an ambulance or CPR. At that point, they saw the two officers lying there dead along the roadside..."
Juror 7 interjects.
"Claude Weeks died after he was charged with the murders. His wife was not called to testify. Why?"
Juror 2 states:
"Let the HJ finish. That's why he was appointed. Keep going...Mr. Chairman.
Head Juror continues.
"The couple said that they figured that the officers had been shot as their bodies seemed pierced, one in the neck and the other in the head. They also claimed that they smelled sulfuric fumes like gunpowder. It then was confirmed in their minds the men could have been shot."

WHO SHOT THE SHERIFF? SERIES

Juror 4 removes his glasses, polishes them thoroughly, and inspects them. Satisfied, he returns them to his face during the Head Juror's disputation.

"Detective Jones and Stevens wanted to believe the couple but had to perform their duty. So, Detective Jones and Stevens, according to their corroborated testimony, had the couple transported to the police station. There, we later questioned the couple more extensively and released them. The two detectives testified."

Juror 7 gets up and paces the room. He finally takes his seat.

The Head Juror notices his move and continues. "The time of death determined by the autopsy indicated that the deaths could have occurred between 8:30 PM and 8:35 PM. Detective Stevens further testified: They arrived at the crime scene at about 9:15 PM."

The Head Juror takes his seat. JUROR 7 quickly relinquishes his seat at the table. He Filibusters and then presides.

"Yes. The Coroner testified and let me unpack: Sheriff John Brown died at 8:33 PM. His Deputy died two minutes later at 8:35 PM. Bubba, the chauffeur for the defendant, testified he dropped her off at the Salon at 8:30 PM."

"Where is he taking this?" Asks Juror 4. He then focuses on Juror 7.

"Are you her lawyer?"

Juror 7 pays no attention to Juror 4's pompousness. Instead, he goes to the board and outlines: "The distance between the Beauty Salon and the Crime Scene is at least fifteen miles. It seems quite unlikely that she could have committed these murders and disposed of the SUV in a ravine. Have her chauffeur pick her up and drop the defendant off at the Salon. There goes her alibi. Based on that alone. Rose Best-Gordon is not guilty."

Juror 4 remarks.

"At this point, after hearing those facts. I have no choice but to change my vote. She was not capable of undertaking such a task." Juror 2 yells.

"You did? Holy smokes!"

Juror 4 responds: "Yep. I'm all in. Count the chips."

Head Juror asks:

"Okay. Is there anyone else siding with the not guilty vote?"

Had Juror is back on his feet.

Juror 5 raises his hand.

"I'm leaning towards it but still doubtful based on her motives. She categorically despised the Sheriff. On the other hand, Sponji Edwards started this whole thing. It could have been him. He was able to make his guns and bullets untraceable. His proficiency scares me. How did he do it?" Juror 7 states: Easy. Firstly, he discovered. Secondly, he tested, and thirdly, he pattern-set.

Juror 7 returns to his seat.
Head Juror asks. "Juror 5 you look puzzled." Juror 5 answers.
"I am." Head Juror asks.
"Okay. So, where do you really stand?"
Juror 5 focuses on the other jurors all seated except for the Head Juror.
Juror 5 states.
"I have to say, I've changed my mind. I have to change my vote. I need to stop fighting my conscience. I vote not guilty."
Juror 2 is inflexible.
"Why didn't you say that all along? You raved, you spun, and now you caved. Very wishy-washy. Now it's 3-9 in favor of the NGs." Juror 5 responds. "At least I'm man enough to walk something back." Juror 2 asks:
"Yeah? What if the defendant were to walk in this room right now and said she would like to walk back her statements?"
The Head Juror assures:
"That would make all of our jobs easier. Don't you think?"
Juror 2 responds:
"I'm thinking. Hypothetically, if we all consented to send that poor woman to the electric chair and later found out it wasn't she who did those killings? That would brand us the worst 12 jurors on the planet. I can't go down that road. I change my vote.

Head Juror states:
"Even if everyone else disagrees. I am holding out..."
Suddenly, the main door opens of its own accord. The JURORS are rattled.
Except for the HEAD JUROR. He states and writes on the board in all caps and quotations:
"DEAD MEN TELL NO TALES!"

WHO SHOT THE SHERIFF? SERIES

About The AUTHORS

John Alan Andrews hails from the islands of SVG in the Caribbean. He began his acting career in New York and took his craft to Hollywood in 1996. He appeared in multiple TV Ad campaigns and films, including John Q, starring Denzel Washington. Andrews later found his niche—writing coupled with filmmaking—and not only starred in but produced and directed some of his work, which won multiple awards in Hollywood.

With over 76 books in his multi-genre catalog, including *Rude Buay* poised for a Jamaican production, Andrews is currently drafting *The PIPS Series,* a police procedural TV series slated for the Mediterranean enclaves. He has also Co-Authored with his sons, *Jonathan Andrews* and *Jefferri Andrews.*

His latest books, Atomic Steps and Make Every Thought Pay You A Profit, are favorites among business leaders, and his twisted NYC Connivers legal thriller series appeals to both women and men ages 16 -85. The Pips Series (Body in a Suitcase). Also, Samuel A. Andrews—*Legacy* (A Biography).

His work can be found at **ALIPNET.COM** or **ALIPNET TV**, his recently launched OTT Streaming Platform.

John Alan Andrews states: "Some people create, while others compete. Creating is where the rubber meets the road. A dream worth having is one worth fighting for because freedom is not free; it carries a massive price tag."

VISIT: WWW.JOHNAANDREWS.COM

LIKE Us on FaceBook

https://www.facebook.com/Whoshotthesherifffilm

WHO SHOT THE SHERIFF? SERIES

WHO SHOT THE SHERIFF? SERIES

WHO SHOT THE SHERIFF? SERIES

WHO SHOT THE SHERIFF? SERIES

WHO SHOT THE SHERIFF? SERIES

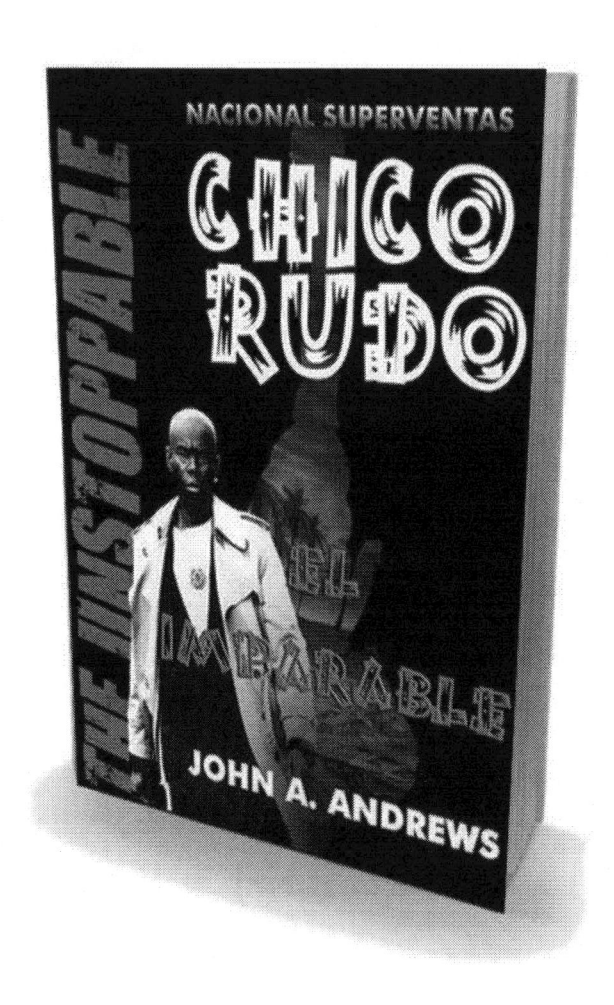

WHO SHOT THE SHERIFF? SERIES

NACIONAL SUPERVENTAS
CHICO RUDO
THE UNSTOPPABLE
EL IMPARABLE
JOHN A. ANDREWS

WHO SHOT THE SHERIFF? SERIES

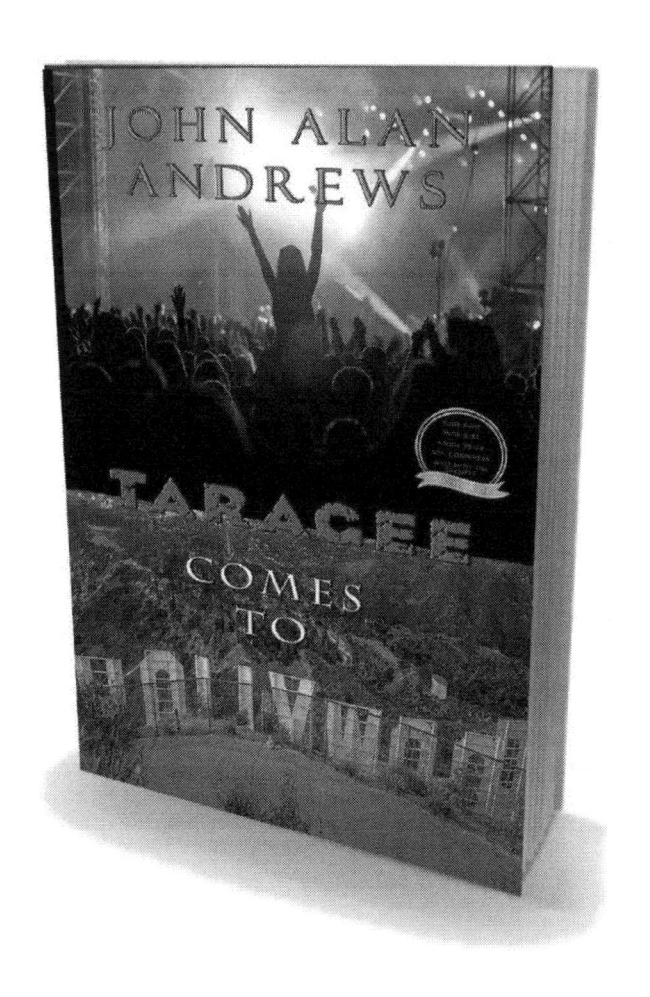

WHO SHOT THE SHERIFF? SERIES

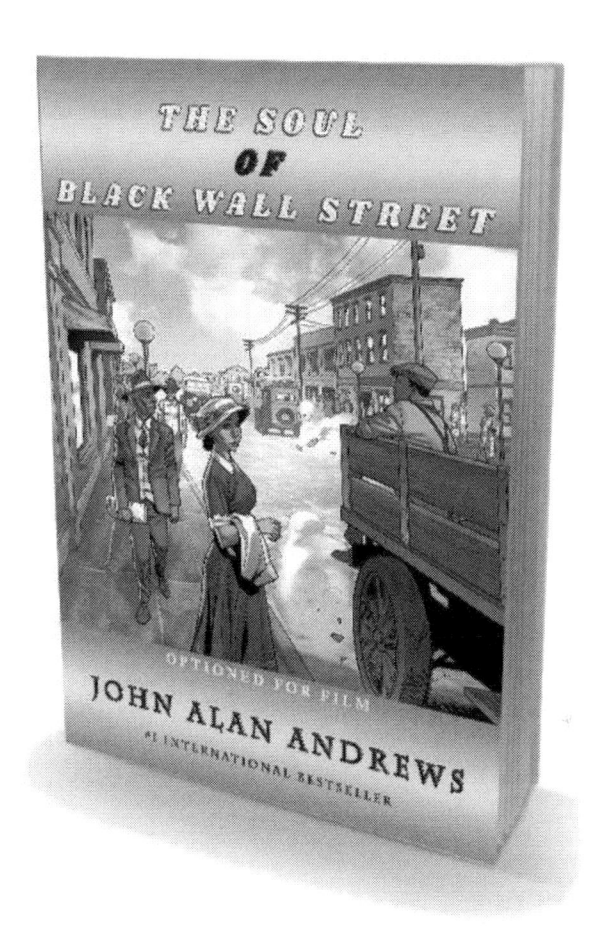

WHO SHOT THE SHERIFF? SERIES

THE SOUL OF BLACK WALL STREET

OPTIONED FOR FILM

JOHN ALAN ANDREWS
#1 INTERNATIONAL BESTSELLER

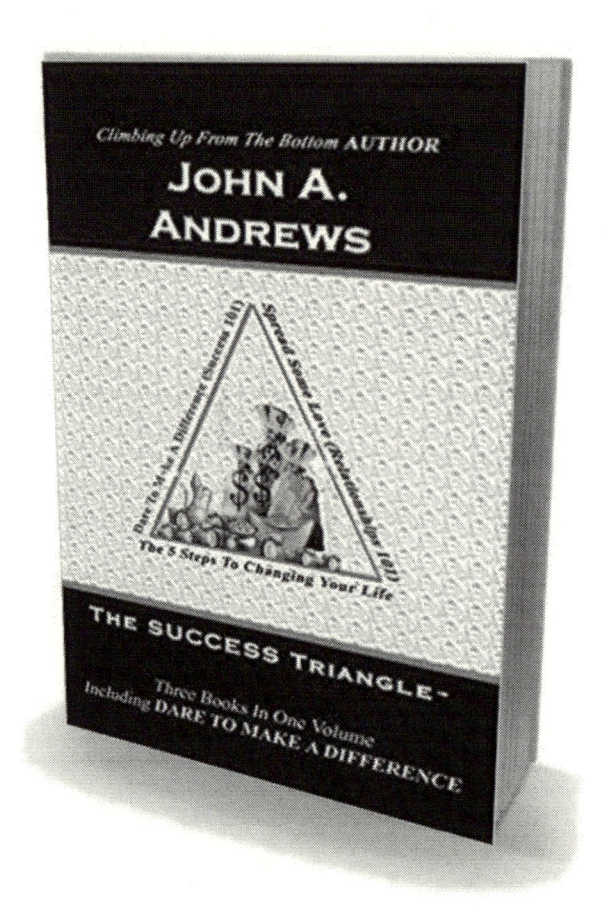

WHO SHOT THE SHERIFF? SERIES

WHO SHOT THE SHERIFF? SERIES

WHO SHOT THE SHERIFF? SERIES

WHO SHOT THE SHERIFF? SERIES

MAKE EVERY THOUGHT PAY YOU A PROFIT

JOHN ALAN ANDREWS

#1 INTERNATIONAL BESTSELLING AUTHOR OF
ATOMIC STEPS
WIN BIG OR GO HOME

WHO SHOT THE SHERIFF? SERIES

WHO SHOT THE SHERIFF? SERIES

WHO SHOT THE SHERIFF? SERIES

How I Wrote 8 Books In One Year

JOHN A. ANDREWS

Author of
TOTAL COMMITMENT
The Mindset Of Champions

WHO SHOT THE SHERIFF? SERIES

By National Bestselling Author of Rude Buay ... The Unstoppable

TOTAL COMMITMENT
The Mindset of Champions

JOHN A. ANDREWS

WHO SHOT THE SHERIFF? SERIES

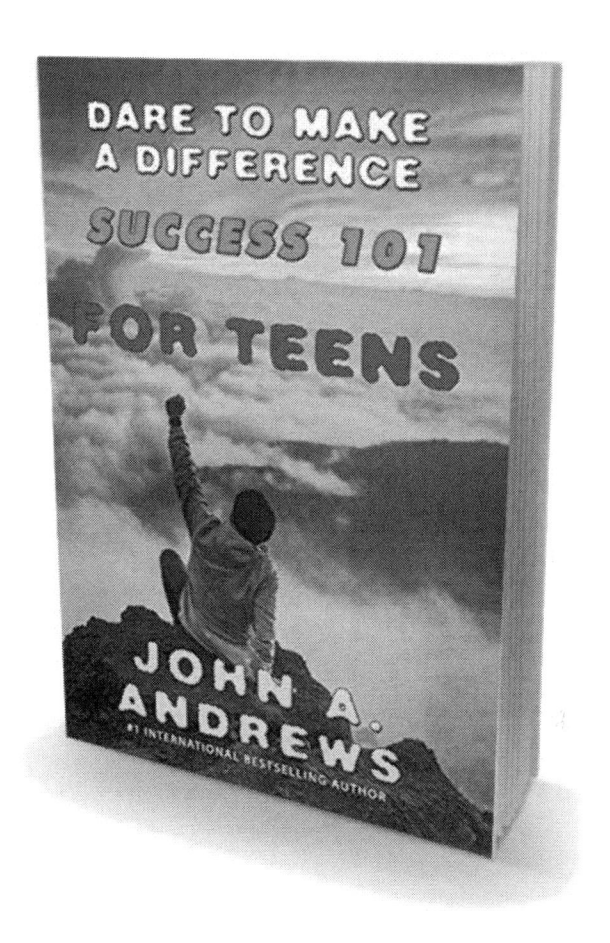

WHO SHOT THE SHERIFF? SERIES

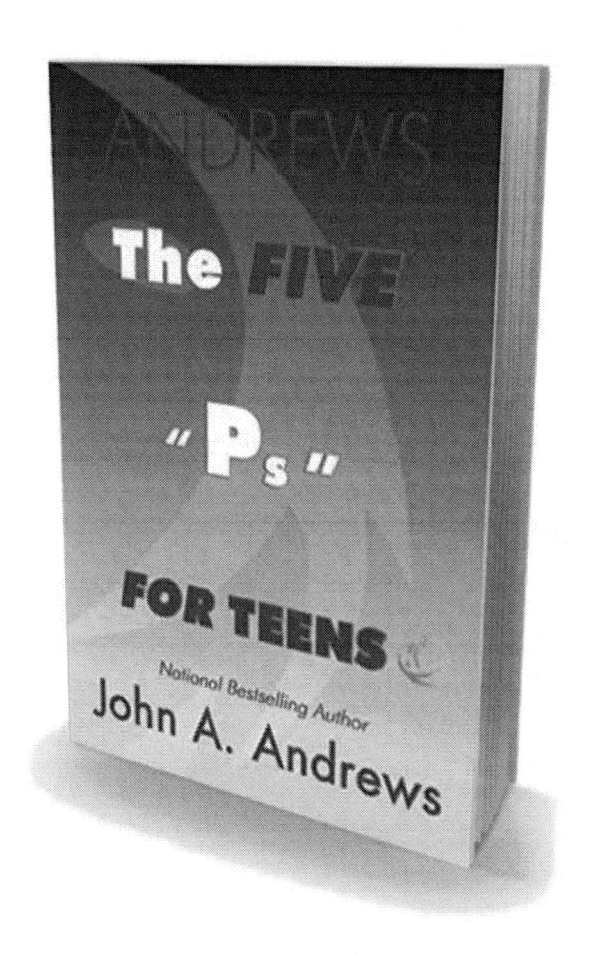

WHO SHOT THE SHERIFF? SERIES

WHO SHOT THE SHERIFF? SERIES

WHO SHOT THE SHERIFF? SERIES

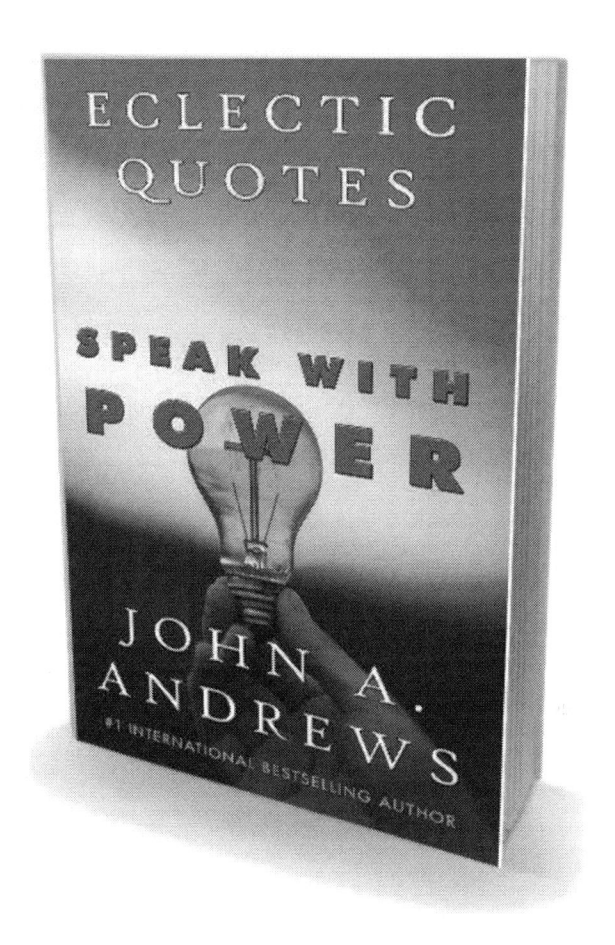

WHO SHOT THE SHERIFF? SERIES

WHO SHOT THE SHERIFF? SERIES

WHO SHOT THE SHERIFF? SERIES

THE 5 STEPS TO CHANGING YOUR LIFE
BY: JOHN A. ANDREWS

"SEE YOU AT THE SUMMIT"

WHO SHOT THE SHERIFF? SERIES

SHADES OF HER

BASED ON A TRUE HOLLYWOOD STORY

WHO SHOT THE SHERIFF? SERIES

NYC

NEW YORK CONNIVERS

FROM THE CREATOR OF *WHO SHOT THE SHERIFF?*

JOHN A. ANDREWS

#1 INTERNATIONAL BESTSELLER

UNTIL DEATH DO US PART

A NOVEL

THE CRIME
THE COVER UP
THE CONCLUSION

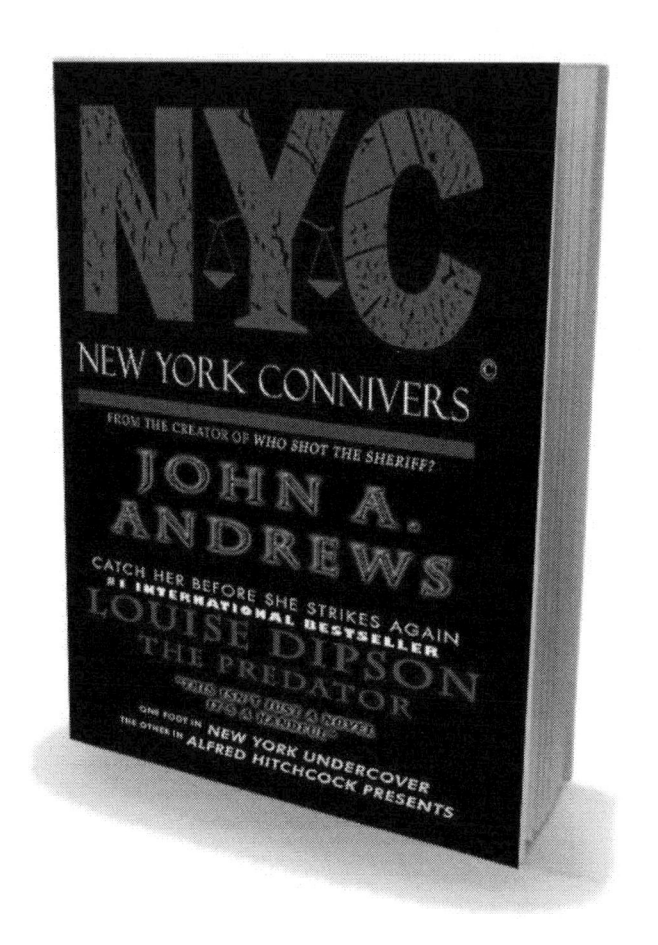

WHO SHOT THE SHERIFF? SERIES

NYC

NEW YORK CONNIVERS

FROM THE CREATOR OF *WHO SHOT THE SHERIFF?*

JOHN A. ANDREWS

CATCH HER BEFORE SHE STRIKES AGAIN
#1 INTERNATIONAL BESTSELLER

LOUISE DIPSON
THE PREDATOR

"THIS ISN'T JUST A NOVEL
IT'S A HANDFUL"

ONE FOOT IN NEW YORK UNDERCOVER
THE OTHER IN ALFRED HITCHCOCK PRESENTS

WHO SHOT THE SHERIFF? SERIES

WHO SHOT THE SHERIFF? SERIES

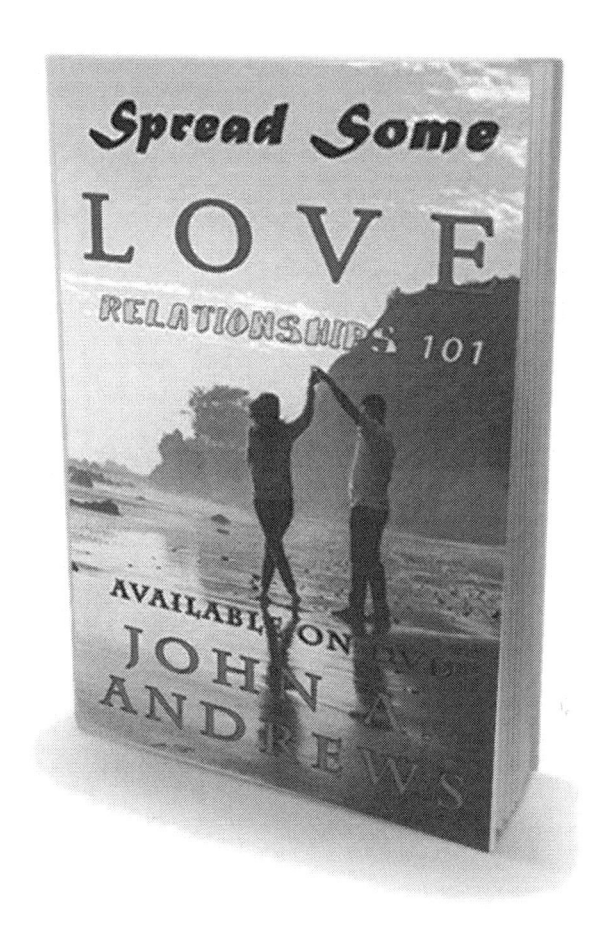

WHO SHOT THE SHERIFF? SERIES

WHO SHOT THE SHERIFF? SERIES

WHO SHOT THE SHERIFF?
The Hustle, The Flow, The Verdict.
#1 INTERNATIONAL BESTSELLER

JOHN A. ANDREWS

WHO SHOT THE SHERIFF? SERIES

WHO SHOT THE SHERIFF? SERIES

WHO SHOT THE SHERIFF? III

JOHN A. ANDREWS

#1 INTERNATIONAL BESTSELLING AUTHOR

THE JURY
DEAD MEN TELL NO TALES

WHO SHOT THE SHERIFF? SERIES

WHO SHOT THE SHERIFF? SERIES

JOHN A. ANDREWS

The Church Is A Hospital?

THE MUSICAL®

FROM THE CREATOR OF
RUDE BUAY
THE WHODUNIT CHRONICLES
&
THE CHURCH ON FIRE

SO MANY ARE TRYING TO GO TO HEAVEN
WITHOUT FIRST BUILDING A HEAVEN
HERE ON EARTH...
#1 INTERNATIONAL BESTSELLER

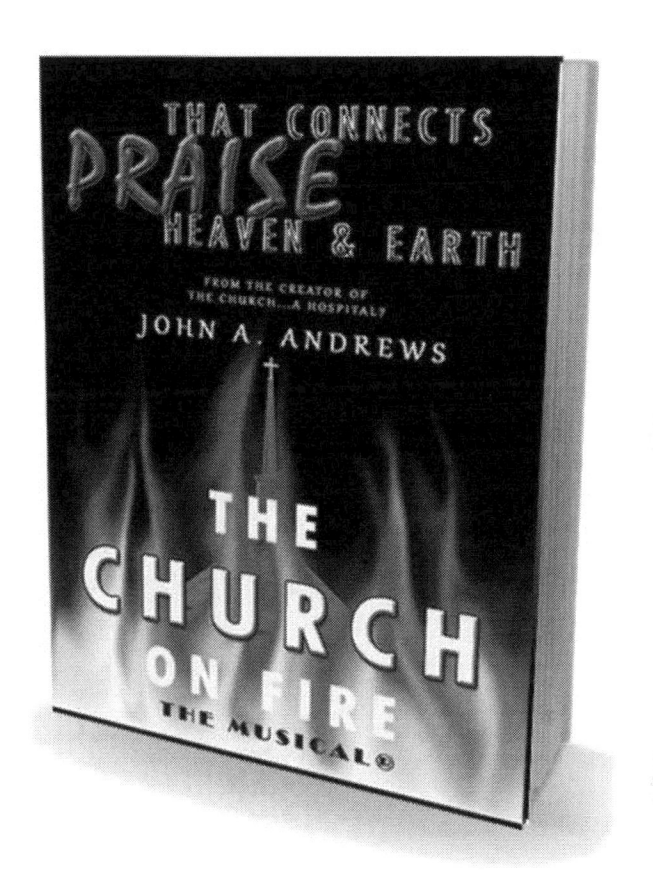

WHO SHOT THE SHERIFF? SERIES

WHO SHOT THE SHERIFF? SERIES

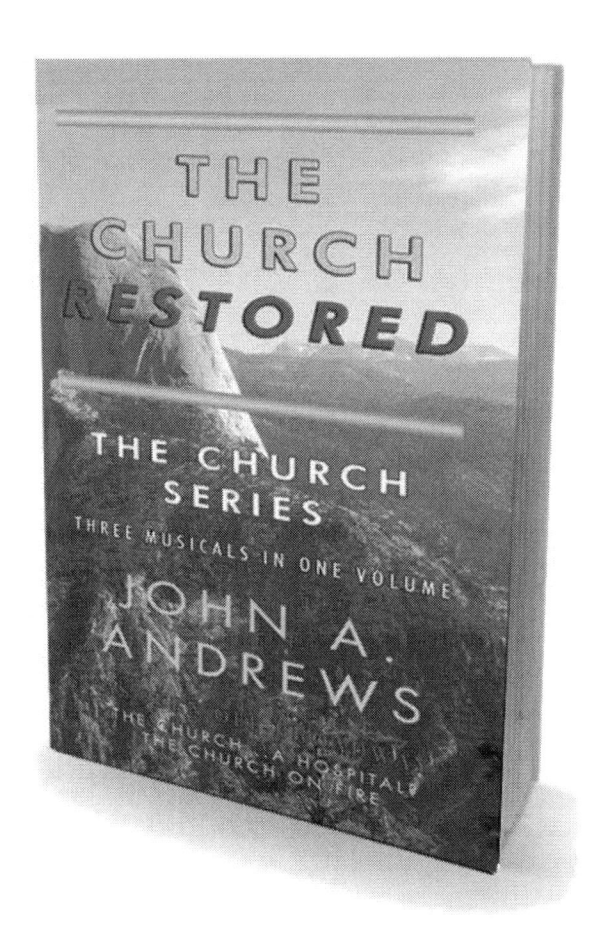

WHO SHOT THE SHERIFF? SERIES

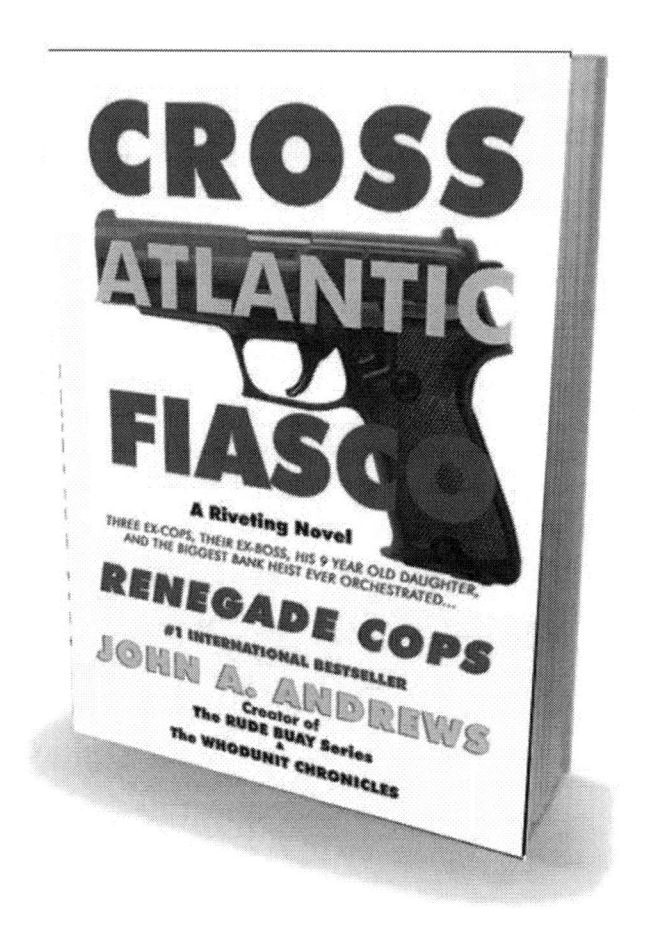

WHO SHOT THE SHERIFF? SERIES

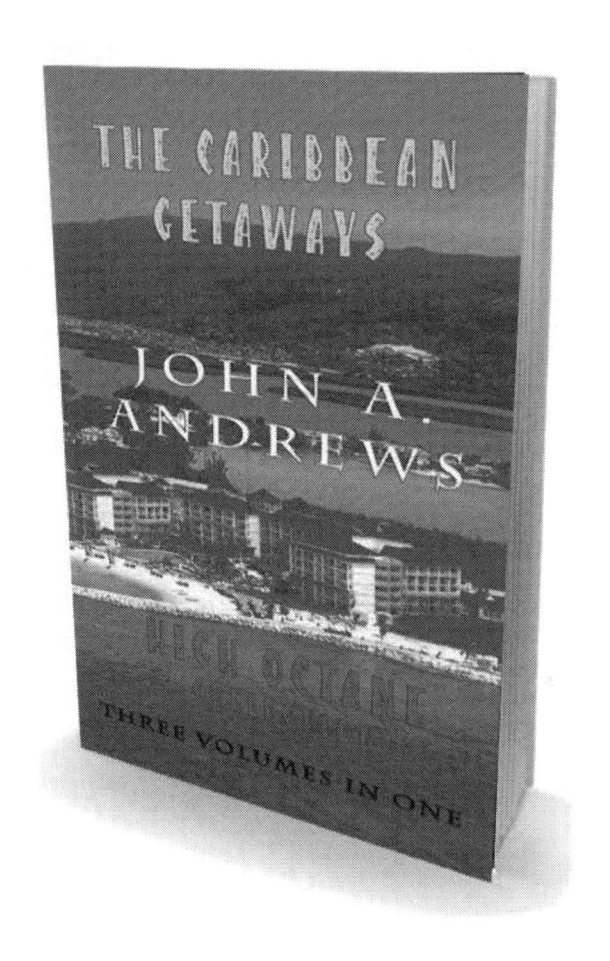

WHO SHOT THE SHERIFF? SERIES

THE CARIBBEAN GETAWAYS

JOHN A. ANDREWS

HIGH OCTANE

THREE VOLUMES IN ONE

WHO SHOT THE SHERIFF? SERIES

THE BOTCHED AMENDMENT

JOHN A. ANDREWS
#1 INTERNATIONAL BESTSELLING AUTHOR

SUPPRESSING THE BLACK VOTE

WHO SHOT THE SHERIFF? SERIES

JOHN ALAN
ANDREWS

BLACK JUSTICE
A SNITCH ON TIME

WHO SHOT THE SHERIFF? SERIES

JOHN & JONATHAN ANDREWS

BLACK JUSTICE
INJUSTICE BAKED IN

WHO SHOT THE SHERIFF? SERIES

CHASING DESTINY

GOT TO HAVE IT!

BASED ON THE NOVEL
A RUDE BUAY SIDEKICK
FROM THE CREATOR OF
RUDE BUAY

JOHN A. ANDREWS

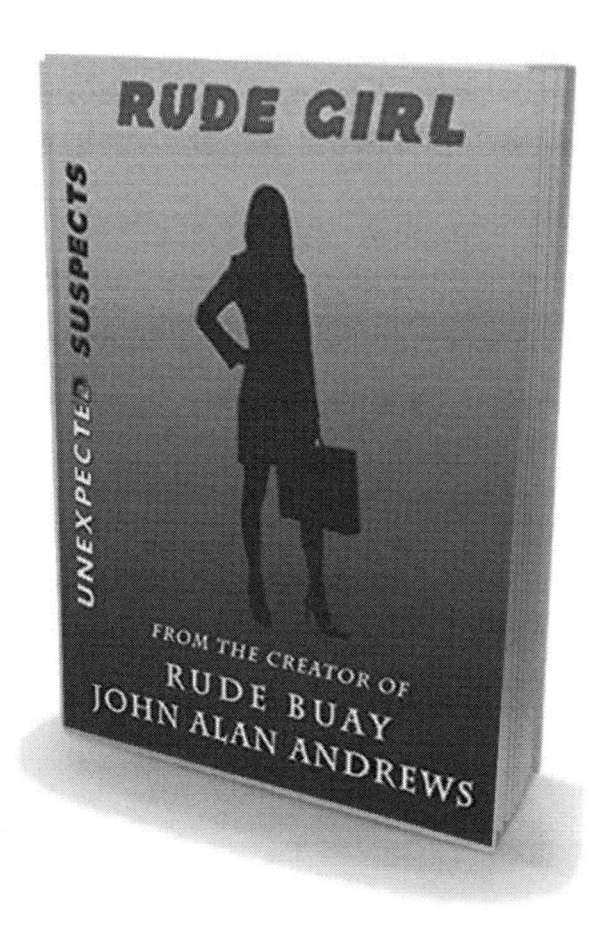

WHO SHOT THE SHERIFF? SERIES

RUDE GIRL

UNEXPECTED SUSPECTS

FROM THE CREATOR OF
RUDE BUAY
JOHN ALAN ANDREWS

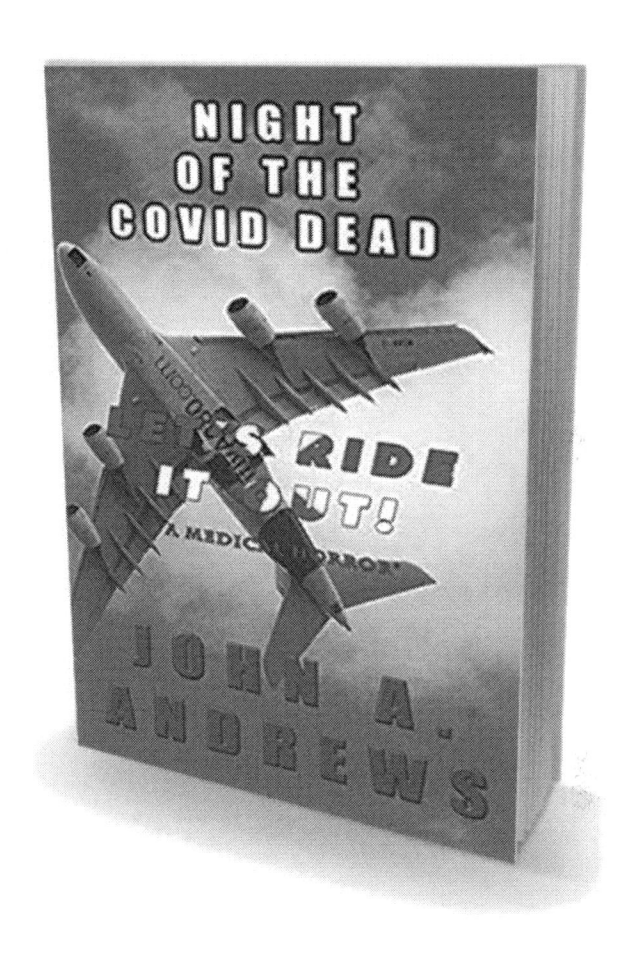

WHO SHOT THE SHERIFF? SERIES

WHO SHOT THE SHERIFF? SERIES

WHO SHOT THE SHERIFF? SERIES

THE PIPS®

ALIPNET
ORIGINAL

WRITTEN BY
JOHN ALAN ANDREWS
CREATOR OF
RUDE BUAY

THE THUMB DRIVES

WHO SHOT THE SHERIFF? SERIES

WHO SHOT THE SHERIFF? SERIES

WHO SHOT THE SHERIFF? SERIES

WHO SHOT THE SHERIFF? SERIES

COMING SOON

WHO SHOT THE SHERIFF? SERIES

WHO SHOT THE SHERIFF? SERIES

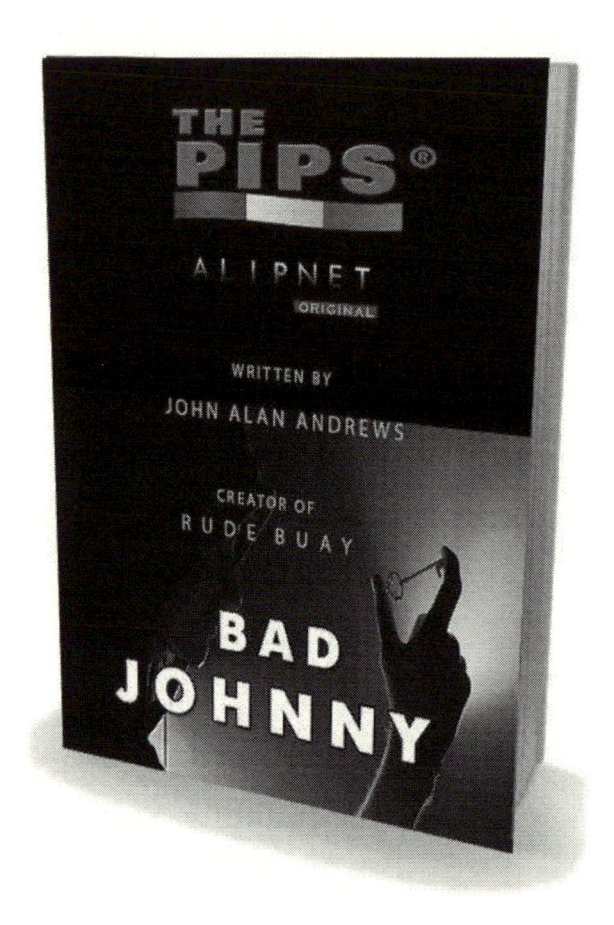

WHO SHOT THE SHERIFF? SERIES

WHO SHOT THE SHERIFF? SERIES

WHO SHOT THE SHERIFF? SERIES

WHO SHOT THE SHERIFF? SERIES

Made in the USA
Columbia, SC
18 January 2025

45507bf3-ecbb-4968-8d7b-bb13006ef34dR01